LOVE'S SHAMELESS PASSION

Awakened by Caroline's soft moans, Ross rose and went to her bed. "Wake up, Caroline."

Her eyes flew open, then she sat up, drew the sheet about her, and fell crying into Ross's arms.

"Sh . . . sh," he whispered, rocking her gently. "It was only a dream."

"No!" she said, tears streaming down her face. "It wasn't a dream. I remember the day the Apaches murdered my parents! I saw it . . . I saw it happen!"

Ross hugged her tenderly, calming her fears. Then, as he began to release her, he noticed that during their embrace, the sheet had fallen from her breasts. He could not stop his gaze from drinking in the beauty of the woman beside him.

Caroline, realizing what had happened, blushed. She started to pull up the sheet but stopped when she saw the blatant hunger in his gaze. Slowly, temptingly, she laced her arms about him and urged his lips to take hers.

When she lived with the Apaches, Caroline's adopted mother had always told her that a woman should answer her man's passion freely. And that was exactly what she was doing—and she was loving every delightful minute of it!

RAPTURE UNTAMED

ROCHELLE WAYNE

PINNACLE BOOKS
WINDSOR PUBLISHING CORP.

For Brenda Zilka
with thanks for helping me achieve
an eight year goal—
to live in the Bluffs!

PINNACLE BOOKS

are published by

Windsor Publishing Corp.
475 Park Avenue South
New York, NY 10016

First printing: August, 1991

Printed in the United States of America

Prologue

1873

Bill Hanley's eyes shone with pride as he studied Caroline, who was his oldest grandchild. He admired her delicate beauty, which was so much like her grandmother's. However, he was also impressed with her spirited ways; a trait inherited from the Hanley side of the family. He had been blessed with three grandchildren, and although he loved them equally, he nonetheless had a special feeling for his only granddaughter. Caroline had two younger brothers, Walter Junior who was five years old, and Daniel who was two.

Now, as Bill Hanley stood on the veranda with Caroline, he placed an arm about her shoulders and drew her close. His gaze swept proudly over his land that stretched as far as the eye could see, and miles beyond. He had lived in New Mexico for nearly forty years, and through hard work and fortitude, he had built his empire. As newlyweds, he and his wife had planned for a large family, but, as fate would have it, they had only one child — Caroline's father. They named him Walter after his paternal grandfather. Through the years as Bill Hanley improved his ranch, expanded his holdings, and grew more prosperous, he was certain that someday he would gladly retire to his rocking chair and hand over the responsibilities to his son. Then when he died, Walter would inherit the Bar-H and reap the benefits of his father's success. However, as Walter grew into manhood, it soon became obvious to Bill that his son didn't want to be a rancher. The revelation was a tremendous disappointment, but he managed to keep it fairly well hidden. Walter had decided to become a minister, and Bill, basically a religious man, could not fault his son for choosing to do God's work. Furthermore, Walter's vocation hadn't been too surprising, for his mother had been a devout Methodist, and her beliefs had made a big impression on her son. Walter's mother died a year before he was ordained, and her sudden death was devastating, but Walter's faith carried him through the tragic loss.

Bill, on the other hand, found his grief more difficult to deal with, and he mourned his wife for years. He had been a widower for ten years when he met Rebecca Rawlins at a church picnic. A widow with two teenage sons, she had moved to the town of Dry Branch to live with her unmarried brother, who was the town's blacksmith. Dry Branch, located on the New Mexico-Arizona border, was ten miles from the Bar-H.

Rebecca Rawlins was extremely attractive, and although she was several years younger than Bill, she seemed to be very taken with him. Flattered, and lonely for a woman's love, Bill began to court the lovely widow. Two short months later they were married at the Dry Branch Methodist Church, the ceremony officiated by the Pastor Walter Hanley.

A long sigh escaped Bill's lips, and his arm tightened about Caroline's shoulders. Marrying Rebecca

6

had been a terrible mistake, but he held his marriage vows sacred.

As he had done numerous times since his marriage, he silently chastised himself for acting so foolishly and rashly—he had actually believed that Rebecca loved him. Soon after their marriage, however, it became quite apparent that she had married him for his money. She was also selfish, demanding, and arrogant. He suspected that she had a lover in Albuquerque, for she often visited the town under the pretext of going shopping. At first, Bill wasn't suspicious, for shopping in the small town of Dry Branch was certainly limited. But as her sojourns became more frequent, and lasted longer, his suspicions were raised. He had finally decided that the next time she went to Albuquerque, he would follow and find out once and for all if she were seeing another man. If so, he'd honor his marriage vows and give her one chance to stay home and be a faithful wife; if she refused, then divorce was inevitable.

A deep frown creased his brow as his thoughts drifted to his stepsons. The two boys were as selfish and demanding as their mother. At the ages of sixteen and eighteen, their ways were set and Bill didn't think their personalities would improve with time. However, they were almost grown, and he hoped they would soon leave. There was no reason for them to linger at the Bar-H, for he had made it quite clear that Caroline would inherit the ranch. He had made his granddaughter his sole heir before Walter Junior and Daniel were born. So far he hadn't changed it, but he planned to include his grandsons in his last will and testament—he just hadn't yet gotten around to it.

As Hanley remained immersed in his thoughts, Caroline turned and looked up into her grandfather's face. His features reflected his worries, prompting her to ask, "Grandpa, is something wrong?"

He tore himself from his troubled reverie. "No, honey. Everything is fine." He smiled warmly, continuing, "Did you have a nice birthday?"

"Yes, it's been a wonderful day!" she replied brightly.

Her grandfather could hardly believe that she was already thirteen years old. It seemed like yesterday when she was born — where did the time go? He studied her thoughtfully; she was blooming into a beautiful young lady. Her long shiny tresses, which framed her heart-shaped face, were the color of golden wheat on a sunny day. She had sensual lips, and a short pert nose, but her charcoal-gray eyes, veiled by thick lashes, were her most captivating feature.

"Caroline," Bill said, his voice conspiratorially low. "You won't say anything to your father about our secret, will you?"

Her eyes sparkled. "Of course not," she assured him. Her grandfather had secretly given her a second birthday present — a brand new Winchester. It was now in Bill's gun cabinet, where it would remain until Caroline returned. She was often allowed to visit her grandfather alone, and would usually stay for several days. He had been teaching her to shoot, and she was a good student. Bill was a firm believer that women should learn to defend themselves. The New Mexico Territory was still partially untamed, for it was sometimes infiltrated by hostile Apaches, and was also frequented by outlaws and Mexican bandits. Bill was teaching Caroline to handle a gun for her own protection. His son, on the other hand, was strongly opposed to Caroline learning to shoot a weapon. He wanted his daughter to be a gentle and refined lady, and, in his opinion, ladies weren't marksmen. But Bill Hanley was stubborn, so he pretended to accept his

8

son's decision, while secretly teaching Caroline to use a rifle.

The Winchester was a secret birthday gift, but Bill had also given Caroline a locket that had belonged to her grandmother. She was wearing it, and now as her fingers caressed the elegant piece of jewelry, she said sincerely, "Grandpa, I love this locket. It's so beautiful, and I promise I'll take good care of it."

"I know you will," he replied affectionately. His eyes regarded her closely. "Caroline, you look so much like your grandmother. She was a very lovely woman, and you're going to be just as lovely — maybe even more so."

His granddaughter blushed. Such compliments always made her feel self-conscious and a little flustered. A painting of her grandmother hung in Bill's den, and she didn't think it was possible for her to ever be as beautiful as the young woman in the picture. Her grandmother's beauty had been too exceptional.

The others were coming outside, and Bill said hastily to Caroline, "I'll come to town next week, pick you up, and bring you back for a long visit. It'll give us a chance to try out your new rifle."

"Promise?" she asked excitedly.

He hugged her tightly. "I promise."

She smiled at him fondly. There was no one she loved more than her grandfather. In fact, she was closer to him than she was to her own father, or even her mother. She loved her parents dearly, but she always felt more comfortable with her grandfather. They were very much alike, for she had undoubtedly inherited the Hanley spirit and zest for life. Her father was quite the opposite — taking more after his mother, he preferred to live quietly and cautiously. He and Caroline's mother were perfect for each other, for she wanted to live the same way.

Walter and his wife, Martha, were the first ones to come outside. Walter was holding his oldest son's hand, and Martha was carrying Daniel.

"Papa," Walter began, "it's been an enjoyable day, but I think we should leave. I want to reach town before nightfall."

"Maybe I should send some of my wranglers with you. They can always spend the night in town, and ride back in the morning."

"That won't be necessary," Walter replied. "We'll be fine."

Bill was worried. "Son, I know you heard about that family who was attacked by Apaches. If those renegades are anywhere in this vicinity . . ."

Walter interrupted, "Papa, that poor family lived seventy-five miles from here. I'm sure the Indians who massacred them aren't anywhere around here. Furthermore, I'm sure they hightailed it back to Mexico."

Bill was still a little uneasy, but before he could try to convince his son to accept the wranglers' protection, his wife and stepsons came outside.

Caroline unconsciously edged closer to her grandfather. She had never liked Rebecca's sons, and now that she was maturing into a young lady, she disliked them even more. The pair were always ogling her with lust-filled eyes. She felt as though they were mentally undressing her.

Bryan, the oldest, was tall and lanky. At eighteen, he was trying to grow his first moustache, and a few dark hairs shadowed his upper lip. It was already apparent that he'd mature into a fairly handsome man, but there was a cruel aspect to his eyes that Caroline found chilling. His younger brother, Alex, better-looking than Bryan, was also tall, but was more muscular. Bryan was by far the smarter of the two. While

10

his brother excelled in school, Alex never went beyond the sixth grade. Rebecca had been assured by more than one teacher that Alex was capable of learning, he simply didn't have the initiative. Although Bryan and Alex were different in a lot of ways, they nonetheless had common traits. They were both selfish and insensitive for instance.

Caroline despised the brothers, but she detested their mother even more. Despite Caroline's young age, she could see through the woman, and knew her for what she was. Caroline was certain that Rebecca didn't love her grandfather and had married him strictly for his money. She also sensed that the woman was making her grandfather very unhappy.

As Walter left to hitch up the buckboard and bring it around to the front of the house, Caroline remained close to her grandfather. She turned her back to Rebecca and her sons, for she preferred not to look at them. She wished fervently that the marriage between her grandfather and Rebecca had never taken place. The woman's presence, along with her sons, always put a damper on her visits to the Bar-H.

Meanwhile, Rebecca, seething inwardly, was glowering at Caroline's turned back. She despised the girl. Bill's will was no secret, and she knew he was leaving his ranch to Caroline. He had assured her, of course, that she would receive enough money to live comfortably for the rest of her life. Well, she didn't want to be simply comfortable, she wanted to be rich! And she wanted to share her riches with her sons! Yes, she most assuredly hated Caroline Hanley, as well as her two young brothers. She'd wish Caroline dead, but a lot of good it would do her—Bill would merely leave the Bar-H to Walter Junior and Daniel. He was determined that she and her sons would not inherit the ranch. She turned her thoughts away from such un-

11

pleasant matters, and concentrated on her lover in Albuquerque. She planned to see him next week, and could hardly wait to be in his arms. He owned one of the saloons in town and he was handsome and a virile lover.

Walter soon had the buckboard hitched and was ready to leave. Bill helped his daughter-in-law and grandchildren into the wagon, and noticed that Walter had brought along a rifle. This put his mind somewhat at ease—at least his son had a means of protection. He quickly cast his worries aside. Walter was right—the Apache attack had taken place a long way off, and the chances that the Indians were in this vicinity were practically nonexistent.

Remembering to tell Caroline that he'd pick her up next week, Bill Hanley waved goodbye to his loved ones. He remained on the veranda until they were out of sight.

Caroline rode in the back of the wagon with Walter Junior, who had fallen asleep. Martha, holding Daniel, sat up front with her husband. As the buckboard rolled across the land, Caroline vacantly watched the familiar scenery. The countryside was mostly open ground interspersed with sagebrush and Apache plume, a shrub so called because of its reddish seed cluster resembling a feathered Indian headdress. Thick tufts of prairie grass, like a plush green carpet, grew vigorously over the plains that were dotted here and there by a few mesquite trees, which sported catkin-like flowers. Distant foothills lay ahead, and Caroline watched as the sun, beginning its journey over the mountain range, bathed the wooded bluffs in radiant sunlight.

Although Caroline was looking at the scenery, she

wasn't consciously seeing it, for her thoughts were occupied elsewhere. She was worried about her grandfather. She knew he was growing unhappier by the day, and she also knew Rebecca and her sons were the reason behind his depression. She wished she could help him, but what could she do? If only he hadn't married Rebecca Rawlins!

Walter Junior's dark-haired head was in her lap, and her legs began to cramp. She managed a more comfortable position without awakening him. She was anxious to reach Dry Branch, for she hated traveling in the slow-moving wagon. She did, however, love to ride horseback. Her grandfather had taught her to ride astride, and there was nothing she liked better than speeding across the plains. Last year, her grandfather had given her a spirited young gelding. Like the Winchester, this gift was also their secret, for her parents were strongly opposed to a lady riding in such fashion.

As the buckboard continued its slow journey, Caroline grew more and more anxious to reach home. Their house was located next to the Methodist Church. It was a modest but comfortable dwelling, and, for the most part, Caroline was happy living there. But her heart was at the Bar-H. She literally adored her grandfather's home, which had been built on the scale of a Spanish hacienda. The two-story house had large, airy rooms, colorful furnishings, and a huge veranda upstairs—as well as one on the ground floor.

The foothills were now much closer, and as Walter turned the buckboard toward the town of Dry Branch, the course placed the mountain range to Caroline's left. A movement caught her eye, causing her to glance over her shoulder. She gasped, terrified by the sight that confronted her. A band of Apache braves, wearing hideous-looking warpaint, were galloping swiftly out of the hills toward the buckboard.

Her mouth went dry with fear, yet she nonetheless managed to cry out to her father, "Papa, look!" He turned, and she pointed at the advancing Indians.

"Dear God!" Walter exclaimed. A bolt of terror shot through him. He quickly slapped the reins against the two-horse team, but even as he did so, he knew the gesture was futile. He couldn't possibly outrun the pursuing Apaches.

The wagon's sudden lurch brought Walter Junior awake with a start, and, sitting up, he spotted the Indians. Terrified, he began to cry, and his arms went about Caroline's neck, holding her so tightly that his grip was choking her. Forcefully, she managed to break his hold. Telling him to stay low, she moved toward the front of the wagon. Her father's rifle lay on the floorboard between her parents. She leaned over the seat, reaching for the weapon, but her mother's hand suddenly gripped her arm, flinging it aside.

"Caroline!" she cried. "Stay back with your brother!"

"Mama, give me the rifle!"

Martha was too scared to make sense out of her daughter's request, but even if she had been calm, Caroline's asking for the rifle would have totally astounded her. She, like her husband, had no idea that their daughter knew how to handle a weapon.

Caroline seldom disobeyed her mother, but she knew this was no time to follow orders, and reaching between her parents, she grabbed the rifle. She moved quickly to the back of the wagon, cocked the weapon, and took aim. The Apaches were drawing dangerously close.

She fired, and the bullet barely missed one of the Indians. She fired a second time, but she missed

14

again, for the jouncing buckboard was making it impossible to hit a target. As she recocked the rifle, she hoped the wagon wouldn't make any more sudden bounces. Once again, she took careful aim, and she leveled the rifle's barrel on a young brave riding in front of the others. He was so close she felt as though she could reach out and touch him. For a tense moment, her finger paused on the trigger. The young Apache was looking straight at her, and although he knew she had him in her rifle's sight, he nevertheless showed no fear. His feral eyes seemed to be daring her to shoot. She swallowed heavily, and broke out in a cold sweat, for she felt sick at the thought of taking a human life. But knowing she must protect herself and her family, she kept the gun aimed at the young Apache. She slowly squeezed the trigger, but, at that precise moment, the wagon's wheels rolled over a large rut, sending the buckboard airborne.

Caroline lost her balance and fell backward. The rifle discharging simultaneously, sending the bullet flying harmlessly into the air. The wagon's wheels hit the ground so hard that the buckboard came close to tipping over.

Moving as quickly as possible, Caroline sat back up. She was raising the rifle to her shoulder to once again take aim when, unexpectedly, the young Apache she had planned to shoot rode up to the side of the wagon. Moving with incredible speed, he thrust his arm forward and jerked the rifle from her grasp. He then rode to her father's side, and pointed the gun at him.

Caroline looked about wildly. The wagon was now surrounded by Indians. Her heart pounded, and she was so terrified that, for an instant, she couldn't move—she could barely breathe. Then, becoming aware of Walter Junior's gasping sobs, she went to him and took him into her arms.

Caroline's father brought the wagon to a stop. His heart was also pounding erratically, and fear knotted and writhed in his stomach. If these were the same Indians who had massacred that other family, then he knew they would certainly kill them as well.

The Apaches, expressing themselves vociferously, swung down from their ponies. Walter, his wife, and little Daniel were jerked off the wagon seat, then thrown to the ground. Three Apaches leapt into the wagon, and Walter Junior was pulled from Caroline's arms. She started to try and draw him back, but a pair of strong arms suddenly lifted her from behind, swinging her over the sideboard as though she weighed no more than a feather.

Her feet touched the ground, and freeing herself from her captor's grasp, she turned about and stared up into an Apache's eyes. It was the same brave who had stolen her rifle—the one she had planned to shoot.

The Apache was called Spotted Horse, and, at the age of eighteen, he was already a hostile warrior, and had killed many settlers, as well as soldiers. The braves riding with him were as bloodthirsty as their leader.

Spotted Horse did nothing as Caroline pushed him aside to run to her parents. They were still on the ground, and their two sons had been placed there beside them. Caroline, her senses now numb with fear, was rushing toward her family when a brave knelt over her father and slit his throat. Her steps came to a sudden halt, and as though she were encountering a nightmare beyond belief, she watched, paralyzed, as the same brave then murdered her mother. When he turned to her brothers, she released a guttural cry of terror, regained feeling in her legs, and rushed forth

16

blindly. Even in her panic, she knew there was no way she could save Walter Junior or Daniel, but, if they had to die, then she wanted to die with them!

As she ran toward her brothers, she heard racing footsteps approaching from behind, but she didn't look back to see who was chasing her—she just kept on running.

She was suddenly struck by a solid blow across the back of the head; the tremendous force sent her sprawling to the ground. Bright stars flashed before her eyes, then everything went black, and she sank into unconsciousness.

Spotted Horse stood over her. He held Walter's rifle, and the gun's butt was stained with Caroline's blood. He hadn't meant to hit her quite so hard, and he wondered if she was dead. He knelt down, and seeing that she was breathing, lifted her into his arms. She came to for a split second, gazed into Spotted Horse's face, then descended back into total oblivion.

Stalking Bear, the warrior who had killed Caroline's parents, moved away from the two boys to ask Spotted Horse, "Do you plan to keep the white girl?"

"Yes. She is brave, and will soon grow into a beautiful woman. Someday, I will marry her."

A scowl crossed Stalking Bear's painted face. He thought Spotted Horse was acting foolishly. He could have his pick of Indian maidens, so why did he want this white girl? He didn't voice his disapproval, however, for he preferred not to anger Spotted Horse. Instead, he asked, "Should I kill the white boys?"

"No. Trade them to the Comancheroes for rifles. Now, I will take the white girl to my uncle's village."

Spotted Horse carried the unconscious Caroline to his horse, draped her face-down across his pony's back, then mounted behind her. As they were riding out of sight, Stalking Bear, along with another brave,

17

untethered the horses from the buckboard. Then they put Walter Junior and Daniel on the horses. They would take the boys into Mexico, contact the infamous Comancheroes, and make a trade.

The Indians, taking their captives with them, galloped swiftly away from the area. They were soon far away, leaving a deathly quiet in their wake.

Reverend Walter Hanley, his life snuffed out like a candle, lay beside his dead wife. The sun, continuing its steady descent, cast a radiant glow over Walter and Martha as though God, in his heaven, was sending a welcoming beam, beckoning them into his glorious kingdom.

Chapter One

Five Years Later

Bill Hanley wasn't expecting Sheriff Jim Taylor, and when the man suddenly showed up on his doorstep, his visit was a complete surprise. But Hanley liked the sheriff, and as he showed him into his study, he was glad he had dropped by.

Bill poured two glasses of brandy and handed one to Taylor, who was seated in the chair facing the desk.

The lawman waited for his host to ease into his own chair, before asking, "Bill, have you heard of Ross Bennett?"

"Yes, I have," he answered frowning, his tone disapproving.

Taylor took a thoughtful drink. He had detected his friend's disfavor. "Bill, don't judge him by his reputation. He hires his gun, true, but for the right causes."

"You sound like you admire him."

"I suppose I do. I've met Bennett on a couple of occasions, and I've always found him impressive. Furthermore, we have a lot in common. We both make a living with a gun, only he earns a helluva lot more money. If I were a younger man, I'd be tempted to try his line of work—the pay's better."

Bill studied the sheriff across the span of the desk top. The two men were close to the same age, but they were still in good physical condition. Bill was somewhat surprised that Taylor hadn't retired.

"Jim, when are you going to hang up your guns, along with your badge?" Hanley asked. "You should quit before some young gunslinger gets the drop on you."

Jim smiled casually. "I've been thinkin' about retiring. But who's gonna take my place?"

"Your deputy."

The sheriff wasn't sure the young man could successfully handle the job. But he didn't come here to discuss himself, or his deputy, and he steered their conversation back to Ross Bennett. "Bill, Bennett's grandmother was an Apache, and he has a granduncle who is a headsman, and is greatly respected by the Apaches."

Hanley's interest was instantly piqued. His body tensed, and his heartbeat increased.

"This granduncle of Bennett's lives in Mexico," Jim continued. "From what I understand, Bennett's free to come and go to his uncle's village as he pleases."

"Dear God!" Bill gasped expectantly. "Do you think I could hire . . . ?"

He didn't finish, but there was no need, for Jim understood. "Hire him to find your grandchildren? Yes, I think there's a chance. That's why I came here—to tell you about Bennett."

"Where can I find him?"

"He's in Dry Branch. He arrived last night. I think he's on his way to Tucson."

Excited, Bill bounded to his feet. "How long does he plan to stay?"

"I don't know, that's why I hurried out here. I think you should ride back with me and talk to him as soon

20

as possible."

"But didn't you ask him when he was leaving?"

"Sure, I asked him—even told him a little about your grandchildren, but he didn't seem too interested. I couldn't get him to confirm when he was leaving, but I got the feelin' he doesn't plan to stick around very long."

"Jim, do me a favor, will you? While I let Rebecca know what's happening, will you saddle my horse?"

He got to his feet. "Sure, no problem."

Rebecca was in her bedroom, sitting at her vanity, studying herself in the mirror. At the age of forty-one, she was still very attractive. Her reddish-gold hair hadn't a trace of gray, and her complexion was smooth and wrinkle-free. Her tall, graceful frame was as firm as when she was twenty.

As she admired her reflection, she was quite pleased with herself. But, then, emitting a long sigh, she turned away from the mirror and began to pace her room. A lot of good it did her to be beautiful! Her beauty was wasted in this marriage! Oh, if only she had the nerve to walk out on Bill Hanley! But if she left, where would she go—where would she live? She certainly couldn't go to Bryan, for he was now a saloon proprietor, he wouldn't want his mother living with him. Alex was no help whatsoever, for he was still living at the Bar-H. Her brother had married and moved away and she hadn't heard from him in over two years.

Rebecca cast all notions of leaving Bill aside. She mustn't let depression get the better of her. Her husband was a rich man, and as Bryan was always telling her, she must be patient. Hanley's new will was no secret—if none of his grandchildren were found within the next year, they would be presumed dead, and the Bar-H and all its profits would go to his widow.

Just one more year, Rebecca reminded herself. She had managed to stay married this long, so one more year should be a breeze. She intended, of course, to become a widow without delay. With her sons' help, they would kill Hanley and make it look like an accident. They hadn't decided yet how to accomplish such a feat, but they would lay their plans when the time was right.

Yes, as Bryan kept reminding her, she must be patient. But patience didn't come easy to Rebecca, for she was too frustrated and unhappy. If only she had a lover to add spice to her life! But she had tried that five years ago, and had gotten caught. She had never dreamed that her husband would find out, for she had foolishly believed that she had pulled the wool over his eyes. But he was sharper than she had realized. He had given her an ultimatum: she could stay home and be a faithful wife, or he would divorce her. She had chosen to be faithful. So far, she hadn't broken her promise, but only because she was afraid of getting caught. Despite her frustrations, she'd continue to be patient and bide her time. Soon she would be a wealthy widow—then she and her sons would live in style! Bryan wanted the ranch—he could have it! She'd take her part of the money and travel to Europe, where she planned to enjoy one lover after another!

Thoughts of greed and lovers had lifted Rebecca's spirits considerably, and her mood was pleasant as Bill rapped on her door before coming into the room.

"Sheriff Taylor's here," he said. "I'm riding back to town with him."

She could sense his excitement. "Oh? Has something happened?"

"There's a man in town named Ross Bennett. His

grandmother was an Apache. I hope to hire him to find Caroline and the boys."

Rebecca frowned. "Honestly, Bill! Just because his grandmother was an Apache doesn't mean he can find your grandchildren." Pretending concern, she went to her husband, took his hand, and said gently, "Darling, when are you going to give up? By now, Caroline and the boys are dead."

"I don't know that for sure!" he remarked gruffly.

"You're chasing a dream," she said. She sounded sympathetic.

"Maybe," he admitted reluctantly. He drew her into his arms, holding her close. In his own way, Hanley loved his wife. He knew she wasn't the loving, considerate woman he thought he had married, but since her affair with the man in Albuquerque, she had tried to be a good wife. Their marriage wasn't as warm as he would like, but they got along well. He was almost twenty years older than Rebecca, and he couldn't fault her for not finding him especially romantic. Their sexual relations were few and far between. Actually, he was still a virile man, and would bed his wife more often if he thought she truly desired him. But Hanley wasn't fooled, on the occasions when they made love, he could sense his wife's adversity. He was sure she craved a younger, more exciting man.

He gave her a chaste kiss on the cheek, told her he'd return this evening, and left.

As the door closed behind him, Rebecca scowled irritably. She wasn't worried that this Ross Bennett would find Caroline and her brothers, for she really did believe they were dead. She was, however, very upset. During the last five years, her husband had spent a fortune hiring men to find his grandchildren, and was foolishly wasting money that, upon his death,

23

would be hers!

Hanley and Sheriff Taylor checked the hotel. Bennett wasn't in his room, and the desk clerk suggested they try the saloon. The town's only saloon was called The Watering Hole. The place was in dire need of repair; bat-wing doors hung on one rusty hinge, and the wood floor was stained with spots of dried blood, for shootouts were not uncommon at The Watering Hole. The walls, covered with paper yellowed from age, were dotted here and there with bullet holes, and the tables and chairs placed randomly about the room were resting on legs that had been restored more than once, for brawls were also common.

As Bill followed the sheriff inside the saloon, he looked about the establishment with disdain. He wondered why Bryan didn't fix the place up, but, more so, he wondered why his stepson had even bought the business. In Bill's opinion, buying The Watering Hole wasn't a good investment, and he couldn't understand why Bryan had wanted the place. He knew his stepson was smart — so why in the world did he purchase a rundown saloon?

Only three patrons were inside. Two were standing at the bar, and the third one was sitting at a corner table. Taylor nudged Bill's arm with his elbow, gained his attention, and nodded at the stranger who was seated. "That's Bennett's cousin. The two are ridin' together. He'll know where Ross is."

They walked over to the table, and as the sheriff pulled out a chair, he asked, "Do you mind if we sit down?"

The man responded with a somewhat cocky grin. "Do I have a choice in the matter?"

"No, not really," Sheriff Taylor answered, sitting.

He waited until Bill was seated, then asked, "Where's Bennett?"

"Upstairs," the man replied tersely.

He didn't need to explain, for the brusque reply was sufficient. Bryan had two prostitutes working for him, and when a customer was upstairs, what he was doing was obvious.

"We'll wait for him," the sheriff remarked.

"Suit yourself," the man replied. If he was curious about the sheriff's reason for waiting, he didn't let on. He simply refilled his glass of whiskey, and leaned back in his chair.

Hanley studied the stranger. He guessed him to be in his early thirties. His face was ruggedly handsome, for he had a strong chin, full lips, and dark eyes shadowed by thick brows. Bill caught a slight whiff of shaving cologne—evidently the man had recently visited the barber shop. His hat was resting on the chair beside him, and Bill's eyes were drawn to the stranger's hair, which appeared to have been freshly cut. His brown hair was full and naturally curly, causing a stray lock to fall haphazardly over his forehead. Bill looked away from the man, he didn't want to be caught staring.

Taylor decided to make introductions. "Mr. Bennett, I'd like you to meet Bill Hanley."

He offered Bill his hand. "Glad to meet you."

Hanley readily accepted the man's firm handshake. "The pleasure's mine, Mr. Bennett."

"Call me Kirk." As he quaffed down his whiskey, his eyes regarded Hanley over the glass's rim. He quickly replenished his drink, returned his gaze to Bill, and said calmly, "The sheriff mentioned you last night. Your grandchildren were abducted by Apaches five years ago."

"Yes, that's right." A glint of hope came to Bill's

eyes. "Do you think your cousin will help me find them?"

"I can't answer for Ross, but I can tell you that the odds of finding your grandchildren aren't very good. Five years is a long time."

Bill sighed miserably. "I know how long it is. My God, each day has been hell for me."

Kirk was sympathetic. "Did the Army try to find them?"

"Yes, they tried, but there wasn't much they could do. They can't go into Mexico. I've hired over a dozen men to try and find my grandchildren, but they have all failed. Ross Bennett is my last hope."

"I'm sorry, Mr. Hanley . . ."

"Bill, please," he interrupted.

"I'm sorry, Bill. I really am, but surely you realize that your grandchildren might be dead."

"I know," he murmured softly. Following a moment's pause, though, he said with conviction, "But as long as there is a shred of hope, regardless of how small . . . well, I just can't give up."

"I understand. In your place, I'd feel the same way."

Bill's expectations rose. He liked Kirk Bennett, and the man seemed genuinely compassionate. Why should he hire Ross Bennett, when he could just as easily solicit Kirk's help?

"Money is no object when it comes to finding my grandchildren," Bill began, speaking directly to Kirk. "Would you consider taking the job? Just name your price."

"I'm not the man to find your grandchildren. You'll have to speak to Ross."

"But I don't understand. Why can't you look for them?"

"If any of them are still alive, they're probably in an Apache village somewhere in Mexico." Kirk smiled

26

faintly. "I can't just ride into these villages."

"Why not?"

His smile widened. "Because I value my life."

"But won't your Apache blood protect you?"

"I'm not part Apache. Ross and I aren't first cousins. Our grandfathers were brothers. His grandfather married an Apache maiden, mine married a white woman. But even though Ross is part Apache, he can't just come and go into any Apache village at will. But he does have a granduncle who is a headsman; through him, he might learn about your grandchildren."

At that moment, Sheriff Taylor, facing the stairway, said to Bill, "Here comes Bennett now."

Hanley turned and looked. He watched Ross as he moved slowly toward their table. He had thought he'd be older, but the young gunslinger couldn't be more than twenty-eight, twenty-nine years old. His tall frame was slim, yet it exuded strength. Bill could see evidence of his Indian heritage—he moved with innate stealth, and his cheekbones were prominently high. Ross was carrying his hat, and Bill noticed that his hair was a mixture of dark brown and black. His bronzed complexion seemed genetic, and not simply the result of hours spent under the hot desert sun. He was wearing dark trousers and a buckskin shirt that laced up the front. The top laces were undone, revealing smooth chest muscles. An embossed holster, holding an ivory-handled Peacemaker .45, was strapped to his hip. As he reached their table, Bill looked up into a pair of eyes that were as black as a moonless night.

"Would you mind joining us?" Sheriff Taylor said to Ross. "We'd like to talk to you."

Ross pulled out a chair, and sat down. He didn't say anything, he merely waited for the sheriff to continue.

"Last night, I told you about Bill Hanley." Taylor

27

gestured toward Bill. "This is Mr. Hanley."

Ross nodded cordially; still, he held his silence.

Bill quickly explained how his grandchildren were abducted, and that their parents were murdered. He went on, telling Ross about all the men he had hired to find the missing children, and that everyone of them had failed. He was nervous, even tense, but he couldn't help it. Somehow, he seemed to know that Ross Bennett was his last hope—if this man refused to help him, he would never see his grandchildren. As he finished his explanation, he paused, caught his breath, then said with conviction, "I know you're about to tell me that the children are most likely dead but, Mr. Bennett, I swear before God that I believe they are still alive!" He placed a hand over his heart. "I feel it here, deep inside—all the way to my soul!" His voice choked, and tears came to his eyes, "My grandchildren are not dead!" He dropped his gaze to his lap, embarrassed that he had come close to breaking down before this man who was a complete stranger.

Silence prevailed about the table, no one moved. Ross, his eyes on Hanley, stared thoughtfully. He was touched by the man's plight, and he had his sympathy. He doubted that the man's grandchildren were still alive, but the chance did exist, regardless of how small. He preferred not to take on the search for the abducted children, but he couldn't bring himself to turn Hanley down. He felt too sorry for him. Furthermore, if his grandchildren were still alive, he was the most likely candidate to find them.

"All right, Mr. Hanley. I'll try to find your grandchildren." Ross's deep voice was soft, and pleasant to the ears.

Bill glanced up quickly, gratitude written all over his face. "Thank you, Mr. Bennett."

"The name's Ross." He had been sitting leisurely, but, now, ready to get down to business, he sat up straight, and asked, "What were the ages of your grandchildren when they were abducted?"

"Daniel was two, Walter Junior was five, and Caroline was thirteen." He reached into his shirt pocket, pulled out a small photograph, and handed it to Ross. "This is a picture of my first wife, Caroline's grandmother. She was eighteen when this photograph was taken, the same age Caroline is now. She has an uncanny resemblance to her grandmother, so this picture might help you identify her."

Ross studied the picture closely. The young woman in the photograph was exceptionally beautiful. "It looks like your wife had fair hair. What color is Caroline's?"

"Blonde, but it's such a beautiful wheat color that it's almost golden."

"As children age, their hair sometimes darkens. Dark hair would make her blend in with the other women. If she's wearing it in braids, a visitor might not even realize she's white. What color are her eyes?"

"Gray."

"That'll help. Apaches don't have gray eyes." He indicated the photograph. "Do you mind if I take this with me?"

"No, of course not."

As the men continued their discussion, they didn't notice Bryan, who had just come into the saloon. Glancing about, he was surprised to see his stepfather sitting with the sheriff and two strangers. Bill rarely visited The Watering Hole, and wondering why he was here, Bryan crossed the room to pause at their table.

Hanley quickly made introductions, he then told Bryan that Ross had agreed to search for Caroline and the boys.

Although Bryan was disturbed, he hid it well, and wished Ross good luck. He then made his excuses, went to the bar, and told his bartender to pour him a shot of whiskey. He didn't down it, he sipped it as though it were brandy. He tried to calm himself, after all, this wasn't the first time Hanley had hired someone to search for his grandchildren. They had all been unsuccessful. There was no reason to believe that Ross Bennett would succeed where the others had failed, but Bryan couldn't completely shake his feeling of uneasiness. There was something different about Bennett, something he couldn't quite put his finger on. For some reason, his intuition was telling him that this man wasn't like the others, and if those kids were still alive, he'd find them!

Bryan finished his whiskey, then put the glass down with a solid bang. Damn it! If Bennett returned with Hanley's grandchildren, then he'd lose any chance of owning the Bar-H.

The bartender, noticing his boss's scowl, asked, "Is anything wrong, Mr. Rawlins?"

"No," he answered, his speech clipped. He shoved the glass forward. "Fill it." As the man complied, he asked, "Do you know Ross Bennett?"

"I don't know him personally, but I've heard about him. He's a hired gun."

"Of course! I thought his name was familiar. I've heard about him, too." Bryan gestured toward Ross, turned back to the bartender, and said, "That's Bennett."

The man was impressed. "Well, I'll be damned! Does he have business with your stepfather?"

"He's hired him to try and find his grandchildren."

The bartender had lived in Dry Branch for a long time, and he knew about the abduction. "Well, if any man can find 'em, Bennett's the one. I've heard he's kin to them damned Apaches."

The information intensified Bryan's uneasiness.

The bartender suddenly shrugged indifferently. "But not even Bennett can bring 'em back from the dead, and mark my word, Mr. Rawlins, them kids ain't alive. They done been dead all these years. Poor Mr. Hanley's just wastin' his money."

A slight smile curled Bryan's lips, and his mood lifted. Of course! He was worrying needlessly! Caroline and her brothers were undoubtedly dead!

Chapter Two

Caroline bundled three willow rods together, then wrapped the rods with a thin strip of willow, and began joining the coil with the top rod of the coil immediately below. She was making a basket that would be used for storing food. Her head was bent over the task, as though she were giving it her full concentration. But weaving baskets came easy to Caroline, and as her fingers worked deftly, her thoughts were elsewhere.

She was inside a wickiup, an Apache dwelling made of slender poles covered with brush and grass. It was her foster parents' home, as well as her own. Her foster sister, Sweet Water, was working beside her. She was also weaving a basket, but she was more experienced than Caroline, and was creating a dark pattern against a beige background. She was using black strips from a plant called devil's-claw in place of the willow.

Although Caroline seemed withdrawn, Sweet Water didn't question her, but went on working diligently. She was used to her foster sister's mood swings, and was certain that she'd soon emerge from her deep thoughts and once again be talkative and cheerful. She didn't blame her sister for having strange moods.

After all, the girl had no memory of her past, and could only remember the last five years of her life. Sweet Water knew if something like that were to happen to her, she would certainly suffer bouts of withdrawal.

As Caroline continued her tedious chore, she unconsciously emitted a deep, depressing sigh. She was disheartened, but she was also impatient with herself. Why couldn't she remember? For the last month or so, she had come so close to recalling her past. It was as though she were on the very brink, and at any moment, her memories would flood forth like a bursting dam.

She thought about last night. She had been on the verge of falling asleep, when a flash from her past passed before her eyes. She had seen the face of an elderly man, but the vision had appeared so quickly that it was gone before she could really think about it. Last night wasn't the first time something like that had happened, glints and shadows from her past life had been playing havoc with her emotions for some time.

Her thoughts meandering, Caroline relived the day Spotted Horse had brought her to live among his uncle's people. Their journey to the village was hazy, for she had spent the whole time drifting in and out of consciousness. Her first clear memory was waking up in bed to find Basket Woman, Spotted Horse's aunt, leaning over her with a bowl of broth. She had been terribly frightened, but she had also been hungry, and had eaten the proffered food.

For weeks, Caroline had lain abed, her mind blank; yet she was terrified. Basket Woman, along with Sweet Water, had taken care of her. Finally, responding to their kindness and concern, Caroline began to recover. Neither of them could speak English, but

33

Spotted Horse's uncle, Leading Cloud, could speak it fairly well. Through him, Caroline learned why she had been with Spotted Horse. The warrior had told his uncle that he had found Caroline wandering in the desert, dazed and incoherent. Leading Cloud, worried about his young charge, had spoken to the village's shaman. Following prayers and chants, the holy man had decided the spirits had taken away the white girl's memory so she could become an Apache. She had been born again, free to reside with the Apaches, and to someday marry Spotted Horse. The warrior had openly voiced his intentions to wed the white girl, and the shaman had taken that into account.

Spotted Horse had remained at his uncle's village until Caroline was well enough to see him. She was in the wickiup alone, lying on a bed of blankets, when he decided to visit. He spoke to her in broken English, however, he very assertively told her that they would never again speak in the white man's tongue. She must learn his language, and forget her own. He also informed her that from this day forward, she would be called White Raven. Caroline didn't have much to say, for she was in awe of the warrior. She found him attractive, yet, at the same time, strangely forbidding. His visit was short, and she was relieved when he left. For some reason, which she couldn't possibly understand, he made her tense and uneasy.

Left alone, Caroline had snuggled into her bed, and had drawn the covers up over her head as though she could find solace in the dark. Amnesia, however, doesn't necessarily change one's personality, and Caroline's spirit couldn't be smothered by blankets. She was too willful, independent, and strong to sink into a state of malaise. Despite the change her life had taken, Caroline emerged from the cocoon she had weaved about her. Although she had no memory of her past, she nonetheless knew her surroundings were unfamiliar. The people and their customs were alien, but she adjusted, and was soon learning Apache etiquette, and proper behavior. She made a point of learning their language as quickly as possible, for she wanted desperately to communicate.

Within a year, Caroline was perfectly at ease in her new environment, and, for the most part, she was content. But her lost past was always there, hovering like a dark cloud. She never stopped trying to remember. Sometimes she would tax her mind relentlessly, but to no avail. Who was she? Why had she been wandering in the desert? Did she have a family somewhere? Should she leave her foster parents, sneak out of the village, and try to find help elsewhere? But striking out on her own would be extremely dangerous. Furthermore, where would she go? No, it would be best to remain here where she was safe, and hope that someday soon her memory would return.

As the years passed, Caroline thought less of her past, and began to live more for the present. She learned to love her foster parents dearly, and she especially loved Sweet Water. They were not only sisters, but good friends as well. Sweet Water had two older brothers, but they were married and lived in their own dwellings.

Caroline never questioned why Leading Cloud and Basket Woman had so generously received her into their family. She knew they were very fond of Spotted Horse, and she supposed they had adopted her to please him. Their reasons didn't matter, for she knew they sincerely loved her.

That Spotted Horse planned to marry her was no secret, and as time passed, Caroline began to accept his decision. Although Spotted Horse's village was only a three days' ride from his uncle's, his visits were few and sometimes far between. After awhile, though, Caroline found Spotted Horse less forbidding, until finally, she forgot that she had ever thought of him in that way. She learned to look forward to his visits, and she eventually accepted him as a friend — and the man she would someday marry.

Now, laying her work aside, she looked at Sweet Water and said, "I think I am close to recalling my past."

"Are you sure?" she exclaimed. Sweet Water had mixed emotions — for White Raven's peace of mind, she hoped that she would remember everything, however, she was afraid that her adopted sister might decide to return to her other life. She knew if that were to happen, she would miss her terribly.

"Yes, I am almost certain," Caroline replied, her voice tense. "I'm right on the edge, I just know I am!"

Sweet Water smiled weakly, then returned to weaving her basket. As she worked, she studied her sister with a sidelong glance. She was somewhat envious of White Raven's beauty, but it wasn't a spiteful envy, for she sincerely admired her. She wished she was as beautiful!

Caroline Hanley was indeed a stunning young lady. Apache women often wore their hair dark loose, held back from their faces with bands adorned with beads. Caroline's tresses were golden like the sun and she wore them unbound, tumbling freely down her back. She wore a headband decorated with hand-polished shell beads. Her complexion was smooth, her cheeks naturally rosy, and her charcoal-gray eyes set off her delicate features to perfection. She was average height, her slender frame exquisitely rounded.

The Apaches wove cloth to make garments, and Caroline was wearing a plain skirt and bodice which was complemented by several pieces of Indian jewelry.

Sweet Water, who was one year younger than Caroline, was dressed similarly. She was also attractive. Her shiny black hair was thick, and her features were pleasant. Although she was shorter than Caroline, she was more voluptuous. However, in her opinion, her beauty couldn't compare to her sister's.

Sweet Water put her own work aside, turned to Caroline, and asked sadly, "White Raven, if you remember your other life, will you leave us?"

Caroline was touched to see tears in Sweet Water's eyes. She placed her hand on her companion's, patting it consolingly. "I don't know. I cannot answer that question until I am able to remember."

"But what about Spotted Horse! How can you leave the man you are supposed to marry? Do you not love him?"

Did she love Spotted Horse? She wasn't sure. She liked him, and considered him a good friend. Among the Apaches, he was greatly respected and admired. To be chosen as his future wife was indeed an honor. But did she love him? She supposed she did; after all, she enjoyed his company, and was always glad to see him. She compared her feelings to those of Sweet Water's. Her sister was engaged to Spotted Horse's good friend, Stalking Bear. The two warriors lived in the same village, and when Spotted Horse visited Leading Cloud, Stalking Bear never failed to accompany him. Sweet Water was always so thrilled to see Stalking Bear that her eyes sparkled, her face glowed, and her pulse raced with excitement. Spotted Horse's presence never had such an effect on Caroline. She was happy to see him, and found his visits pleasant, but that was as far as her feelings went. If she were truly in love, wouldn't she react like Sweet Water?

Caroline shrugged the question aside. Maybe she just wasn't as emotional as Sweet Water. Her love for

Spotted Horse was born out of friendship, instead of passion. Once they were married, her feelings would certainly grow amorous.

"What about Spotted Horse?" Sweet Water asked again.

Caroline sighed heavily. "It is hard for me to think about marriage now that my past is so close. Once I remember my other life, I might want to go back to it. I might even have a family who loves me, and whom I love in return."

"You have a family here," Sweet Water murmured.

"Yes, I know. And I love all of you very much. But my past keeps calling out to me."

Before Sweet Water could reply, Basket Woman entered the dwelling. A large smile was on her chubby face, and her rotund body was practically dancing with excitement. "Guess who is riding into the village?" she asked happily.

Sweet Water bounded to her feet, exclaiming, "Stalking Bear and Spotted Horse?"

"Yes," her mother replied. She laughed heartily as Sweet Water rushed outside to greet her future husband.

Caroline followed her sister, but she did so with less gusto. She was looking forward to seeing Spotted Horse, but, as always, she wasn't as delighted as Sweet Water. Actually, she wished she was as thrilled, for it must be wonderful to be so ecstatically in love! She wondered if she would ever feel that way.

Spotted Horse, riding beside Stalking Bear, watched Caroline closely as she waited in front of Leading Cloud's wickiup. He was relieved to see there was no hostility on her face. Evidently, the spirits had not given her back her memory. He was beginning to

38

believe that they never would. If she was going to remember, she would have done so by now. Apparently their future marriage had the spirits' blessings, otherwise, they would have returned her memory.

A pleased smile crossed his face. It was time to set a wedding date. The next time he visited his uncle's village, it would be to claim his wife.

Several people came out of their homes to call greetings to the two visitors. Dozens of children ran alongside the warriors' ponies, and camp dogs barked rapidly. Spotted Horse and Stalking Bear always received a boisterous welcome, for visitors were a reason for gaiety and celebration. Also, the travelers brought news from other bands, messages from loved ones living in other villages, and general gossip.

As they neared Leading Cloud's home, Stalking Bear said quietly to Spotted Horse, "White Raven is smiling. That means she still has no memory of her other life." An imperceptible scowl deepened his brow. He had hoped the white girl would remember, for he was against his friend's future marriage. He hated all whites, and his hatred extended to Caroline.

"The spirits have made their feelings clear. My marriage to White Raven has their blessing."

Stalking Bear sulked silently. More than once, he had been tempted to tell White Raven about her parents' deaths, but respect, love, and even fear, of Spotted Horse had kept him silent. He had prayed earnestly to the spirits, beseeching them to return the white girl's memory, but his prayers had gone unanswered. Evidently, his friend would marry White Raven. Stalking Bear's heart grew heavy, for he knew the marriage would make his sister very unhappy. She was in love with Spotted Horse, and he had hoped that Spotted Horse would love her in return. But his friend was too blinded by the white girl's beauty to

39

notice another woman. His sister, One-Who-Laughs (so named because she laughed out loud at an early age) would make Spotted Horse a good, obedient wife. Stalking Bear seriously doubted White Raven's ability to do the same. Despite her loss of memory, she was still white, and in his opinion, white women didn't make good wives. A horse can't fly like a hawk, and a white woman can't become an Apache!

He steered his thoughts away from Spotted Horse and White Raven. Thinking about the pair not only depressed him but angered him as well. He set his gaze upon Sweet Water, who was watching him with sparkling eyes. As he admired her voluptuous curves, he grew anxious to set a wedding date. Stalking Bear was not capable of loving a woman deeply, but he was very fond of Sweet Water, and he intended to be a good husband and provider. He was also eager to have sons, and Sweet Water was obviously strong and healthy — she would give him many children.

The warriors drew in their ponies, and dismounted in front of the wickiup. Leading Cloud, standing beside his wife, stepped forward and greeted the young men warmly. Basket Woman welcomed them next, and it was then proper for Sweet Water and White Raven to murmur their hellos.

Spotted Horse turned to Caroline, and his intense gaze raked her from head to foot. She grew uncomfortable beneath his scrutiny, for she could see passion stirring in his eyes. Embarrassed, she started to move away, but his hand was suddenly on her shoulder, stopping her.

"White Raven," he said huskily. "I will return at the next full moon, and we will be married."

The announcement immediately sent Basket Woman embracing her adopted daughter, and by the time she released her, happy tears were stinging her eyes. Then Sweet Water, also shedding joyful tears, took Caroline into her arms.

Caroline's response was less than enthusiastic, for she suddenly felt very empty inside. This should be one of the happiest days of her life, so why did she feel so . . . so alone?

Caroline was sleeping fitfully. She shared a bed with Sweet Water, but her companion was so sound asleep that she wasn't disturbed by Caroline's tossing and turning.

In her dream, Caroline was held in a man's arms. She somehow knew that she had been knocked unconscious, and was coming to. Her eyelids seemed as heavy as lead, and it took great effort for her to open them. She was terribly frightened, and as she raised her gaze to the man holding her, she did so with reluctance. She didn't want to look into his face, for she was afraid of him, but, her eyes had a will of their own. Then, as she lifted her gaze to his, the dream faded abruptly.

Caroline awoke with a start. Her heart was pounding, and her skin was layered with cold perspiration. Why had the dream frightened her so? Was it a shadow from her past? Had some man really held her in his arms? Had she been terrified of him? Had she looked into his face? If so, then why had her dream blocked it out of her memory? Why couldn't she remember him?

She threw off the covers, rose quietly, slipped into her clothes, and stepped outside. Perhaps the night air would help clear her head as well as her thoughts.

Not all of the village had retired, quite a few people were still lingering about. In honor of their guests, a gay celebration and a huge feast had taken place.

41

Merriment was still alive, for Caroline could hear soft laughter coming from several wickiups, as well as from the people outside.

Looking about, she caught sight of Spotted Horse and Stalking Bear. They were standing off to themselves, but, unlike the others, they didn't appear to be in a festive mood. Quite the opposite. She could tell by their hand gestures and body movements that they were disagreeing. They were too far away, though, for her to hear what they were saying. She was confused. They were good friends, so why were they arguing?

The two warriors, unaware that Caroline was watching, continued their discussion.

"If you marry White Raven," Stalking Bear was saying, "and she gets back her memory, she will turn on you!"

"Apache women do not turn on their husbands."

"But she is not an Apache!" Stalking Bear's eyes bore into his friend's. Why couldn't he make him understand that it would be a mistake to marry a white woman? "Also, there are many in our village who know about her parents. What if someone should tell her what happened to them?"

"No one would dare!" he remarked gruffly. He suddenly shrugged as though unconcerned. "Even if she learned the truth, it would not matter. She does not remember her parents. How can she grieve for people she does not know?"

"If you really think that way, then you are thinking like a fool!"

"Enough!" Spotted Horse bellowed. "I do not want to hear any more! Besides, I did not kill her people — you did!"

"That will make no difference. You are just as guilty, because their deaths are what you wanted.

42

When White Raven remembers, she will know this is true."

"She will never remember!" he declared emphatically. "The spirits have stolen her memory, and they will never give it back!"

Stalking Bear placed a tentative hand on his friend's shoulder. "Spotted Horse, I love you like a brother. Please take my advice. Forget the white girl, and marry my sister. One-Who-Laughs will make you a much better wife."

Spotted Horse threw off his companion's hand. "I will marry White Raven! If you want us to remain friends, then you will not speak against my marriage again! Do you understand?"

Stalking Bear gave up, albeit reluctantly. "As you say, my brother."

Spotted Horse grinned. "Good!" he replied, his mood much improved. Hearing footsteps, he whirled about. He was surprised to see Caroline approaching.

Excusing himself, Stalking Bear departed quickly.

"White Raven, why are you not asleep?"

"I had a worrisome dream. I thought a breath of fresh air might make me feel better."

"Tell me about your dream." Spotted Horse was upset. Was her memory coming back to her in the form of dreams?

Caroline came close to revealing her nightmare, but some unknown force warned her to be silent. The warning was intuitive, but Caroline took heed. She didn't want Spotted Horse to know that her memories were trying to return.

Speaking as though the dream was unimportant, she said with a smile, "Now, I can't even remember that much about it. You know how dreams can be— they simply fade away."

Spotted Horse was relieved. "When we are married,

I will keep all bad dreams away."

Her smile widened sincerely. "How do you plan to do that? Will you spear them with your arrow, or shoot them with your rifle?"

The warrior laughed gustily. "Neither. I will fill all your dreams, and make them happy ones."

Caroline regarded her fiance with fondness. He was an impressive warrior, his stocky frame was muscular, and his face was classically Apache—high forehead, pronounced cheekbones, broad nose, and eyes so dark that they were almost black. His long straight hair was shoulder-length. Among the Apaches, he was considered exceptionally handsome, and Caroline agreed that he was indeed a striking figure.

"You should not be out here," Spotted Horse warned her gently. "If Basket Woman finds you are not in bed, she will come looking for you. Then we will both be in trouble. We cannot be alone like this until we are married."

She knew he was right. She was still a maiden, and under Leading Cloud's and Basket Woman's protection. "I will see you in the morning," she replied, then turned to leave.

"White Raven, he called, detaining her. "I plan to leave tomorrow, but I will be back soon to make you my wife."

She nodded slightly. "Very well, Spotted Horse."

He watched as she hurried back to his uncle's wickiup. Although he was anxious to marry White Raven, he was nevertheless apprehensive. When he brought her to his village, she would certainly learn that he was a fierce warrior, and had killed many whites. Would she be repulsed by his many killings? Or had the spirits made her a true Apache? He conveniently convinced himself that she was now an Apache in every sense of the word. She would not be displeased.

Quite the contrary, she would be proud of her husband's prowess.

Inside the wickiup, Caroline crawled back into bed. It was hard for her to imagine herself married and living in a strange village. She would miss Basket Woman and Leading Cloud. But at least when Sweet Water married Stalking Bear, she would move to the same village.

Closing her eyes, Caroline slowly drifted into sleep, where she was again haunted by shadowy dreams.

Chapter Three

Bryan eyed his mother intensely. Like Rebecca, he was fairly certain that Caroline and her brothers were dead; nevertheless, he couldn't completely convince himself. Earlier in the day, when the bartender had stated his belief that the children were dead, Bryan had agreed. Later, however, doubts had crept back into his mind. What if they were still alive? Would this Ross Bennett locate them? He had a nagging suspicion that he might indeed.

Bill Hanley had invited Ross and his cousin to the Bar-H for dinner—the invitation had included Bryan. During dinner, Bryan had paid close attention to Ross. He had found the man impressive, and sensed that Bennett was a man to be reckoned with. Bryan had also been impressed with Kirk, who seemed a lot like his cousin. Both men possessed an aura of dauntless strength, yet they seemed totally relaxed, and handled themselves confidently. Their conversations had consisted of straight talk and direct answers. Bryan had found the Bennetts friendly, yet somehow intimidating.

Following dinner, Bill had walked outside with his guests. Bryan, Rebecca, and Alex had retired to the parlor, where Bryan had voiced his worries. Alex had listened avidly, his intuition agreeing with his brother. Rebecca, on the other hand, thought her son was worrying unnecessarily. She was certain that Caroline and the boys were dead, and she said as much to Bryan.

Now, his nerves on edge, Bryan said with exasperation, "Mother, how can you be so sure they're dead? They could very well be living with the Apaches."

"Nonsense," she replied. "Everyone knows that Apaches seldom take prisoners."

"Then how come their bodies were never found?"

She shrugged nonchalantly. "There's a lot of country out there, and their bodies could be most anywhere. Their bones are most likely rotting somewhere in the desert."

"Well, I hope you're right."

"Of course I'm right," she said confidently. She went to her son and embraced him briefly. "Bryan, you worry too much."

Alex felt left out, but when the three of them were together, he always felt that way. He knew he wasn't smart like Bryan, but that was no reason for them to always ignore him. They never asked his opinion on any matter. Now, wanting to assert himself, he said eagerly, "I could get a couple of my ,friends, and we could follow the Bennetts. If they find Caroline or the boys, we could kill 'em all."

Bryan laughed. "Alex, are you crazy, or just plain stupid? What chance do you think you and your friends would have against men like the Bennetts? These guys are professionals!"

Sullen, Alex mumbled, "Oh yeah? They don't look all that tough to me."

"Your brother's right," Rebecca said. "When you're around the Bennetts, you keep your gun holstered, or you won't live very long." She moved to the sofa, and sat down. A coffee service was placed on the table,

47

and as she filled three cups, she thought about Ross and Kirk Bennett. She had found both men extremely attractive. Their masculine presence had aroused the passionate woman inside her that had lain dormant for so long. What she wouldn't give to share a romantic interlude with either one of them! If she had her choice, however, she would choose Ross. She was a good judge of men and was sure that he was not only sensually handsome, but beneath his controlled demeanor, lay a very passionate and aggressive lover.

She sighed desolately. Well, maybe someday when she was a rich widow, her path would again cross with Ross Bennett's — then she would find a way to get him in her bed. She'd not let the difference in their ages be a deterrent.

Meanwhile, Bill was still outside, talking to his guests. There were several comfortable chairs on the veranda, and the men were seated, smoking cigars, and sharing an amicable conversation.

Now, after spending time with Ross, Bill understood why the sheriff admired the young man. He was nothing like his reputation. He was polite, interesting, and respectful. These were admirable traits, but Bill wasn't blind to them, and he knew there was another side to Bennett. Confronted with violence, Bennett would meet it with deadly intent, utter courage, and steady nerve.

Bill turned his attention to Kirk, and asked, "Do you plan to ride with Ross?"

"To search for your grandchildren?" Kirk clarified.

Hanley nodded.

"Yeah, I guess I might as well ride along." He grinned at his cousin, then looked back at Bill. "I'll keep him out of trouble."

"Since when?" Ross said, amused.

Hanley smiled. Apparently, the cousins shared an

easy rapport. He sincerely liked both men. He had loved Walter with all his heart, yet he couldn't help but wish he'd had sons like these two. They would make a father proud. His thoughts prompted him to ask, "Are your fathers still alive?"

The question, coming out of the clear, seemed a little strange. After a moment, Kirk answered, "No, they aren't. My pa's been dead a long time, and Ross's died in the War between the States."

"Your mothers?" Bill was still curious.

"My mother died in childbirth," Kirk replied. "Ross's mother died years back. The only family we have is each other, except Ross still has kin among the Apaches." He lifted an eyebrow questioningly. "Why are you so interested in our parents?"

"Forgive me for prying. I guess I'm just as old man asking too many questions."

"No harm done," Ross said, getting to his feet. "Kirk and I will leave early in the morning. I hope we'll return with your grandchildren."

Bill also rose. "So do I. God, so do I!"

The Bennetts shook Hanley's hand, bid him a quick farewell, and moved down the steps to their horses. Untethering them from the hitching rail, they mounted, waved goodbye, and soon disappeared into the night.

Hanley remained on the veranda a long time, his thoughts on his grandchildren. Tears stung his eyes, and his heart ached over his loss. Praying, hoping, that the Bennetts would find Caroline and the boys, he turned about and walked sluggishly into the house.

The Bennetts rode back toward town at a leisurely pace. It was a pleasant night, for a cool breeze was blowing gently. They traveled quietly, both engrossed in their own thoughts.

Ross was wondering how much time he should spend searching for Hanley's grandchildren. He intended to do as good a job as possible. Hanley had paid him half the money up front — he was determined to earn it — he'd receive the remainder if he found one or more of the children. Ross still doubted that they were alive, but for Hanley's sake, he hoped they were.

Kirk's thoughts weren't on Hanley or his grandchildren, he was thinking about Ross. He knew his cousin well, and he was sure that deep inside, where no one could see, Ross was hurting, and hurting deeply. He didn't doubt that his cousin was still infatuated with Emily Parker. Ross and Emily had been engaged, but two months ago, Emily had broken their engagement. Her father, Henry Parker, owned a prosperous ranch outside Albuquerque. Emily was his only child, and he had spoiled her extravagantly. Henry had been firmly against Emily seeing a man like Ross, for he had higher expectations for his daughter. He wanted her to marry a refined gentleman, perhaps a lawyer, a doctor, or even a rich rancher like himself. He certainly didn't want her involved with Ross Bennett — a man who not only made a living with his gun, but was also part Apache. He had finally given Emily an ultimatum; if she didn't stop seeing Ross, he would disinherit her. Emily, loving riches more than Ross, had conceded to her father's demands. She told Ross that she never wanted to see him again.

Now, his thoughts still on his cousin and Emily, Kirk sighed deeply. Losing Emily had hit Ross hard, and for weeks he had drowned his sorrow in whiskey. Then, overnight, he made a complete turnabout. He stopped drinking to excess, and pulled his life back together. He never spoke of Emily, and Kirk never brought up her name. It was as though she had never existed. Although Kirk was tempted to talk about her with Ross, he thought it wiser to let it be.

The two cousins continued to ride without talking. Their friendship was too deep and secure for long lapses of silence to be uncomfortable.

Ross had been born in Texas, and at the onset of the War between the States, his father had joined Hood's Texas Brigade. Ross had been eleven at the time; he was twelve when his father was killed in battle. A year later, his mother, who had always been frail, died following a short illness. The Bennetts were poor, the old homestead was falling to ruin, and Ross abandoned the place without misgivings. He knew his father had kin living in Tucson, Arizona. At the young age of thirteen, he made the trip alone, inquired about town, and learned that Kirk Bennett was the sheriff's deputy. Although Kirk was only eighteen, he was already good with a gun, and the kind of deputy that a sheriff could depend on. The two Bennetts had never met each other, and Kirk had certainly been surprised to learn that Ross was his kin. He had his own house on the outskirts of Tucson, and he gladly took in his homeless relative. The five years separating the cousins wasn't a factor, and they quickly became good friends. Kirk continued his job as deputy, and Ross went back to school. A few years later, the Bennetts decided it was time to leave Tucson and see more of the West. For the most part, the two stayed together, but they would sometimes go their own way. However, they would inevitably meet up again.

Although they were a lot alike, in some ways they were quite different. Kirk was a taciturn man, and somewhat of a loner. He made his living in different ways. During his lifetime, he had been a wrangler, an Army scout, and had taken several jobs as a deputy. Ross, on the other hand, ended up working as a bounty hunter. But the work wasn't really to his liking, and he started hiring out his gun. He was particular about which jobs he took, as Sheriff Taylor had pointed out to Hanley, Ross hired his gun for the right causes. He had been twenty years old when he had decided to try and locate his Apache kin. Infiltrating Apache territory had been dangerous, but coming through it unscathed, he had located his grandmother's band, and had found that his granduncle was still alive. He had been welcomed into the village, and, now, eight years later, he was still warmly received.

Ross's granduncle, called Slow Bull, belonged to the Lipan Apaches, but Ross suspected that Hanley's grandchildren were abducted by the Chiricahua Apaches, who were reputed as the fiercest of all Apaches. He was worried that his granduncle might be of no help whatsoever, for there were so many Apache tribes that Slow Bull couldn't possibly know if one or more of them had white captives. There were Apache bands in Arizona and New Mexico, but Ross tentatively ruled them out. If the Hanley children were their captives, the Army would most likely have found them. If Caroline and the boys were still alive, they were probably in Mexico.

Kirk's thoughts were now on the same wave length as Ross's. "Even if those kids are alive, it's gonna be hard for us to find them."

Ross agreed. "If Slow Bull can't help us, then we might as well be looking for a needle in a haystack."

Kirk stifled a yawn. "I don't know about you, but I'm ready to hit the sack."

Ross felt the same way, and he urged his mount into a fast gallop. Kirk rode alongside him, and they were soon in Dry Branch, where they stabled their horses, then went to the hotel.

* * *

Ross awoke in the middle of the night. He had been dreaming about Emily, and unable to go back to sleep, he got out of bed, dressed, and went across the street to the saloon. He ordered a bottle of whiskey, sat down at a table by himself, and filled his glass.

A deep scowl was on his face, for he was aggravated with himself. Why the hell couldn't he forget Emily? She had chosen her father's inheritance over him; that alone should give him the initiative to completely wipe her out of his mind. She hadn't even jilted him for another man, but for money!

He took a long drink, leaned back, and propped his feet on a chair. He tried to put his feelings for Emily in perspective. Did he still think about her because he hadn't stopped loving her, or was bitterness keeping her in his thoughts? Was he tormented by a wounded heart, or wounded pride? He couldn't be sure, but he supposed it was a little of both. After all, he had never loved a woman until Emily. Then, the first time he had left himself vulnerable, he had taken a hard fall. Well, it had taught him a valuable lesson — he'd never again lay his heart on the line!

"Mind if I join you?" Kirk suddenly asked.

Ross glanced up with surprise.

Kirk drew out a chair, sat down, and said, "I couldn't sleep, so I decided to have a couple of drinks. I didn't think I'd find you here."

"Well, that goes both ways. I certainly wasn't expecting you."

"I woke up, and started thinking about Hanley and his grandkids, and I couldn't fall back asleep. I suppose that's why you're here, too."

"Actually, Hanley had nothing to do with it — it was Emily."

Kirk didn't say anything, but he had known that

sooner or later, Ross would talk to him about Emily.

"I was trying to figure out if I'm still in love with her."

"Love doesn't die quickly, Ross. It'll take time."

"Do I detect a note of experience?"

Kirk grinned wryly. "Well, I haven't exactly been celibate all my life." He watched Ross closely, as he asked, "When Emily chose her father's money over you, why didn't you tell her about your own finances? Hell, Ross, you've got a tidy sum of money stashed away."

"I didn't want Emily's love if I had to buy it."

Kirk was silent for a long moment, then still regarding his cousin closely, he questioned, "Ross, are you sure you were really in love with her? Maybe you were just blinded by her beauty. Besides, she wasn't the right woman for you—she's too damned wishy-washy. You need someone who's exciting, straightforward, and strong-willed. A man can love that kind of woman for a lifetime."

"Does that kind of woman even exist?" Ross asked with an amused smile.

"Sure she does, you just have to find her."

Basket Woman found Caroline sitting at the river's edge. The morning sun was peeking over the horizon, and it would soon be full light.

"White Raven," Basket Woman said, joining her. "I awoke to find you gone. I was worried, so I decided to look for you. Why are you sitting here alone? And why are you up so early? Leading Cloud and Sweet Water are not even awake yet."

Caroline turned and looked at her. The woman was concerned to see such torment on her daughter's face.

"I couldn't sleep," Caroline answered. "Too many

54

dreams keep swirling through my mind! I know these dreams are memories, but before I can make sense out of them, they are gone like fleeting wisps of smoke."

Basket Woman placed her hand on Caroline's, patting it soothingly. "White Raven, do you really want to remember? Does your other life mean that much to you?"

Caroline thought her answer over carefully, then answered candidly, "Yes, it means everything to me! Mother, please understand. I love you, and Sweet Water, and Leading Cloud very much, and I'm grateful to you and to them. I'm also thankful to everyone in this village for treating me so nicely, and accepting me as one of their own. But I had another life before this one, and I believe that is where I belong. In my dreams, I keep seeing a man's face. He's an older man, so he must be my father, or maybe my grandfather. I see such sorrow on his face, and I know he's grieving for me! I just know it!"

"You have no memory of this man?"

"No, but I think I'll remember him very soon. I also know that I loved him. We must have been very close."

Basket Woman got to her feet. "Wait here; I will be right back."

She hurried back to the wickiup, slipped quietly inside, then returned momentarily. Sitting beside Caroline, she handed her a piece of jewelry. "You were wearing this the day Spotted Horse brought you here. He told me to destroy it, but I hid it instead. It is such a beautiful necklace, and it looks as though it is very old. Maybe it will help you to remember." Basket Woman loved Caroline as though she were really her daughter; it was a mother's unselfish love. If White Raven truly longed for her other life, then Basket Woman wished her to have it. She wanted her to be happy, and she had a feeling that she might never be happy living as an Apache.

Caroline dropped her gaze to the dainty locket. She stared at it intensely, then she suddenly lifted her eyes to Basket Woman. She was trembling, and her voice quivered with excitement, "My grandfather gave me this locket! It belonged to my grandmother!" She bounded to her feet, exclaiming, "I remember! I actually remember!"

Basket Woman stood up quickly. "Do you now remember your other life?"

"No, I don't really remember all that much. But I do know that this locket was my grandmother's." Her gray eyes sparkled with expectancy, and she continued eagerly, "But now that a small part of my memory has returned, surely it's only a matter of time before I remember everything!"

The two women had been too involved to notice Spotted Horse approaching, and when he suddenly stepped to Caroline, jerking the locket from her hand, they were taken totally off guard.

Anger radiating from the dark depths of his eyes, he uttered fiercely to Basket Woman, "Why didn't you destroy this? Why did you disobey me?"

Fighting back tears, she answered meekly, "Forgive me, Spotted Horse, but it was too pretty to destroy. Also, I wanted to save it for White Raven."

"The spirits do not want her to have anything from her other life!" He threw the necklace into the river, grabbed Caroline's arm, and held her forcefully at his side. He continued to chastise Basket Woman. "I can no longer trust you! I will take White Raven to my village, and we will be married there!"

"Spotted Horse!" Caroline cried furiously, trying vainly to free herself from his tenacious hold. "Why are you so angry? It was only a necklace! Besides,

56

Basket Woman was right! It belonged to me, and you had no right to tell her to destroy it, nor did you have the right to throw it into the river!"

Spotted Horse was fuming. "See what the white man's necklace has done to you? It has made you forget your place! You are an Apache woman, and Apache women do not talk back to a warrior!" His wrath returned to Basket Woman. "Go inside your wickiup and pack White Raven's belongings! We leave very soon!"

As Basket Woman left to carry out his orders, Caroline managed to break Spotted Horse's firm grip on her arm. Eyes flashing defiantly, she argued, "I don't want to leave here! You have no right to take me away until we are married!"

"You belong to me, White Raven! You have been mine since the day I brought you to this village. No one will stop me from taking you!" He was dressed simply in a breechclout, and crossing his arms over his bare chest, he eyed Caroline threateningly. "You will do as I say!"

She controlled her temper; angering him further would only make matters worse.

She didn't say anything, and he took her silence as concession. He smiled complacently. Despite her white blood, she would make a good Apache wife. She was strong, spirited, yet she would be submissive to her husband.

"I will pack my things, and tell Stalking Bear that it is time to leave. In the meantime, go to your wickiup and tell your family goodbye." With that, he whirled about and walked away.

Caroline waited until he had disappeared into the dwelling he shared with Stalking Bear. Then, removing her moccasins, she moved to the bank, and stepped into the shallow water. Dawn had made its full ascent, and the river was so crystal clear that the sun's rays fell across the necklace's gold chain, causing it to sparkle like tiny diamonds. She reached down, picked it up, and slipped it into her pocket. The locket was hers, and she was going to keep it, regardless!

Caroline was putting on her moccasins when Sweet Water, rushing from their wickiup, called out to her. Running as fast as she could, she reached Caroline, and flung herself into her arms.

"Mother told me what happened! Oh White Raven, I will miss you so much!"

"We'll see each other again. Stalking Bear will marry you soon and bring you to his village."

"Yes, I know," she murmured, wiping at her tears. She stepped back, smiled shakily, and continued, "But, until then, I will miss you, and so will Mother and Father."

"I will miss all of you, too," Caroline replied, meaning it sincerely. She put an arm about Sweet Water's waist, and they started back to the wickiup. Suddenly, however, Caroline stopped dead in her tracks, and remarked with astonishment, "My grandfather's name is Bill Hanley! And my name is . . . is . . ."

"My sister!" Sweet Water exclaimed. "You remember!"

"No, I can't remember very much. But I am starting to recall so many things. It's as though my grandmother's locket is the key to my past, and its gradually unlocking my memories." She gripped Sweet Water's shoulders, smiled radiantly, and announced, "Now I remember my name—it's Caroline!"

Chapter Four

Spotted Horse's parents had died years ago, so when they reached his village, he took Caroline to Stalking Bear's family. He told her that she would live with them until they were married. Caroline was miserable from the moment she entered their dwelling, for Stalking Bear's parents merely made a pretense of welcoming her. She could sense their hostility. She was white, and like their son, they hated anyone who was white. They had one unmarried daughter who was still at home, One-Who-Laughs. She didn't even pretend to welcome Caroline, but was openly resentful. Stalking Bear, like Spotted Horse, lived in a communal wickiup exclusively for bachelors.

The journey to Spotted Horse's village had been an agonizing one for Caroline. Stalking Bear, who had never been very friendly, had seemed less sociable than usual, and Spotted Horse had been withdrawn and moody. It had become obvious to Caroline that Spotted Horse didn't want her to regain her memory, and she resented him for that. She had always liked Spotted Horse, and had considered him a friend, but now her feelings were starting to change. Furthermore, he had revealed a cold, authoritative side to his nature that she didn't like. Moreover, she was beginning to distrust him. This made her feel guilty, for Spotted Horse had saved her life the day he had found her wandering in the desert. In addition, he had taken her to his uncle's village, where she had been warmly welcomed. She should be more loyal! Still almost without knowing it, she began to doubt Spotted Horse's sincerity. In the beginning, most of Caroline's memories were hazy, but some she could recall with clarity. She vividly remembered her grandfather and the Bar-H, but memories of her parents and brothers were still shadowy. With each passing day, however, she began to recall more and more about her family. Her past life was like a jigsaw puzzle that she was slowly piecing together. As the pieces fell into place, and the first thirteen years of her life grew clearer, her heart ached to return home. She still couldn't remember why she had been wandering in the desert. Her mind had totally blocked out her parents' deaths and her brothers' abduction. That day remained a total blank.

Now that Caroline knew who she was, and could even remember most of her life, she wanted desperately to leave Spotted Horse and return to Dry Branch. She knew she didn't belong with the Apaches, but with her own kind. She had warm feelings for Leading Cloud, Basket Woman, and Sweet Water. The years she had spent with them had been pleasant ones. But now her life had changed drastically, for living in Spotted Horse's village was a lot different than living in Leading Cloud's. Here, the people treated her coldly, and Stalking Bear's family could barely tolerate her presence. Well, the feeling was mutual — she wanted to leave their home as badly as they wished she weren't there. Also, at Leading Cloud's village, she had been free, but here she was treated like a prisoner. Apparently Spotted Horse was afraid that she might run away, for he had told Stalking Bear's mother, Sun Flower, to watch her closely. When this wasn't possible, Sun Flower always had another woman keep a sharp eye on Caroline. Escaping would be extremely difficult, but Caroline hoped to find a way. She certainly didn't want to spend the rest of her life as Spotted Horse's wife.

Her recollections had finally brought her to her thirteenth birthday—she even remembered spending the day at the Bar-H. Her grandfather had given her the locket, and had secretly presented her with a new Winchester. She vaguely remembered leaving the ranch with her parents and brothers, but, from that point on, her mind was a complete blank. Had something happened on their way home? Had they been attacked by hostile Indians or Mexican bandits? Why had she been wandering in the desert? Had she been in New Mexico, or had Spotted Horse found her in the Mexican desert? Dear God, why had she been separated from her family? Where were her parents and brothers? Were they still alive? These questions were now haunting Caroline. They not only disrupted her sleep, but also plagued her during the day.

She considered questioning Spotted Horse. He might know something that could help her, but she was now wary of the warrior, and she didn't want him to know that she was remembering her past.

Caroline had been living in Spotted Horse's village for three days when he came to Sun Flower's wickiup, told Caroline he needed to talk to her, and took her outside. He led her down to the river's bank where they could be alone.

She stood before him, pretending docility. She didn't want to do or say anything that might put Spotted Horse on his guard. She wanted him to believe

61

that she was willing to marry him and live in his village.

Spotted Horse seemed in no hurry to explain why he wanted to see Caroline. He simply stared at her as though he were trying to read her thoughts, as indeed he was! He didn't quite trust White Raven, for he was afraid that the spirits were returning her memories. If she were to remember her parents' deaths, she'd certainly turn on him with a vengeance. Well, it would make no difference, for he would still marry her! If he had to resort to force to bend her to his will, then he would do just that! She was spirited, true, but he could make her submissive. He hoped it wouldn't come to that, for he admired her vitality. After all, it had been her spirit and courage that had attracted him in the first place. Her exquisite beauty, of course, had been equally important.

Now, regarding her closely, he tried to discern her thoughts, but there was nothing in her expression to make him suspicious. She was watching him patiently, waiting for him to speak. He looked deeply into her charcoal-gray eyes, and, as always, he found them enchanting. His gaze then traveled over her body, and he was greatly pleased with what he saw. White Raven was most assuredly a beautiful maiden. The day he had kidnapped her, he had known that someday she would be a vision of loveliness. Over the years, his body had ached for hers, but he had been patient. Before they married, he wanted her to act and think like an Apache. As the mother of his children, her influence would undoubtedly play a big role in their upbringing. If she were an Apache in heart and soul, then she would raise them properly.

Spotted Horse had begun to believe that his dreams would come true, but he was now having doubts. It had all started with Basket Woman giving White

Raven the locket. That morning, he had seen something in White Raven's eyes that had put him on edge. He couldn't quite pinpoint what it was — had it been a spark of rebellion? He wasn't sure, but his confidence was now somewhat shaken. He hoped it was only his imagination, and that he was worrying needlessly.

"White Raven," he said, finally talking to her. "I plan to leave today, and I will be gone for some time. When I return, we will be married. In the meantime, Sun Flower and One-Who-Laughs will help you build our wickiup."

"Very well, Spotted Horse," she replied respectfully. She wondered where he was going, but she didn't dare ask, for she knew it wouldn't be proper. She was glad that he was leaving. Escaping would be easier with him gone.

Spotted Horse, and the warriors leaving with him, were planning to raid Arizona and New Mexico, where they intended to kill and loot. Spotted Horse, wondering how White Raven would react to this information, decided to put her to the test. Out of the clear, he disclosed where he and the others were going, and what they hoped to accomplish.

Caroline hid her disapproval, and feigning a modest smile, asked, "Will you bring me back something pretty?" She didn't doubt that Spotted Horse was testing her, and she knew it was vital that she pass.

Spotted Horse was pleased. He wondered if he had been wrong to distrust White Raven's sincerity. Although he was beginning to believe in her again, he nevertheless decided to remain cautious. Smiling, he asked, "What would you like me to bring you?"

"A necklace, perhaps?" Her eyes teased his. "After all, you threw mine away."

He chuckled heartily, for he enjoyed her sense of humor. "I will see what I can do." He wrapped an arm about her waist, and urged her back toward the heart of the village.

His laughter echoed in Caroline's ears, and it touched a tender chord deep inside her. She had always liked Spotted Horses's laugh, for it was full, deep, and infectious. She supposed she should loathe Spotted Horse, for if he were a killer of whites, then he was actually her enemy. But she couldn't bring herself to hate him. Still she now knew that she didn't love Spotted Horse — had never loved him. She didn't want to marry him now, or ever!

As they neared Sun Flower's wickiup, Caroline's steps hesitated. She didn't want to go back in there where she wasn't welcomed. Tears misted her eyes, but she inconspicuously wiped them away, she didn't want Spotted Horse to catch her crying. She wished for complete privacy, then she could cry until there were no tears left to shed. She had a feeling it would make her feel better.

Despite an aching heart, she walked proudly with her head held high. An observer, Spotted Horse included, would never imagine that deep inside she was tormented. She was longing to see her grandfather — and her parents and brothers, if they were still alive! She thought about escaping. If she were to slip away during Spotted Horse's absence, would Stalking Bear's father, Gray Feather, come after her? She was afraid that he would, for Spotted Horse had entrusted her in Gray Feather's care, and he would probably feel responsible.

Caroline, worried that she would never see her family, prayed for a miraculous escape. Now that she could remember her grandfather with clarity, she was positive that he had made every effort to find her; by now, he had certainly given up. In the beginning, he had probably hired men to search for her, but now that so many years had passed, he most likely believed she was dead. She seriously doubted that anyone was still out there looking for her.

Ross and Kirk arrived at Slow Bull's village in the late afternoon. After they were graciously welcomed, one of the warriors took them to Slow Bull's wickiup. As the visitors waited outside, the warrior went in to tell the headman that he had guests. He returned momentarily, letting Ross and Kirk know that Slow Bull was ready to receive them.

The two men entered the dwelling. The interior was dark compared to the sunlight outside, and it took a moment for their eyes to adjust. Slow Bull's two wives were sitting at the back, weaving baskets. They smiled and nodded cordially to Ross. He greeted them respectfully, and asked about their health. One of the women, who was Slow Bull's first wife, was very old. Although the other wife was years younger, she was still well into middle-age.

Ross motioned for Kirk to follow, and moved to Slow Bull's bed, where the old man was resting. He and Kirk sat down, crossing their legs Indian-fashion.

The Apaches had no central tribal government, so bands within each tribe had headmen, whose positions were maintained through their persuasiveness and warlike prowess. In his time, Slow Bull had been a courageous and enthusiastic leader, but he was now approaching ninety years of age. Although he was crippled with arthritis, and was even growing blind, he was still greatly respected, for the people knew a man of his age was very wise.

Ross reached out and placed a hand on his grand-uncle's. The man's skin felt clammy. Slow Bull's eyes were open, but Ross wasn't sure if he were actually seeing him. The old warrior's face was weathered and wrinkled, and his long, straight hair was snowwhite.

"He-Who-Wanders," Slow Bull murmured, calling Ross by his Apache name. "I am glad you are here. Do you come alone?"

"No, my uncle. My cousin is with me."

Slow Bull had met Kirk before, for this was the third time Kirk had accompanied Ross.

"Tell him he is welcome," the old man said. His voice was so weak that Ross had to strain to hear.

Ross and Slow Bull were speaking in Apache, and Ross turned to Kirk to give him Slow Bull's message. Kirk understood some Apache, and he had grasped the old man's words.

"I understood," he said to Ross. "Tell him I am pleased to see him again."

Ross, following Apache etiquette, continued with proper amenities for a time, then he got down to his reason for being here. "My uncle, I am looking for three white children. They were abducted by the Apaches five years ago. The two boys would now be ten and seven years of age. The girl would be eighteen. She is no longer a child, but a young maiden. Can you help me find them?"

Slow Bull was silent for so long that Ross wondered if he had even heard him. He was about to repeat himself, when the man finally answered, "I have heard nothing about two white boys living with the Apaches."

"The girl?" Ross asked.

"It is rumored that Spotted Horse plans to marry a white woman."

"Who is Spotted Horse?"

"He is a fierce warrior, and is greatly respected. He is a Chiricahua. You will not be welcomed in his village."

"But it's very important that I see him."

"Then I will ask Standing Elk to go with you. But you must not enter Spotted Horse's village. You are considered white, and you will be killed. Standing Elk must go in your place. He will talk to Spotted Horse."

"You say it's only a rumor that Spotted Horse will marry a white woman. Where did you hear such a rumor, and do you believe that it's true?"

"The rumor has been heard for many moons, it travels from village to village. I do not know if it's true. I know no one who has seen this white woman."

Ross knew it was a lead he had to follow. "Thank you, my uncle. I will stay here tonight, and leave in the morning. I will let you rest now, then come back later. Where is Standing Elk? I did not see him when I rode into the village."

"Standing Elk is hunting, but will return before the sun sets. He will be happy to see you."

"As I will be happy to see him," Ross said, getting to his feet. Standing Elk and Ross were the same age, and Slow Bull was also Standing Elk's granduncle. Eight years ago, when Ross first found his Apache kin, he and Standing Elk had become instant friends. It was Standing Elk who had taught him the Apache language and customs. In return, Ross had taught the warrior English.

With Kirk following, Ross left his uncle's wickiup, and stepped back outside into the bright sunlight. Leading their horses and a pack mule, they walked to a dwelling located on the outskirts of the village. Regardless of where Slow Bull's people set up camp, an empty wickiup was always erected in the same general area. It was put there for Ross to use when he visited.

As he and Kirk entered the home, they found three young maidens inside, chaperoned by a matron. The women were preparing the wickiup. They had a lodge fire burning, and a pot of cooked stew was warming over the hot coals. Now, they quickly spread blankets over dry grass, which would suffice for beds. Then the older woman, ready to leave, ushered the young maidens past the two men. The girls, casting Ross and Kirk flirtatious glances, giggled merrily as they were practically pushed outside.

The men were carrying their carpetbags and provisions. They pitched the bags onto their prospective beds, then went to the lodge fire. Ross unpacked what he needed to make coffee, and soon had a pot brewing.

"Exactly what did Slow Bull have to say?" Kirk asked. "I only understood some of it."

Ross explained everything in detail.

"Maybe this woman Spotted Horse plans to marry is Caroline Hanley."

"Maybe," Ross murmured. He reached into his pocket and withdrew the picture of Caroline's grandmother. He studied it for a long time. He wondered if Caroline was as beautiful as her grandmother. He supposed she was, for Hanley had said their resemblance was remarkable. If Caroline Hanley was Spotted Horse's woman, then Ross didn't blame the warrior for wanting to marry her, for she must be very lovely. He slipped the picture back into his pocket.

"Ross," Kirk continued, "what if this woman is Hanley's granddaughter, but she doesn't want to leave Spotted Horse? What happens then?"

Ross shrugged. "I don't know. I'm not sure we have the right to force her to leave. If she wants to stay with Spotted Horse, then I guess we go back to the Bar-H, and break the bad news to Hanley."

"What about the boys? Where do you suppose they are?"

"They could be with an Apache band somewhere.

68

But if they were, I think Slow Bull would know about it." He paused, then said with a heavy sigh, "I'm afraid the boys are dead."

"Yeah, I am too," Kirk said softly.

Caroline lay in bed, waiting for the others to fall deeply asleep. It was well into the night, and she was certain that she was the only one still awake. Nevertheless, she didn't move, for she wanted everyone to be sound asleep before she left. Gray Feather was a light sleeper, and she didn't want to take any unnecessary risks. She was planning to run away. She knew that if she didn't succeed on her first try, she might not get a second chance. If Gray Feather were to catch her, he would probably have her bound in the evenings, which would stop any further nighttime escapes. During the day, Sun Flower would certainly start watching her more closely.

Caroline knew it was now or never. But slipping away from the village was the easy part, making her way alone in the wilderness was where the biggest danger lay. She could be captured by bandits or hostile Indians. Furthermore, the land itself posed a threat, for it could be more deadly than her worst enemy. To reach the Rio Grande, she would have to travel across desert terrain. What if her horse were to suffer a mishap, and she was left afoot? Could she possibly survive, or would the hot sun eventually drive her mad? Would she wander in the desert, dazed and incoherent, until she dropped dead? A shiver ran through Caroline, for she had heard of such things happening to travelers.

She forcefully pushed the possibility from her mind. If she started thinking the worst, then she'd lose the courage to escape. And she desperately wanted to run away! She wanted so badly to see her grandfather and her family! Remembering them with clarity had made her painfully aware of how much she loved them.

Deciding it was time to leave, Caroline slipped furtively out of bed. She slept next to One-Who-Laughs, but the young woman didn't even stir as Caroline moved away cautiously. Caroline was nude, for the Apaches preferred to sleep uninhibited. She grabbed her clothes, which were folded neatly beside her bed, and tucking them under her arm, she sneaked across the wickiup, stepping stealthily outside. She dressed quickly, then hurried to where Gray Feather kept his horses tethered. She planned to take the pony Spotted Horse had given her when they left Leading Cloud's village.

The young pinto remembered her, and it didn't even whinny as she approached with its lead and blanket. Praying no one would step out of their wickiup and see her, she hastily slipped the lead over the pony's head, threw the blanket across its back, and led it away from the other horses.

Earlier in the day, she had found the opportunity to hide a bag filled with provisions. Sun Flower's sister had given birth that afternoon, and Sun Flower had been so occupied with the event that Caroline had managed to temporarily escape the woman's watchful eye.

Leading the pinto down to the river's bank, Caroline retrieved her provisions, which were stashed behind a tree. Without stirrups, or a handup, mounting the pony wasn't easy, but Caroline managed on her first try.

She kept the pinto at a steady walk until she was a good distance from the village, then she sent the pony into a fast gallop. She wanted to put as many miles as

70

possible between herself and Gray Feather.

Unknown to Caroline, her escape hadn't gone undetected. Moments after she left the wickiup, One-Who-Laughs had awakened. Finding White Raven gone, she had dressed and had stepped outside to look for her. Standing in the shadows, she had watched Caroline's every move. But the young woman wasn't about to thwart Caroline's escape, for she was glad to see her leave. She was certain that with White Raven gone, Spotted Horse would marry her instead. She was very much in love with the warrior, so she did nothing to stop Caroline from leaving. In fact, she was smiling as Caroline rode away.

Now, slipping back into her wickiup, One-Who-Laughs returned to bed. She prayed earnestly to the spirits, begging them to aid White Raven's escape.

Chapter Five

The sun was midway in the sky before Caroline decided to stop and let her pony rest. Although she wasn't in the least tired, she knew it was vital that the horse not overexert itself. She was so eager to reach home she felt as though she could travel nonstop. She knew, however, that her adrenalin would eventually slow down.

The countryside was mostly open terrain, but spotting a section of mesquite trees, she rode over, dismounted, and removed her provisions. The land was dotted with clumps of grass, and the pony began to nibble at the long blades. A gentle breeze, stirring the treetops, made the area a comfortable place to stop.

Caroline sat in the shade of a mesquite, leaned back against its trunk, and considered her situation. She wasn't sure of her exact location, but she knew she was somewhere in Mexico. How far away was the Rio Grande? A day's ride, a week's, or even longer? She couldn't remember ever feeling so insecure. She felt as though she were alone in the middle of nowhere. What if she couldn't find the Rio Grande? She quickly thrust the notion aside. If she kept heading north, she'd surely run across the river — wouldn't she?

Caroline's enthusiasm began to falter. Had it been a mistake to run away from Spotted Horse's village? Would her rebellion inevitably lead to her own death? She knew the journey ahead was precarious, and she wished for a weapon, for she had no way to protect herself. If only she could have stolen one of Gray Feather's rifles!

Her thoughts drifted back in time, and she remembered her grandfather teaching her to shoot. She hadn't shot a rifle in five years, but she was quite certain that she hadn't forgotten how.

She shrugged. Well, wishing for a rifle was a waste of time, she didn't have one, and one wasn't going to drop in her lap! She was defenseless, except for her own wit, caution, and instinct. It wasn't much, and she supposed her chances of reaching the Rio Grande were slim. Nevertheless, she was determined to try!

"How much farther to Spotted Horse's village?" Ross asked Standing Elk.

"We will be there at sunset," the warrior replied.

Ross, along with Standing Elk and Kirk, had been traveling since dawn. The men had decided to get an early start. They had stopped at noon to eat and rest their horses, otherwise, they had been riding steadily.

"He-Who-Wanders," Standing Elk said to Ross. "Remember, you are not to enter Spotted Horse's village. You are part Apache, true, but you are not really one of us. The Chiricahuas will see you as a white man, and they consider all whites their enemies. You and Kirk must set up camp away from the village, and I will ride in alone."

Ross agreed. He wasn't about to turn this mission into a suicidal one. A white man riding uninvited into a Chiricahua village was certain death.

Standing Elk, his pony cantering beside Ross's, studied his friend with a sidelong glance. Although they shared the same forefathers, he could see little resemblance between himself and Ross. Standing Elk was typically Apache, dark complexion, stocky build, and broad features; Ross was tanned, tall, his face finely sculpted.

They were riding through an abra, a narrow pass between hills, but Standing Elk suddenly turned his pony to the left, and started up the gradual slope. Ross and Kirk followed close behind. As they reached the top of the hill, they reined in their horses. The countryside below was grassless except for a few dry clumps flecked here and there. Mesquite trees, along with clusters of sage brush, grew sparsely.

The men were about to continue onward when they suddenly spotted a lone rider. The traveler appeared to be an Apache woman, for she was dressed in Apache garb and was riding an Indian pony.

"I didn't think Apache women traveled alone," Kirk remarked.

Standing Elk, speaking English, replied, "They do not ride alone. Something is wrong, or this woman would not be by herself."

"Let's catch up to her, and see if she needs help," Ross said, kneeing his horse into motion.

Ross, leading the way, started down the hillside with his companions close behind.

Caroline's thoughts were on Gray Feather. She wondered if he was trailing her. If so, would she be able to outrun him? She estimated she had at least six hours head start. But was six hours long enough to elude an experienced warrior like Gray Feather? She was afraid that it wasn't.

The sudden sounds of approaching horses sent Gray Feather fleeing her thoughts, and glancing over her shoulder, she was unnerved to see three riders advancing. They were still at a distance, but she could make them out fairly well, and could see there were two white men and an Indian. For a moment, she was hesitant. Should she stop and wait? They might be able to help her. But what if they were renegades? Stopping could be a terrible mistake. She didn't know these men, and they could very well be up to no good. She quickly chastised herself for even considering stopping. How could she be so foolish, so naive?

Now, fear peaking, Caroline urged her pinto into a full run. The pony's hoofs were pounding against the dry terrain when a rattlesnake, hidden behind a small rock, struck quickly. The poisonous fangs missed their mark, but panicked by the dangerous reptile, the pinto's eyed rolled in terror. Bucking wildly, it threw its rider to the ground.

Caroline's whole body was jarred painfully as she hit the dirt with a solid thump. The impact was so severe that for an instant, she couldn't catch her breath. Then, scrambling to her feet, she looked about, searching for her pony, which was standing close by. As she raced toward the horse, she dared to glance over her shoulder. The riders were drawing extremely close.

Caroline, having no idea why her pony had panicked, didn't see the recoiling snake. She was halfway to her horse when she heard the ominous rattle that came before the strike. She tried to jump back, but it was too late, and the reptile's fangs dug sharply into her leg. Meanwhile, the pinto, frightened again by the snake, bolted, leaving its rider behind.

Caroline turned to flee her slithering attacker, but her leg was already paining her considerably, and instead of running, she hobbled. She didn't get very far before collapsing. She tried futilely to get back up, but her head was swimming, and there was a terrible roaring in her ears. She wondered if she were about to faint.

Despite her condition, she was aware of the three riders' arrival. She was lying on her stomach, but managing to turn over, she watched as one of the men drew his pistol, aimed it at the snake, and fired.

Holstering his gun, Ross dismounted lithely, went to Caroline, and knelt beside her. As he gazed down into her face, he could hardly believe his own eyes. It was as though he were looking at the photograph he carried in his pocket. My God, this lovely young woman must be Caroline Hanley!

He didn't question her, for there was no time. Kirk had dismounted, but Standing Elk was still on his pony. Speaking to him, Ross said quickly, "Go after her horse."

The warrior kneed his pony, and was gone in a flash.

Ross turned back to Caroline, and lifted the hem of her skirt. As he had feared, two puncture marks, located above her low-cut moccasins, were already starting to swell. Glancing toward Kirk, he said, "Get that flask of whiskey."

Caroline, halfway between awareness and unconsciousness, heard Ross's words. They sounded somewhat strange, but were nevertheless soothing, for he had spoken in English. She hadn't heard her own language spoken aloud in years. She had always heard it in her mind, though, for she had never stopped thinking in English.

Ross drew his knife from a sheath strapped to his waist, then held it toward Kirk, who poured whiskey over the sharp blade.

"I'll have to make an incision," Ross said gently to Caroline. She nodded, feeling too faint to say anything. Despite her weakened state, she was very taken with Ross's good looks, as well as with his kindness.

Quickly, and as painlessly as possible, Ross made the small incision across the wound. He then sucked out the venomous poison, spitting it onto the ground. Finished, he gazed tenderly into Caroline's pale face, placed a hand on her brow, and was concerned to find that she was already feverish.

Caroline, on the brink of losing consciousness, tried to thank the stranger for helping her, but before she could utter a word, she was immersed in a sea of blackness.

"She passed out," Ross said to Kirk. "We'll have to hole up somewhere until she's able to travel."

Kirk, recognizing Caroline from her grandmother's picture, shook his head with amazement. "I can hardly believe what I'm seeing. I thought finding Caroline Hanley would be next to impossible, but I'll be damned if she didn't just materialize out of nowhere."

Ross agreed totally. "I know what you mean."

Then, catching a movement, Kirk whirled about stealthily. In the distance, a lone Indian sat astride his pony. "Ross, take a gander at that," Kirk said softly.

Ross was still kneeling beside Caroline, but the distant threat put him on guard. Rising, he edged closer to his horse, and unsheathed his rifle.

"You suppose he's after Caroline?" Kirk asked.

77

"That'd be my guess," Ross replied. He kept a close vigil on the warrior. He hoped he would turn around and leave, for he didn't want to kill him.

The lone Indian was Gray Feather. He had awakened at dawn, two hours sooner than Caroline had speculated. Learning that his ward had run away, he had set out immediately to find her. Swifter and more experienced than Caroline, he had steadily shortened the miles between them.

Now, his next move was uncertain. Should he try to steal White Raven from the two white men? It would be risky, and could very well cost him his life. He knew Spotted Horse would be enraged to learn that White Raven had escaped. Although Gray Feather loved Spotted Horse as though he were his own son, he nonetheless thought him a fool to love a white woman. In his opinion, he should marry One-Who-Laughs. Gray Feather knew his daughter would make Spotted Horse a much better wife than White Raven. Spotted Horse was not thinking rationally, but was blinded by White Raven's beauty.

A sigh of resignation escaped the warrior's lips. He was loyal to Spotted Horse, and would try to get White Raven back. The odds were two against one, but he wasn't dissuaded. In his estimation, one Apache warrior's prowess equaled that of two white men.

He was considering a plan of attack when he suddenly spied Standing Elk returning with White Raven's pinto. The arriving warrior gave him reason to reconsider. He now believed the odds were in his enemies' favor, and he decided to leave without White Raven.

Gray Feather recognized Standing Elk, for he occasionally visited his village. If Spotted Horse decided to pursue White Raven, he could tell him

78

where to start looking—at Standing Elk's village.

Leaving, Gray Feather turned his pony about, galloped away quickly, and was soon out of sight.

Standing Elk led the way, for he knew a good place to set up camp. It was a short ride, no more than thirty minutes from where Caroline had been bitten. The small area was well-hidden by shrubs and mesquite trees.

Caroline was placed on a bed of blankets, and sitting beside her, Ross bathed her warm brow with a damp cloth. Although he was worried, he wasn't overly alarmed, for he knew most victims survived snake bites, especially if they were tended to immediately. He was fairly sure that he had gotten to Caroline in time. Nonetheless, he knew she would be ill for the next twenty-four hours.

Delirious with fever, Caroline rambled incoherently. Sometimes, she would speak in Apache, other times in English. Most of what she mumbled was gibberish and made little sense. There were moments, however, when she would call Spotted Horses's name.

Ross was now certain that Caroline Hanley was the white woman Spotted Horse planned to marry. He wondered if Caroline was in love with the warrior. He supposed she was, otherwise, why would she call his name?

Although Ross tried to keep his feelings detached, he couldn't help but find Caroline enchanting. She was lovelier than words, in fact, he couldn't recall ever seeing a woman more beautiful. She was even more attractive than Emily, and his ex-fiance was indeed striking.

Caroline tossed and turned in her delirium, and

79

Ross spoke to her soothingly. Deep within her mind his calming voice made contact, and his soft, sedate tone lulled her into a deep, restful sleep.

Standing Elk and Kirk had gone hunting, and they returned with two rabbits. Kirk immediately checked on Caroline.

"How is she doing?" he asked Ross.

"She's resting peacefully. I think she's going to be all right."

"I wonder why she was traveling alone, and why Gray Feather was trailing her." Standing Elk had recognized the warrior, and had told Kirk and Ross who he was.

"I don't know," Ross replied. "I guess we'll find out why when she's able to talk to us."

"She might not want to return to her grandfather, you know. What do we do if she refuses to leave with us?"

"Like I said before, I won't force her to return. She's no longer a child. She has a right to make her own decisions."

Kirk's eyes traveled briefly over Caroline. "She's no child, that's for sure. She's very beautiful, isn't she?"

"I suppose," Ross mumbled. "I hadn't really noticed."

Kirk chuckled. "You'd have to be blind not to notice." Kirk could read his cousin like a book. "Yeah, she's beautiful, all right. Just like Emily Parker. And just like Emily, she's heir to a prosperous ranch and lots of money. Are you worried history's gonna repeat itself, Ross?"

"No, because I learn from my mistakes. Besides, you're talking nonsense. I don't even know this girl."

"That's true, you don't know her—not yet, that is."

* * *

Caroline's fever broke about an hour before dawn. She awoke slowly and sat up, but the movement caused her head to ache terribly. Groaning, she rubbed her throbbing temples, hoping to ease the pain.

Ross's bedroll was close to hers. He was a light sleeper, and her soft moans had awakened him instantly. He got up, went to her side, and sat beside her.

"How do you feel?" he asked quietly.

Her brow creased. She knew he was speaking something familiar . . . but her hazy mind could not quite grasp it. He seemed to sense her confusion and spoke again.

"How do you feel?" he said once more, but this time in the Apache tongue.

"My head hurts," she groaned in the Indian language.

"Head," he said in English as he pointed to his own head. "Do you understand?" he asked in the Apache tongue, then repeated the question in English.

She nodded her head. Their eyes met, and she understood that he wanted her to speak the English. "I un-de-stan . . ." she murmured, the language feeling both strange yet comfortingly familiar to speak after many years.

"Head," he said again.

"Head," she repeated in English. The cobwebs were beginning to be brushed away as her mouth responded to the language that had never been abandoned by her mind, but merely pushed aside until she needed it again.

"My head hurts," Ross said then looked expectantly at her. "Say it."

Caroline's memory helped as she struggled to say the words. "M-m-y head hu . . . hu . . ."

Ross's gaze met hers, and he smiled. "Hurts."

"M-m-y head . . . hu—hurts!" exclaimed Caroline, then groaned with the effort. Now her head hurt even more!

"Otherwise, how do you feel?" Ross asked.

Her leg was aching, and she moved a hand to her wound. She wasn't surprised to find it was bandaged. "My l . . . leg . . ." she paused to find the right word. "My leg . . . hurts," she said with a grimace.

"That's expected, but you're going to be fine." He touched her brow, saying with a smile, "Your fever has broken . . . Understand?"

Caroline nodded, realizing at the same time that the touch of his hand was having a strange effect. The contact was pleasant; yet, it triggered a sensuous sensation, one she had never experienced. The feeling brought a warm tingle to her depths, for she was indeed attracted to this handsome stranger.

The attraction was mutual. Ross wanted to reach out and take her into his arms; the need was so strong that it was almost tangible. With effort, he controlled the urge. His mission was to return Caroline Hanley to her grandfather, and there was no reason to become emotionally involved. A vision of Emily Parker flashed across his mind. He had left himself vulnerable once, he'd not do so a second time.

"I'll get you some broth," Ross said, getting to his feet. Caroline watched as he crossed to the low-burning campfire, knelt, and dished up a bowl of warm broth. Returning, his eyes met hers. He smiled. It was a disarming smile, yet, so sensuous that it went

82

straight to Caroline's heart. She not only instinctively liked this man, but also felt an immediate and total attraction to him. She was very impressed with his good looks, she liked the way his brown hair was streaked with black, the warmth in his dark eyes, and his charming smile. His tall, tightly-muscled frame moved with the grace and stealth of an Indian.

Ross handed her the bowl and sat beside her. As she ate, he spoke softly and gently to her in English and coaxed her to speak back. With Ross's warm smile as encouragemen, Caroline found herself regaining command of her first language at a rate that seemed to astonish Ross. But Caroline was not surprised. In the past days, as the memory of her identity was gradually coming back to her, it seemed only right that the language of that identity be restored to her as well. After only a short time talking with Ross, Caroline felt that the English was very natural, even comforting, to speak.

Finally, the conversation turned from simple topics to the questions Ross had been waiting to ask. "I must ask you some questions now. Why were you riding alone?"

"I run away," she replied.

"From Spotted Horse?"

She was startled. "You . . . know Spotted Horse?"

"Not much," he answered. "You're Caroline Hanley, aren't you?"

She was so surprised that, for a moment, she was left speechless. "You — you know who I am!" she stammered, incredulous.

"Your grandfather hired me to find you." He reached into his pocket, withdrew the photograph, and offered it to Caroline. "I recognized you from this picture of your grandmother."

Placing the bowl aside, she took the photograph

and stared at it intensely. Then, lifting her gaze to Ross's, she asked timorously, "My f . . . family — are they still alive?"

Ross was surprised at her question. He'd assumed she would've already known that her parents had been murdered after she had been taken away. He wished he didn't have to be the one to break such tragic news. "I'm sorry, Caroline. You're parents are dead. They were killed five years ago."

"Dead!" she cried. "But how . . . why?"

"They were killed by Apaches."

"No! Surely, you are wrong!" She couldn't fathom the people she had lived with all these years murdering her parents. "My brothers?" she questioned, dreading the worst.

"I don't know if they're still alive. Like you, they were abducted . . . taken against their will."

"I was . . . taken by Apaches?" she asked, evidently shocked.

Ross was as confused as Caroline. "Don't you know what happened to you?"

"No, I do not." She quickly explained her loss of memory. He asked a few questions, she answered them, then continued, "Spotted Horse found me wandering in the desert, and he took me to his uncle's village. For years, I had no memory of my past. Only recently did I start to see the memories again. That was why I was running away. I wanted to go home!" She paused, and a trace of tears appeared. "I still cannot remember what happened that day when my family and I left the Bar-H."

Her shock began to wear off, its waning bringing her parents to mind. They had been dead all these years! Murdered by Apaches! Grief cut into her painfully, tearing cruelly into her heart. Tears fell from her eyes, and her shoulders shook with deep, rasping sobs.

Ross was quick to take her into his arms, and he held her closely as she wept for the parents she had loved so dearly.

A long time later, her grief somewhat appeased, she moved out of his embrace. Wiping at her tear-reddened eyes, she said softly, "Forgive me for crying like this, but . . . but . . ."

"It's all right," he whispered soothingly.

"My grandfather, he is well?"

"He's fine," Ross hastened to answer, glad he had at least one piece of good news to deliver.

Kirk and Standing Elk, ensconced in their bed-rolls, were not asleep. They had remained where they were because they didn't want to infringe on Caroline's grief. But now that the sun was rising, they knew it was time to start moving about.

As the men were rolling up their blankets, Ross emptied the broth that by then had turned cold. He quickly dished up another bowl, gave it to Caroline, and told her that she must eat to keep up her strength.

She accepted the proffered food, for she knew he was right.

"Would you like to stay here and rest another day, or do you feel well enough to travel?" Ross asked her.

She didn't want anymore delays, she was too anxious to see her grandfather. "I can travel," she replied.

"We'll make you a travois," Ross decided. He didn't want her riding horseback, she should remain recumbent for at least another day.

He turned to leave, but Caroline detained him. "What is your name?"

"Ross Bennett," he replied, then he introduced

Kirk and Standing Elk. He started to walk away, but again Caroline stopped him. "Ross, why was I wandering in the desert? Was I not with my brothers? If I was taken by Apaches, how did I get away from them?"

"I don't know. Maybe Spotted Horse didn't really find you in the desert." He watched her closely, wondering how she would react to what he was about to say. "It's a strong possibility that Spotted Horse was with the Apaches who killed your parents."

Caroline couldn't — wouldn't — even consider such a thing. It would be more than she could bear! Like fleeting wisps of smoke, memories of Spotted Horse swirled through her mind. For five years, he had been her friend. They had gone horseback riding, he had taught her how to find food in the plains, which plants and roots to use for medicine. They had talked together, even laughed together! And, yes, he had chivalrously courted her! No, he couldn't be involved in her parents' murders! She didn't love Spotted Horse, true, but she still felt a certain loyalty. Recently, her confidence in Spotted Horse had been shaken, but not to this degree! Spotted Horse involved in her parents' deaths? No, he couldn't be that devious! She had lived with the Apaches for five years, and they weren't capable of such deceitful trickery!

Her eyes met Ross's, and she spoke firmly, "Spotted Horse did find me in the desert. I know him, and he would not lie about something like that."

Ross didn't say anything, he merely walked away. It was now obvious to him that Caroline was in love with Spotted Horse. After all, she had called his name during her delirium, and now she was standing up for him. He wondered why she had chosen to leave him. Well, maybe she just intended to see her grandfather, then return to Spotted Horse. She would definitely have to do so without Spotted Horse's permission, for Ross was certain that the warrior would never have agreed.

He shook his head slightly. He felt a little sorry for Caroline Hanley. Someday she might recall her parents' deaths, and he suspected that, when she did, she would remember that Spotted Horse was there! Ross's instincts seldom steered him wrong, and he had a feeling that Spotted Horse hadn't found Caroline in the desert, but had abducted her after leading the raid that had cost her parents their lives.

Chapter Six

Ross and the others had stopped for the noon break when they were found by Lone Tree, a brave from Slow Bull's village. He rode into camp, and reported that Slow Bull was dying.

Ross hadn't planned to return to Slow Bull's village. He and Standing Elk intended to part company following lunch. The warrior would head home, and Ross, Kirk, and Caroline would start for the border. But, now, Ross felt he must see his granduncle one last time. Even though he had known for a long time that the headsman's health was declining, it didn't ease the pain. He sincerely loved his granduncle, and there was no one he respected more.

As Standing Elk offered Lone Tree some food, Ross turned to Caroline, who was resting beneath a tree, leaning back against its trunk.

She had heard Lone Tree's announcement. "I've never met Slow Bull," she said. "But his name is well known among the Apaches."

Ross sat beside her. "He's my granduncle."

"You're part Apache?" She was obviously surprised.

"Yes. My grandmother was Slow Bull's sister. So, really, I'm only a quarter Apache."

She supposed that mixture of white and Apache was the secret that made him handsome in a sensuous yet savage sort of way. She was undeniably attracted to Ross Bennett, but she had a feeling that he had that same effect on most women. She was certain that she wasn't the first, nor would she be the last woman to fall victim to his blatant sensuality. She couldn't help but wonder if he was in love with someone — he might even be married. But she didn't dare ask. The years she had spent with the Apaches had its effect, and a young maiden didn't ask such questions.

Ross was curious about her thoughts, and he wished he knew what was going through her mind. He admired Caroline, for in his opinion, she was a strong and courageous young woman. She had suffered amnesia, lived with the Apaches for five years, but had evidently come through the ordeal unharmed. He wondered if she had witnessed her parents' murders, and if that trauma could have brought on amnesia. She told him that she had received a head injury, and he knew a severe blow could also cause a loss of memory.

"Ross," Caroline began. "Are we going to Slow Bull's village?"

It was a moment before he answered, and his tone was somewhat apologetic, "I know you're anxious to see your grandfather, but considering . . ."

"I understand," she interrupted. "You must visit Slow Bull now while you still can."

He smiled warmly. "Are you sure you don't mind?"

"I have waited five years to return home. A short delay won't matter."

He reached over and took her hand, squeezing it gently. It was an impulsive move, and out of character for Ross. He rarely demonstrated his emotions, especially to strangers. But for some inexplicable reason, he didn't think of Caroline as a stranger. It was as though he had known her all his life.

Caroline's feelings were the same as Ross's. She had known this man for such a short time, yet she felt perfectly at ease with him. He was disarmingly friendly, and very likeable. Also, she was fully aware of his masculine appeal, and her attraction to him. He was still holding her hand, and she couldn't help but respond to his touch. She suddenly had an overwhelming urge to throw herself into his arms, but she resisted doing any such thing. She could never be so bold! Her thoughts moved to Spotted Horse. The warrior had often held her hand, but his touch certainly had never evoked such a response. She wondered if she were falling in love. The rapid beat of her heart told her that she was, but her common sense disagreed, for love couldn't happen this quickly — could it?

Ross let go of her hand, and got to his feet. "As soon as Lone Tree finishes eating, we'll leave. We're not far from Slow Bull's village. I'll come back and help you onto the travois."

"Ross, a travois is not necessary. I can ride horseback."

"Maybe, but I'd rather you didn't." A charming twinkle sparked in his dark eyes. "Go along with me, please."

Her response was an enticing smile, but it was so innocently provocative that it hit Ross with a startling force. He had never felt anything like it. He was wary of these feelings, for he had been terribly hurt once before, and he didn't intend to let it happen a second time. He had fallen prey to Emily Parker's beauty and charm; he'd not be so reckless again.

He turned about and moved away with the grace of one who was in total control. It was a misleading perception, for Caroline Hanley was weakening his resolve to keep a firm rein on his emotions. Stubbornly, he tightened those reins, for he wasn't ready for an emotional involvement.

When they reached Slow Bull's village, Ross took Caroline to the wickiup he and Kirk had used the night before. Leaving her there with his cousin, he went to see his granduncle.

The shaman was directing a ritual in the heart of the village, and several male dancers were taking part in the ceremony. The dancers, along with the shaman, were chanting prayers to the spirits, and most of all to Yusn — the Giver of Life. It was from this godhead that all life was generated.

Ross paused to watch the ritual. He knew that the Apaches always appealed to Yusn for help, even for such everyday problems as drought and shortage of game. Now, however, they were praying for Slow Bull. The dancers, their bodies painted, were wearing ceremonial skirts, black masks, and spectacular head-dresses.

Ross watched for a moment, then moved on to Slow Bull's wickiup. The headsman's second wife was standing at the opening, and she waved Ross inside.

A group of elderly men were watching over Slow Bull, but they left quickly, giving He-Who-Wanders time alone with his granduncle.

Ross sat beside the old man's bed. His breathing was shallow, rasping. Ross could tell that he had to fight for each breath.

"Slow Bull," he said softly.

The man's eyes didn't open, but it didn't matter, for he was now completely blind. He recognized his grand-nephew's voice. "He-Who-Wanders, I am glad you are here. I will soon go to the spirit world. When I see my sister, your grandmother, I will tell her what a fine man you are."

Ross didn't know what to say, he simply placed his hand on Slow Bull's, and held it gently.

"He-Who-Wanders," the headsman continued, a trace of anxiety now in his voice. "You must not come back to the Apaches. You are not really one of us. Only my presence has kept you safe. There will soon be much war between my people and yours. There is talk of returning to our homeland. The white soldiers will fight us."

Ross was confused. "But I've always been welcomed here."

"The young warriors greet you with false smiles. Inside, they hunger for war with anyone who is white. They want to leave Mexico and return to the land the whites call Arizona." The headsman's bony fingers tightened weakly about Ross's hand. "My nephew, you must stay away from all Apaches. There will be much war, much bloodshed."

Ross didn't doubt the old man's prediction. If the people returned to Arizona, war was inevitable. A feeling of sadness came over Ross. With Slow Bull's passing, he would lose his last link to his Apache heritage. It was as though two deaths were approaching, his granduncle's, and the demise of his own ancestry. He felt as though a part of himself would die along with Slow Bull.

Caroline sat on a bed of blankets, and Kirk was seated across from her. Silently, they listened to the prayers, chants, and wailing coming from outside. The people knew Slow Bull's death was certain, and they were already mourning his passing.

Kirk shifted uneasily. The high-pitched voices, expressing grief, sounded a little eerie. A cold chill prick-led the back of his neck.

"There is no reason to be afraid," Caroline said qui-etly, for she had detected his discomfort.

Kirk smiled tentatively. "I suppose you've heard all this wailing before."

"A few times. The Apaches never let a loved one pass into the spirit world without expressing a lot of grief."

"Do you believe in a spirit world?"

She laughed lightly. "Spirit world—Heaven—is there a difference?"

"No, I suppose not," he replied.

They fell comfortably into discussing the Apaches, and time passed quickly. Kirk was just about to ask Caroline if she'd like some coffee when Ross returned.

He was carrying a carpetbag, and as he took a seat beside Caroline, he placed it at his feet. His strong shoulders were slumped, and his face was etched with grief. "Slow Bull is dead," he said softly.

"I'm sorry," Caroline replied. She placed a hand on his arm in a sympathetic gesture. "You loved him?"

"Yes, I suppose," Ross answered. "He was a great man." He turned his attention to Kirk. "We need to get our horses and pack mule. It's time to leave."

"Now?" Kirk questioned. "It'll soon be dark."

"All the same, we should get away from here."

"Is there something you aren't telling me?" Kirk asked, watching Ross closely.

"It seems the young warriors in this village are itch-ing for war with the whites. You're white, and so is Caroline. And my drop of Apache blood is no longer a shield. I'm sure most of the older men, as well as Standing Elk, don't harbor hard feelings, but just to be on the safe side, let's leave as soon as possible."

"You don't have to tell me twice," Kirk said, bound-

93

ing to his feet. "I don't like the odds facing us here. I'll get the horses and the mule." He was gone in a flash.

Ross turned to Caroline. "I'm sorry about this. You should be resting instead of traveling."

"I will be fine," she assured him.

He lifted the carpetbag, and handed it to her. "There's a change of clothes in here. Your grandfather borrowed a set of riding clothes from his wife." He grinned wryly. "An optimistic gesture, I suppose, that we would find you. There's no reason for you to dress like an Apache woman. I'll help Kirk with the horses while you change."

Caroline waited until he was gone before looking inside the carpetbag. Her grandfather had also sent a pair of riding boots and a western hat. She slowly withdrew the clothes and accessories, looking at them as though they were somehow alien. It had been a long time since she had worn such finery. All at once, she was eager to change into the garments.

It was only natural that Caroline should find the clothes thrilling, and she could hardly wait to put them on. As she was dressing, she suddenly remembered to whom they belonged. Rebecca Rawlins! She knew she had never liked the woman, or her sons. She wondered if the threesome were still as unlikable as they had been five years ago.

Alex, eyeing Bryan testily, said with determination, "I tell you, if I hole up in El Zarango, I'm bound to find out if the Bennetts have Caroline or the boys. They gotta stop at El Zarango 'fore crossin' into New Mexico."

"They don't have to stop," Bryan replied impatiently. "They might have enough supplies to see them through to Dry Branch. There's no guarantee that they'll stop at the town of El Zarango."

The two brothers, along with their mother, were in Bryan's office. Rambunctious noises from the saloon drifted into the room, and Rebecca found the commotion disrupting. How were she and her sons to carry on a discussion with so much racket in the background? As she had done a dozen times before, she inwardly berated Bryan for purchasing the establishment. It was beyond her comprehension why he had wanted to own a saloon, and such a rundown one at that.

Bryan had his own reason for buying the Watering Hole—he wanted to get away from the Bar-H. When he was living there, his stepfather had expected him to work as hard as the hired help. That he had found galling. He considered himself socially far above the wranglers who worked for Hanley. He was willing to bide his time, keep things as they were, and wait for the Bar-H. Soon now, Caroline and her brothers would be declared legally dead, and upon Hanley's death, his mother would inherit the estate. Then she would give him the Bar-H. The prosperous ranch would make him rich!

Now, leaning back in his chair, and crossing his arms over his chest, he regarded his brother irritably. "If you want to go to El Zarango and hang around that miserable little town waiting for the Bennetts, then by all means do so. Just remember, it could be weeks, maybe even months, before they show up."

His reasoning got through to Alex. He certainly didn't relish spending so much time in a poor Mexican town. He liked the comforts afforded at the Bar-H too much.

"All right," he gave in. "I won't go to El Zarango."

"Even if you did," Rebecca began, "what good would it do?"

"If the Bennetts have any of Hanley's grandkids, I

95

could kill 'em, and the Bennetts too."

Bryan chuckled heartily. "You'd just get yourself killed."

Alex was offended. "Damn it! I'm good with a gun, and furthermore, I've been practicin'!"

Bryan didn't argue, for he knew Alex was a fast draw and an accurate shot. But was he good enough to go against the Bennetts? He didn't think so.

Rebecca got up from her chair. "I'm supposed to meet Bill at the general store. If I don't hurry, I'll be late." She looked at Alex. "Are you coming?"

"No," he answered sullenly. "I'm gonna stay in town for awhile."

She told Bryan goodbye, left by the back door, and walked around to the street. The stagecoach was arriving, and its large wheels stirred up loose dirt, sending it swirling through the air. As the dirty particles fell over Rebecca's hair and clothes, she silently cursed this western town, as well as all others. She could hardly wait to visit the East, and then Europe, where she intended to fully enjoy their modern cities. How desperately she longed for civilization!

To reach the town's general store, she had to pass by the stage depot. Seeing that Bill was standing there with Sheriff Taylor, she hurried to join them.

Her husband smiled at her. "I know I was supposed to meet you at the store, but Jim wanted me to wait here with him. His niece is on the stage."

The passengers were leaving the coach, and Rebecca watched as a very attractive woman stepped down from the stage and into the sheriff's awaiting arms.

After hugging his niece, and welcoming her to Dry Branch, he led her to the Hanleys, and told her, "This is Rebecca and Bill Hanley." Smiling largely, he continued the introductions, "This is my niece, Mary Murphy."

Rebecca's eyes scanned the visitor. She didn't like meeting any woman who was as pretty or prettier than herself. She guessed Mary's age to be in the late twenties. She was a striking woman, for her curvaceous frame was slim, and her thick auburn hair shone with radiant highlights. Her emerald-colored eyes were large, and veiled by thick lashes and arched brows.

Rebecca uttered a quick, and somewhat cold hello, then ushered her husband along. She had no wish to become acquainted with the sheriff's niece.

As Bill assisted her into their carriage, he said reproachfully, "You could have been friendlier to Mary. After all, she's a stranger in town."

Rebecca heaved a deep sigh, waited until her husband was seated, then replied, "Honestly, Bill! What did you want me to do? Fawn all over her?"

He slapped the reins against the horses, and headed the carriage out of town. "Jim's niece is very pretty, isn't she?"

"Oh? I hadn't noticed."

"Jim told me she's a widow."

"What else did he say?" Although Rebecca had no desire to become friends with the woman, she was nevertheless curious.

"Seven years ago, her husband and two children were killed by the Apaches. Her sons were twelve and ten when it happened."

"The boys would now be nineteen and seventeen," Rebecca said. Remembering Mary's youthful appearance, she added, "Mary Murphy's looks are deceiving. I thought she wasn't a day over thirty."

"Jim said she's thirty-nine. She was living in Albuquerque with her mother-in-law, but the woman passed away last month. Jim invited her to come here and stay with him and his wife. Mary's a schoolteacher."

"Dry Branch already has a teacher."

"Jim said his wife's arthritis is getting real bad. Mary will be a lot of help to her."

Bored with Mary Murphy, Rebecca withdrew into silence. She closed her eyes and daydreamed about Europe, and all the exciting lovers she would undoubtedly enjoy.

Jim and his wife showed Mary into her room, then left her alone to unpack. She was glad for the privacy, for putting up a cheerful front was difficult. Her mother-in-law's death still weighed heavily on her heart, for they had been very close. The deaths of Mary's husband and children had placed a strong bond between the two women, and both had drawn strength and courage from the other.

Mary finished unpacking, then moving to the window, she gazed thoughtfully outside. Her bedroom faced the street, and she watched with little interest as two horsemen rode by. The sheriff's home, located at the edge of town, was isolated and quiet. A white picket fence, surrounding the front yard, protected Mrs. Taylor's prized flowers from wandering dogs and cats. Despite the dry climate, her garden was filled with colorful blooms.

Mary's mind, however, wasn't on flowers. She was wondering if she would find work. She wasn't trained for anything except teaching, and this town already had a schoolteacher. She suddenly felt very depressed. Her future didn't look very promising. But, then, why did she even think about such things? Her future had died with her husband and children. Only her mother-in-law's strength and understanding had given her the initiative to go on. Now she no longer had the woman's support, and Mary felt as though she was losing the will to continue. Her family's deaths had shattered her heart, and her mother-in-law's passing had broken what was left of it.

She leaned her head against the window pane, tears slowly filled her eyes, then rolled down her face.

Chapter Seven

The small Mexican town of El Zarango was rowdy and lawless, frequented by renegades, outlaws, and bandits. Ross had misgivings about taking Caroline to El Zarango, but they needed to replenish their supplies. The town had a hotel of sorts — a two-story adobe building that was in dire need of repair. However, Ross knew that the rooms were surprisingly clean, for he had stayed at the establishment on several occasions. He intended to rent two rooms, one for Kirk, and one that he and Caroline would share. He hadn't yet told her of his plans, he wasn't quite sure how to go about it. He certainly didn't want her to get the wrong idea. He wasn't trying to compromise her, he was trying to protect her. It wasn't safe for a woman, especially one as lovely as Caroline, to be alone in a town like El Zarango; not even if she were locked in a hotel room. Ross had considered not spending the night in town, but he had a feeling that Caroline would enjoy a hot bath and a comfortable bed. The journey from Slow Bull's village had been long and tiring. Caroline had ridden for days, and had slept on the hard ground at nights without uttering a single complaint. In Ross's opinion, she deserved a little comfort, and although El Zarango wasn't much of a town, it did have clean beds, hot baths, and halfway decent food.

The sun was setting as the travelers entered the Mexican town. The main street, which was a narrow dirt road, was crowded with riders either leaving or coming; dogs, chickens, and even a few pigs wandered the road undisturbed. Animal droppings were everywhere, and that stench, mixed with the smells of greasy food, permeated the air.

Caroline made a face, for the odors were overwhelming.

Ross, noticing her distaste, was quick to say, "The hotel's at the far end of the street, and in a cleaner part of town."

Caroline managed a faint smile. She knew they only planned to stay one night in El Zarango, and she felt she could tolerate anyplace for one night. In fact, she was glad they had decided to stop, for she longed desperately for a hot bath. She hoped the hotel could send a tub to her room, for then she could soak for a long time.

The town had three cantinas, two on one side of the street, the third and largest one on the other side. Guitar and piano music, mingled with loud voices, and even a gunshot or two, carried from the cantinas into the street. A couple of stores — a livery and a few other buildings — made up the town. Caroline wasn't surprised to find that El Zarango lacked both a church and a lawman's office.

Caroline's first glimpse of the hotel was a letdown, for the building didn't look very promising; but, then, considering what she had seen of the town so far, what had she expected? In fact, comparatively speaking, the hotel was grand.

When they arrived at the hotel, Ross was somewhat surprised to see a large group of vaqueros mounted outside. There was also a wagon loaded with luggage, as well as a sturdy carriage.

Ross helped Caroline dismount, then as he led her into the hotel, Kirk left to take the horses and the pack mule to the livery.

A room, cluttered with threadbare furniture, was the hotel's version of a lobby. As Caroline stood back, Ross went to the desk and rented the rooms. The proprietor, an obese middle-aged man, handed over the keys. He remembered Ross from his previous visits, and was glad to welcome him back. The man's dark eyes, which were nearly hidden in his pudgy face, kept going back and forth from Ross to Caroline. The lovely lady had aroused his curiosity, for Señor Bennett had never before arrived with a woman.

As Ross was returning to Caroline, a distinguished-looking couple with their young son came down the stairs and into the lobby. Recognizing them, Ross smiled congenially, offered the man his hand, and said, "Fernando, it's good to see you again."

He shook Bennett's hand heartily. "Ross, it has been a long time."

Courteously, Ross greeted Fernando's wife and son, then he introduced Caroline.

"What are you doing in El Zarango?" Ross asked the man. Fernando Mendoza was a wealthy landowner, and a Mexican aristocrat who was personally acquainted with the country's president, Porfirio Días. Ross certainly hadn't expected to find a man with Fernando's connections in El Zarango.

With a sudden angry glint in his eyes, Fernando replied, "I came here to kill a man!"

Ross was obviously shocked. "But why?"

"My sister, Eugenia, was attacked by one of my vaqueros. He was a young drifter that my foreman hired. He worked for me only two weeks before he raped and killed my sister."

"Eugenia dead?" Ross gasped. He remembered the

102

young woman very well. She had been quite lovely.

"Her murderer, who calls himself Alfredo, was seen in El Zarango, but he is no longer here. I do not know where he is, but someday I will find him." He turned to his wife, smiled warmly at her, then said to Ross, "Leonora wishes to go home." He gestured toward his son. "So does Ricardo. I brought my son along because I wanted him to watch as I killed Alfredo."

"Isn't he a little young for that?" Ross asked.

"A Mendoza is never too young to learn how to mete out justice."

Caroline, listening, looked closely at the boy. She guessed him to be about seven or eight years old. He was standing close to his mother, one small hand was gripping her long skirt, and his body was halfway hidden behind the dress's voluminous folds. For a moment, his brown eyes met Caroline's, and a somewhat bashful smile crossed his face. As she returned his smile, she couldn't help but think about her brothers. Where were they? Were they still alive?

"Señor, I am glad that I came across you," Fernando was saying to Ross. "I would like to hire you to find Alfredo."

"I'm already working on a job," Ross replied.

The man was vividly disappointed. "I am sorry to hear that. Well, when you are finished, please come to my hacienda. If Alfredo is still at large, I will pay you a handsome fee to find him."

"I'm not free to obligate myself."

Fernando understood. "That is too bad. If any man could find Alfredo, it would be you." He shrugged aside his disappointment, and said, "My vaqueros are waiting out front. We must leave." Again, he and Ross shook hands, then taking his wife by the arm, he escorted her and his son outside.

Watching them leave, Caroline said, "Mrs. Mendoza

looks Mexican, but her husband doesn't."

"Fernando is Spanish. He claims he's a direct descendent from Antonio de Mendoza, who came to Mexico three hundred years ago. He was a Spanish viceroy sent here by the king."

"Are you close friends with Fernando Mendoza?"

"We're not especially close friends, but I've worked for him a couple of times." Ending the subject abruptly, he suggested they go upstairs.

They moved to the narrow stairway, and made their way to the second floor. Ross unlocked the first door on their left, then stood back for Caroline to enter.

The room was quite plain, but appeared to be relatively clean. A large bed, spread neatly with sheets and a blanket, dominated the limited space. A small wardrobe, which was badly chipped, stood in a corner. The one window was open, and a warm breeze drifted in from outside.

"I told the proprietor to send up a bath," Ross said. He didn't enter the room, but stood poised in the open doorway.

Caroline smiled brightly. "A bath! How wonderful!"

Ross grinned. "I thought you'd be pleased."

As always, Ross's smile sent warm, intense feelings rushing through Caroline. She was not only attracted to him, but liked him immensely. She wished she knew him better. They had been traveling together for days, but she knew very little about him, for he seldom talked about himself. But, then, it was the same with Kirk, he was as secretive as Ross.

"I'll be back for you later," Ross said, stepping into the hall. "There's a place to eat a couple of doors down. It doesn't look like much, but the food's pretty good."

He left, closing the door behind him. Going to the stairs, he sat down on the top step, where he intended

104

to wait for Kirk. He wasn't about to leave Caroline unguarded.

Ross was there only a few minutes when his cousin showed up, carrying their carpetbags. Ross asked Kirk to keep a close watch on Caroline's room, then he hurried down the stairs and outside. He had a few errands to take care of.

Ross proceeded to buy more supplies, he also purchased Caroline a change of clothes. Then he visited the barber shop, where he had a shave and a bath. Afterwards, he went to the telegraph office and sent a wire to Hanley, letting him know that Caroline had been found.

Returning to the hotel, he found Kirk sitting in front of Caroline's room. Kirk, wanting a shave and a bath himself, left Caroline's care in Ross's hands.

Going to the other room, Ross quickly put away the supplies, changed into clean clothes, then left to knock on Caroline's door.

She let him in, and he handed her a package wrapped in brown paper. "What is this?" she asked.

"A change of clothes. I had to guess at the size. My choices were limited, but I managed to find you a skirt and a blouse. The owner's wife does laundry, so if you'll give me your other clothes, I'll take them to her."

Caroline, naturally, was wearing them. She had taken her bath and washed her hair, but had put her riding attire back on.

Ross stepped to the door, saying, "I'll wait in the hall."

Caroline was pleasantly surprised when she opened the package. Ross had bought her a Mexican-style skirt and blouse, which were bright in color. The full skirt was barely long enough to cover her ankles, and the blouse was designed to be worn off the shoulders.

Earlier, Kirk had delivered her carpetbag, she now opened it and drew out her moccasins. She removed her boots, and slipped her feet into the soft leather shoes. They didn't quite match her outfit, but they certainly looked better than riding boots.

She re-admitted Ross, and gave him the clothes to be laundered. Caroline, having no idea that she presented a provocative image, didn't understand why Ross was staring at her so strangely.

He tried very hard to see her only as the young woman he intended to return to her grandfather. After he delivered her to Hanley, chances were good that he'd never see her again. He planned to go back to Tucson and build a ranch. He was through with hiring his gun.

Ross's effort to remain unmoved by Caroline's enchanting beauty was in vain. His eyes studied her with a will of their own. Caroline's golden hair was loose, and the shiny tresses tumbled seductively down her back to her tiny waist. Her heart-shaped face was enhanced by high, delicate cheekbones, and her jawline was strong, yet exquisitely feminine. Thick lashes fringed her beautiful gray eyes, which were now watching Ross with puzzlement. At first, she didn't understand his sudden silence, nor did she recognize the hunger in his gaze. But, then, the woman in her came alive, and sensations that were new and compelling held her spellbound. As she stood before him, his gaze caressed her body. A thrill like she had never felt before coursed through her with a powerful jolt. It was as though she could actually feel his heated gaze touching her flesh, and awakening her deepest passion.

Ross's eyes roamed over every inch of her. He had never seen a woman so perfectly desirable. The blouse she wore revealed her soft shoulders, and emphasized the fullness of her breasts. Her skirt clung seductively to her rounded hips before falling gracefully to the tops of her moccasins.

Caroline was returning Ross's scrutiny. She not only thought him extremely good-looking, but she also admired him a great deal. He had shown her such kindness and concern. Yes, he was most assuredly a gentleman, yet, she seemed to instinctively know that there was another side to Ross Bennett. A side she hadn't seen. She suspected a somewhat savage side to his nature; one that men found intimidating, and women found exciting. She sensed that to really know Ross Bennett, one had to be acquainted with both sides of his nature. She wondered if she, or any woman, would ever know him that well.

He had shown her tenderness and respect, true, but she also felt a tremendous physical attraction to him. Now, as her gaze traveled over him boldly, she noticed the tight fit of his shirt across his masculine chest, and the way his dark trousers moulded to his slim hips. He had his gun strapped on, and her eyes were drawn to the pistol's ivory handle. She wondered if Ross ever went anywhere without his gun—she had a feeling that he didn't.

She lifted her gaze to his face. Ross's eyes, filled with desire, met hers. She flushed as a rush of longing flashed over her. Her heart began to pound, and warm perspiration beaded up on her brow. If Ross's gaze alone could evoke such a response, then she shuddered to think what his touch could do. She knew she would not only be helpless in his embrace, but would also be his for the taking. It was a somewhat frightening revelation, yet, at the same time, wonderfully exciting!

Ross took control of his emotions. He had read the desire in Caroline's eyes, and he knew it was sincere, for she wasn't flirtatious, nor was she coy. But he wasn't about to succumb. Emily Parker still ruled too much of his heart for him to even consider another serious involvement.

He turned about brusquely, and headed for the door. "I'll see about your laundry, then come back and take you to dinner." He made a quick retreat into the hall, but as he was hurrying down the stairs, he wondered why Caroline had so obviously desired him. After all, she was in love with Spotted Horse. Wasn't she?

Roberto's Restaurante wasn't much of a restaurant, for it consisted of one small room, which was furnished with stained tables and chairs in poor condition. The establishment, however, served good food, and the place was crowded.

The owner showed Ross and Caroline to a table, took their order, then brought them a bottle of wine.

Caroline's eyes were drawn to a young dark-haired boy who was busy removing dirty dishes from one of the tables. Although he was working quickly, he kept glancing nervously over his shoulder. When the owner suddenly bellowed a command to the boy, Caroline supposed the youngster was nervous because of his boss. The man was probably a tyrant to work for. She wondered if the owner was the child's father. The boy had dark features, but he didn't especially look Mexican. Thinking about the boy brought her brothers to mind once again.

"Ross," she began, "do you plan to search for my brothers?"

It was a moment before he answered, "I don't think I can find them. My only real connection with the Apaches was through Slow Bull."

"But surely you have friends among the Apaches who would help you."

108

"Not really," he replied heavily. "The only ones I know well live in Slow Bull's village, and the young warriors want to return to Arizona. Reclaiming their homeland is uppermost in their minds. They certainly wouldn't offer to help me locate two white boys who might be living with an Apache band somewhere. Without a warrior's escort, I'd never be allowed to ride randomly into villages."

"But what about Standing Elk? Wouldn't he help you?"

"Considering the unrest among his people, he wouldn't feel free to leave them." Ross sighed deeply. "I'm sorry, Caroline, but I don't think it's possible for me to find your brothers. Also, you must realize that they're probably dead. If they were living with the Apaches in Mexico, I think Slow Bull would have heard about it. After all, he knew about you."

Caroline fought back tears. "But what if they aren't dead? Do we just give up and leave them to the Apaches?"

"If they are alive, then they were adopted. Chances are they're perfectly happy where they are. You were content, weren't you?"

"Yes, as long as I couldn't remember. When my memories started returning, I could think of nothing but going home."

Ross started to question her feelings for Spotted Horse, but, at that moment, Kirk joined them. He pulled out a chair and sat down. Speaking to Ross, he said with a note of worry, "The Mackennas are in town. I saw them as I was leaving the barber shop."

"Who are the Mackennas?" Caroline asked.

Ross answered, "They're thieves and murderers. Last year, I got into a card game with their youngest brother. He accused me of cheating, jumped up from the table and drew his gun. I was faster . . ."

"And?" Caroline coaxed.

"I killed him."

"It happened in El Paso," Kirk explained. "The sheriff was in the saloon at the time, and he saw it was self-defense. The two Mackenna brothers didn't see it that way. They swore that they'd get even. The sheriff ran them out of town. Until now, our paths haven't crossed, but they saw me leaving the barber shop, and they'll come lookin' to see if Ross is with me."

Alarmed, Caroline turned anxious eyes to Ross. "What are you going to do?"

"Have dinner." He appeared undisturbed.

"But aren't you worried that they'll find you?"

"I hope they do. Their threat has been hanging over my head for a long time. The sooner it's settled, the better. When men like the Mackennas are gunning for you, you can spend your whole time watching your back."

"Ross," Kirk said, gesturing toward the door. "Jake Mackenna just came in."

Caroline watched anxiously as the man paused to scan the room. He was tall, heavy-set, and a scraggly beard covered his face. He spotted Ross, and a look of unadulterated murder came to his eyes. Then, suddenly, he whirled about and left the restaurant.

"One of 'em will be watchin' the back door," Kirk said. "The other one will watch the front. They'll try to gun you down when you leave."

"Yeah," Ross agreed calmly. "They'll try."

Caroline noticed the way in which Ross stressed the word "try." She was amazed, for he didn't seem the least bit scared. She wondered if she was about to see the other side of Ross Bennett.

Chapter Eight

Caroline merely picked at her dinner, for she was too tense to eat very much, but Ross and Kirk ate with hearty appetites. Their behavior astounded Caroline. With the Mackennas waiting outside to gun them down, how could they be so calm and collected?

Finally the men had their fill of food, pushed their plates aside, and leaned back in their chairs.

Ross finished his glass of wine, then looked at Kirk and said as calmly as though he were discussing the weather, "Well, I don't know about you, but I'm bushed. I guess it's time to get rid of the Mackennas, then go to the hotel and get some sleep."

Caroline questioned quickly, "How do you intend to do that?"

Ross quirked a brow, smiled wryly, and asked, "Do what?"

"Get rid of the Mackennas?" She was impatient, for she knew he was toying with her.

"I'm not sure, but I have an idea." He got up and went to the youngster who worked for the proprietor. The boy was setting a table with clean dishes.

Caroline watched as Ross spoke quietly to the boy before handing him some money. He then returned to the table, sat down, and said to Kirk, "The boy's going to bring us two ponchos and two sombreros. You take the back door, and I'll take the front."

Caroline understood Ross's ploy, but she wasn't sure it would work. "Do you really think the Mackennas will mistake you for Mexicans?"

Ross shrugged casually. "Mexicans have been leaving this place all night, and I haven't heard any gunshots."

The boy arrived with the ponchos and hats. He placed them on the table, asking, "Will these do, señor?"

"They'll do fine," Ross assured him.

He and Kirk quickly slipped on the ponchos before putting on the wide sombreros. Ross moved to Caroline, who was still in her chair. His gaze met hers, and he spoke firmly, "Stay here until I return. Don't come outside under any circumstances."

He glanced over at the young boy. The youngster hadn't moved away. Flipping him a coin, Ross asked, "Will you stay with the lady?"

Putting the coin into his pocket, the boy answered, "Sí, señor. I will not leave her."

Caroline, her heart beating rapidly, watched as Kirk hurried to the back door as Ross moved toward the front. Ross pulled the sombrero low over his brow, then arranged the poncho so that his gun was in the open. Moving confidently, he stepped outside. At that same moment, Kirk went out the back door.

Minutes dragged by, seeming interminable to Caroline. Then, suddenly, a gunshot rang out. Caroline jumped to her feet, and actually took a step toward the front door before catching herself. Ross had told her to stay inside. Two more shots exploded. They sounded like they came from the back of the restaurant.

Caroline, her body taut with fear, stood as though fastened to the floor. A low gasp sounded deep in her throat, causing the boy to touch her arm and ask, "Are you all right, señorita?"

She didn't answer, for she hadn't even heard him. She was too scared, a vision of Ross lying dead had flashed before her mind. It was a terrifying sight, and it caused her heart to pound irregularly.

She watched with bated breath as the front door slowly opened. Ross walked inside, and she was so happy that she flung herself into his arms. "Thank God, you're all right!" she cried.

Caroline's actions came as a surprise to Ross. He hadn't realized that her feelings for him were so strong.

As Kirk came through the back door, Ross released Caroline with reluctance. He had liked the way she felt in his arms.

"I think I nicked Jake," Kirk said to Ross. "But he got away. You want me to go after him?"

"No. By the time you can get your horse saddled, he'll be too far away."

"What about his brother, Pete?"

"He's dead. If you'll take Caroline to the hotel, I'll find the undertaker."

The young boy had been listening to the two men. Now, as Ross said Caroline's name, the youngster tensed. The name seemed familiar. Where had he heard it before?

Kirk removed his poncho and sombrero, went to Caroline, took her arm, and escorted her outside.

In the meantime, Ross handed over his own borrowed garb, then paid the proprietor for the meal and left.

The owner, seeing that the boy was standing idle, lumbered over to him, and said angrily, "Get back to work, Carlos!" He held out his large hand. "But first give me the money you got from the gringo. I saw him give it to you."

The boy gave him the money, then began cleaning off the table. He thought about the pretty señorita.

113

The man had called her "Caroline." He knew he had heard the name before, but he couldn't remember where. He shrugged his shoulders briefly, and dismissed the name as unimportant. He turned his attention to his chore, and gave no more thought to Caroline.

Caroline paced her room anxiously. She hoped Ross would stop by before retiring. She wanted to question him about the shooting. Why had he killed Pete Mackenna? Had it been in self-defense, or had he coldly shot him down? She shuddered to think that Ross could kill a man in cold blood. She quickly chastised herself for thinking the worst. Considering the kindness and consideration Ross had shown her, how could she think for one minute that he was a killer? No, Ross Bennett wasn't a murderer; however, she knew he was a man to be reckoned with.

A warm blush colored her cheeks as she recalled the way she had thrown herself into Ross's arms. *What must he think of me,* she wondered. She had never before been so bold. Basket Woman had taught Caroline, as well as Sweet Water, to always be demure. A maiden should never throw herself at a warrior, but should reveal her feelings subtly. Then, when it was right for her to love him, she should do so passionately and without inhibition. Caroline supposed she had made a spectacle of herself. Ross probably thought her entirely too brazen. Why had she reacted so impetuously, so foolishly? Had she rushed into his arms because she loved him?

Stopping her pacing, she went to the bed and sat on the edge. Yes, she was in love with Ross Bennett. The revelation brought her no joy, for she had a feeling that Ross wasn't in love with her. Why should he be? What

114

did she have to offer a man like Ross? She had spent her most impressionable years with the Apaches. She was practically unschooled, for her education had stopped when she was thirteen. She still had so much to learn. Moreover, she wasn't yet at ease living as a white woman: eating in a restaurant — sheltered by an adobe roof instead of a wickiup — and tonight she would actually sleep in a bed on a feather mattress! These comforts were still strange to Caroline, and she knew it would be awhile before she could take such things for granted.

A soft rap sounded on the door. Hoping it was Ross, Caroline hurried to answer it. She wasn't disappointed, and she admitted him with a radiant smile.

He was carrying two blankets and a pillow, and as he placed them on the floor, he said somewhat hesitantly, "All things considered, I've decided to sleep in here tonight."

Caroline was indeed surprised. "I'm not sure I understand."

He made a terse gesture toward the closed door. "That lock wouldn't keep anyone out if he really wanted to get in. This is a lawless town, Caroline. Kirk and I are the only protection you have."

His reasoning made sense to Caroline, and she didn't argue with him.

"I'll step into the hall while you get undressed and into bed," Ross offered, moving to do so.

"Wait," she called. "Ross, tell me what happened between you and Pete Mackenna."

"I found him lurking in the shadows. I gave him the choice to shoot or leave. He made the wrong choice."

Caroline swallowed heavily. "Ross, how many men have you killed?" She wasn't sure why she asked the question, nor was she sure if she wanted to hear the answer.

"Not as many as you probably think."

"Fernando Mendoza offered to hire you to find his sister's killer, and my grandfather hired you to find me. Exactly what do you do for a living?"

He smiled easily. "What do you think?"

"Are you a hired gun?"

"For the moment."

"What does that mean?"

"After I return you to your grandfather, I plan to build a ranch. I own some land outside Tucson. It's good grazing land, and good cattle country." His smile widened charmingly. "Any more questions?"

"No, I don't think so."

"Then I'll leave so you can get undressed."

He stepped into the hall, and Caroline got ready for bed. She didn't have a nightgown, so she undressed and crawled between the sheets. She was used to sleeping nude, for the Apaches never wore garments to bed.

"You can come in now," she called loudly so Ross would hear.

Ross entered, locked the door, then spread out his blankets. Extinguishing the lamp, he unbuckled his gun belt, and slipped off his shirt and boots. "Good night, Caroline," he said softly.

The moon's saffron glow shone through the open window, and Caroline could make him out as he lay down on his blanket. She wished him a pleasant good night, then rolled to her side, and waited anxiously for sleep to overtake her. She knew that falling asleep wouldn't be easy, for she was too aware of Ross's presence. He had awakened Caroline's passion, and she yearned to go to his bed. She didn't find these feelings shameful, for the Apaches accepted love between a man and woman as a natural and most pleasant part of life. If she had spent her adolescent years with her parents, then their puritan ways would undoubtedly have influenced her, and she would be ashamed to desire Ross so passionately. But Caroline wasn't raised to think that way, and she felt no shame. She did, however, feel frustrated, for she didn't think that Ross cared for her in the same way she cared for him.

She closed her eyes, and eventually sleep took over.

An hour or so later, Ross was awakened by Caroline's soft moans. He rose at once and went to her bed. She was tossing and turning in her sleep, and rasping, almost mournful groans sounded deep in her throat. Gently, he sat on the edge of the bed, touched her shoulder, and said soothingly, "Wake up, Caroline. You're having a bad dream."

Her eyes flew open, and, for a moment, she stared at Ross as though she didn't know him. Then as she left her nightmare to return to reality, she sat up, drew the sheet about her, and fell into Ross's arms. She was crying heavily.

He rocked her gently as though she were a child. "Sh . . . sh," he whispered. "It was only a dream."

"No!" she said, sobbing. "It wasn't a dream, not really." She moved out of his embrace, and with tears still streaming down her face, she cried, "I remember the day my parents were murdered! Stalking Bear cut their throats, and I saw it!" Her voice rose wretchedly, "My God, I saw it happen!"

Ross drew her back into his arms, and held her close until her sobs finally abated. Then, releasing her, he lit the lamp, and turned the wick down low. "Were you dreaming about their deaths?" he asked gently.

"For some time now, I have been having the same dream. In this dream, I am being held in a man's arms. I do not know who he is, but I do know that I'm terrified of him. Before I can see his face, the dream always vanishes."

"But not this time?"

"No, this time I saw his face, and when I did, everything came back to me."

"Whose face was it?" Ross asked, suspecting he already knew the answer.

"Spotted Horse!" she gasped.

Ross had guessed right.

"He didn't kill my parents, Stalking Bear did. But Spotted Horse wanted their deaths. He did nothing to save them!" A morbid chill coursed through her. "My God, all these years I was friends with the men who murdered my parents! I was always polite and kind to Stalking Bear, and I — I was engaged to Spotted Horse. I thought he was special." A look of abject misery crossed her face. "I feel so ashamed!"

"You can't blame yourself. How were you to know that Spotted Horse lied? It was only natural that you should believe him. After all, you were only a child."

"Yes, but later I should have known! I should have sensed it. You don't even know Spotted Horse, yet you suspected that he was there when my parents were killed."

"It's easier to be objective when you aren't personally involved."

She supposed he was right, but it didn't ease her pain, nor her guilt.

"Caroline, do you remember what happened to your brothers?"

"They were on the ground beside my parents. Stalking Bear killed Papa and Mama, he then turned to my brothers. I rushed over to help them, but I was hit over the head. I blacked out, but I came to for only a moment. Spotted Horse was holding me. I looked up into his face, then I sank back into blackness. I remained

118

that way for a long time. When I woke up, I was traveling with Spotted Horse. I had no memory, I was in a daze. My next clear memory is waking in Basket Woman's wickiup. She and Sweet Water were tending to me."

Caroline had told Ross about her adopted family, and he knew who she was talking about. He was quiet for a moment, then said gravely, "Well, there's at least two people who know what happened to your brothers—Stalking Bear and Spotted Horse."

Excitement shone in Caroline's eyes. "I must go back to Spotted Horse's village and wait for him! I'll make him tell me where my brothers are!"

"You'll do no such thing!" Ross demanded gruffly. "If you go back to him, he'll never give you a chance to escape again. You'd gain nothing by returning except your own imprisonment. Furthermore, how the hell do you think you could make him tell you about your brothers? He'd tell you only what he wanted you to know, and nothing more. And even that might not be the truth!"

Caroline wasn't so sure. She thought there was a chance that she could convince Spotted Horse to cooperate.

She did, however, look terribly disheartened; Ross, brought her back into his embrace. He hugged her tenderly, then as he let her go he noticed that, during their embrace, the sheet had fallen from her breasts. His eyes raked her hungrily.

Caroline, realizing what had happened, blushed. She started to pull up the sheet, but, against her own volition, she responded to the hunger in Ross's gaze. Slowly, temptingly, she laced her arms about him, pressed a hand to the nape of his neck, and urged his lips to take hers in a fiery exchange.

The passionate kiss left them breathless, but eager

for more. Again, Ross's mouth branded hers in a heated, questing caress that was demandingly stimulating.

Caroline, free of inhibition, returned his fervor with equal passion. She had never been kissed like this before, but her response was so total that it belied her inexperience.

Although Ross was completely caught up in their embrace, he was nonetheless surprised by Caroline's fervent response. Tentatively, he moved a hand to her breast, almost expecting her to stiffen and push him away. Caroline, however, moaned rapturously as she returned his kiss with wild abandon. A streak of jealousy now coursed through Ross — had she and Spotted Horse been lovers? She certainly seemed to know what she was doing! Suddenly, Ross cursed his jealous thoughts. He had no right to think this way. Her relationship with Spotted Horse was none of his business. She undoubtedly gave herself to the warrior out of love, and he should respect her for that; not judge her!

Meanwhile, Caroline, totally immersed in ecstasy, had no way of knowing that she was acting as though she were experienced. Basket Woman had always told her that a woman should answer her man's passion freely. And that was exactly what she was doing — and she was loving every minute of it!

Ross eased her all the way down onto the bed, he then lay beside her. Flinging the sheet aside, he bared her beauty to his devouring gaze. He found her body perfect, for her breasts were full, her hips delicately rounded, and her shapely legs were long and slim.

He drew her close, and as his mouth explored hers, his hand skimmed over her flesh. His touch aroused such exquisite sensations that Caroline's response was shameless, total, and uncontrolled. She was conscious only of his demanding kiss, and the raging fire his caresses were sending through every nerve in her body.

Ross could no longer keep his passion leashed, and leaving the bed, he hurriedly drew off his trousers. The low-burning lamp illuminated his masculine physique. He was indeed a fine figure of a man. Ross's tall frame was slim, yet powerful muscles rippled over the smooth skin of his manly chest, and his arms were vividly strong. Caroline was watching him intensely, and her gaze dropped to his manhood. It was erect and throbbing. Raised in an Apache village, the male body was no secret to Caroline, and her perusal wasn't one of curiosity, but admiration.

She held out her arms, and he went eagerly into her embrace. Again, his hand caressed the smooth textures of her body as, in turn, Caroline's fingers explored his hard, muscular frame.

Ross, his hunger now ravenous, kissed her so urgently that she trembled with excitement. His naked chest was molded to hers, and she could feel the pounding of his heart against her breasts.

Ross's arousal was now beyond the point of control, and he moved between her legs. Eager tremors of ecstasy raced through his veins as he prepared for penetration.

Caroline felt his powerful male hardness against her, and she readied herself for the pain she knew would follow. Basket Woman had thoroughly rehearsed her adopted daughter for this moment.

Ross, thinking she was experienced, plunged into her deeply and demandingly. She cried out; Ross, realizing she was innocent, froze in place. Angry at himself for taking her innocence, he damned his own foolishness.

Caroline's discomfort subsided, and she now became aware of how wonderful it felt to have him deep inside her. As an exultant sensation wafted through her body, she moved against him erotically.

Her response rekindled Ross's passion, and his need again became a leaping flame. Pushing her innocence to the far recesses of his mind, he surrendered to the twisting desire in his loins. With the rhythm of sex beating in his heart, he kissed her aggressively as his hips thrust against hers, sending his hard member far into her velvety depths.

Caroline's ecstasy was absolutely fathomless, and she gladly abandoned herself to Ross's steady thrusts of possession. Together, they soared to a lover's paradise, where they wished such rapture would never end. They were completely consumed by love's breathtaking fulfillment.

Afterward, they lay in silence. It was an uncomfortable moment, for the silence between them was so thick that it was almost tangible.

Caroline didn't know what to say. She longed to confess her love, but she wasn't sure if Ross wanted to hear such a confession. Although he lay beside her silent and unmoving, she could nonetheless feel his tension. Why had such a strange mood come over him? Had she been a disappointment? Was she a poor lover? She had tried so hard to please him. He had certainly pleased her, for she had found their intimacy thrilling. She now loved him all the more! Did she dare hope for a marriage proposal?

"Caroline," Ross said suddenly. "Why didn't you tell me you were an innocent? If I had known, this would never have happened."

His remark, thrown at her so carelessly, was like a slap in the face.

When she didn't offer a reply, Ross got out of bed, slipped on his trousers, and moved to stare thoughtfully out the window. He felt sick over what he had done. Hanley had entrusted his granddaughter in his care, and he had failed him inexcusably. But, damn it, Caroline had responded so willingly that he had taken too much for granted.

A long sigh escaped his lips. He cared about Caroline, there was no denying his feelings. He just wasn't ready for this kind of involvement, not so soon after Emily Parker. Their relationship had been a romantic whirlwind. He had foolishly believed she was the right woman for him, but he hadn't known her; not really. Nor did he now truly know Caroline Hanley. Had she surrendered her body to him because she loved him, or had she merely been swept away by the heat of the moment? Once she was back at the Bar-H, surrounded by her grandfather's riches, would she scorn him the way Emily had?

Ross's emotions were understandably insecure, for his experience with the opposite sex, except for Emily, had consisted of prostitutes and bawdy women. The one and only time he had handed over his heart, it had been thrown back in his face.

Minutes passed before Ross finally turned back to look at Caroline. She tried to read his expression, but his countenance was inscrutable.

"I'm not a man to shirk my duty," he said calmly, still determined to do the right thing. "I took unfair advantage of you, and I feel I owe you a marriage proposal. I don't know what kind of a husband I'll make, but I suppose you could do a lot worse."

Quickly Caroline drew up the sheet, and holding it over her breasts, she sat up, met Ross's gaze, and answered coldly, "I would not marry you if you got down on your knees and begged me!"

It wasn't the answer Ross had been expecting.

Chapter Nine

Ross didn't blame Caroline for being angry, for his proposal certainly hadn't been very flattering or romantic. It was, however, the best he could do. He simply didn't have the heart to fall in love, not so soon after Emily.

He cared about Caroline, and he hoped to make amends. Perhaps if he explained his feelings, she would understand. He drew up a hard-backed chair, placed it beside the bed, and sat down.

"Believe me," he began, "I never intended to hurt you. Considering the way you responded, I thought you had been with a man before."

"The way I responded?" she questioned sharply. "I merely gave myself to you willingly. What was I supposed to do, lead you on then push you away?" Her gray eyes flashed angrily. "Well, I am not like that!"

"No, you're a very straightforward and honest young lady. What happened between us is my fault. But I meant it when I offered to marry you. I know my proposal was lacking, but right now love is a sore subject with me."

Caroline was suddenly more curious than angry. "Why?"

He told her about Emily Parker, and the way she had broken their engagement. He concluded by saying,

"I'm not ready for love right now, I guess it's still too soon."

Caroline wondered if he was fooling himself. Was he truly guarding his emotions, or was he protecting his wounded pride? She wasn't sure, but at the moment, she was too hurt and angry to care.

With a proud lift to her chin, she said smoothly, "Ross, you do not need to feel shame for what happened tonight. We behaved foolishly. There is no harm done."

Ross thought otherwise. Damn it, he had stolen her innocence! He decided not to press the issue, but he did, however, intend to make his feelings clear. "Caroline, my proposal stands. If you should change your mind—"

"I will not!" she interrupted tartly.

He left his chair brusquely, moved to the lamp, extinguished it, then returned to his pallet. He still had more to say, and speaking softly into the darkness, he told her, "If you should find yourself with child, we'll have to get married for the baby's sake."

Caroline held her tears in check.

Silence prevailed for a long time, and Caroline had begun to believe that Ross was asleep when he suddenly asked, "Now that you know the truth about Spotted Horse, how do you feel about him?"

The question had passed Ross's lips impetuously. His thoughts had been on Caroline and Spotted Horse. He didn't understand why he couldn't stop thinking about the two of them.

It was a moment before Caroline answered, "I'm not sure how I feel about him. I suppose I should hate him, but I don't."

"I understand," he replied. "It's hard to hate someone you loved."

She knew he was speaking introspectively. Well, he

might have been in love with Emily Parker, but she had never been in love with Spotted Horse. She had been very fond of him, but that was as far as her feelings had gone. She started to say as much to Ross, but then decided not to bother. Let him think she was in love with Spotted Horse — what difference did it make?

She closed her eyes, but sleep was impossible with Ross so close. She had to continuously fight the urge to go to his bed, lie with him, and make love. If only she had the power to rout Emily Parker from his heart! But how could she compete with a woman like her? Ross had told her enough about Emily for Caroline to surmise that she was not only beautiful, but schooled and sophisticated. Caroline didn't see herself as beautiful, her education was certainly limited, and she was more familiar with Apache customs than parlor proprieties.

As sleep continued to elude her, she sat up, and looked toward Ross's pallet, which was lit softly by the moon. "Ross," she said clearly. "Will you please go next door and ask Kirk to sleep in my room?" Surely, with Ross gone, she could finally fall asleep.

Ross thought her request uncalled for. "You don't have to worry, Caroline. I don't plan to return to your bed and seduce you."

His retort sparked an angry reply, "Seduction was not on my mind. I simply prefer not to be in the same room with you."

"You're stuck with me whether you like it or not. There's no reason to disturb Kirk."

"You are a stubborn, inconsiderate devil!" she lashed out.

Ross chuckled lightly. "Go to sleep, Caroline. We'll be leaving at dawn, and you need your rest."

She turned her back, and rolled to her side. She didn't see any reason to argue with him; he wasn't about to relent. She tried vainly to fall sleep, then giving up, she wrapped the sheet about her and moved quietly to her carpetbag.

"What are you doing?" Ross asked.

"Before Leaving Spotted Horse's village, I packed some provisions. I brought along some medicine just in case I needed it."

"Are you sick?" Ross asked, concerned.

"No," she replied.

She lifted a little leather pouch, reached inside and brought out a pinch of dry powder. She wasn't sure of its origin, for most plants and roots used for medicinal purposes were well guarded by the medicine men. She did know, however, that this particular powder was used to ease pain and induce sleep.

"If you aren't sick, then why are you taking medicine?" Ross asked.

"I am taking it to help me sleep."

Ross didn't try to stop her. He had confidence in Indian remedies, and had never known one to be harmful.

Caroline, finding her way by moonlight, stepped to the water pitcher, filled a glass, sprinkled the potent powder into the water, then drank the entire contents.

She returned to bed. The medicine soon took effect, and she fell into a deep, restful slumber.

They left at dawn, and although Caroline was still groggy from the powder, she was glad to leave El Zarango behind. She now wished they had never stopped. If she and Ross had never been alone in that hotel room, then what had happened would never have taken place.

Dry Branch was a three days' ride, and Caroline was now more anxious than ever to reach home. Ross would turn her over to her grandfather, receive his pay, then would most likely leave for Tucson. She wondered if she would ever see him again. She supposed it would be best if she didn't. That way, it would be easier to get over him.

Ross was also looking forward to reaching the Bar-H. The sooner he left for Tucson, the sooner he could put all this behind him. He wasn't deluding himself, he knew it wouldn't be all that easy to forget what had happened with Caroline. Their passionate interlude would stay with him for a long time.

Kirk could sense the tension between Ross and Caroline. It didn't take extraordinary insight for him to figure out what had taken place. From the beginning, Kirk had seen the attraction between the two. He supposed what happened had been inevitable. Kirk knew his cousin well, and he didn't doubt that Ross had now put up a barrier between Caroline and his feelings. In Kirk's opinion, he was a fool. If Ross wasn't so blinded by Emily's treachery, he would see that Caroline was a treasure. Kirk was hopeful that, in time, Ross would come to his senses. But, for now, he knew that Ross had met Caroline too soon after losing Emily. It took time for a man's heart to heal.

They were half a day's ride away from El Zarango when Ross decided to scout ahead. A rocky bluff stood in their path. Beyond it lay open ground, and Ross didn't want to encounter any surprises. His horse's agile hoofs climbed the gradual incline, then horse and rider disappeared over the rise.

Within moments, Ross was speeding back over the rise and down the bluff. Returning to Caroline and Kirk, he reined in sharply, and reported, "There's a band of Apaches headed this way." He pointed toward a cluster of trees standing in the distance. "Let's take cover over there!"

They raced to the shelter, and had barely arrived

when the Indians' ponies crested the rocky bluff. The warriors descended in single file, and Caroline gasped softly when she saw that Spotted Horse was the first in line.

Ross, detecting her gasp, looked at her questioningly.

"Spotted Horse," she whispered. She remembered that day when Spotted Horse had told her that he planned to raid Arizona and New Mexico. A chill coursed through her as she wondered if Spotted Horse and his warriors had left death and destruction in their wake. She looked closely at the Indians passing before her. She didn't see any prisoners or loot. Maybe their mission had failed. She certainly hoped so.

Caroline continued staring at the band until they had ridden out of sight. She actually had an impulse to chase after them. She knew that Spotted Horse loved her, and she wasn't afraid of him, nor could she imagine him ever hurting her. She wished she could ask him about her brothers. Now that she knew the truth, he would certainly understand why she couldn't marry him. What would he gain by refusing to help her? Ross believed if she returned to him, he would keep her against her will. Caroline wasn't so sure. After all, Spotted Horse wanted her as his wife, not his prisoner.

Reluctantly, she cast aside the notion to go after him; Ross would never allow it.

They continued onward, but as hard as Caroline tried, she couldn't quite shake the impulse to pursue Spotted Horse. This might be her only chance to learn what had happened to her brothers. Ross had said that he wasn't going back into Mexico to search for them, and Kirk had told her that Ross had been Hanley's last hope.

She tried to bring a vision of her brothers to mind, but after five years, their faces had grown hazy. But her love for them was still as strong as ever! She longed so desperately to find Walter Junior and Daniel! They were her little brothers, and she felt that she had somehow failed them.

They set up camp at sunset, and as Kirk tended to the horses and the pack mule, Ross built a small fire. Caroline, sat off by herself and watched Ross intently. She found him irresistible, and just looking at him stirred her passion. She wondered if she would ever desire another man as much as she desired Ross. She seriously doubted it, for he was her first love. She had a feeling she would never truly stop loving him.

She looked away from Ross and cast her thoughts elsewhere. Thinking about him was depressing, and a waste of time. He'd soon ride out of her life, and that would be the end of it!

As Walter Junior and Daniel returned to her mind, she literally ached to see them again. Were they still alive? For some unknown reason, she felt that they were. If only she could have intercepted Spotted Horse and asked him about her brothers! But, of course, that had been impossible. Such an act would have placed Kirk's and Ross's lives in jeopardy. However, if she had been alone, she most certainly would have confronted Spotted Horse. She didn't think he would hold her against her will, for now that she had regained her full memory, he would understand why she could never love him. Nonetheless, she knew the chance that he might take her prisoner did exist, but she considered it a slim one. She was willing to take that risk in order to find her brothers.

She wondered how many miles were between her and Spotted Horse. He and his warriors were most likely setting up camp this very minute. If she were to leave soon, she could reach their camp before morning. But how in the world was she to get away from Ross and Kirk? She couldn't sneak off while they were asleep, for they slept in shifts. One was always standing guard. She didn't bother to hope that one of them might fall asleep while on watch; neither of them was the type to be so reckless.

Suddenly, she was struck with an idea. Why not lace their coffee with sleeping powder? That would leave them vulnerable should an enemy stalk the camp. Well, she wouldn't give them enough to knock them out all night, but enough to put them to sleep for a couple of hours. By then, she would have a good head start. She prayed that Ross and Kirk would remain safe during the short time they were asleep.

She couldn't help but feel pangs of guilt. Kirk and Ross trusted her, and she was about to betray that trust. But all she wanted was to question Spotted Horse. She was hopeful that she'd receive the answers she sought, then she'd meet up again with Ross and Kirk. She knew they would follow her.

This mission she had decided to attempt was dangerous, but her brothers' welfare was at stake! She believed she was their last hope, for who else could help them? Spotted Horse loved her; if it became necessary, she would use that love to get the truth!

Her mind made up, she moved to the campfire where Ross was heating their supper. Taking the coffee pot, and filling it with water from a canteen, she said matter-of-factly, "You can help Kirk with the horses — I will finish here."

Caroline hoped desperately that he'd cooperate. She was very tense, but it didn't show.

"All right," he said, glad to hand over the chore. He grinned wryly. "I usually burn dinner anyhow."

"I have noticed," she replied pertly.

Ross didn't leave, for he had become totally enraptured by Caroline's beauty. The fire, casting a golden glow across her face, illuminated her delicate features. She was beautiful beyond compare. Ross knew Caroline wasn't aware of how lovely she was, and this he found extraordinary, as well as touching. Her modesty was sweetly innocent. Deep, tender emotions began to swirl within him, and he suddenly longed to take her into his arms. He felt the need to hold her close, to protect her, and, yes, to love her! His feelings jolted him. Could he possibly care more about her than he realized?

He was about to admit his thoughts to Caroline when, anxious for him to leave, she said coaxingly, "You should hurry if you are going to help Kirk."

He decided to wait and give himself more time to sort out his feelings. There was no reason to rush into anything. After all, that had been his mistake with Emily. He had thoughtlessly dived headlong into their relationship. He wasn't about to make that same blunder again!

The moment Ross walked away, Caroline hurried to her carpetbag, removed the pouch holding the powder, returned to the fire, and poured an estimated portion into the coffee pot. She hoped she had guessed the right amount. She didn't want Kirk and Ross to sleep too long.

She quickly returned the pouch, and was dishing up supper when the men came to the fire. They drank water with their food, but Caroline knew from past meals that they always had coffee afterward.

As soon as they were finished, she poured two cups of coffee and handed them over.

"Aren't you having coffee?" Ross asked her.

"No, it keeps me awake," she murmured, uncomfortable with such a statement. This was one time when it would have a completely opposite effect.

She watched the pair guardedly as they took their first sips. Although she knew the powder was practically undetectable, there was always the chance that one or both of them might catch on. When they didn't question the coffee's taste, but continued to drink, she released an inward sigh. As the men conversed quietly, Caroline removed a pan of heated water from the fire, and washed the dishes. She then dried them and stashed them into a burlap bag.

Ross offered to take the first watch. He took his rifle and moved off into the distance. Kirk decided to have a second cup of coffee before retiring. Caroline was reluctant to pour him another cup, but she could find no justifiable reason to refuse without arousing his suspicion.

She watched as Kirk drained his cup. He then told her good night and went to bed.

She put away the cups, then moved to her bedroll, where she sat down and waited anxiously for the powder to take effect. She was eager to leave, and she had to force herself to be patient. When ample time had finally passed, she dared to leave her blankets and move stealthily to Kirk. Looking down at him, she could tell by his deep, methodical breathing that he was sound asleep.

Nervously, she then walked softly to where Ross was keeping watch. He was sitting beneath a tree, his back propped against the trunk. She noticed that his rifle was lying on the ground at his side.

She whispered his name, but when he didn't respond, she knelt down and took a closer look. As she had suspected, he was asleep. His handsome face, relaxed in repose, made him appear vulnerable, and a tender, loving smile touched Caroline's lips.

Knowing he couldn't hear her, she confessed, barely

above a whisper, "Ross Bennett, I love you. I think I will always love you." Daringly, she leaned over and placed a light kiss on the corner of his mouth.

Then, taking his rifle with her, she returned to camp, hastily gathered her belongings, saddled her pony, and rode off into the quiet night.

She hadn't ridden very far, though, before she turned around and headed back toward camp. Despite her desperation, she just couldn't leave Ross and Kirk defenseless!

Caroline knew Ross wouldn't sleep very long, for he'd had only one cup of coffee. Kirk, of course, would be out much longer. That, however, fit into her plans. Ross wouldn't be able to leave until Kirk was awake, which would still give her time to be far away.

She took up a position a distance from camp. She was well hidden, yet from her vantage point, she could keep a vigilant watch. She cradled Ross's rifle in her arms; she would use it if necessary. She loved Ross, and was very fond of Kirk; she'd not let anything happen to them!

Two hours later, the sleeping potion wore off, and Ross came awake. At first he was too groggy to think sharply. He was, however, clear-headed enough to curse himself for falling asleep. It wasn't like him to do such a crazy thing!

Gradually, as the powder lost its lingering influence, his thoughts sharpened. There was a bitter taste in his mouth, and he was quite certain he knew what had caused it. Caroline had apparently drugged his coffee. He remembered the sleeping powder she had taken the night before.

He bounded angrily to his feet, bent over to pick up his rifle, and saw that it was gone. He was so furious that he failed to detect the distant sound of a horse's hoofs. Caroline, knowing Ross was awake, was leaving her post.

In the meantime, Ross, storming into camp, wasn't surprised to find that Caroline was missing. He hurried to Kirk, and knelt beside him. He shook his cousin's shoulder, but the man didn't budge. He figured Kirk had probably drunk a second cup of coffee, which meant he'd be out for hours. Although Ross was determined to go after Caroline, he couldn't leave Kirk. Drugged, he'd be easy prey to any thief or murderer who happened along.

Knowing he couldn't leave until Kirk awakened, Ross moved to the low-burning campfire, built it up, then made a fresh pot of coffee. As he waited for the coffee to brew, his thoughts were raging. Damn Caroline! She had not only deceived him and Kirk, but had also left them unable to defend themselves. Asleep, they had been totally helpless.

Ross didn't wonder where she was going, for her destination was obvious—she was running after Spotted Horse. He wasn't sure if she was returning to Spotted Horse to question him about her brothers, or if love was the compelling force. Earlier, when she had seen the warrior, had the sight of him renewed her feelings? Did this flight mean she had chosen Spotted Horse over her grandfather?

Ross didn't know the answers to these questions, and he saw no reason to ponder them. Regardless of her reasons for leaving, he was bent on finding her. He not only had a score to settle with her, but Hanley was paying him to bring her home, and he intended to do just that—if he had to hog-tie her to get her there!

Chapter Ten

Following Spotted Horse and his warriors was easy, for they had made no attempts to cover their tracks. Spotted Horse had taught Caroline to read telltale signs, but, in this instance, the trail was so obvious that it wasn't necessary for her to use such skills.

As Caroline rode across the dark countryside, her thoughts were running deeply. Her mind was indeed troubled. She hoped Ross would forgive her treachery. Surely, he would understand her desperation. She believed she was her brothers' only hope. Spotted Horse knew what had happened to them, and she was sure she could persuade him to talk. Her thoughts settled intensely on Spotted Horse. She supposed she should hate him with a vengeance, but she couldn't find it in her heart to loathe him. He had been her friend for five years, and they had spent too many pleasant days together. Furthermore, he had been a very important part of her life. Now, she wasn't sure how she felt about him. She did know that remembering her parents' deaths destroyed any warm feelings she had for Spotted Horse. It was strange, but her emotions toward the warrior were empty, devoid of sentiment. She simply felt nothing at all.

Time passed slowly for Caroline as she continued her trek over the lonely plains. Except for the occasional howling of a coyote, silence reined supreme. The hours dragged by interminably, and Caroline was growing drowsy when, suddenly, a campfire in the distance brought her wide awake. She halted her pony, and considered her next move. Should she ride into the camp unannounced? No, that would be too dangerous. A warrior might shoot her before realizing who she was. All at once, Caroline berated her own stupidity. There was no guarantee that this camp was Spotted Horse's. It could be a fatal mistake to make her presence known.

The site was bordered by low shrubbery, and deciding to sneak in closer, she dismounted. Leading her pony, she moved cautiously toward the distant fire. She didn't dare take the horse too close, for it might whinny and give her away. She came upon a cottonwood and wrapped the reins about a limb. Then opening her carpetbag, she removed her moccasins. Knowing her riding boots might make too much noise, she quickly took them off.

Now, wearing her moccasins and taking Ross's rifle, she left the horse behind and moved closer to the campsite. Her Indian shoes moved soundlessly over the land, which was dotted with clumps of dry grass. Overhead, a skimming cloud covered the moon, its maneuver darkening the countryside.

Keeping the glowing fire in her sights, Caroline made her way to the bordering shrubbery. Now that she was within easy earshot, she could hear two men talking in low tones. She took a quick intake of breath, like she was about to plunge into icy water. The men were speaking in Spanish, not Apache! She didn't know whose camp she had come across, but it certainly wasn't Spotted Horse's!

She didn't bother to part the shrubbery to take a peek, for she was too anxious to leave. Moving as quietly as possible, she was about to sneak away when a rough, calloused hand was clamped over her mouth. A strong arm knocked her rifle to the ground, then it went about her waist, pulling her back flush against her captor's burly chest. She squirmed wildly, but to no avail, for the man's hold was too powerful.

"If you scream, I will be forced to hurt you," he said in a heavy Mexican accent. Carefully, he removed his hand.

Caroline wasn't about to scream.

She was suddenly lifted into his arms and carried into camp. She estimated at least twenty or twenty-five men asleep in their bedrolls. She was amazed by the group's size.

The man carried her to two men who were sitting at the campfire. Roughly, he placed her on her feet. She supposed these were the Mexicans she had heard talking.

The men stood up quickly, for they were shocked to find a woman in their midst. A cold chill coursed through Caroline as she recognized lust in the men's examining gazes. They spoke to each other in Spanish, but Caroline didn't need to understand their words to know what they were saying. Their lecherous expressions told it all.

The younger of the two men took a step toward her, but Caroline's captor grasped her arm and jerked her to his side. He spoke gruffly to his comrades, who, in turn, responded angrily. The three men bantered back and forth for a couple of minutes, but Caroline's captor apparently won the argument, for the other two left and went to their bedrolls.

The man still had a firm grip on Caroline's arm. Then he released her and told her to sit at the fire.

Doing as she was told, she asked, "You saved me from those two men, didn't you? Why?"

He sat beside her, poured himself a cup of coffee, then answered, "They wanted to take you. I told them you are not to be touched until Rolando returns."

"Rolando?" she gasped. Even among the Apaches, the name of Rolando Sánchez was well known. He was the most infamous of all Comancheros. She swallowed nervously, then asked, "Do you mean, Rolando Sánchez?"

"Sí, señorita. You have heard of him, yes?"

In my nightmares, she thought to herself. She was suddenly more frightened than she had ever been in her life. Apaches, visiting Leading Cloud's village, had often given terrifying accounts of Sánchez and his bandits. They were reputed as vicious villains and bloodthirsty killers. Had she fallen into a fate worse than death?

For the first time, she took a close look at the man who had found her. He was middle-aged, and there was a gentleness in his eyes that gave her hope. Maybe she could persuade him to set her free.

"Please let me go!" she pleaded. "I can do you or the others no harm. There is no reason for you to keep me here."

"Rolando would think otherwise. No, señorita, I cannot let you go. You must stay here until he returns."

"Where is he?"

"He is visiting a friend. He will be back soon."

"A friend out here in the middle of nowhere?"

"You ask too many questions, señorita. You must be quiet, or I will gag you."

Caroline withdrew into silence, for she didn't want a gag stuffed in her mouth. She wondered about Sánchez's nighttime visit. Who could he possibly see at this hour, especially in an unpopulated area? He had to be visiting other travelers. Was it Spotted Horse?

Could it be possible that Spotted Horse and Sánchez were friends? Considering her parents' murders, she could no longer put anything past Spotted Horse. No, she wouldn't be surprised to learn that he had dealings with the Comancheros.

Realizing that her relationship with Spotted Horse might save her, she began to hope that her suspicions were right. Surely, Sánchez wouldn't harm the woman Spotted Horse intended to marry!

As Caroline waited for the notorious Sánchez, she held on to that hope.

Caroline had been gone for two hours when Ross forcefully awakened Kirk, then urged him to drink coffee. He was on his third cup before the sleeping powder began to lose its lingering effect. Slowly, Kirk's head started to clear, and his senses grew alert.

Kirk was still in his bedroll, but as Ross returned to the pot to get him a fourth cup, Kirk got up and joined him at the fire. Sitting, he asked, "What the hell did Caroline give me?"

"An Indian sleeping medicine."

"Yeah? Well, she oughta patent it and sell it, 'cause it sure as hell works."

Ross handed him a cup of coffee. "Here — drink this, then we'll go after her."

"Where do you think she went?"

"To find Spotted Horse," Ross answered dryly.

Kirk was surprised. "Why would she want to do that?"

"I can think of two reasons. Last night, she remembered that Spotted Horse was involved in her parents' murders. She might hope to question him about her brothers' whereabouts. Then, again, maybe she went after Spotted Horse because she loves him."

"I doubt if she's in love with him." He sipped his coffee for a long moment, then continued, "You know, I can't blame her for what she did. I'm sure she was only thinking of her brothers."

Ross frowned angrily. "That's no excuse to drug us and leave us defenseless."

"Maybe she didn't think about that."

"She thought about it all right! Caroline's no fool!" Standing, Ross kicked loose dirt over the campfire, smothering the flames. "Let's pack up and get out of here. By now, she's miles ahead of us."

"Don't worry, Ross, we'll find her."

Ross's eyes swept anxiously over the dark countryside. Despite his anger, he was deeply worried. "A lot of things can happen to a woman riding alone in these parts," he murmured gravely.

Kirk agreed. "Let's go; we're wasting time!"

Caroline had been sitting at the fire for over an hour when the sounds of approaching horses sent the man guarding her bounding to his feet. Standing beside him, she watched as four men rode into camp.

Rolando Sánchez was about to dismount, but seeing Caroline caused him to hesitate. He could hardly believe his own eyes. Where had this beautiful woman come from? Why was she in his camp? He doubted that she had come here looking for him, for he was certain he didn't know her. He couldn't, of course, remember all the women in his life, for there were too many. He would have remembered this one—she was too lovely to forget!

With his eyes still on Caroline, he slowly got down from his horse, and ambled lithely toward the campfire.

Caroline knew she was about to meet Rolando Sánchez. She was surprised to see that he was young. She had always pictured him much older, but he couldn't be more than thirty. She was also amazed to find that he was exceptionally good-looking. For some reason, she had never imagined a bandit could be handsome.

Sánchez was most certainly a striking figure. He was dressed all in black, his shirt fitting snugly across his muscular chest, and his trousers adhering to his long, manly legs. A silver-embossed holster, holding two pearl-handled pistols, was strapped about his narrow waist. His Mexican sombrero, held in place by a braided thong, was resting at the back of his neck. His hair was coal-black, his dark eyes were framed by thick brows, and his lips drooped sensuously at each corner. His complexion was smooth, dark, and blemish free.

Although Caroline was impressed with his appearance, there was something undefinable about him that sent a cold chill up her spine. She sensed that his good looks were deceiving.

"What is she doing here?" Sánchez asked the man who had found her. Caroline understood for he spoke in English.

"I found her in the bushes spying on us."

Rolando turned to Caroline. "Is that true, señorita? Were you spying?"

"No, not really. I was looking for another camp, and came upon this one by mistake."

A rakish smile curled the outlaw's lips as his perusal traveled boldly over Caroline. His penetrating eyes seemed capable of seeing through her clothes. His lustful scrutiny made Caroline very uncomfortable.

"What is your name, señorita?"

"Caroline Hanley."

"Whose camp were you looking for?"

"Spotted Horse's."

His incredulity was evident. He couldn't imagine why a white woman was searching for an Apache warrior. "Why do you seek Spotted Horse?"

"I lived with the Apaches for five years, and Spotted Horse and I . . . well, we are supposed to be married." She wasn't about to tell him that she had run away from Spotted Horse, for she still hoped that her relationship with the warrior would save her from Sánchez. She eyed Rolando speculatively. "You know Spotted Horse, do you not? In fact, did you not just come from his camp?"

"Sí, señorita, I know Spotted Horse quite well, and you are right, I just came from his camp. He is about three miles from here."

"Then if you'll please let me leave, I'll return to my horse and ride to Spotted Horse's camp."

Sánchez chuckled brusquely, turned to his comrade, and said, "She wants me to let her leave, Pedro. What do you think, *amigo?* Should I let her go?"

"That is up to you, *capitán.*"

Rolando's eyes returned to Caroline. "I think maybe I will keep you." He stepped forward, placed his hands on Caroline's shoulders, smiled down into her face, and said, "You will be my woman, *sí?*"

Taking him by surprise, she flung off his grip. "No, I won't be your woman!" She proceeded with a touch of desperation in her voice, "If you keep me against my will, Spotted Horse will be furious!"

"I do not fear Spotted Horse. He is nothing but a stinking savage!"

"I thought you were his friend!"

"Spotted Horse and I do business together, but we are not friends."

Caroline's hopes were dashed. Her relationship with Spotted Horse was not going to save her. She was at this bandit's mercy, and there was no one to help her. A hopeful glint suddenly came to her eyes. Ross and Kirk! They would surely follow her! Her expectations, however, took a quick plunge. They were only two men, they couldn't possibly rescue her from so many!

"Caroline," Rolando began, his tone caressing her name. "Pedro will fix you a bed, then you will get some sleep. We will leave in a couple of hours."

"Where are you taking me?" she asked.

"To my home, of course. There, you will be my woman."

Her anger stronger than her fear, she lashed out, "I'll never be your woman willingly!"

Sánchez grinned expectantly. "I like a woman with spirit. Maybe I will keep you for a long time." He spoke to Pedro, "Fix the señorita a bed, then find her horse."

As Pedro moved away, Sánchez turned back to Caroline and said with serious intent, "If you do not do as you are told, I will not hesitate to hurt you. Do you understand, señorita?"

"Yes, I understand," she replied. Her steady voice belied her fear.

The Comancheros broke camp at dawn. For breakfast, they had coffee and spicy beans. Caroline accepted a cup of coffee, but she didn't want anything to eat. She was told to ride beside Sánchez, and everyone was mounted and ready to leave when two riders appeared on the horizon.

Caroline, recognizing them, gasped deeply.

"Do you know these two who are about to die?" Rolando asked her, his eyes regarding her intensely.

"Please don't kill them!" she cried. "I'll do anything you say if you'll spare their lives!"

144

"Who are they?" he asked. The riders were still too far away for Sánchez to get a good look at them.

"Ross and Kirk Bennett," she replied.

"Ross Bennett!" Rolando exclaimed. He suddenly smiled.

"Do you know Ross?"

"Sí, señorita." He told Pedro, who was mounted on his other side, to stay with Caroline. He then slapped the reins against his horse's neck, and rode out alone to greet Ross and Kirk.

Ross knew it was Sánchez, and he and Kirk halted their horses, dismounted, and waited for him.

"*Amigo!*" Rolando said heartily, reining in. He got down from his horse quickly, shook Ross's hand, and asked with a big grin, "Do you always live so recklessly? Only two of you riding toward so many?"

"I knew it was you."

"But how could you know?"

"I sneaked up to your camp before anyone was awake. You were in your bedroll beside the fire, sound asleep."

Sánchez was astounded. "Did you sneak up from the rear?"

Ross nodded.

"But that is impossible! My man, Juan, was keeping watch."

"He was taking a nap. I made sure I didn't disturb him."

"Juan Martínez is an imbecile! I am lucky, *amigo,* that it was you, and not soldiers, *sí?*"

"That all depends," Ross said flatly.

Rolando understood. "You came for the señorita, Sí?"

"I hope you'll hand her over peacefully."

"But why do you want her, *amigo?* She is not your woman, she is Spotted Horse's."

145

"Did she tell you that?"

"*Sí,* she did."

Ross hid his disappointment. Apparently, she was returning to Spotted Horse because she still loved him. He wondered how she could love a man who was responsible for her parents' deaths. Putting all this to the back of his mind, he spoke calmly to Rolando, "Caroline's grandfather hired me to find her. I intend to earn my pay, and deliver her safe and sound."

Sánchez considered the situation seriously. He was reluctant to hand over such a beautiful woman, and if it were any man but Ross Bennett, he would flatly refuse. "Very well, *amigo,* I will give her back to you." He stepped to his horse, mounted, then looked down at Ross. "Maybe this, señor, will make us even."

"Maybe," Ross replied softly.

"Wait here; the señorita will come to you." With that, Sánchez sent his horse into a gallop and returned quickly to camp.

Halting beside Caroline, he told her with a somewhat cocky grin, "You are free to leave, señorita." Pedro had confiscated Ross's new Winchester, but Rolando took it from him, and handed it to Caroline.

Caroline was too incredulous to say anything.

"Go!" he ordered gruffly, reaching out and slapping her pony's flank. The unexpected whack sent the pinto on its way.

Caroline's mind was swirling crazily as she raced toward Ross and Kirk. Why did Sánchez set her free? He certainly didn't fear Ross and Kirk, for they were only two men against all his Comancheros. As she drew closer to the Bennetts, however, her thoughts went from Sánchez to her own treachery. She wondered apprehensively if Ross and Kirk were terribly angry.

The Bennetts were mounted, and waiting when she

arrived. She looked first at Kirk, but his expression was unreadable. She then dared to meet Ross's gaze, and the fury she saw in his eyes gave her a start. She sensed he was a lot more than simply angry. He was outraged, to say the least!

"What you did was not only stupid, but inexcusable!" Ross said furiously. "Do I have to put you under restraint to keep you from running away?"

"I won't leave again. You have my word."

"Your word?" he questioned skeptically. "Let's get one thing straight, Miss Hanley, I don't trust you any farther than I can see you!" He took back his Winchester, then looked over at Kirk, and said, "I'm gonna ride ahead. Keep a close watch on her!"

As he galloped away quickly, Kirk and Caroline followed at a more leisurely pace. "He'll never forgive me, will he?" she asked Kirk.

"Sure he will. Just give him a little time."

"I knew he'd be angry, but I didn't think he'd be this mad."

"He trusted you, Caroline. It's going to be hard for him to forget what you did. I mean, after all, you drugged us, took off, and left us defenseless."

"But I didn't!" she exclaimed. "I started to, but I just couldn't! I returned close to camp, and kept watch until Ross woke up."

Imagining Caroline's vigil placed a warm smile on Kirk's face. Although he doubted her ability to protect him and Ross, he was nonetheless pleased that she had chosen to do so. "You should let Ross know what you did. It might cool his temper a degree or so."

"I doubt it," she replied glumly. They rode in silence for a couple of minutes, then Caroline asked, "Why did Sánchez set me free?"

"If it had been any man but Ross looking for you, I

don't think Sánchez would have let you leave. But he feels he's in Ross's debt. Also, regardless of their differences, there's a certain camaraderie between them."

She looked at him curiously.

"About eight years ago," Kirk explained, "Ross was traveling through Mexico searching for his Apache kin. He came upon Sánchez. A band of Navajos had staked him out in the sand, and had left him there to die. He was already half dead when Ross found him. Well, Ross took care of him until he was better. They struck up a friendship, and Sánchez swore he'd always be grateful to Ross for saving his life. Back then, Sánchez hadn't made a name for himself. They parted company, and went their separate ways, but off and on, they'd come across each other. Sánchez started making a name for himself as a Comanchero, and Ross as a hired gun. Sánchez is a thief and a killer; Ross is just the opposite; yet they've managed to remain on friendly terms."

"So Sánchez let me go because he feels indebted to Ross."

"Yeah, something like that, I guess."

Caroline withdrew into her own thoughts. She had believed her relationship with Spotted Horse would save her. How ironic that instead, it had been Ross's friendship with Sánchez.

Chapter Eleven

Ross remained withdrawn for two days and nights. Although he and Caroline traveled in close proximity, he nevertheless kept her at a distance. Caroline supposed she could force his hand, and make him talk to her. She knew he had a lot to get off his chest, and once he had his say, maybe then he could forgive her for running away. She wasn't sure why his forgiveness was so important. After all, once he delivered her to her grandfather, he'd leave for Tucson, and she'd probably never see him again. Nevertheless, she wanted them to part on a friendly note.

On the last day of their journey, they crossed the Rio Grande. Passage across the water was easy, for due to infrequent rainfall, the river was shallow. They set up camp on the other side, and by the time the sun had made its full descent, dinner had been eaten and the dishes washed and put away.

Caroline was longing for a bath, and she was pleased when Ross suggested that they take turns washing in the river. Leaving Kirk to watch over Caroline, he gathered up a change of clothes, a bar of soap, and headed downstream.

Later, when Ross returned, Caroline's gaze was admiring as she took in his appearance. His dark hair, still damp, was somewhat mussed; the look was quite sensual. He had changed into buckskins, and the soft cream-colored leather fit his tall, tightly muscled frame like a glove. The fringed shirt was partiall unlaced, laying bare an apex of muscles that rippled smoothly across his chest. He had strapped on his gun, and the holster hung loosely about his slim hips.

Caroline raised her eyes to his face. She was a little startled to find he was watching her. Their gazes locked, and the fiery intensity in his coal black eyes gave her quite a turn. She wasn't sure if he was looking at her with passion or rage.

Ross was the first to glance away, and speaking to Kirk, he said, "You'd better go with Caroline. It's not safe for her to go downstream alone."

The last two days had been uncomfortable ones for Kirk. The tension between Ross and Caroline had been difficult for him to deal with. In his opinion, they were both behaving foolishly. If they would talk to each other, they might settle their differences. So far, Kirk had minded his own business and had stayed out of their quarrel. Now, however, he decided to intervene. He would send Ross down river with Caroline.

The coffee pot was still on the hot coals, he picked it up, and filled his cup. "You go with Caroline. I feel like another cup of coffee. Hell, she's your responsibility, but for the past two days, I'm the one who has been takin' care of her."

It wasn't like Kirk to be cantankerous. Ross, as well as Caroline, found his mood peculiar.

Ross, however, decided he couldn't really blame him. What he had said was true. In an effort to avoid close contact with Caroline, he had been shirking his duty and putting all the responsibility on Kirk.

"All right," Ross replied. "I'll go with her." He motioned for Caroline to follow him.

She intended to wash her riding clothes, and opened her carpetbag and drew out the skirt and blouse Ross had purchased in El Zarango.

Ross had started downstream, and she quickly fell into step behind him. She was bothered by Kirk's refusal to accompany her, and she wondered if she had done something to upset him. Because he was on her mind, she glanced back over her shoulder to look at him. She wasn't surprised to find that he was watching her, but she was surprised to see him smile, then wink at her.

Confused, she turned her eyes straight ahead, and followed in Ross's footsteps. Suddenly, she understood what Kirk was up to, and a warm smile brightened her face. Kirk, bless his heart, had intentionally sent her off alone with Ross. Until now, she wasn't sure how Kirk felt about her relationship with Ross, but it was now apparent that he was on her side. She was pleased to have him as an ally, but she believed his ploy to get her alone with Ross was for naught. She couldn't foresee a future between them, and she was sure that Ross wasn't in love with her. She had a depressing feeling that he was still very much smitten with Emily Parker.

Ross stopped at an area bordered by low shrubbery and a few trees. He handed Caroline the bar of soap, then moved to sit beneath a full-branched cottonwood. He said, "I'll wait over here. I'll also be a gentleman and keep my back turned."

Caroline didn't see any reason to say anything. Apparently, he wanted to avoid a discussion, have her bathe as quickly as possible, then return to camp. Well, she'd cooperate, up to a point. She'd take her bath, wash her riding clothes, but then she'd insist on Ross talking to her. After all, time was running out. Tomorrow evening they'd arrive at the Bar-H, Ross would receive his pay, then he'd most likely leave for good. If she was going to make amends, it was now or never.

She believed that she did indeed owe Ross an apology. Drugging him was a serious thing; however, she felt he should understand.

As Caroline was bathing, Ross remained sitting beneath the cottonwood. His back, propped against the wide trunk, was turned toward the water. He lit a cheroot, and as he puffed on the cigar, he tried to keep the image of Caroline, beautifully nude, and washing in the shallow river, out of his thoughts. The effort was hopeless, for the vision kept flashing before his eyes.

Annoyed with his own weakness, he inwardly cursed himself. Damn, hadn't he learned his lesson with Emily? She had made a complete fool of him; and, now, if he wasn't careful, Caroline was going to do the same. Emily had jilted him for her father's money; he didn't know how Caroline would react to her grandfather's riches. He did know that she was still loyal to Spotted Horse. He had a feeling his efforts to return Caroline to Hanley would be for nothing. The first chance she got, she'd certainly go back to Spotted Horse. She had already tried it once, so why not a second time?

Ross found it very hard to understand why she still loved Spotted Horse. The man had actually taken an active part in her parents' murders! It wasn't as though Caroline had been abducted as a small child

152

and couldn't remember her mother and father. My God, she had been thirteen!

Ross, remaining engrossed in his thoughts, lost track of time, and before he knew it, Caroline was calling to him.

"Ross, I'm ready to go back to camp."

He got up, dropped his half-smoked cheroot, then smashed it with the toe of his boot. He turned to go down to the bank, but as his gaze fell across Caroline, he froze as though riveted to the ground. Her beauty was spellbinding!

A light breeze was causing Caroline's windblown hair to fall in seductive disarray, and the thin fabric of her blouse, pressed against her damp skin, temptingly outlined the fullness of her breasts. Her colorful skirt, fitting her small waist snugly, gracefully hugged her rounded hips before falling down to touch the tops of her moccasins.

Ross approached her slowly, reluctant to shorten the distance between them. He didn't trust his emotions, for he was totally enchanted with the lovely woman standing before him.

He came to her side, and gazed down into her beautiful dove-colored eyes. He wondered if she knew that her eyes had the power to bring a man to his knees. He didn't think so, for Caroline didn't seem to be aware of her own extraordinary beauty and the effect it had on others.

Meanwhile, Ross's proximity was causing excitement to mount within Caroline, and she tried vainly to still the wild pounding of her heart. But she had seen desire in his eyes, and her need for him had come alive. She had to forcefully control the urge to fling herself into his arms.

Ross, with effort, managed to get a tenuous hold

on his emotions, and adhering to his resolution to remain uninvolved, he drew his gaze from Caroline's, and said with belying calm, "Let's get back to camp. Kirk's probably anxious to take a bath."

"I do not think he will mind waiting a little longer," Caroline replied firmly. "Surely, you know that he wanted us to be alone. That is why he pretended to be so nasty."

Ross wondered if she was right. "But why would he want us to be alone?"

"He hopes we will resolve our differences."

"There's nothing to resolve," Ross muttered flatly.

"Oh yes, there is!" she responded angrily. "Since that night I drugged your coffee, you have not only treated me coldly, but on occasion, downright rudely!"

Her anger sparked Ross's. "What was I supposed to do? Thank you for what you did?" Releasing his pent up rage, he continued harshly, "Kirk's right! You and I do need to talk! I've got a score to settle with you, and, damn it, I'm gonna have my say! I think what you did was unforgivable. You knew the danger you were placing Kirk and me in when you drugged us and left us defenseless!"

"I didn't leave you defenseless!" she came back sharply. "I guarded the campsite until you woke up."

"You did what?" he snapped.

"You heard me! I had your rifle, and I wouldn't have hesitated to use it. Thank goodness, it didn't come to that."

For a moment, Ross gaped at her as though incredulous. Then, suddenly, he laughed outrageously.

Caroline fumed inwardly. How dare he laugh at her!

He stifled his humor, and said flippantly, "Well,

154

that makes everything all right. Kirk and I were perfectly safe, for we had you watching over us. If I had known that, I might have slept longer."

His sarcasm was infuriating. "You are unfair! Just because I am a woman does not mean I cannot protect you!"

"Is that right?" he questioned, arching a brow. "If you're so good at protection, then why couldn't you protect yourself from Sánchez?"

She hated him! What she wouldn't give for a good retort, but she couldn't think of one. Damn him, he had her cornered! Forgetting her earlier plan to apologize, she let her frustrated temper get the upper hand, and stamping her foot childishly, she said furiously, "Ross Bennett, you are a mean, terrible man!"

She turned to leave, but his hand suddenly grasped her arm, whirling her back around to face him. "Mean and terrible?" he questioned with quiet rage. "Look who's calling the kettle black!"

She tried unsuccessfully to break his firm grip. "If you were not so stubborn, you would understand why I just had to find Spotted Horse!"

Oh, he believed he understood all right! Love was a powerful force, and it had sent her fleeing after an Apache warrior!

Again, she tried to wrest free, her struggles causing her to fall against him.

Caroline's body, pressed closely to his, was a temptation Ross couldn't overcome. Unable now to tame his desire, his lips assaulted hers in a heated kiss that set fire to his smoldering passion.

Caroline surrendered without a struggle, for, like Ross, she had no control over her desire. Returning his kiss with all her heart, she leaned against his strong frame. Her knees had weakened, and her head was swimming. Her passion was like a sudden and powerful gust that was threatening to sweep her off her feet.

Ross lifted her into his arms, carried her to the cottonwood, and gently laid her down under its canopied branches. He lay beside her, holding her body flush to his.

Their exploring hands skimmed anxiously over each other, every touch, every caress, intensifying their wild, uncontrollable need. Passion burned as hotly as their blazing kisses, which were explosively overpowering.

When Ross lifted her skirt, Caroline made no move to stop him; quite the contrary, she helped him remove her undergarment, for she, too, was anxious to consummate their union. Unbuckling his gun belt, he placed it at his side, then pushing his trousers past his hips, he moved over her.

His mouth, warm and demanding, pressed against hers as his manhood entered with firm aggression. A small sound of ecstasy came from her throat. Wrapping her legs about his waist, she took the full length of him.

They made love with an intensity, as though firebolts of desire were arcing through every nerve in their bodies. Passion, like a consuming flame, engulfed the lovers, leaving them conscious only of their burning need for each other.

Their rapture drew to an explosive, fulfilling finish that left them both shaken by this wondrous passion between them.

Ross's thoughts were in turmoil as he moved away from Caroline to straighten his clothes. During his lifetime, he'd certainly had his share of women, but no woman had ever set fire to his loins like Caroline.

Her beauty, of course, had the power to arouse any man's passion. But Ross knew his desire for Caroline was more than physical. His emotions were too strong and too tightly-coiled for him to take lightly. He had to look beyond his physical attraction for Caroline, and into his own heart. What he saw there was disturbing. He was falling in love with Caroline, but she was already in love with Spotted Horse. Furthermore, she loved the warrior so deeply that she had even confessed her feelings to Rolando Sánchez. Obviously, she hadn't hesitated to let Sánchez know that she was Spotted Horse's woman. Ross found Caroline quite perplexing. If she loved Spotted Horse, why had she no qualms about making love to him? Caroline was indeed a mystery. How was he to understand a woman who could love a man who was involved in her own parents' deaths—and probably even the deaths of her brothers? No, Caroline Hanley went beyond his comprehension, and calling on his last source of willpower, he once again decided to cast her out of his life.

Meanwhile, as Ross was sorely misjudging Caroline, she was trying to keep her expectations in check. She wanted so desperately for him to profess his love, and ask her to be his wife. He had to know how much she cared! After all, if she didn't love him, she couldn't give herself to him so passionately.

To Caroline's disappointment, Ross didn't profess his love; he got to his feet, helped her up, and said dryly, "We'd better get back to camp."

His attitude was not only chilling, but infuriating. Caroline, however, was more angry with herself. She had been such a naive fool to succumb to Ross's charms. Twice now, she had been his for the taking. Well, there wouldn't be a third time!

157

With a defiant tilt to her chin, she looked him squarely in the eyes, and remarked frigidly, "Ross Bennett, do not dare to ever touch me again! If you do, I will send a bullet right into your unfeeling heart!" With that, she twirled about, stepped to the riverbank, gathered her washed clothes, and started back toward camp.

Ross followed, his thoughts now more perplexed. What had he done to Caroline to cause such an outburst? His own anger was suddenly ignited, and he decided to hell with it! He was through trying to figure her out. Besides, her outburst was probably a reflection of her own guilt—twice now she had cheated on Spotted Horse!

Returning to camp, Caroline spread her clothes out to dry, then went to her bedroll, crawled inside, and turned her back. She was hurt as well as angry. Damn Ross Bennett! He was undoubtedly still infatuated with Emily Parker! Caroline felt used and degraded. She was nothing more to Ross than a physical release!

Meanwhile, as Caroline lay fuming, Ross was pouring himself a cup of coffee. He moved to his own bed, sat down, and stared straight ahead at nothing in particular.

Kirk, watching the two, frowned testily. Obviously, his ploy to get them together hadn't worked. He retrieved the bar of soap, and headed downstream. He reminded himself not to play cupid again, for he apparently wasn't very good at it.

Bill Hanley sat in the parlor, the telegram from Ross clutched in his hands. He had received it two days ago; the paper was now frayed and worn, for he had read it several times. The missive had been short and straight to the point. It had simply read: We found Caroline and are bringing her home.

Bill felt it was a miracle come true. His granddaughter was actually coming home! The boys weren't mentioned, obviously the Bennetts had failed to locate them. Despite Bill's joy over Caroline, he was nevertheless worried that Kirk and Ross had learned that his grandsons were dead.

Rebecca, along with Bryan and Alex, were also in the room. The family had finished dinner a few moments before, and had retired to the parlor for coffee and brandy.

Rebecca was extremely annoyed with her husband. In her opinion, he was making a spectacle of himself sitting there holding that telegram. He was acting as though if he let it out of his hands, Caroline would somehow slip through his fingers. Rebecca was more than annoyed, however—she was also very upset. Caroline alive! Damn the bad luck!

Bryan, like his mother, was cursing Caroline's miraculous return. Hanley would, without a doubt, leave the Bar-H to the little chit! Steaming inwardly, Bryan refilled his brandy glass. He intended to get drunk.

Unlike his mother and brother, Alex wasn't wasting his time cursing their misfortune, for he had every intention of changing it. He was merely waiting for Hanley to go to bed, then he'd tell Rebecca and Bryan what he planned to do.

A few minutes later, Bill cooperated, bid his family good night, and left for his bedroom. Rebecca noticed with disdain that he took that blasted telegram with him.

Alex, taking note of Bryan's and Rebecca's long faces, chuckled heartily.

159

"What's so funny?" his brother asked, irritated.

"You two," Alex answered, smiling. "You'd think the world has come to an end."

"Well, in a way, it has," Rebecca murmured sourly.

"No, it hasn't," Alex said. "Caroline can be eliminated. That telegram came from El Zarango, which means her and the Bennetts will be gettin' here sometime tomorrow evenin'. I got a couple of buddies who'll help me ambush 'em." Alex spoke directly to Bryan, "Course they won't do it for nothin'. You're gonna have to pay 'em. I'd offer to pay part of it, but I'm broke."

"Honestly, Alex!" Rebecca complained. "What do you do with your money? Bill pays you a handsome salary, and you don't work half as hard as his wranglers."

"I'll tell you what happens to his money," Bryan put in. "What he doesn't lose playing poker, he spends on my two prostitutes."

"If you were any kind of brother at all," Alex whined, "I wouldn't have to pay for them whores. You'd let me have 'em for nothin'."

"If I did that, you'd never let them out of bed. I can't make any money that way."

"Stop it!" Rebecca ordered sharply. "Alex, do you really think you and your friends could pull off an ambush?"

"Sure, why not? The Bennetts ain't gonna be suspectin' nothin' like that to happen. There ain't no reason why we can't take 'em by surprise."

Rebecca turned to Bryan. "What do you think?"

"I think it's a big risk, but right now I'm so desperate, I'll try anything."

"I agree," Rebecca replied, wondering if her youngest son could be the answer to their dilemma.

160

Alex smiled confidently. For once, he was the one in charge. Bryan and Rebecca were both looking at him expectantly, waiting to hear what else he had to say. For the first time in his life, he felt important in their presence.

Chapter Twelve

To reach the Bar-H, it wasn't necessary to ride through Dry Branch, and since there was no reason to stop, Ross decided to by-pass the town.

The countryside was now familiar to Caroline, and she recognized the scenery that lay between Hanley's ranch and town. She grew anxious to reach the Bar-H, and could hardly wait to see her grandfather.

As they approached a pass bordered by shrubbery on one side, and a rocky bluff on the other, Ross and Kirk didn't anticipate danger, for they weren't expecting trouble this close to the Bar-H.

Alex, along with two companions, had taken up positions on top of the bluff, and from their vantage point, they had a full view of the pass below. The three men had their rifles aimed and ready to fire. But the ambush wasn't going as Alex had planned. He had thought it would be another hour or so before Caroline and the Bennetts got this far. Due to the time, the setting sun was shining in their eyes, and the bright rays were blinding. Alex silently cursed his bad luck. He actually considered terminating his mission and waiting for a better opportunity, but he dreaded telling Bryan and Rebecca that he had failed. He knew, in their eyes, he had always been a failure. He set his jaw firmly, and mustered his confidence. Damn it, this time he wouldn't fail! He'd get rid of Caroline and the Bennetts, sun or no sun!

He cast his companions a sidelong glance. They, too, were squinting against the sun. The one called Nick he knew quite well, for they had been buddies for a long time. The other one was a stranger who had drifted into town a few days ago. He was a young Mexican named Alfredo. He had struck up an acquaintance with Alex and Nick. The three of them had hit it off right from the start, for they were a lot alike. They were a dangerous threesome, for not one of them possessed a shred of decency. Bryan had offered Nick and Alfredo fifty dollars a piece to kill Caroline and the Bennetts, the men had accepted without hesitation. Alex had chosen his conspirators well, for they placed little value on human life.

Now, as Alex and his fellow snipers awaited their victims, they were forced to squint against the sun's glaring rays. They cursed the blasted sun, but they weren't about to give up. Alfredo and Nick were too anxious to earn their fifty dollars, and Alex was still determined not to fail!

Caroline was riding between the Bennetts, but as they entered the narrow path, Kirk took the lead, followed by Caroline. Ross brought up the rear.

Since leaving the Rio Grande, they had made exceptionally good time, and Ross was pleased at their progress. They would reach the Bar-H sooner than he had estimated.

For no apparent reason, Ross happened to glance up at the bluff; fortunately, at that same moment, the sun's glare fell across the barrel of Alex's rifle. Ross, recognizing the flash, spurred his horse for-

163

ward, for his first instinct was to protect Caroline. He drew up alongside her, his body shielding hers; at that exact instant, Alex, intending to kill Caroline, fired his rifle. As the shot exploded, Ross fell from his horse.

Caroline dismounted quickly, went to Ross, and knelt beside him. A scream lodged in her throat. In the meantime, Kirk had freed his rifle and was shooting back.

Alex and his comrades fired a barrage of ammunition, but the blinding sun, coupled with Kirk's rapid counter shots, caused their bullets to go awry.

Although Ross was badly wounded, he was conscious, and with Caroline's assistance, he managed to take cover behind a large shrub. Kirk took time to daringly grab Ross's Winchester before he, too, took shelter behind the bush. He started to hand the rifle to Ross, but Caroline took it instead. She knew Ross was too seriously injured to fire accurately.

Five years had passed since Caroline shot a rifle, but she handled herself as though it had been yesterday. Along with Kirk, she returned their attackers' gunfire.

As Alex and the others were dodging flying bullets, it was apparent that their mission had failed. Nick was the first one to retreat. "Hell, I'm gettin' out of here!" he said, turning to run for his horse.

Alfredo, fleeing also, yelled over his shoulder to Alex, "If you stay, amigo, you are loco!"

Alex was fuming. Damn the rotten luck! If only the sun hadn't been in their eyes! Knowing it would be useless to continue the battle alone, he followed behind his comrades.

Reaching their horses, they split up. Nick and Alfredo headed toward town as Alex started for the Bar-H. He hoped to arrive unseen, sneak into the house from the rear, then slip upstairs to his room. It was imperative that he avoid Hanley, for he didn't want him suspecting that he was involved in the ambush. Maybe he wouldn't know that he had even left the house.

As Alex was racing for home, Caroline was helping Kirk bandage Ross's wound. He had been shot in the side, and blood was flowing freely. Ross was barely conscious, but he was determined not to pass out.

"Are you able to ride?" Kirk asked him.

"I can make it," Ross said raspingly.

Kirk helped him onto his horse, but he was so weak that he could hardly stay in the saddle. Kirk hesitated for a moment as he tried to decide whether to take Ross to Dry Branch or to the Bar-H. The ranch was closer. His mind made up, he hurried to his own horse, mounted, then told Caroline, "Take Ross to the Bar-H. I'll ride into town, get the doctor, and bring him to the ranch." He swung his horse about, and raced away.

Caroline was frightened, for Ross was losing so much blood. The bandage was already soaked a bright red. She knew his condition was grave, and she marveled that he could stay on his horse. Most men would have passed out by now.

They had to travel slowly, for Ross was too weak for them to move quickly. It seemed to Caroline's frantic mind that they were moving at a snail's pace. At this rate, it would take well over an hour to reach the Bar-H. Could Ross hold out that long? God, would he bleed to death by then?

Caroline turned anxious eyes to Ross. Somehow, he managed to summon a shaky smile and murmur, "I'll make it, Caroline."

She prayed that he would.

* * *

Bill Hanley was pacing his front porch when Rebecca and Bryan stepped out of the house. Rebecca had been watching him from the parlor window. She saw the way he would pace restlessly, then pause to gaze down the lane leading up to the house, then resume his pacing. Caroline's expected arrival was making her husband extremely nervous. Well, if Alex was successful, Bill's nerves would soon be shattered, for his darling Caroline would be dead!

"Will you please stop pacing back and forth like a corralled mustang!" she complained.

"I can't help it," Bill answered, although he did manage to stand still. "Caroline could be here anytime now." He paused for a moment, then continued excitedly, "Maybe I should saddle up and ride out to meet them."

Rebecca was against the idea. What if Bill should come upon the ambush? He could spoil everything.

Bryan was the first to object, "Bill, why don't you just settle down and wait?"

"Yes!" Rebecca put in. "There's no reason for you to leave. Besides, waiting here for Caroline will make for a much nicer reunion. Don't you think?"

"Yes, I suppose you're right," he agreed. "I'm just so jittery. I hate this waiting!"

Rebecca, pretending concern, took his hand and squeezed it gently. "You've already waited five years, now your wait is almost over."

"Furthermore," Bryan added, "it might be an hour or longer before she shows up." If she shows up at all, Bryan concluded to himself. He wasn't too optimistic, for he didn't have much confidence in Alex.

The sudden sound of a speeding horse arrested their attention, and they watched as one of the wran-

166

glers raced up to the house. Reining in abruptly, he said to Hanley, "Boss, me and Carl were on our way home for supper when we came across your grand-daughter and Ross Bennett. The girl's fine, but Bennett's been badly shot, and I'm gonna go back after 'im in the buckboard."

"Where are they?" Bill asked at once.

" 'Bout two miles south. They were ambushed back yonder at the pass."

"Give me your horse," Bill ordered, fleeing down the porch steps. As the wrangler dismounted, he swung agilely into the saddle. "Get that buckboard hitched. I'll ride ahead!"

Hanley turned the tired horse about, and sent it racing back down the lane.

Rebecca waited until the wrangler had left to get the buckboard, before saying disgustedly, "Damn that Alex!"

"He's a blundering idiot!" Bryan seethed.

"I heard that!" Alex said suddenly, opening the door and stepping out to the porch.

"What happened?" Rebecca asked him. "And how long have you been home?"

"I've been back for quite awhile. I slipped in through the back door, and went up to my room."

"How the hell did you manage to foul everything up?" Bryan demanded.

"Caroline and them Bennetts reached the pass 'fore I thought they would. The goddamn sun was in our eyes. I got off a shot, but I hit Bennett instead of Caroline."

Bryan threw up his hands in despair. "I've heard enough! Damn it, Alex, you've never done anything right in your life! You're an imbecile!"

"You ain't got no right to call me that!" Alex shouted.

Bryan stormed into the house, slamming the door. He headed straight for the den, where he fixed himself a glass of brandy. He was soon joined by his mother.

"Pour me one, too," she said.

"Where's that idiotic brother of mine?"

"Outside, pouting like a little boy."

"Mother, you should have drowned him the day he was born."

She didn't see any reason to disagree.

Caroline spotted the lone rider approaching, but he was too far away for her to recognize him. As he drew closer, however, she realized it was her grandfather. Although she longed to send her pinto into a fast gallop, meet him halfway, and throw herself into his loving arms, she couldn't bring herself to leave Ross.

By now, Ross had grown dangerously weak. The wrangler called Carl was riding double with him, for he needed the man's support to keep from falling.

They reined in and waited for Hanley to reach them. Caroline dismounted shakily, then moved to check on Ross. He was braced by Carl's arm wrapped about his waist. Caroline's heart pounded frightfully as she noticed that Ross was deathly pale. He was still conscious, but on the brink of passing out.

Arriving, Hanley brought his horse to a stop, leaped from the saddle, rushed to Caroline, and took her into his arms.

She held her grandfather tightly, and the tears she had kept suppressed, rose to the surface and overflowed. Her tears were a mixture of happiness and grave concern. She was indeed overjoyed to be reunited with her grandfather, but Ross's life was uppermost in her mind.

"Caroline!" Bill exclaimed, his voice ringing ecstatically. He held her at arms' length so that he could get a good look at her. "You're beautiful, absolutely beautiful." His eyes grew misty. "You still look so much like your grandmother."

Caroline was slightly taken aback by her grandfather's appearance. These past five years had aged him considerably.

Losing his family had taken its toll. However, he did seem to be in good health.

"Grandpa, we have so much to talk about, but right now I can only think about Ross." Fresh tears gushed from her eyes. "I'm afraid he's going to die!"

Bill wondered if she was in love with Bennett. The thought was a little startling, but only for a moment. After all, Caroline was no longer a child. He wasn't displeased, though, for he liked Ross.

Hanley was in full accord with Caroline—their reunion would have to wait—tending to Ross was too imperative. He moved over to Carl and said, "Hand Bennett down to me. I'll check his wound while we wait for the buckboard."

"I can get down by myself," Ross groaned, his voice so weak that he could barely be heard.

Despite Ross's determination to do it on his own, he was compelled to accept Carl's assistance. He had no patience with his enfeebled condition, and he cursed his helplessness.

Caroline hurried to the pack mule, got the medicine kit, then grabbed a blanket off her horse's back, and spread it out on the ground. With Hanley's support, Ross made it to the blanket, then giving in to his weakness, he allowed Bill to help him lay down. A devouring gulf of blackness tried to overtake him, but Ross willfully fought it back.

"Where's Kirk?" Bill asked Caroline, as he tended to Ross's wound.

"He went to town for the doctor."

Caroline watched as her grandfather carefully removed Ross's blood-soaked bandage. The ghastly wound sent her heart to pounding. Waves of grayness suddenly passed over her, and, for a moment, she thought she might faint. She drew in several deep breaths, and the feeling passed. Fear was knotted in her stomach, and her nerves were at full stretch. She prayed that God wouldn't let him die!

"Exactly what happened?" Bill asked her. He removed a clean bandage from the kit and pressed it against Ross's wound.

"We were ambushed."

"Did you see who it was?"

"No," she replied.

"How many were there?"

"I don't know. Three, maybe four."

He held her hand. "Thank God, you weren't hurt." He shuddered to think that he could have found her, only to lose her.

"I don't understand," Caroline began, "why someone wanted to kill us."

Ross, listening, whispered hoarsely, "Maybe it was Jake Mackenna."

"Who's he?" Bill asked.

As Caroline was explaining what had happened with the Mackennas in El Zarango, Hanley's wrangler arrived with the buckboard. Against Ross's protests, the men lifted him and placed him in the back of the wagon. Caroline climbed in beside him.

Bill hefted himself up onto the seat, picked up the reins, then told his ranch hands, "I'll drive, you two get the horses and the pack mule."

170

As the buckboard started in motion, Caroline placed her hand gently into Ross's. She was about to speak to him, but his weakness had finally overcome his willpower, and he had passed out. She leaned over and kissed his lips softly. "I love you," she murmured intensely. "I won't let you die! I won't!"

Caroline, closeted in the den with Hanley and Kirk, paced the room anxiously. The doctor was upstairs with Ross. Caroline had wanted to assist the physician, but her grandfather, worried about her fatigue, had sent his housekeeper instead. Although Caroline was reluctant to let the woman go in her place, she didn't argue. She remembered the housekeeper very well, and the woman had tended to the ill and wounded several times. She was undoubtedly better trained to help the doctor.

Sheriff Taylor had ridden as far as the pass with Kirk and the physician. He had remained behind to look over the area, and to perhaps pick up a trail.

The door opened, and, Caroline, hoping to see the doctor, was disappointed, for Bryan was the intruder. She watched him somewhat curiously as he helped himself to a glass of brandy. She had seen Bryan when they arrived, but she hadn't paid him much attention. Now, though, she took time to examine him closely. He hadn't really changed all that much in five years, he had simply matured. He was the same height, but he had put on a little weight. At eighteen, his moustache had been noticeably thin, but it was now thick and well-groomed. He wasn't exceptionally handsome, but he was nice looking and made a good appearance. Caroline wondered if the years had improved his personality, or if he was still as self-centered and arrogant as she remembered.

Bryan was inconspicuously returning Caroline's scrutiny. He wasn't surprised to see that she had grown into a beautiful woman, for she had been an extremely lovely girl. As his gaze traveled over her furtively, he imagined her naked and in his bed. The lustful vision not only triggered his desire, but also gave birth to an idea. Why should he kill such a gorgeous woman, when he could marry her instead? If Caroline was his wife, he would also inherit the Bar-H; in addition, she would be his to do with as he pleased. Yes, his idea was delightful, as well as practical! It didn't dawn on him that Caroline might not find him irresistible, for he had every confidence in his suavity. He couldn't imagine her not succumbing to his sophisticated charms. Furthermore, after living with savages for five years, she'd most certainly be grateful that a white man even wanted her. He didn't doubt that she had been sexually abused by several warriors. She was not only used goods, but contaminated goods at that! But Bryan didn't consider her tainted past a deterrent. He wanted the Bar-H, and he also wanted Caroline. He was determined to have both!

The door opened again, admitting Rebecca and Alex. Caroline gave them her full attention. Like Bryan, they hadn't changed very much. Rebecca was still a strikingly attractive woman, and her youngest son was boyishly handsome. Earlier, Caroline had gotten a glimpse of the two, but she had been too worried about Ross to pay much attention.

"Leave the door open, Alex," Hanley said. "That way, Doctor Gordon can find us when he comes downstairs."

Secretively, Rebecca cast Kirk an admiring glance, then bustling over to Caroline, she exclaimed, "Caroline, darling, it's so wonderful to have you home!"

172

She embraced her exuberantly.

Caroline returned the woman's hug hesitantly, for she doubted her sincerity. She knew that Rebecca hadn't liked her as a child, and she didn't think her feelings had changed.

They were interrupted by Bryan, who swept Caroline smoothly into his embrace. "Forgive me for not welcoming you home sooner, but considering everything . . ."

"I understand," she replied, wishing he would let her go. She didn't like being so close to him.

Bryan was forced to release her quite suddenly, for her nearness had sexually aroused him.

Meanwhile, Alex was standing beside the door, too glum to even pretend to welcome Caroline. He merely nodded at her, and mumbled, "It's good to see you again."

At that moment, the physician entered the room. Doctor Gordon was tall, middle-aged, and the fatherly type. "The patient's going to make a complete recovery," he said, smiling. "It'll be awhile before's he's up and about, but he's out of danger."

"May we see him?" Caroline asked, her heart racing joyously.

"Sure, but don't stay too long."

Hanley took his granddaughter's arm and escorted her to the stairs. They were followed by Kirk and the doctor.

Alone with his family, Alex mustered a semblance of self-assurance, and said strongly, "I ain't gonna give up. I'll get rid of Caroline. I just need another chance."

Bryan turned on him with a fury. "You are to stay the hell away from Caroline! This matter is now in my hands, and I'll take care of everything! You just keep out of it!"

Rebecca was confused by Bryan's outburst. "What do you plan to do?" she asked him.

"I plan to marry Caroline," he answered simply.

Chapter Thirteen

Caroline was alone with Ross. Her grandfather, along with Kirk and the doctor, had gone downstairs for brandy. The housekeeper, Inés, was in the kitchen getting Ross a bowl of broth.

Ross was barely awake, for Doctor Gordon had given him a mild sedative. Caroline was sitting in a hard-back chair placed close to the bed. Although Ross was awake, his eyes were closed; and, Caroline, thinking he had fallen asleep, took his hand, brought it to her lips, and kissed it.

Her caring gesture touched Ross profoundly, it also surprised him. Did her feelings for him run deeper than he thought? He opened his eyes to find that she was watching him. A warm blush colored her cheeks.

"Did you think I was asleep?" he asked softly.

Her blush deepened. "Yes, I did," she replied, obviously embarrassed.

Ross decided not to mention that she had kissed his hand, for it would only increase her embarrassment. "Caroline," he began, his voice distinctly weak, "through this whole ordeal, I kept telling myself that if I lived through it, I was going to apologize to you."

"Apologize?" she questioned.

"During the ambush, you handled yourself very well. I saw the way you shot my rifle, and you knew what you were doing. That night when you drugged Kirk and me, then kept watch over us, we were in capable hands. I'm sorry that I reacted so sarcastically when you told me what you had done."

"Shall we just forget it? We both said things we did not really mean. I told you if you ever touched me again, I would send a bullet into your unfeeling heart." She smiled warmly. "I could never shoot you, no matter what."

The door opened, and Inés entered, carrying a tray. She placed it on the bedside table, then spoke to Ross, "The doctor said that you must eat, señor. I brought you some broth."

"I'll feed him," Caroline was quick to offer.

"No, you won't," Ross objected. "I'm not a helpless invalid. I'll feed myself." Grimacing, he sat up in bed, as Inés placed the pillows at his back.

Carefully, Caroline balanced the tray on his lap. She didn't insist on Ross letting her feed him, for she knew he wouldn't allow it — he was too proud.

His weakened condition, coupled with his painful wound, made eating a little difficult, but he managed to finish half the bowl before the need for sleep took over.

Caroline removed the pillows from his back. He stretched out, and was asleep before she placed the tray back on the table. She stood over him, and her gaze was filled with love. Inés, watching, saw the devotion in her eyes.

"You are in love with Señor Bennett, sí?" she asked tenderly.

"Is it so obvious?" Caroline asked, smiling.

"Sí, it is," she replied. "Does he know how much

you care?"

"No, I do not think so," Caroline said. There was a touch of sadness in her voice.

"You should tell him," Inés remarked firmly. "Otherwise, you might lose him."

Caroline disagreed, for Ross wasn't hers to lose. He still belonged, heart and soul, to Emily Parker. She kept her speculations to herself, and simply responded to Inés's advice with a heartwarming smile. She was very fond of Inés. The woman had come to work for Hanley a few years after his first wife died. She was an attractive woman in her late fifties. She wasn't very tall, and her matronly curves were on the plump side, but the extra weight looked good on her, and it caused her round face to appear more youthful than her years. Her long black hair, streaked with silver, was pinned up into a tight bun at the back of her neck. Her olive complexion was smooth and almost wrinkle free.

Inés, who had been returning Caroline's scrutiny, said admirably, "Señorita, you have grown into a very beautiful woman. Your grandfather must be very proud."

As though her words had conjured up the man, Hanley came into the bedroom, and asked Caroline, "Honey, haven't we waited long enough for our reunion? Can't we please be alone for awhile?"

"Of course we can," she replied readily. She, too, was anxious for them to spend time alone. They had so much to discuss!

Inés watched them as they left the room. She hoped the señorita would not make the same mistake she herself had made so many years ago. She must tell Señor Bennett of her great love before he married someone else. Perhaps, if she had been honest with Señor Hanley, he would have married

177

her instead of Señora Rawlins. But she had foolishly kept her love hidden, hoping that someday he would come to her. Her pride had led her to make a serious mistake. She hoped Caroline would not be as foolish!

Caroline and Hanley went to the den, where they talked for a long time. Caroline gave her grandfather a full account of the last five years—she told him of her amnesia, her life with her adopted family, and her relationship with Spotted Horse. She explained how her memories had slowly returned, which had led to her desperate flight to come home!

As Bill listened, he was grateful to Leading Cloud and his family for taking good care of Caroline, but his feelings toward Spotted Horse weren't quite so charitable. If the warrior and his friend, Stalking Bear, dared to leave Mexico to make their home in the New Mexico territory, he would see to it personally that the Army arrested them for murdering his son and daughter-in-law.

A long moment of silence came between Hanley and Caroline, for they were both deep in thought. It was Bill who spoke first, and his somber tone reflected his mood, "I've lost my grandsons, haven't I? I'll never see them again." A trace of tears came to his eyes. "Dear God, they've probably been dead all these years!"

"We don't know that for sure!" Caroline declared. She and Hanley were sitting on the sofa, but, now, bounding to her feet, she continued with excitement, "But Spotted Horse knows what happened to Walter and Daniel! If I could only talk to him!"

Jolted, Bill stood up quickly, and grasped Caroline's shoulders. His eyes bore authoritatively into hers, and he spoke inflexibly. "I know what you're thinking, and you can forget it! Under no circumstances will I allow you to return to Spotted Horse! My God, I lost you once, I couldn't bear losing you again!"

Caroline understood his fear, and she also knew it wasn't idle—there was no guarantee that Spotted Horse would cooperate. That he might keep her against her will was indeed a possibility. She longed to tell her grandfather that, for the sake of her brothers, she was willing to take such a gamble. It wasn't easy for Caroline to succumb to his wishes, but she didn't see where she really had any other choice. She couldn't bring herself to defy him and return to Spotted Horse on the chance that he might reveal her brothers' whereabouts, if they were even still alive. Furthermore, if she were to travel alone across the plains, she would probably never make it to Spotted Horse's village, even if she could locate it! She wished desperately that she could find her brothers, but she knew it wasn't possible.

She went into her grandfather's arms, and hugged him tightly. "I love you, Grandpa. And please don't worry. I will not do anything foolish."

He returned her hug, kissed her cheek, then moved to his gun cabinet. Taking out a rifle, he brought it to her. "Do you remember this?" he asked.

"Yes, I do," she replied, accepting it. "You gave me this Winchester on my thirteenth birthday."

"It's still yours."

She returned it to him, saying, "I will be right back." She hurried to the foyer, where she had left her carpetbag, opened it, and withdrew her necklace. She quickly went back to the den, and showing her grandfather the piece of jewelry, she said, "You also gave me this. Spotted Horse told Basket Woman to destroy it, but she kept it for me. It helped me to remember."

Bill studied it through blurry eyes. "Why aren't you wearing it?"

"I wanted to wait for you to put it on me, just like you did on my birthday."

He took the dainty locket, and clasped it about her neck. Then he gently turned her so that she was facing him. "You look so much like your grandmother, only you're more beautiful."

Caroline couldn't help but blush. She was about to thank him for the compliment, but was interrupted by a knock on the door.

"Come in," Hanley called.

Sheriff Taylor entered. "Bill," he began, "I hate to disturb you, but I need to borrow some of your wranglers."

"Did you pick up a trail where the ambush took place?"

"No, I'm afraid I didn't. That's not why I'm here. While I was looking over the area, my deputy found me. It seems my niece went riding this afternoon, and hasn't returned home."

"We'll begin a search immediately," Bill replied.

"I saw Kirk when I rode up to the house. He offered to help find Mary. In fact, he already left."

Seeing the sheriff's grave concern, Caroline was quick to say, "Try not to worry. I'm sure Kirk will find her."

As Kirk's horse galloped across the dark plains, he tried to figure out which direction a woman riding alone would decide to take. He omitted the mountain region, for it would be too dangerous. No, she'd mostly likely stick to open ground. If she was riding leisurely, and giving her horse free rein, it would probably take her to the river that meandered across a portion of Hanley's land.

Deciding on that course, Kirk headed toward the river. He hadn't traveled very far before he came upon a saddled horse nibbling at the tall blades of grass. It didn't shy away as Kirk rode up to it. He grabbed the horse's reins, and taking it with him, he continued onward. He wondered if Mary Murphy had been thrown from her horse. If so, he hoped she wasn't injured.

The sky was cloudy, causing the night to be extremely dark and treacherous. Kirk figured if Mary was afoot, then she was probably scared half to death. When he found her, he'd most likely have an hysterical woman on his hands.

Mary Murphy was annoyed, but she certainly wasn't scared. She was a skilled rider, and she hadn't been thrown from her horse. She was afoot because she had been careless. Earlier, when she had arrived at the river, she had dismounted, and simply flung the reins over a tree branch. She had removed her boots, and was already in the river when her horse, panicked by a snake, had bolted. Scared, the animal had run away at full speed.

Now, as Mary trudged her way toward town, she hoped she would come across the runaway horse. Surely, it stopped somewhere close by. Although she was more annoyed than scared, she was nonetheless cautious. She was aware of her precarious predicament.

She also knew that she was on Bill Hanley's prop-

181

erty, but she didn't know where his house was located, so she had no choice but to keep heading in the direction of town. If she tried to find Hanley's home, she might get lost.

Mary heard the sound of horses before the black night revealed a lone rider approaching. Uncertain, she paused as she tried to decide if she should wait or take shelter.

Before she could decide, however, the man called out to her, "Mary Murphy? Don't be frightened, I'm a friend of your uncle's."

She was relieved. Thank goodness, she had been found!

Kirk rode up to her, dismounted, and asked, "Are you all right?"

"Yes, I'm fine, thank you."

Due to the darkness, they could barely see each other, and Mary had no idea that Kirk was so handsome, nor did Kirk realize that she was so lovely.

Kirk, thinking her foolish to ride alone, said with some annoyance, "You know, a woman doesn't have any business riding around this countryside unescorted. You're damned lucky getting thrown from your horse was the worst that happened."

Mary resented his criticism and thought him rude. She moved to her horse, put her foot in the stirrup, mounted, then said curtly, "Just for the record, sir, I didn't get thrown. My horse ran away while I was wading in the river." He was holding the reins, and she held out her hand, saying, "If you'll give me the reins, I shall return to town."

"You're going to the Bar-H," Kirk replied. "By now, the sheriff's probably got Hanley's wranglers scanning the countryside for you."

Mary felt a little remorseful. "I'm sorry I worried my uncle, and I'm also sorry that I caused so much trouble."

Kirk was impressed with Mary's composure—he'd certainly been wrong to think she'd be hysterical. He handed her the reins, then swung up onto his own horse. "The house isn't very far," he told her. "We'll be there in a few minutes."

Mary, preferring to avoid further conversation, rode behind Kirk. She was grateful to him for finding her, but she didn't especially care for his attitude. She found him brusque and discourteous. She wondered who he was—he probably worked for Bill Hanley.

As they rode up to the ranch house, Caroline, Hanley, and Rebecca were standing on the front veranda. Five wranglers, intending to search a different area from the others, were mounted and ready to pull out, but seeing that Kirk had found the sheriff's niece, they started back toward the corral.

Hanley called to one of his men, "Carl, ride out, find Jim, and tell him his niece is here."

"Yes, sir," the wrangler replied, sending his horse into a fast canter. He waved tersely to Kirk and Mary as he rode past them.

Bill hurried down the veranda steps and helped Mary dismount. With an arm about her shoulders, he escorted her into the house. The others quickly followed.

They went into the parlor, where Bill offered his guest a glass of sherry. She declined, and asked instead for a drink of water. Caroline left to get it, and Bill and Mary sat on the sofa.

"What happened?" he asked her.

She quickly explained why her horse had run away. Kirk was at the liquor cabinet, pouring him-

183

self a glass of brandy. He turned about, and for the first time since entering the house, he looked at Mary. He was taken aback, for he hadn't realized that she was so alluring. Her auburn hair was unbound, held back from her face with two ivory colored combs. He studied her youthful features. She had a slightly turned-up nose, dark green eyes, and a sensually shaped mouth. A few freckles, splashed haphazardly over her face, lent her a girlish look that was most flattering.

Kirk's perusal continued. Although Mary was sitting, he could see that she was of average height. She was wearing riding clothes, and they fit her slender frame flawlessly.

Mary, feeling Kirk's intense scrutiny, returned his gaze. She couldn't help but find him impressive. Outside, in the darkness, she'd had no idea that he was so handsome. He had doffed his hat, and she could see that his hair was thick and curly—as usual an unruly lock was falling across his forehead. He hadn't shaved since morning, and a shadow of a beard covered his tanned face. His soft brown eyes were framed by thick brows and long lashes, on some men such a feature would border on the effeminate, but not on Kirk, for his masculinity was too dominant. As Mary's eyes swept over his tall, powerfully built frame, she was duly impressed. She noticed that he wore his holster low on his hip, a common trait among gunslingers. She began to doubt that he was one of Hanley's wranglers.

She looked away from Kirk. There was no reason for her to find him attractive or interesting. She still didn't approve of his manners; in addition, he was too young for her—he was most likely in his early thirties. She would soon be forty years old.

The pair's secretive glances didn't escape Rebecca. She found herself growing jealous of Mary. It was a selfish jealousy. She didn't especially want Kirk, she just wanted a man!

When Caroline returned with the glass of water, Bill was asking Mary about her profession. "Jim told me you're a schoolteacher," he said.

"Yes, I was. But as you know, Dry Branch already has a teacher."

Caroline brought Mary the water. As she accepted the glass, she tried not to stare at Caroline too curiously. Her uncle had told her about Hanley's granddaughter, and she knew that she had recently been rescued from the Apaches. Come to think of it, Jim had said that the Bennetts found her. Mary wondered if she had also been found by one of the Bennetts.

"Mrs. Murphy," Bill continued, "would you consider tutoring my granddaughter? I'll pay you handsomely." Earlier, Caroline had mentioned to him that she wished to further her education. "My library is well supplied, and I'm sure you'll find it sufficient."

Mary was pleased, and she didn't need to think about her answer, for she was determined to be self-supporting. "Mr. Hanley, I'm grateful for your offer, and I accept the position gladly."

Rebecca, slumped sullenly in her chair, wasn't glad at all. Having Caroline home was bad enough, but now she'd be forced to endure Mrs. Murphy's presence. She had hoped to seduce Ross or Kirk, but now that would be impossible, for Caroline and Mary would no doubt inveigle the Bennetts. After all, the women were not only attractive, but they were also free. Oh, if only she wasn't married! Rebecca felt sorry for herself, and murmuring a lame excuse, she hurried upstairs to her room.

Bill, used to his wife's peculiar moods, thought nothing of her hasty departure. He continued speaking to his guest, "I'll come to town tomorrow, and we'll discuss your salary."

"Grandpa," Caroline began, "it'll be a terrible inconvenience for Mrs. Murphy to ride back and forth every day. Don't you think she should stay here?"

Bill concurred; however, he didn't know where to put her. His home consisted of six bedrooms, but they were presently in use. Normally, he'd have spare rooms, but due to Caroline's return, plus with Ross and Kirk staying, his home was filled to capacity.

Kirk was sure he knew the reason behind Hanley's hesitancy. "Why don't you give Mrs. Murphy my room? I'll stay in the bunkhouse."

"I wouldn't dream of putting you out!" Mary objected.

"It's all right, ma'am. I don't mind bunkin' with the wranglers. Besides, it won't be all that long. As soon as Ross is able to travel, we'll be leavin' for Tucson."

Caroline's mood had been chipper, but Kirk's words dashed her spirits. Would Ross really leave for Tucson? She couldn't bear the thought of him riding out of her life. Did she dare hope that he would marry her and take her to Tucson with him? It wasn't easy for her to keep her expectations in check, but she somehow managed. She couldn't let her aspirations fly too high, for Ross might very well send them crashing back to earth. He probably wouldn't marry her, or any woman, as long as there was a chance that he could win back Emily Parker.

186

"Mrs. Murphy," Bill said. "I'll come to town tomorrow in the buckboard, so we can bring your luggage back with us."

"Very well," she replied. "But please call me Mary."

"I'd be honored. You must call me Bill." He motioned toward his granddaughter. "This is Caroline—" he then indicated Kirk—"And this is Kirk Bennett. But then, I guess you two already know each other's names."

"Mr. Bennett knew mine, but I didn't know his." Mary cast Kirk a reproachful glance. "He didn't bother to introduce himself."

Kirk was inwardly amused. "Excuse my manners, ma'am."

The sounds of arriving horses carried into the parlor. Bill started out of the room. "That'll be Jim and my wranglers."

Moments later, after telling Mary that she'd see her tomorrow, Caroline excused herself and left to check on Ross.

Mary was uncomfortable to find herself suddenly alone with Kirk. There was something about the man that made her uneasy.

Kirk, on the other hand, wasn't the least disturbed. Earlier, the sheriff had mentioned to him that his niece was a widow, so Kirk saw no reason to deny his attraction to Mary. He had been searching a long time for the right woman, for he was ready to settle down and have a family. Like Ross, he owned good grazing land outside Tucson. His spread wasn't quite as large, but it was more than ample. He didn't know if he would fall in love with Mary, but he certainly found her desirable. He was not only taken with her beauty, but he also admired her spirit. Kirk considered himself a good judge of character, and it was his initial opinion that Mary had the grit to stand resilient beside her husband—through thick as well as thin. It would take a strong-willed woman to help him build his future.

Kirk put down his half-empty glass, and moved to join Mary on the sofa. She, however, reading his intent, got quickly to her feet. She preferred to avoid close contact with him. She wasn't sure why; she only knew that his presence was overwhelming. She chastised herself for letting Kirk unsettle her emotions. She certainly had no intentions of getting to know him better—he was not only too young for her—but she had heard of Ross and Kirk Bennett before coming to Dry Branch. The cousins' reputations were not above reproach. Mary's husband had been a quiet, peaceful man, and there was an untamed aura about Kirk Bennett that she found intimidating.

She made a quick dash for the doorway, saying over her shoulder, "I'm sure my uncle is anxious to see me. Good night, Mr. Bennett."

Kirk let her leave without trying to detain her. After all, she'd soon be living at the Bar-H. They had plenty of time to get better acquainted.

Chapter Fourteen

Caroline was in her grandfather's den, her chair placed close to an open window. Outside, the wranglers were gathered around the corral, for they were getting ready to break some wild mustangs. Their boisterous voices carried into the house, and Caroline was tempted to put her history book aside, hurry outdoors, and watch the excitement. Decisively, she put the temptation behind her—education was more important.

The book was in her lap; she opened it, and thumbed through the pages until she found the chapter Mary had told her to read. Although she really tried, she couldn't make herself concentrate. At the moment, history held little interest, for she was too concerned with the present.

Three weeks had passed since the ambush, and Ross's recovery was almost complete. Caroline knew he would soon leave for Tucson, and to her dismay, he hadn't said or done anything to make her believe that he intended to take her with him. They were on friendly terms, and during Ross's convalescence, they had spent a lot of time together. But their relationship was noticeably strained, for their past intimacy was always there between them. Several times, Caroline came close to bringing up the subject, but she could never find the right opportunity, or else she would lose the nerve. She wondered if she subconsciously found excuses to avoid the topic because she dreaded Ross's response. Was she too afraid that he would scorn her affections? Was she clinging to the adage that what she didn't know wouldn't hurt her? Reluctantly, she had to admit to herself that she was indeed. She knew she was behaving cowardly, which made her very angry at herself. It wasn't like her to be so afraid.

She slammed her book closed. It was time to face Ross, as well as her emotions. She would muster the nerve to confront him, for if she kept putting it off he'd leave for Tucson.

Her mind set, she was about to leave to find Ross when Mary came into the room. "Have you read the chapter already?" she asked, surprised.

"No, I haven't even begun," Caroline admitted a little sheepishly. She heaved a deep sigh. "I'm sorry, Mary, but I'm not in the mood for studying."

"I know what you mean," she replied. "The day's too beautiful to stay indoors." A bright twinkle came to her eyes. "Let's play hooky, shall we? I thought maybe we could have a picnic."

Caroline found the idea delightful. "That's a wonderful suggestion. But I think we should invite Ross and Kirk."

Mary was hesitant. "Are you sure?"

"I'm positively sure," Caroline answered, springing enthusiastically from her chair. She pitched the book onto Hanley's desk, then as she headed for the door, she told Mary she'd have Inés prepare a picnic basket.

Mary started to go after her, and ask her not to invite Ross and Kirk, but she changed her mind. After all, it would be best to have their protection. It was rumored that a small band of Apaches had been seen in the vicinity. She wasn't sure if it was true, but it never hurt to take precautions.

She went to the open window, and looked outside. She could see the corral, where the men had congregated. She picked out Kirk among them, standing between Ross and Hanley. She wasn't sure how she felt about Kirk Bennett. He had been very nice to her during these past weeks. There was a masculine force about him that generated awe in her. She was usually confident in mixed company, but, for some unexplainable reason, Kirk made her very uneasy.

Still gazing out the window, Mary caught sight of Caroline as she hastened to the corral to talk to the Bennetts. She wondered if Ross and Kirk would agree to accompany them on a picnic. She was doubtful, for the cousins didn't seem like the type. She pictured them in more venturesome surroundings — like tracking down dangerous fugitives.

Ross and Kirk accepted Caroline's invitation readily. They were not only looking forward to spending the afternoon with the ladies, but thought it safer that the women not go alone. The Apaches had everyone on their guard.

Standing at the corral, Ross watched Caroline intensely as she hurried back to the house. He knew he was in love with her, nonetheless, the past three weeks had been cautious ones, for he had guarded his emotions carefully. He had decided, though, that it was time to lay his insecurities aside. Just because Emily had jilted him didn't mean that Caroline would do the same. Also, she was apparently content to let Spotted Horse remain a part of her past, for she had shown no symptoms of missing him.

For the past few days, Ross had been well enough to

leave for Tucson. Only his love for Caroline had held him back. He couldn't bring himself to ride out of her life. This morning, he had awakened with his mind set, for he had spent a restless night going over his feelings. He finally had to admit to himself that Caroline meant the world to him, and that he loved her more than he had ever loved anyone. In fact, he began to realize that his feelings for Emily had been simply infatuation, and that their parting had wounded his pride much more than his heart. Sleep had at last put his mind to rest, and he had slept quite soundly. The moment he awoke, he knew exactly what he must do—he would ask Caroline to marry him! He loved her, and wanted to spend the rest of his life with her.

Caroline's asking him to the picnic fit perfectly into his plans. After they ate, he would take her for a walk and ask her to be his wife. Despite Ross's state of mind, he couldn't help but be somewhat insecure, for he knew there was always the chance that she might refuse to marry him. It would be a blow, and the biggest disappointment of his life. Still, he was determined to put aside his damnable pride, and lay his heart on the line.

Like Ross, Kirk had also made a firm decision. He didn't plan to stay at the Bar-H indefinitely, and if he didn't soon get up the nerve to pay court to Mary, then it would be too late. The picnic was to his advantage, for it would give him a chance to really talk to her. For the past three weeks, she had treated him pleasantly, but with an air of indifference. More than once, he had attempted to get her alone, but she had always managed to elude him. Kirk was not one to fight a losing battle, and he would gracefully bow out of Mary's life if he truly believed it was hopeless. But despite Mary's reserved composure, he had seen desire buried deeply in her emerald-green eyes.

It was there every time she looked at him.

They chose to have their picnic beside the river. Leaving the carriage close by, they spread out a blanket beneath a large, full-branched cottonwood. The temperature was warm, but a gusty breeze stirred the air, ruffling the tree tops and making the afternoon very pleasant.

Ines had packed a delicious lunch, filling the basket with fried chicken, biscuits, potato salad, and a bottle of wine. The foursome ate with hearty appetites until they swore they couldn't eat another bite.

Now, as they relaxed with second glasses of wine, Kirk looked closely at Mary. He had noticed throughout the meal that she would periodically glance apprehensively about the area. Seeing that she was doing it again, he asked, "Is something wrong? You act like you're expecting trouble."

She smiled haltingly. "I suppose I am a little nervous. After all, Apaches were spotted in this vicinity."

"We don't know that for sure," Kirk reminded her. "It's only a rumor. I don't know anyone who has actually seen any Apaches."

Mary stifled her apprehensions. "Yes, it's probably nothing more than a rumor. Besides, the day's too beautiful to worry about Apaches."

Mary was not the only one who was uneasy. Ross was also on edge. His nervousness wasn't caused by Apaches—he was trying to get up the courage to ask Caroline to take a walk. He was determined to propose to her, but he was as nervous as a school boy. He had no patience with his jitters, and inwardly cursed himself for being such a coward. During his lifetime, he had dauntlessly faced professional gunmen, hostile Indians, and dangerous fugitives, so why the hell was he scared of love? His gaze went furtively to Caroline as he wondered why this lovely, delicate young woman had such power over him. He hadn't felt this kind of anxiety when he proposed to Emily. Ross smiled to himself, for he hadn't really been in love with Emily Parker; Caroline Hanley was his heart, soul, and his very reason for living.

Ross took control of his emotions, and taking the wine glass from Caroline's hand, he placed it on the blanket, then asked her to take a walk.

She accepted without hesitation, for she was still adhering to her resolve to confront him. She planned to insist that he lay his feelings on the line, once and for all! If there was no place for her in his life, then she wanted him to make that fact perfectly clear. If he didn't share her feelings, it would break her heart, and she knew she might never truly recover. Nevertheless, she had to know where she stood with him, and she had to know now!

Kirk was glad they had decided to leave, for it gave him the opportunity to be alone with Mary. As Ross and Caroline strolled downstream, he moved over and sat closer to her. Although the tree trunk was at Mary's back, she was sitting ramrod straight. Kirk, however, leaned back against the tree, stretched out his legs, and made himself comfortable.

"Why don't you relax?" he asked her.

His closeness was unnerving, and Mary wished he had stayed where he was. "I am relaxed," she said. Despite her efforts to appear composed, there was a slight quiver in her voice.

Her back was toward him. "Why don't you sit where I can see your face?" he asked.

She moved so that she was looking at him. "Mr. Bennett, that wouldn't be necessary if you had remained where you were."

194

"I didn't like it over there. I was too far away from you. By the way, I wish you'd call me Kirk."

Her poise was faltering, she didn't know how to handle a man who was so bold. Nervously, she patted her auburn curls as though the tresses were mussed.

"Mary," Kirk began, "why do you keep avoiding me? You've got to know that I'm attracted to you. I can feel something between us, and so can you."

She was determined to keep their relationship casual. "There is nothing between us, except in your imagination. I admit that you are a very nice-looking man, but I'm not attracted to you. That is, not romantically."

"Can I ask why?"

"You're entirely too young for me."

"What makes you think that?"

"How old do you think I am?"

"I already know. Bill told me."

She was somewhat offended. "How dare you discuss me with Bill Hanley!"

"You don't have to get all huffy about it," he replied calmly. "It's only natural that I should be curious about the woman I'm going to marry."

"Marry!" she exclaimed. "You must be out of your mind!"

He grinned wryly. "You might be right."

"Mr. Bennett—"

"Kirk," he insisted.

She began again, "Kirk, I'll soon be forty years old. How old are you?"

"Thirty-three," he said.

"I'm almost seven years older than you. That is entirely too many years. Have you ever been married?"

"No, I haven't."

"Well, I was not only married, but I had two chil-

195

dren. Don't you think I'm just a little too experienced for you?"

"Just because I'm a bachelor doesn't mean I can't marry a widow."

She was impatient. "You're listening to me, but you aren't hearing what I'm saying. You're still a relatively young man who deserves a wife who can give you children. My childbearing years are probably behind me. If not, they soon will be."

"Not necessarily. My grandmother had a baby at forty-two, then another one at forty-four."

"Well, I'm not your grandmother!" she remarked curtly.

"You sure aren't," he replied, smiling suggestively. Before she could dissuade him, he had her in his arms, kissing her passionately. His lips, pressed aggressively against hers, melted her defenses, and she leaned into his embrace.

When he finally released her, she was visibly shaken. She hadn't been kissed since her husband, and the touch of Kirk's lips revived feelings she thought had died years ago. Still, she held firm to her belief — Kirk was too young for her. She was about to tell him this when they were interrupted by one of Hanley's wranglers.

The man rode up to them, reined in, and asked, "Where's Ross?"

"He and Caroline took a walk," Kirk answered, pointing downstream.

"Mr. Hanley wants Ross to come back to the ranch immediately. He has a visitor."

Kirk was curious. "Do you know who it is?"

"Yeah. Hanley said his name is Henry Parker." The wrangler urged his horse in the direction Ross and Caroline had taken.

"Parker!" Kirk remarked, surprised. "I wonder

what the hell he wants."

"Who's Henry Parker?" Mary asked.

"Ross used to be engaged to a woman named Emily. Henry Parker's her father. I don't know what he's doing here, but it probably means trouble."

Ross and Caroline talked of nothing in particular as they strolled beside the shallow river. They kept their conversation trivial and sporadic. They both had much to say, but neither of them knew quite how to begin.

Finally, Ross took her hand, and led her to the edge of the water. They stood there, looking across the river to the cattle grazing on the other side. Ross intentionally kept her hand enclosed in his. He studied her with a sidelong glance, she was breathtakingly lovely in her white summer gown. Caroline, with Ines's help, had sewn herself a new wardrobe. The dress she was wearing had been made with hot summers in mind. The material was soft cotton, and the V-shaped neck was complimented by short, puffed sleeves.

Ross, his gaze still on Caroline, said with feeling, "Someday, I plan to own a spread as prosperous as your grandfather's. I have the land, and the money, all I need to do is build it." He was leading up to asking Caroline to share this future with him, but before he could, she intervened.

"Ross, are you saying that you're wealthy?"

He smiled easily. "Well, I'm not exactly rich, but I do have a tidy sum put away. I've made quite a lot of money in my profession."

"Yes, I suppose you have."

He watched her closely. "Do you disapprove?"

"Disapprove?" she questioned, not understanding.

"Of my profession. Or I guess I should say, my past

197

profession. I already told you that I've quit that line of work. My gun's no longer for hire."

"No, I don't disapprove, but I am glad you've decided to quit. It's a very dangerous way to make a living."

She was facing him, and he gazed deeply into her charcoal-gray eyes. As always, he found them spellbinding, and beautiful beyond compare. The summer breeze was ruffling her long, shiny tresses, and he reached out and wrapped a blonde curl about his finger.

Caroline felt the surging power of his closeness, and her heart reacted immediately, pounding rapidly against her chest. She was wary of her vulnerability—why did Ross have such dominance over her? His nearness alone could bend her to his will.

He brought her into his arms, and she didn't resist. Hope streamed through her heart as his lips seared hers in a fiery caress. Did this mean he loved her, or was he merely taking advantage of her weakness? She swept the questions aside, for his kiss had stolen her thoughts, and she was conscious only of their passionate embrace.

Ross, his desire burning rampantly, released her with reluctance. He longed to kiss her into wonderful submission, then make love to her to his heart's content. But this was not the place, nor the time. But, more importantly, the next time they made love, he wanted her to be his wife.

Holding her at arms' length, he regarded her lovely features tenderly. Did she now love him instead of Spotted Horse? Had he won her heart, as she had won his? He knew there was only one way to learn the truth. All he had to do was ask.

In the meantime, Caroline was plagued with similar doubts. She was hoping, praying, that Ross was no longer in love with Emily, but was now in love with her. She decided it was time to confront him.

"Ross," she began, "we need to talk."

"Yes, I know," he replied. "But first, I have something to ask you." He drew her close, and was about to propose; but, at that moment, he heard Hanley's wrangler riding up to them.

They broke apart, and watched as the man reined in. "Ross," he began, "Mr. Hanley wants you to come back to the house. You have a visitor who needs to see you at once."

"Do you know who it is?" Ross asked.

"Henry Parker."

Ross was astounded. "Parker!" he exclaimed.

Caroline's heart sank, for she knew the man had to be connected to Emily.

Ross turned to her. "Henry is Emily's father." He grasped her arm. "Come on — we'd better get back to the house and find out what he wants."

Her feelings went numb, and she allowed Ross to usher her along. His zealousness to see Parker hit her profoundly. Apparently, she had been a fool to think she could make Ross forget Emily!

Ross's thoughts were running chaotically. He couldn't begin to imagine why Henry wanted to see him. He was somewhat annoyed, for he didn't need Parker showing up to complicate his life. Damn it, all he wanted was to marry Caroline and build their home! He had a feeling, however, that Parker's visit was a prelude to trouble.

Chapter Fifteen

Henry Parker stood at the parlor window, anxiously awaiting Ross's arrival. He dreaded facing Bennett! If there had been any other man he could have turned to, he would have done so gladly, but he didn't feel he had that choice — he believed Ross was the only one who could save Emily!

Bill, seated in a chair beside the sofa, watched his guest closely. He wished he could say something to ease the man's fears, but he knew from his own experience that at a time like this, words were useless. "Mr. Parker," he began, "why don't you have a seat? Ross will be here shortly."

Henry turned away from the window, went to the sofa, and sat down. He wrung his hands nervously.

"Are you sure you wouldn't like a glass of brandy?" Bill asked. Earlier, he had offered Parker a brandy, but he had declined.

"Yes, maybe it would calm my nerves."

As Bill moved to the liquor cabinet, Henry glanced about the room. He was impressed with Hanley's home. It was furnished in a way that tastefully reflected its owner's wealth. The parlor furniture consisted of large, comfortable pieces made of dark mahogany. A tall case clock, with a shimmering brass face, stood elegantly in the far corner. The walls were decorated with expensive paintings, and the windows were framed by multicolored drapes. A plush, brightly hued rug, which covered the center of the floor, added the final touch to the parlor's decor.

Bill poured the brandy, and was bringing it to Parker when Rebecca came into the room. She was surprised to find they had a visitor. She had been napping when Parker arrived, and no one had let her know about their guest. Upon her entrance, Parker got politely to his feet, and Rebecca's gaze went over him quickly, but thoroughly. She was impressed, for he was a fine figure of a man. She guessed him to be in his late forties. He was tall, slim, and his black hair was graying attractively at the temples. A well-groomed moustache shadowed his full lips, and his brown eyes were enhanced by dark, prominent brows. His tan trousers and white shirt were obviously tailor-made, and the attire fit his trim frame perfectly. He was indeed very distinguished-looking. She was pleased to note that he wasn't wearing a gun. Apparently, he was above such crude western ritualism—the man was undoubtedly a gentleman.

Rebecca's impression was correct, to a point. Henry Parker was most assuredly important-looking, strikingly handsome, and when it suited him, could be a perfect gentleman. However, Rebecca Hanley didn't awaken Henry's chivalry—instead, she aroused the lustful side to his nature. He knew about the illicit affair she'd had five years ago. Her lover, who owned a saloon in Albuquerque, was a friend of Henry's. The man had confided in him, and had given him an explicit account. Henry also knew that Bill Hanley had learned of his wife's adultery, and that she had broken off her affair to save her marriage. Henry couldn't help but wonder if she had remained faithful these past years. If so, it was probably out of fear of being caught. Rebecca had foolishly confided in her ex-lover who, in turn, had divulged her secrets to Henry; he knew that she had married Bill Hanley for his money. He supposed she was now impatiently waiting for her husband to die. Henry was somewhat amused—Hanley appeared to be in robust health—Rebecca most likely had a long wait!

Henry's gaze traveled over her discreetly, and he was impressed, for she was very provocative. He was seeing her for the first time, for during her past visits to Albuquerque, their paths had failed to cross.

Hanley, unaware of the pair's secret, admiring exchanges, handed Henry his brandy, then made introductions. "Mr. Parker, this is my wife, Rebecca."

She walked over to their guest lightly, but with the right amount of hip sway to make her long skirt swirl gracefully. Offering him her hand, she flashed him her most alluring smile, and asked, "Are you Henry Parker?"

"Yes, I am," he replied, taking her hand and kissing it lightly. "Have you heard of me?"

"Why, Mr. Parker, everyone in these parts has heard of you." She knew who he was all right; she also knew that he was an extremely rich widower. What she didn't know was that her former lover and Parker were good friends. Having no idea that Parker was familiar with her lascivious past, she played the role of a refined hostess to the hilt.

"Please, Mr. Parker, do sit down," she said, gesturing a dainty hand toward the sofa. As he obliged, she stepped gracefully to a wing-backed chair. Picking up a folded fan from the table, she opened it, and began to wave it coquettishly in front of her face. "Tell me, Mr. Parker, why have you come to the Bar-H?" She lowered the fan, smiled warmly, and added quickly,

"Not that we aren't honored to have you as our guest."

"I heard that Ross Bennett was staying here," Henry answered. His countenance concealed his thoughts, for he found Rebecca Hanley's facade amusing; after all, he knew from his friend that she made love like a wildcat! He had seen the scratches she had left on her lover's back.

"Rebecca," Bill explained, "Mr. Parker's daughter has been kidnapped by a group of Comancheros. He's hoping to hire Ross to deliver the ransom and to bring his daughter back safely."

"Your daughter kidnapped?" Rebecca exclaimed, her face displaying more concern than she actually felt. "How terrible! You must be half out of your mind with worry!"

"I am," he replied tersely. Concern for Emily wiped Rebecca from his mind, and as he took a big drink of brandy, he wished Ross would show up. God, how he dreaded asking the man for help! He didn't like Bennett, and considered him a low-bred renegade, and coming to him for assistance was a bitter pill to swallow. But he had no other choice; Emily's welfare was more important than his pride.

The sounds of an arriving carriage carried into the parlor. "That's probably Ross and the others," Bill said, heading toward the front door to greet them.

Apprehensive, Henry put down his glass, and got to his feet. He hadn't seen Ross since the night Emily had obeyed his wishes and broken her engagement. He was certain that Ross blamed him entirely, and he doubted if the man would even treat him civilly.

Bill returned with Ross and the others, and courteously introduced Parker to Caroline and Mary.

Following the amenities, Henry turned and met Ross's gaze for the first time. He tried to discern his feelings, but Ross's expression revealed nothing.

"Mr. Bennett," Henry said to Ross. "May we talk alone?"

A bitter smirk touched Ross's lips. The last time he had talked to Parker, the man hadn't been so polite. Then, it had been just "Bennett," now it was "Mister Bennett."

"You're welcome to use my study," Bill told them.

Ross motioned for Parker to follow, and leaving the parlor, they moved down the hall.

Caroline was unable to suppress her curiosity, and she asked her grandfather, "Do you know why Mr. Parker wants to see Ross?"

"Yes, I do. His daughter has been kidnapped by the Comancheros. He hopes to hire Ross to deliver the ransom, and bring her back safely."

Despair pressed down upon Caroline as she saw her dreams wither and die. Ross would certainly accept Parker's request and go to Emily's rescue. Then once they were together again, they would most likely stay that way! Caroline believed Ross was still in love with Emily, and thus would undoubtedly do everything within his power to win her back. Would Emily succumb to his wishes? Caroline couldn't imagine her turning away Ross's affections, especially after he had so gallantly rescued her!

"I'll be in my room if you need me," Caroline murmured to no one in particular. She left the room quickly.

Ross showed Parker into the study, sat at Hanley's desk, and leaning back in the chair, asked with a calmness he didn't really feel, "Why are you here?"

Henry remained standing, for he was too uptight to try and relax. "Emily has been kidnapped by the Comancheros."

Ross sat rigidly. "What?"

"Please, let me start at the beginning. Emily and I had a disagreement, and she stormed out of the house. It was late at night, and I thought she merely intended to take a walk. Instead, she saddled her horse and left. At the time, I didn't know this. When she didn't come back, I went in search of her. When I discovered that her horse was gone, I realized what she had done. I gathered up a few of my wranglers and we tried to find her. We searched all night and into the morning. There wasn't a trace of her—it was as though she had disappeared into thin air."

Parker fell silent for a moment as he assembled his thoughts. He continued somberly, "My men and I searched all that day, and through the next night. By morning, I was half out of mind with worry. It was about noon when Emily's horse came home. There was a note attached to the saddle. It was a ransom demand."

He reached into his pocket, drew out a piece of paper, and unfolded it. "This is the note, and it's in Emily's handwriting. Proof, I suppose, that they really have her. I'll read it to you." He removed his spectacles from his shirt pocket, put them on, and began to read, "If you want to see your daughter alive, then you will send ten thousand dollars in cash to El Zarango not later than two weeks after you receive this note. You are not to bring the money yourself. It must be delivered by someone else, and he must be alone. This man is to tell the town's blacksmith that he needs to see Rolando Sánchez. You must not contact the law, and if you are seen in or around El Zarango, your daughter will die."

His emotions suddenly drained, Parker dropped into a chair. He placed the note on the desk. "Here—if you wish, you can read it for yourself."

Ross did just that, then handing it back to Henry, he asked, "Do you want me to deliver the ransom?"

"Yes! You're the perfect man for the job. Emily once told me that you and Sánchez were friends." A deep scowl creased his brow. Ross's friendship with the infamous Comanchero was only one of several reasons why he had been opposed to Emily marrying him.

"You said that you and Emily had a disagreement. What was it about?"

"Does that matter?"

"It might."

Parker didn't answer right away. He wasn't sure if he should be candid with Ross. He was hoping Ross was still in love with Emily, which would compel him to deliver the ransom. If he knew the truth, however, he might refuse. Even though he and Sánchez were friends, the Comanchero was a violent man, and there was no guarantee that he'd allow Ross to come through this alive. Ross was no fool—he had to be aware of the situation. The more Parker thought about it, the more he realized that he couldn't be honest with Ross. If he were to tell him the real reason why he and Emily had argued, it could very well destroy not only his love for Emily, but also his respect. The final result could be disastrous, for Ross might flatly refuse to help.

The night Emily had ridden away, her father had caught her in bed with one of his wranglers. Parker had been in town, and Emily hadn't expected him back so soon. Parker had been more than outraged—he had reacted violently, for the week before, he had found her in a similar situation, with a different wrangler. Now, he couldn't bring himself to admit Emily's disgrace. He was not only ashamed, but was also afraid that the truth would sway Ross's decision.

Parker drew a deep breath, and lied with calculated deceit. "Emily never got over you. From the day you

206

left, she slowly sank into a state of malaise. I could do nothing with her. She was too depressed, and too broken-hearted. The night our argument started, she told me that she was going to find you, and beg you to take her back. She said my money meant nothing to her, and that she didn't want to live without you. I tried to dissuade her, which led to a very heated disagreement. I'm sure she didn't just go for a ride that night, she was running away to find you."

Henry was pleased with his story. Now, how could Bennett possibly refuse? That he would eventually learn the truth was inevitable, but Parker wasn't concerned. By then, Bennett would have the ransom delivered, and he'd bring Emily back safely, for there would be a big reward waiting.

"I'll pay you five hundred dollars to deliver the money; there will be a thousand more waiting when you bring my daughter back to me. If you agree, I'll get a room in town at the hotel. I'll stay there until you and Emily return."

Ross intended to deliver the ransom, however, Parker's reward had nothing to do with it. Although he was no longer in love with Emily, he certainly couldn't leave her at the mercy of Comancheros. He didn't think Rolando would actually harm her. He was a killer, true, but he had never heard of him murdering a woman. But the other Comancheros might feel differently. Sánchez had a lot of power over them, but his influence could falter at any time.

Ross had listened to Parker's story without questioning him, but he wasn't sure if he believed what he said. He couldn't picture Emily in a state of malaise, nor could he imagine her broken-hearted. If she had truly loved him, she wouldn't have called off their engagement in the first place.

"All right, Mr. Parker, I'll deliver the ransom. Do

you have the ten thousand with you?"

"Yes, I do. I brought a couple of my men with me. They're at the hotel, and the money is with them."

"I'll ride back to town with you, get the money, and leave right away."

Parker was relieved. Despite Emily's shame, she was his only child, and he loved her. Once he got her back, he planned to send her to St. Louis to live with his sister. She was married to a very prominent businessman, and through their connections, Emily would certainly meet a man of class, marry him, and become the lady she was meant to be.

Ross got up and walked around the desk, but he was quickly intercepted by Parker, who held out his hand, "Thank you, Mr. Bennett, for agreeing to help."

"Let's get one thing straight," Ross said, "I don't want your handshake, and I don't want your money."

Parker was flabbergasted. "You don't want to be paid? But I don't understand! You make your living hiring your gun, don't you?"

"Not any more." With that, Ross left the room to find Caroline.

Learning that Caroline was in her room, Ross hurried upstairs and knocked on her door. He had to wait only a moment before she let him in.

"You're going to deliver the ransom, aren't you?" She hit him with the remark the second he entered the room.

"Yes, I am. I take it that Bill told you what happened?"

"He told me as much as he knew." She regarded him suspiciously. "I thought you quit your profession."

"I'm not doing this for money. Parker offered to pay me, but I told him to keep his damned money."

Caroline turned away, moved to the bed, and sat on the edge. Naturally, Ross refused Mr. Parker's money—he wasn't doing this for money, but for love. She started to say as much to Ross, but decided not to bother. "When are you leaving?"

"Right away," he answered.

She was surprised. She had thought he'd at least wait until morning. "Why so soon?"

"There's no reason to wait. Besides, the sooner I leave—" He was going to add "the sooner I'll get back," but Caroline didn't give him a chance.

"Then why don't you leave?" she cut in brusquely. Oh, he was indeed anxious to see Emily!

"I thought we should talk first."

"I'm sure whatever you have to say can wait." Caroline could have bitten her tongue! There was no reason to be disagreeable. She and Ross had so much to discuss!

She was about to apologize, but Ross, concurring, said, "You're right. We'll talk when I get back." He took a hesitant step toward her, for he wanted to kiss her before leaving. He decided not to, however, for there was a strange coldness about Caroline that held him back. Damn it, if he only knew where he stood with her! Well, once he got this matter with Emily over with, he'd settle things between them!

"Goodbye," he said softly, although he longed to say so much more.

"Goodbye," she replied. She withheld her gaze from his, for she was afraid if she looked at him, her composure would crumble. The moment she heard the door open and close, she fell limply across the bed. Although she feared losing Ross to Emily, she nonetheless hoped that Ross would find Emily, and return her safely to her father.

Kirk was standing in the hall, waiting for Ross to

leave Caroline's room. "Do you want me to go with you?" he asked.

"No, I think I better go alone. It's Sánchez who has kidnapped Emily, and he made it clear in the ransom note that he wanted only one man to deliver the money. Where's Parker?"

"In the parlor."

"Tell him I'll be ready to leave shortly. Will you have my horse saddled and brought to the house?"

"Sure," Kirk replied.

Ross hastened to his room and packed his carpetbag. He walked down to the parlor, and told Parker, "I'm ready to leave."

Ross said a quick goodbye to Hanley, Rebecca and Mary, then followed Parker to the front door. Kirk was standing there, waiting.

Ross smiled hesitantly at his cousin. "See you later."

"I'm counting on it," Kirk answered. He stood in the open doorway, watching until Ross and Parker had ridden out of sight.

Chapter Sixteen

Caroline merely picked at her breakfast; she was too concerned to have an appetite. Although Ross had been gone less than a day, to Caroline it seemed much longer. She was not only unhappy, but worried as well. That Ross might lose his life rescuing Emily was a distinct possibility. Why was he so willing to take such a risk? Did he still love Emily that desperately? She sighed with discontent, and told herself that Ross did indeed love Emily Parker. She supposed, in a way, he also loved her, but it was minimal when compared to his feelings for Emily.

Bill, Mary, and Kirk were also at the table. Rebecca was still in bed, and Alex had spent the night in town. Inés had prepared a savory breakfast, but the food was mostly ignored. Like Caroline, the others had poor appetites, for Ross's trip into Mexico had them worried.

The meal was suddenly interrupted by a loud knocking at the front door. Bill, excusing himself, left to answer it. He returned momentarily with Sheriff Taylor.

"Caroline," Bill said. "Jim needs to talk to you."

The sheriff sat in the chair next to Caroline, say-

211

ing, "I'm sure you're aware that a small band of Apaches was spotted in this vicinity."

"Yes," Caroline answered. "But I thought it was only a rumor."

"Well, it wasn't. However, the band was merely three braves and a squaw."

Bill handed his guest a cup of coffee. He took a drink, then continued talking to Caroline, "There was some trouble in town last night. This young Mexican named Alfredo killed a man over a card game, then ran away. I rounded up a posse, and we took after him. I figured he'd head for the border. Well, we didn't catch up to Alfredo, but we did come upon these Apaches who were about to set up camp for the night. I decided we oughta arrest 'em, and hold 'em for the Army. They didn't surrender peacefully, and one of the warriors was killed. I've got the other two locked up in my jail, along with the woman. I thought you might want to come to town and take a look at 'em."

"Caroline," Bill explained, "if these warriors are Spotted Horse and Stalking Bear, then we'll let the Army know that they killed Martha and Walter. They're cold blooded murderers, and they should pay for their crime."

Conflicting emotions swirled within Caroline. She knew her grandfather was right—Spotted Horse and Stalking Bear should be brought to justice! But, God, why must she be the one to send them to the gallows? She felt sick inside.

Kirk understood her dilemma, and he spoke to her gently, "Caroline, this is something you have to do."

"Yes, I know," she replied regretfully. She turned to the sheriff. "If you don't mind waiting, I'll change into my riding clothes."

He assured her that he didn't mind.

"Caroline," Kirk said. "I'll ride to town with you."

She hurried upstairs to her room, her thoughts churning. She had believed that she'd never see Spotted Horse again, and that belief had brought her a certain solace. A part of her wanted to forget those five years when Spotted Horse had been such an important figure in her life. She often wished she could put him in the past and let him remain there. There was another part of Caroline, however, that refused to give up. As long as there was a chance that her brothers were alive, Spotted Horse couldn't be forgotten!

If Spotted Horse was one of these warriors in Sheriff Taylor's jail, could she possibly convince him to tell her what had happened to her brothers? God, she prayed, if it is Spotted Horse, please make him cooperate! And please, please let Walter and Daniel be alive!

Bill decided to accompany them to the jail, for he hoped to come face to face with Spotted Horse and question him about his grandsons.

Sheriff Taylor led the way inside, his young deputy was seated at the desk, but at his boss's entrance, he stood up quickly. The cells were separated from the office by an adjoining door. The sheriff grabbed a ring of keys hanging on a peg, unlocked the door, and held it open.

Caroline moved hesitantly. Her body was tense, and her heart was pounding. Bill, walking at her side, placed a comforting arm about her shoulders. The gesture, though appreciated, did little to ease her anxiety.

A narrow corridor ran the length of three cells. Caroline, glancing into the first one, was astounded to see One-Who-Laughs. The woman was glaring at her, and Caroline was nonplussed to see such loathing in her eyes.

Moving past One-Who-Laughs, Caroline looked at the two warriors inside the second cell. She wasn't at all surprised to see Spotted Horse, she was however shocked to find Leading Cloud. Why was he riding with Spotted Horse? He was a kind, peaceful man, and he didn't deserve to be behind bars!

Caroline, her gaze on Leading Cloud, didn't see the cold fury in Spotted Horse's feral eyes. He wasn't sure if he loved White Raven or hated her—he only knew that he was still obsessed with her.

When Spotted Horse had returned to his village to find that White Raven had escaped, he had reacted like a man insane. He was determined to go after her. Stalking Bear and others pleaded with him to forget White Raven, but their entreaties fell on deaf ears. Spotted Horse wasn't sure where White Raven had gone, but he did remember where he had captured her five years ago. He was certain that he would find her somewhere in that area. He was content to go alone, but Stalking Bear loved him like a brother, and he wasn't about to let Spotted Horse leave without him. Also, he had been hopeful that, during their journey, he could persuade his friend to forget White Raven. She was a white woman, and she belonged with her own people. It had been Stalking Bear who had invited One-Who-Laughs to accompany them. The invitation was a ploy, for if Spotted Horse were to stay in close contact with One-Who-laughs, surely he'd come to realize that she would make him a much better wife than White

214

Raven. Stalking Bear had never given up his hope that Spotted Horse would marry his sister.

It was merely by chance that Leading Cloud visited the village the day before Spotted Horse planned to leave. He had stopped by to check on White Raven, for he still loved her as though she were his daughter. Leading Cloud, wary of the fury in Spotted Horse, insisted on riding with him. He was afraid that the warrior's anger might drive him to hurt White Raven, maybe even kill her. Thus, his only reason for riding along was to protect White Raven, should it become necessary.

Now, as Leading Cloud found himself facing his adopted daughter, he was glad to see that she was well. Apparently, her escape had been successful. He glanced at Hanley, who was standing close to Caroline. He wondered if this man was kin to White Raven.

Caroline moved closer to the cell, and in the Apache language asked Leading Cloud, "Why are you here?"

"It does not matter," he answered in his Apache tongue. Spotted Horse was listening, and he didn't feel free to tell Caroline that concern for her safety had driven him to accompany Spotted Horse and the others.

Sheriff Taylor stepped to Caroline, indicated Leading Cloud, and asked, "Is this man Spotted Horse or Stalking Bear?"

"No," she replied. She turned to Hanley, and said urgently, "Grandpa, this is Leading Cloud! You must tell Sheriff Taylor to set him free!"

Bill quickly explained to the lawman that the warrior had been Caroline's foster father, and that he had taken good care of her.

"I'm sorry, Caroline," the sheriff said. "I can't set him free. I have to keep him here until the Army arrives. I sent a wire to the fort this morning. A troop should be here by tomorrow afternoon."

"Caroline," Hanley began, his voice intense, "is the other warrior Spotted Horse or Stalking Bear?"

Spotted Horse was listening, and he spoke enough English to understand Hanley's query. "I am Spotted Horse," he remarked proudly.

"Where are my grandsons?" Bill asked strongly.

Spotted Horse didn't answer, he merely stared coldly into Hanley's eyes.

His body rigid, his fists clenched, Bill moved closer to the cell. He barely had his rage under control. "Damn you! What happened to my grandsons?"

Again, Spotted Horse held his silence.

Caroline, intervening, asked Leading Cloud, "Do you know where my brothers are? What happened to them? Are they alive?"

"I know nothing about your brothers," he replied honestly.

Hanley's anger erupted. Spotted Horse was standing close to the bars, and Hanley reached through them and wrapped his hands about the warrior's neck. "Talk, damn it! Where are my grandsons? Did you kill them like you killed my son and daughter-in-law?"

"Grandpa!" Caroline cried, trying to pull him away from Spotted Horse. With Kirk's help and the sheriff's, they managed to break Bill's death grip.

Hanley regained a tenuous hold on his emotions. "I'm sorry," he murmured. "But, my God, that man knows what happened to those boys! If he would only talk!"

216

Desperate now, Caroline said pleadingly to the others, "Please let me talk to Spotted Horse alone! I want to be locked in the cell with him."

The sheriff was hesitant to agree; Bill was firmly against it. "No!" he bellowed. "Caroline, don't you realize why Spotted Horse was in this vicinity? He was obviously looking for you? If we leave you locked in that cell with him, he might kill you!"

Caroline didn't think so. Despite everything that had happened, she couldn't imagine Spotted Horse actually harming her. But she knew it would be impossible to convince her grandfather of this. Instead, she replied, "I'll be perfectly safe. Leading Cloud will be in the cell, too. He loves me like a daughter, and he'd never let anyone hurt me. Not even Spotted Horse."

Hanley knew she had made a valid point, for Caroline had spoken often of Leading Cloud's compassion.

"Bill," Kirk said, deciding to help Caroline. "If anyone can persuade Spotted Horse to talk, it's Caroline. For your grandsons' sakes, and for your own peace of mind, give her this chance."

Hanley had grave reservations; nevertheless, he relented. "All right, she can go inside the cell." He spoke directly to Caroline. "You have only ten minutes, then I'm coming back for you."

She had hoped for more time, but she didn't push for it. She was grateful for the time she had, and saw no reason to press her luck. Her grandfather could change his mind at any moment.

Sheriff Taylor unlocked the cell, admitted Caroline, then locked it again. The men moved down the corridor to the sheriff's office. Intentionally, they left the adjoining door open.

217

Caroline went to Leading Cloud and embraced him fondly. Lapsing easily into Apache again, she said respectfully, "My Father, I am happy to see you are well. How are my mother and sister?"

"Basket Woman and Sweet Water are fine." A look of sadness crossed his face.

"What's wrong?" Caroline asked.

"Sweet Water will never marry Stalking Bear. The sheriff and his men killed him. Sweet Water will be in great mourning, for she loved Stalking Bear very much."

Caroline was grieved, but her sorrow was for Sweet Water, not Stalking Bear. Knowing time was of the essence, she moved away from Leading Cloud and approached Spotted Horse. She paused before the warrior, and her gaze went over him fleetingly. He was dressed in Apache garb, his long pants tucked into high-topped moccasins, and his shirt was unbuttoned to the waist, revealing his smooth, bronze-colored chest. His straight black hair, worn shoulder-length, was held back from his face by a beaded band wrapped about his forehead. His dark, deeply-set eyes were staring unwaveringly into hers, and their expression was chilling.

Spotted Horse's gaze moved to examine White Raven more closely. His perusal swept over her intensely. Her riding skirt, fitting snugly, hugged her slim hips, the fringed hem barely touched the tops of her western-style boots. She wore a short-sleeved blouse, and the first two buttons were undone, exposing the smooth hollow of her throat. His eyes were drawn to the locket clasped about her neck. Anger stirred within him. Apparently, White Raven had disobeyed him and retrieved the necklace from the river. Despite his anger, Spotted Horse couldn't help

218

but admire her rebellious spirit. He lifted his gaze to Caroline's large, provocative eyes, and, as always, he found them captivating.

There were two narrow cots inside the cell, and moving to the one closest to Spotted Horse, Caroline gestured for him to sit beside her.

He did so hesitantly.

"Spotted Horse," she began, "you must tell me what happened to my brothers."

He ignored her plea. "Why did you run away from me?"

"When my memories returned, I knew I belonged here with my own people."

"You are mine. Your place is with me."

"I don't love you, Spotted Horse. I never did, not really. But even if I did love you, I couldn't marry a man who was involved in killing my parents."

"I did not kill them. Stalking Bear did."

"I remember that day clearly. You wanted them to die. You're just as guilty as Stalking Bear. But I'm not here to discuss your guilt, or our feelings for each other. I'm asking you—No, I'm begging you to tell me what happened to my brothers!"

Spotted Horse withdrew into silence, he stayed that way for quite some time. His thoughts were running fluidly. He knew the white soldiers would hang him for killing White Raven's parents. Although he wasn't afraid to die, he longed desperately to live! He had to find a way to break out of this jail, and flee back into Mexico. He wondered if White Raven was the key to his escape. Could he persuade her to help him? Yes, he was certain that he could, for he would bargain with her.

"White Raven," he finally began, "I will tell you about your brothers, but first you must break me and the others out of this jail."

She was astounded. "Break you out of jail? That's impossible!"

"You must find a way. If you refuse to help me, than I will refuse to help you. I will never tell you about your brothers. You will never know if they are alive or dead. When the soldiers hang me, the truth will die with me."

"They're alive, aren't they?" she cried, her hand unconsciously grasping his arm.

He pried her fingers loose, flung her hand aside, and answered firmly, "Leave, White Raven. You have much thinking to do. It will not be easy for you to break us out of this jail. You must plan carefully, but quickly. The soldiers will arrive tomorrow to take us away."

Before she could continue their discussion, she was interrupted by her grandfather's return. The sheriff was with him, and he quickly unlocked the door, motioning for Caroline to step out.

She rose from the cot, leaned toward Spotted Horse, and whispered, "I don't think I can break you out of here. You're asking for the impossible."

He smiled without humor. "White Raven, if you fail me, you will also fail your brothers." He spoke too quietly for anyone else to hear.

"What do you mean by that?" she demanded, keeping her voice low.

His expression turned into stone, and he acted as though he hadn't even heard her. Caroline knew he was through talking.

"Caroline," her grandfather called. "Come on, honey, it's time to leave."

She embraced Leading Cloud, then walked out of

the cell. Despite her inner turbulence, she appeared calm.

"Did he tell you anything about the boys?" Hanley asked hopefully.

"No," she murmured. She spoke so quietly that he barely heard her.

"Try not to be too disheartened," the sheriff remarked. "Maybe the Army can do something. They have a way of makin' these Indians talk."

Leading Cloud watched as the two men escorted Caroline into the office, then turning at once to Spotted Horse, he asked commandingly, "If White Raven helps us to escape, will you tell her about her brothers?"

Anger flared in Spotted Horse's eyes. "You act as though she is really your daughter. She does not belong to you! She is mine! Remember that, my uncle, for I do not want to hurt you!"

"Answer one question for me, Spotted Horse."

"What is that?" he asked testily.

"Do you plan to kill White Raven?"

The warrior was clearly surprised. "Kill her? I could never kill White Raven. She is the only woman I have ever loved."

In the next cell, One-Who-Laughs was listening avidly. Spotted Horse's love made him weak! Well, he might not be able to kill White Raven, but she had no qualms about murdering her! Thanks to White Raven, Stalking Bear was dead! One-Who-Laughs hated Caroline with a vengeance. The white woman had stolen the man she loved, and now One-Who-Laughs blamed Caroline for her brother's death! She was determined to have revenge!

Caroline spent an agonizing afternoon. The moment she returned home, she went to her room where she battled with her conscience. The hope that her brothers might be alive kept tempting her to help Spotted Horse escape. On the other hand, breaking him out of jail was wrong. But she didn't feel it would be wrong to help Leading Cloud. He didn't deserve to be locked up, and there was no way of knowing how long the Army would hold him. They might think he was a troublemaker, and keep him indefinitely. How well could Basket Woman and Sweet Water survive without him? They were wholly dependent on Leading Cloud!

As the afternoon wore on, Caroline grew more frustrated. Even if she decided to help Spotted Horse and the others, how could she conceivably break them out of jail? There didn't seem to be any possible way.

She had been in her room for hours when Mary knocked on her door. As Caroline let her in, she told her that she was going into town to spend the weekend with her uncle and his wife. Then, she let her know that Bryan was in the parlor, and that he wished to see her.

Caroline had no wish to see him, but she didn't want to be rude. For the past three weeks, Bryan had been trying to court her, and she found his wooing distasteful. She wasn't in the least attracted to him. As a child she had sensed a cruel aspect about Bryan that the years hadn't erased. She didn't like him, and she didn't trust him. He was, unfortunately, her grandfather's stepson, and she felt she had to be civil to him.

She went downstairs to the parlor, where she found Bryan alone. He was seated on the sofa, but at her entrance, he hastened over, took her hand, and kissed it softly. The touch of his lips sent a repulsive shudder through her.

"Caroline," he said, his voice dripping with concern. "I heard about your dreadful experience this morning. My dear, it must have been terrible for you to face Spotted Horse."

"It wasn't terrible at all," she replied. "Bryan, why did you wish to see me?"

"I was worried about you," he answered. Caroline's cold aloofness was irritating. The woman was exasperating and uncooperative. She had scorned every attempt he had made to win her affections. Still, Bryan wasn't ready to admit defeat.

"There was no reason for you to worry," she replied. There was a final note in her tone, for she was about to leave the parlor.

Bryan's next words, however, dissuaded her. "I won't mention any names, but there's talk of a lynching. It was discussed in my saloon, and I overheard everything that was said." Bryan didn't have to strain to eavesdrop, for the group had talked freely.

"A lynching?" she questioned. "You can't be serious!"

"Caroline, surely you must realize how intensely Apaches are hated. I don't imagine there's a family in these parts who hasn't lost a loved one to those savages. Now there's two warriors locked in our jail with only the sheriff and his deputy to protect them."

"Have you mentioned this to Sheriff Taylor?"

"He's aware of what's going on. He broke up the crowd, and told everyone to go home. I'm sure he thinks he has the situation under control." Bryan shrugged casually. "And who knows? Maybe he does."

Caroline was extremely upset. A vision of Leading Cloud swinging from a rope flashed horribly before her eyes. It was a terrifying picture, and it sent fear racing through her veins.

Bryan had arrived in his carriage, and had offered to give Mary a ride into town. Now, as Mary came into the parlor with her packed bag, Caroline took advantage of the woman's intrusion, and made a quick retreat back to her room.

She closed her door, then paced the floor anxiously. Dear God, what if the sheriff didn't have the situation under control? Those men might very well carry out their plan to lynch Leading Cloud and Spotted Horse. If so, they probably wouldn't do anything until after dark, which meant she still had a couple of hours to form a jailbreak. But how? How? She had absolutely no idea, she only knew that she couldn't leave Leading Cloud at the mercy of a raging mob. Furthermore, Spotted Horse didn't deserve such a fate either. He had the right to a fair trial. A bitter laugh escaped her lips. Was there such a thing as an Indian receiving a fair trial? She seriously doubted it. But, at the moment, that was beside the point.

As she continued her pacing, she passed by her dresser. The top drawer was open a crack, and she caught a glimpse of the small pouch that held her sleeping powder. Her steps came to a sudden halt, and her hand shook slightly as she reached out and picked up the medicine. An escape plan quickly germinated in her mind. The sleeping powder, of course! It was the answer! She must find a way to slip it to Sheriff Taylor. It was harmless, and would only put him to sleep. Then, while he was sleeping,

she would help Leading Cloud, Spotted Horse, and One-Who-Laughs to escape.

Her mind set, Caroline stuck the leather pouch into her skirt pocket, hurried downstairs, found Inés, and told her that she had a slight headache and planned to take a nap. She made it clear that she didn't want to be disturbed until it was time for dinner.

Now that she had seen to it that she wouldn't be missed for at least two hours or longer, she returned to her room and packed a small bag. Then slipping to the stables, she saddled her pinto, and rode unseen away from the ranch. She traveled at a relatively slow pace, for she didn't want to catch up to Bryan and Mary. She supposed what she planned to do was wrong, but she didn't see where she had any other choice. She couldn't, wouldn't, let Leading Cloud be lynched! Also, if she successfully broke Spotted Horse out of jail, he would tell her about her brothers.

Deep in her heart, she felt that Walter and Daniel were still alive, and that they needed her! Nothing, or no one, was going to keep her from finding them!

Chapter Seventeen

Dusk blanketed the town as Caroline rode toward the livery. She hoped to find the Indians' ponies there, and move them to the rear of the jail. A group of men were gathered in front of the stables, and Caroline spotted the liveryman in the crowd. She wondered if these men were plotting a lynching. If so, she knew she must move even faster, for time was running out.

She guided her horse to the back of the livery, dismounted, and slipped quietly through the rear entrance. She was relieved to find the ponies, and since the Apaches didn't use saddles, only blankets, it didn't take Caroline long to have the horses ready to leave. The Indians' provisions were also stored in the livery, so she attached them to the horses and left by the back, leading the ponies behind her. Taking the reins to her own horse, she kept to the back street, which brought her to the rear of the jail. She secured the horses, then hurried around the building to the front entrance.

She opened the door, walked inside, and was glad to find that Sheriff Taylor was alone.

The lawman was surprised to see her. He was seated at his desk, but getting to his feet, he asked, "Caroline, what are you doing here?"

"I came into town with Alex," she lied. "He's having a drink at the saloon, so I told him to pick me up here. I hope you don't mind." She cringed inwardly, for she was uncomfortable with deceit.

Taylor found her request a little peculiar. Why did she choose to wait here for Alex? He thought his home would have been more appropriate, for his wife and Mary were there.

Caroline read his confusion, and without giving him a chance to suggest she wait elsewhere, she stepped to the coffee pot, which sat atop a wood burning stove. She picked up the pot, and was pleased to find that it was full.

The sheriff, watching her, said, "I just made fresh coffee. Help yourself."

"You'll join me, won't you?" Caroline poured two cups, and keeping her back turned to the sheriff, she slipped her hand into her pocket and withdrew the small pouch. Cautiously, she glanced over her shoulder. The sheriff was again seated at his desk, taking care of paperwork. He wasn't paying much attention to Caroline, and she quickly sprinkled the right amount of powder into his cup.

She handed him his coffee, then sat in the chair facing the desk. "Where's your deputy?" she asked, hoping the sheriff wasn't expecting him.

"I told him to go home and get some sleep. He'll have to relieve me in a few hours. Considering we have Apaches for prisoners, I think one of us should stand guard through the night." He took a big drink of his coffee; the powder was undetectable.

"Are you expecting trouble?"

"You never can tell. A lot of people in these parts hate Apaches." He decided not to tell Caroline that he feared a possible lynching, for it was probably noth-

227

ing more than talk — there was no reason to upet her.

He went back to his paperwork, and Caroline watched intently as he continued to sip his coffee. He soon had the cup drained, shortly thereafter, he leaned wearily back in his chair. Stretching his cramped muscles, he tried unsuccessfully to suppress a yawn.

"Excuse me," he murmured. "For some reason I suddenly feel very tired."

"You work too hard," Caroline said. She disliked herself for deceiving him. But learning about her brothers, and Leading Cloud's freedom, were more important than anything else; including honesty.

As Caroline waited for the powder to take full effect, her nerves grew taut. Cold perspiration dotted her brow, and her hands turned clammy. Her escape plan was shaky, to say the least. It could so easily be foiled — a visitor to the jail would ruin everything!

A few minutes after drinking his coffee, Sheriff Taylor leaned over his desk, placed his head on his folded arms, and fell sound asleep.

Caroline bounded from her chair, grabbed the keys, and hastened to the adjoining door. She unlocked it, moved quickly to the warriors' cell, and freed them. Leading Cloud took the keys from her hand, and hurried to release One-Who-Laughs.

Spotted Horse was very proud of Caroline. "White Raven," he said, "I knew you would find a way to help us." No wonder he was so obsessed with her — there was no other woman like her! She was as clever as she was beautiful!

"Your horses are out back," Caroline said hastily. "Come; we must hurry!"

They followed her into the office. Seeing the sheriff slumped over his desk, Leading Cloud asked with surprise, "White Raven, did you kill him?"

"No, of course not."

Spotted Horses spatted angrily, "Since he is not dead, I will kill him!"

"No!" Caroline cried.

"Why not? He and his men killed Stalking Bear. It is only right that I seek revenge!"

"If you kill him, then you'll have to kill me, too!" Caroline's eyes flashed furiously.

At that moment, the front door opened, and Mary stepped inside. She was carrying the sheriff's dinner tray, but the sight confronting her, caused her to hesitate. She suddenly dropped the tray, and made a halfway turn to flee; but, Spotted Horse, seeing her intent, jerked her farther into the room, then slammed the door closed.

"Mary!" Caroline gasped. "What are you doing here?" It was a foolish question, she was obviously delivering her uncle's dinner. But Caroline was too upset to think rationally.

Mary rushed over to the sheriff. "My God!" she cried. "Is he dead?"

"No," Caroline was quick to assure her. "He's only asleep. I laced his coffee with a sleeping powder."

Mary was shocked. "You mean, you're actually helping these Indians escape? But why? Why?"

"Enough talk!" Spotted Horse interrupted gruffly. "We must leave!" He went to Mary, and his arm snaked about her waist, pulling her back flush against his chest. "We will take this woman as a hostage!"

"I forbid it!" Caroline said sharply.

"Our flight will be safer if we have a hostage." Spotted Horse's temper softened as his eyes met Caroline's. "She will not be harmed." The words passed his lips impulsively, for his only thought was to ease

White Raven's mind. But if he should find it necessary, he would kill their hostage.

"White Raven," Leading Cloud said gently, "Spotted Horse is right. We need the woman as a hostage. Do not worry, she will be safe."

They were speaking in Apache, and although Mary didn't understand what they were saying, she nonetheless knew she was the topic of their discussion. She was terrified.

Caroline, seeing her friend's fear, told her as soothingly as possible, "Don't be afraid, Mary. No one will harm you. They're going to take you as a hostage, but I promise you that you won't be hurt."

Mary's anger surged, and struggling vainly against Spotted Horse's tenacious grip, she yelled to Caroline, "You traitor! How can you side with these savages?"

Caroline, knowing Leading Cloud understood English, cast him a loving glance, then turned back to Mary. "You might think of them as savages, but I don't." She indicated Leading Cloud. "That man was my father for five years."

Spotted Horse, anxious to leave, told Leading Cloud to unlock the rifle case and to get weapons and ammunition. He did so quickly, then taking their hostage with them, they hurried to the rear entrance.

There were only four horses, so Leading Cloud shared his pony with Mary. He didn't completely trust Spotted Horse, and decided to guard their hostage himself.

As Caroline rode down the back street and out of town with the others, she felt deeply distraught. If only Mary hadn't shown up! She began to blame herself—maybe she should have been more assertive. if she had stood her ground, maybe Spotted Horse

230

would have relented and left Mary behind. They could have tied her up and gagged her.

More questions swirled through her mind. Had she been wrong to break Spotted Horse and the others out of jail? Should she have left them to their fate? But, then, remembering the men gathered in front of the livery, she told herself that she had done the right thing. The group was most likely planning a lynching. A fleeting vision of Leading Cloud hanging at the end of a rope flashed before her eyes. The picture eased her conscience. Leading Cloud was a fair, compassionate man, and he deserved to be saved! She was sorry that Mary had inadvertently become involved, but no harm would come to her. When they neared El Zarango, she would insist that Spotted Horse set her free. The town had a telegraph office, and Mary could send a wire to her uncle.

Caroline began to feel a little better—everything would work out. She knew they would have to cross the border before stopping to rest their horses and make camp, but when they did, she was determined to question Spotted Horse about her brothers. The upcoming confrontation caused her to have mixed emotions. Her feelings seesawed back and forth from high to low. One moment she was ecstatic at the thought of finding her brothers, the next moment, however, she was afraid she would learn that they were dead.

A creeping uneasiness settled in the pit of her stomach. It didn't go away.

Hours later, they crossed the Rio Grande, but Spotted Horse insisted on continuing. He knew a posse would be on their trail, and he wanted to cover more miles. There was no guarantee that the sheriff and his men wouldn't pursue them into Mexico.

Spotted Horse set an exhausting tempo, and they rode through the night and into the next day. The sun was midway in the sky when they came upon a small oasis.

Fatigued, Caroline was glad when Spotted Horse announced that they would rest here for a couple of hours. The warrior handed each of them a strip of jerky, and told them to fill their canteens, for they would be traveling across desert terrain.

Mary was sitting alone, and Caroline moved over and sat beside her. They were beneath a mesquite tree, and its branches, filled with catkin-like flowers, afforded cool shade.

"Mary," Caroline began, "I know you're angry with me."

"Angry is putting it mildly!" she cut in bitterly. Mary was miserable, not only was she terribly upset, but she was also tired, afraid, and uncomfortable. She wasn't dressed to ride horseback, for she was wearing a gingham gown, and it had a long, full skirt. Underneath, her voluminous petticoat was tangled about her legs.

Caroline, conscious of Mary's discomfort, told her, "I brought a change of riding clothes. You better change into them. But first I want to talk to you." She hoped to make Mary understand why she felt she had to break Leading Cloud and the others out of jail. Before she could explain, however, Spotted Horse called to her.

"White Raven; come here," he said authoritatively.

"You'd better leave!" Mary spat. "Your lover wants you!"

Caroline stood up wearily, looked down at Mary, and said, "He isn't my lover. I broke him out of jail

232

because he knows what happened to my brothers."

She turned about and walked over to Spotted Horse.

"We must talk," he said. He took her arm, and led her away from the others.

Leading Cloud watched them leave. He was worried, for he didn't think Spotted Horse would tell White Raven about her brothers. Suddenly, he was distracted by Mary moving to Caroline's horse. He hurried to her and asked, "What are you doing?"

Removing Caroline's carpetbag, she answered, "I'm getting a change of clothes." She took out what she needed, then asked, "Where can I change?"

"Here," he replied.

She couldn't imagine undressing in front of him. "I need privacy."

"I will leave. One-Who-Laughs will stay."

Mary's eyes followed him as he moved away. The warrior's manners surprised her. She had always thought Apaches were uncivilized savages and murderers, but Leading Cloud certainly contradicted that belief. Since leaving Dry Branch, she had ridden on the same horse with him, and he had treated her kindly. Was she wrong to judge all Apaches by the ones who killed her family?

She turned to the matter at hand, and began changing clothes.

One-Who-Laughs obediently kept a vigil watch, but their hostage didn't really interest her. She didn't care if the woman escaped or not. Her sole concern was White Raven. She was still determined to find a way to kill her. One-Who-Laughs was totally consumed with revenge, and she despised Caroline with a vengeance. Now, as she waited for Spotted Horse and White Raven to return, she grew insanely jealous. For years, she had done everything in her power to win

Spotted Horse's affections, but he had been too blinded by White Raven's beauty to notice her. One-Who-Laughs was through fighting a lost cause; Spotted Horse would never choose her for his wife, no matter what! She would avenge Stalking Bear and kill White Raven. Afterwards, One-Who-Laughs was certain that Spotted Horse would take her life, but she didn't care. She would rather be dead than live without him.

Spotted Horse and Caroline didn't walk very far before stopping. The warrior was silent for quite some time, then he said calmly, "White Raven, after we are married, I will tell you about your brothers."

"Married!" Caroline exclaimed angrily. "That's not the bargain we made! You said you'd tell me what happened to my brothers if I broke you out of jail! Well, I lived up to my part of the deal, now you live up to yours!"

Spotted Horse raised his chin arrogantly. "I have spoken. We will not talk again about your brothers until you are my wife. Do you understand, White Raven?"

"Oh, I understand all right! You tricked me, and you lied to me! I have never had less use for anyone than I have for you! Marry you? I'd rather be dead!"

She whirled about to leave, but Spotted Horse grasped her arm. "You belong to me, White Raven. You always have. I do not want to hurt you, but I will if you leave me no other choice. Obey me, or else!"

Taking him by surprise, she jerked free from his grip. "I'm leaving, and I'm taking your hostage with me!"

She started back, but the warrior's long strides easily surpassed hers. Going to her horse, he took her rifle, turned to her, and said furiously, "You will not

234

leave! You are mine, White Raven! Remember that!"

She didn't say anything, she merely glared at him. She knew Spotted Horse meant what he said, and it would be useless to argue. Well, she had escaped him once before, and she would do so again! Her eyes went anxiously to Mary. She didn't have only herself to consider, but Mary as well. What if Spotted Horse refused to set his hostage free? What would become of Mary? Would Spotted Horse kill her? She was suddenly fearful for her friend's life.

Caroline was not the only one who feared for Mary's life, Sheriff Taylor and Kirk were also worried. About an hour or so after the jailbreak, Kirk had stopped by the sheriff's office. He revived Taylor, and as the man recovered from the effects of the sleeping powder, Kirk went to the Watering Hole, and asked Bryan to ride to the ranch for Hanley. When the sheriff was sufficiently recovered, he rounded up a posse, and by the time Bill arrived, everyone was ready to leave. Hanley insisted on riding with them.

They traveled through the night. There was no need to follow tracks, for Caroline and the others would unquestionably head straight for the border.

The sheriff crossed the Rio Grande. He wasn't concerned with jurisdiction, he was too bent on finding his niece. Now it was important that they pick up a trail, and, with luck, Kirk was quick to find it. They followed it to the oasis, but there, the trail ended. Apparently, Spotted Horse had decided it was time to start covering their tracks.

They stopped at the area to fill their canteens, and water their horses. The sheriff drew Kirk aside.

Taylor looked spent, physically as well as emotionally. "Kirk, I've got to go back. I shouldn't have brought these men this far. I'm out of my jurisdiction." He sounded angry. "Jurisdiction? Hell, I'm out of the country! This posse is my responsibility, and I need to get them back across the border. I can't go any farther, but you can. Will you . . . ?"

Kirk interrupted, "Yes, I'll keep looking."

The sheriff gestured toward Hanley, who was sitting beneath the mesquite where Caroline and Mary had rested hours before. "Bill looks completely drained. I'm worried about him."

Kirk had noticed it too. "I know what you mean. He looks like he's about to collapse."

"This has been too much for him. Damn Caroline! Didn't she realize what losing her would do to him?"

"He hasn't lost her. She didn't break Spotted Horse out of jail to live with him, she wants him to tell her what happened to her brothers."

"We don't know that for sure. And I certainly don't think Mary is with them of her own free will."

"Neither do I," Kirk agreed.

Taylor spoke reluctantly, "Well, let's tell Hanley I've decided to go back. He won't like it. He'll probably insist on going with you."

"I don't think he's up to it."

Hanley stood at their approach. He could see by the sheriff's expression that he was bringing disturbing news.

"Bill, we've got to turn back. But Kirk's going to keep looking for Mary and Caroline."

"Then I'm going with him." He looked at Kirk. "You don't mind, do you?"

"Yes, I do mind. You'll slow me down."

"I might be old, but I'm not decrepit!" Hanley was visibly upset.

236

Kirk reasoned with him. "I'll stand a better chance of finding Caroline alone. You're already so exhausted that you can barely stay in the saddle. You're right, you aren't decrepit, but you're too old for this kind of work."

Hanley knew he was right. Age had gotten the better of him. "All right," he relented. "You can go on alone. But, God, do you have any idea how much this galls me?"

Kirk understood. in Hanley's time, he was no doubt a fine specimen of a man.

Suddenly, Bill reached out and grasped Kirk's arm. He sounded desperate, "Caroline broke Spotted Horse out of jail to learn about her brothers. No one can make me believe differently. Kirk, if it's possible, help her learn what happened to them. With God's help, maybe you'll not only bring back my granddaughter, but my grandsons as well!"

Chapter Eighteen

Bryan watched his mother a little suspiciously. He wondered if she was up to something. They were having dinner at the hotel, and the date had been Rebecca's idea. He suspected she had an ulterior motive, for he had lived in town for over a year, and she had never done anything like this before. If she had some other reason for planning this evening, though, he couldn't imagine what it was.

Bryan's suspicions were correct, for his mother did indeed have an ulterior motive—she was hoping to see Henry Parker! Since the day he had visited the Bar-H, she hadn't been able to get him out of her mind. He was handsome, sensual, and delightfully rich! Why should she stay married to Bill when Henry Parker was fair game? He was not only younger than her husband, but was also wealthier!

Three nights had passed since Caroline had broken the Apaches out of jail. That first night, when Hanley joined the posse, Rebecca had hoped Henry would ride out to the ranch to see her. Rebecca was certain the man found her attractive, for she had seen desire in his eyes the day they had met. She had thought he'd take advantage of her husband's absence and come to the Bar-H, but she had been disappointed. Bill returned home the next day, emotionally and physically drained. He needed solace from his wife, but Rebecca was so fed up that she couldn't even pretend sympathy. She cloistered herself in her bedroom, and stayed there for two full days. She finally decided it was time to make a change in her life. She was tired of staying married to Hanley on the chance that she might inherit his money. She was still a relatively young woman, and she wanted to live again! She craved excitement and romance! She believed Henry Parker was the answer to her dreams. She wouldn't mind being married to him, not at all. Parker, apparently, wasn't going to make the first move, so she would have to find a way to encourage him. After all, he probably thought she was happily married. Well, if she found the chance to be alone with him, she'd certainly set him straight on that point. She'd let him know quite clearly that her marriage wasn't happy.

Rebecca had plotted this evening carefully—a late dinner with Bryan meant, of course, that she'd have to spend the night at the hotel. She couldn't very well travel back to the Bar-H at night. She hadn't asked Bill's permission, she had simply told him what she intended to do. She had been worried that he'd decide to accompany her, but she needn't have bothered, for he was too upset over Caroline to think of anything else. He had merely told her to go on and have a good time.

A good time was exactly what she was planning to have, but things weren't going the way she had thought they would. She had been certain that Parker would have dinner at the hotel, but, so far, he hadn't shown up. It was late, and she had a depressing feeling that he was having dinner in his room.

Earlier, her mood had been chipper, but depression was slowly taking over. Having no appetite, she ignored her food, and concentrated on her wine.

Bryan, watching her, said, "If you keep drinking like that, you're going to get tipsy."

She frowned testily. "So what?"

"Mother, what's wrong?"

"Everything," she replied. Her tone was sullen.

"Do you want to talk about it?"

"Bryan, I'm just so tired of my life! For years, I've been stuck on that ranch living with a man I can barely tolerate!"

"Mother," he said cautiously, "don't give up. Things are just now looking good."

"How can you say that?"

"Caroline's gone. All we have to do is get rid of Hanley, and his money is ours."

"Caroline isn't gone for good. She'll be back."

"I don't think so. She obviously wants to live with that savage."

"Bill believes she broke Spotted Horse out of jail to question him about her brothers."

"Yeah? Well, he's lying to himself because he won't admit that she's in love with an Apache warrior."

Rebecca wasn't convinced. "I think she's in love with Ross Bennett." She shrugged. "However, I could be wrong."

"She's apparently in love with someone. I couldn't get anywhere with her, and I damned well tried!" Failing to win Caroline's affections had been a big disappointment for Bryan and a terrible blow to his pride. He continued calmly, "But it doesn't make any difference whom she loves. The Bar-H will be ours. If she comes back someday and tries to claim her inheritance, we'll say she's deranged. There's not a judge alive who won't believe us. Any woman who would break her parents' murderers out of jail would have to be insane."

Bryan gloated inwardly. Naturally, in court, he would volunteer to take care of Caroline—in more ways than one!

He gave his mother an encouraging smile, reached across the table, and patted her hand. "Things will work out splendidly. Bill is depressed, and everyone knows this. We'll get rid of him by making it look like a suicide. Just be patient, Mother, and give me time to plan everything."

She arched a brow irritably. "Well, my patience is about to wear out, so don't take too long." She got shakily to her feet. Her head was swimming, and her knees were wobbly. She had drunk too much wine. "I'm going to my room. Good night, Bryan."

"I'll come by and have breakfast with you in the morning," he offered. She had already started out of the room, and he wasn't sure if she heard. It didn't matter, he'd stop by anyway.

Rebecca was making her way down the hall when the door on her left opened. She was pleasantly surprised to find herself face to face with Henry Parker.

"Mrs. Hanley," he said, smiling affably. "What are you doing here?"

"I came to town to have dinner with my son, and since it's so late, I'm spending the night here in the hotel."

"Is your husband with you?"

241

She gleamed invitingly. "No, I'm alone."

Henry was intrigued. Why not? Rebecca Hanley was a stunning woman. His gaze raked her appreciatively. She was dressed provocatively, her low-cut evening gown revealing the deep cleavage between her ample breasts. The dress was enchantingly black, and the dark color contrasted beautifully with her reddish-blond hair.

Parker made a sweeping gesture toward his room. "Won't you come in and join me for a drink? I was just on my way to the saloon, but I'd much rather enjoy your charming company."

Rebecca could barely conceal her delight. "Yes, I'd love to have a drink." Despite the amount of wine she had consumed, she managed to walk gracefully inside.

Henry closed the door, then discreetly locked it. "A sherry?" he asked.

"Yes, thank you."

Although Henry was eager to take her to bed, he behaved as a gentleman. He wanted her, and he thought she wanted him—but there was no reason to rush. They had all night.

He poured a sherry for Rebecca, and a brandy for himself. They sat on the sofa, sipped their drinks, and kept their conversation trivial.

Time passed pleasantly, and they were on their second drinks when Henry decided it was time to make a move. He placed his arm on the back of the sofa, letting it slide gently down to her shoulders.

"Do you mind?" he asked softly.

"No, I don't mind." She looked at him as though she were deeply distressed. "I hope you don't think badly of me, but my marriage is not a happy one. Bill treats me abhorrently."

"You poor dear," he murmured, feigning sympathy.

She forced tears to her eyes. "I've been unhappy and lonely for so long. That day when I met you, I knew this night was inevitable. Did you feel that way too?"

"Yes, I certainly did," he answered. Taking her into his arms, he kissed her fervently. She quickly slid her hands about his neck and responded without hesitation.

After a few minutes of kissing and caressing, Henry stood, reached for her hand, and led her to the adjoining bedroom. A lone lamp was burning softly, and its golden glow was quite romantic. He sat on the edge of the bed, then told Rebecca to undress in front of him.

She found his request stimulating, and was more than ready to cooperate. Inspired, she removed her clothes slowly and temptingly. She knew her body was superb, and she proudly revealed her voluptuous attributes to Parker's watching eyes.

When she took off her final undergarment, Henry stood and drew her into his arms. His lips seared hers as his hand moved down her back to cup her firm buttocks.

He picked her up, placed her on the bed, then hastily shed his own clothes. His passion was raging, and he could hardly wait to totally ravish her.

She beckoned him with open arms, and he went eagerly into her embrace. Parker was an excellent lover, and he knew how to drive a woman to the brink of rapturous torment. He soon had Rebecca writhing and squirming, and begging him to take her completely.

He moved over her, entering her suddenly and

aggressively. She cried aloud with ecstasy as she slid her legs about his waist, allowing him even deeper penetration.

Henry made love to Rebecca skillfully, but with no emotional involvement. He cared nothing about her, for he knew her for what she was. Rebecca, on the other hand, responded to him as she had never responded to any man, for she was totally infatuated. She equaled her lover's passion, and reveled in their union. Her husband never crossed her mind.

Bill, seated on his front veranda, was thinking about Rebecca. He knew his wife wasn't happy, and he wondered if he were somehow to blame. He had tried to be a loving, considerate husband, but despite his efforts, their marriage was growing colder by the day. In his own special way, he still loved Rebecca, but like their marriage, his love was dying. Maybe he should offer her a divorce and a generous settlement. She would probably be happier without him. But Bill hated the thought of divorce. He took marriage seriously, and considered it a lifetime commitment.

"Patrón?" Iné's said, opening the door, and stepping out to the porch. She was worried about Hanley, for he didn't look well. "Are you all right? Is there anything I can get you?"

He smiled at her fondly. "I'm fine, Inés." He indicated one of the chairs. "Why don't you sit down and talk to me for awhile?"

She was happy to accommodate him. "I suppose you are worrying about Caroline, sí?"

"Actually, I was thinking about Rebecca. I'm concerned about her."

Inés hid her annoyance. She disliked Rebecca intensely, but jealously had nothing to do with it. If the woman was a loving wife, then Inés would have been happy for Hanley. She loved him, true, but it was an unselfish love. Also, if she had lost him to a woman worthy of his affections, the loss would have been easier to take. Inés would have left years ago if Hanley's marriage had been successful. But the hope that someday he would send Rebecca packing had kept her hanging on.

"Why are you concerned about the señora?" she finally asked. "She acts no differently."

"No, she's changed. She seems almost . . . almost desperate."

"Maybe she is worried about growing old."

Amused, Bill laughed heartily. "You might be right."

"The señora does spend a lot of time in front of her mirror."

"Well, we both know that vanity is her middle name." He sighed heavily. "Inés, if only I had been wiser. I was so blinded by her beauty that I couldn't see what lay beneath it. Marrying Rebecca was a terrible mistake."

"You can get a divorce," she said quickly.

"That's strange advice coming from a Catholic."

Inés, though a religious woman, knew if Bill were free she would go against the Church. Divorce would not stop her from marrying him. She loved him too deeply.

Bill got to his feet. "Well, it's late. I guess we should call it a night."

"But what about a divorce?" she persisted.

He shrugged as though defeated. "There's an old saying — you make your bed, you lie in it."

"But sometimes, señor, it is best to change the sheets."

Again, he chuckled heartily. "Inés, you're a jewel. What would I do without you?"

She rose to stand before him. Hanley's admitting that his marriage was a mistake gave her courage. "I do not know what you would do without me. But maybe when you are lying alone in your big bed, you should think about it." With that, she turned about and went into the house.

Hanley was baffled. Exactly what point had she been trying to make? He wasn't sure. He did, however, try to imagine the Bar-H without Inés. She had been here so long that she was like a member of the family. If she left, he would sorely miss her. She was his companion, his confidant, and his closest friend. She was everything a wife was supposed to be, except his lover.

Bill thought about Inés in that respect. She was indeed a fine figure of a woman. He quickly brushed the notion aside. After so many years, thinking of Inés in that way was foolish.

He went into the house, and upstairs to his room. Later, however, as he lay in bed, Inés's words kept coming back to haunt him. Against his own volition, he imagined Inés lying there beside him. It was a sexually arousing vision, and he forced it out of his mind. He might be old, but he wasn't dead! He hadn't bedded his wife for months, and he needed a woman.

Steering his thoughts elsewhere, he wondered about Kirk. Had he found Caroline? Hanley was gravely worried about both of them, as well as Mary.

Kirk was troubled as he rode into the town of El Zarango. Spotted Horse had covered his tracks so well that he hadn't been able to find them. Kirk wasn't giving up, but he had decided to detour to El Zarango. He was hoping Ross was still there. Kirk needed his help.

He took his horse to the livery, then checking at the hotel, he learned that Ross was still registered, and that he was having dinner at *Roberto's*.

Kirk went to the restaurant, where he found Ross dining alone. As he was heading toward Ross's table, he happened to glance up. He was surprised to see Kirk, but he was also a little annoyed.

"Kirk, what the hell are you doing here? Sánchez made it clear that he wanted only one man to deliver the ransom."

Kirk pulled out a chair, and sat down. "I'm not here because of that."

Ross was understandably confused.

"About three nights ago, this Mexican named Alfredo killed a man over a card game. The other guy wasn't even armed. Alfredo left town, and Sheriff Taylor rounded up a posse and took after him. He didn't catch Alfredo, but he arrested Spotted Horse, Leading Cloud, and an Indian woman. Stalking Bear was with them, but he was killed."

The young boy who worked at the restaurant came to their table. "Can I get you some dinner, señor?" he asked Kirk.

Kirk waved a hand at Ross's plate. "Bring me whatever he's having."

The youngster left, and Kirk continued, "Caroline broke Spotted Horse and the others out of jail.

247

They took Mary with them, supposedly as a hostage."

Ross was astounded. "How the hell did she break them out of jail?"

Kirk couldn't help but smile. "She flavored the sheriff's coffee with her favorite secret ingredient."

"I should have known!" Ross said irritably. "Damn it! I thought she was over Spotted Horse!" He was not only angry, but hurt as well. He had begun to believe that Caroline loved him.

"I don't think her feelings for Spotted Horse had anything to do with it."

Ross looked at him questioningly.

"I could be wrong, but I bet he made a bargain with her. If she got him out of jail, he'd tell her what happened to her brothers."

"Maybe," Ross mumbled, but he wasn't convinced.

"Anyway, to make a long story short, I joined up with the sheriff and his posse, and we tracked them into Mexico. We lost their trail at the oasis. The others turned back, and now I'm on my own. The only chance I have of finding Caroline and Mary is to find Spotted Horse's village. For that, I need your help. We'll have to ask Standing Elk to take us there." He noticed Ross's carpetbag on the table, he wondered if it held the ransom. "Has Sánchez contacted you yet?"

"No, he hasn't."

"You don't have the money in that bag, do you?"

"Of course not."

"Where is it?"

"Safely hidden."

"Well, the way I have it planned, I'll go with you to deliver the ransom, and from there we'll

248

head to Standing Elk's village."

"Haven't you forgotten a couple of things? I'm supposed to deliver the money alone."

"And?"

"What about Emily?"

"We'll take her with us."

Ross wasn't so sure Kirk's plan would work. He was about to say so, but was interrupted by three men approaching their table. They were Mexicans, and they didn't look friendly. The biggest one looked familiar to Ross, then he remembered seeing him at Sánchez's camp. He was the one who had fallen asleep on duty.

In the meantime, Kirk was giving the youngest man a second glance. He recognized him, for he had seen him in Dry Branch. It was Alfredo.

The large one stepped forward. "The blacksmith said you were looking for Sánchez. Which one of you has the money?"

"I do," Ross answered.

"Where is the money?"

Ross pointed at the bag.

"You were told to come alone."

"I am alone."

"It does not look that way to me, señor."

"Juan," Alfredo cut in, "these men are cousins. If you leave one behind, he will follow."

Juan considered the situation, then decided to take them both along. "You will both come," he said, gesturing for them to leave with him.

The youngster, bringing Kirk's dinner, watched as the men left. Puzzled, he looked down at the filled plate, then to the now empty table. Apparently, the gringo had changed his mind. With a shrug, he turned about and carried the food back

249

to the kitchen.

He remembered the two men from the last time they had been in El Zarango. The pretty señorita had been with them—the one called Caroline. The name still rang a familiar bell with him. If he could only remember!

The proprietor, coming into the kitchen, was furious to find the boy loafing. He drew back his arm, and slapped the child across the face. "Carlos, if you have nothing better to do than stand around, then you can mop the floor!" He gave the boy a hard shove. "Get to work!"

Carlos, holding back tears, stumbled to the pantry to get the mop and the bucket.

The cook, who was a kind, middle-aged woman, waited until the proprietor left, then going to the child, she said gently, "Do not fret, Carlos. I keep praying that God will help you, and I know that soon He will answer my prayers."

"How do you know that?" he asked, sniffling.

She placed a hand on her chest. "I feel it here, deep in my heart."

Carlos hoped her feeling was right, but he didn't see how God could help him.

Chapter Nineteen

Spotted Horse continued setting an exhausting pace, and everyone was physically drained. After three days of hard traveling, the warrior decided that it was safe to slow down. He was certain a posse wasn't trailing them.

For the first time, they stopped and made camp before the sun had made a full descent. Leading Cloud went hunting, and returned with two rabbits, which One-Who-Laughs prepared for dinner.

Mary's appetite was poor, and she ate very little. Leaving the campfire, she spread her blanket beneath a tree, sat down, and stared blankly into space.

Caroline, watching, was concerned about her. Due to the arduous journey, she hadn't had a chance to really talk to Mary. She knew the woman was still harboring a lot of anger, and she didn't blame her. Caroline left the campfire and followed Mary. She hoped to make her understand why she had felt compelled to break Spotted Horse and the others out of jail.

Joining Mary on the blanket, Caroline said, "I must talk to you."

"Don't bother!" she replied testily.

251

"You're going to hear what I have to say," Caroline insisted. "Spotted Horse said if I got him out of jail, he'd tell me what happened to my brothers. Mary, try and set your anger aside, and listen to me with an open mind. You had two sons who were killed by the Apaches. What if they had been captured instead, and you had a chance to learn where they are. Would you let anyone or anything stand in your way?"

"No," she admitted, suddenly ashamed. "I'd lie, steal, and even kill to find them." Tears filled her eyes, and holding Caroline's hand, she said sincerely, "Forgive me for being so mean to you! I've been so scared and upset that I haven't been thinking fairly. I never once tried to see this from your point of view."

Caroline intended to be perfectly truthful. "My brothers aren't the only reason why I planned a jailbreak. There was talk in town of a lynching. I couldn't leave Leading Cloud at the mercy of a mob. He was like a father to me for five years. Believe me, he's a very fair and compassionate man."

Mary didn't find that hard to accept, since her capture he had shown her respect as well as kindness.

Caroline continued, "Now Spotted Horse refuses to tell me what happened to Walter and Daniel. He says I'll have to wait until after we're married."

"Do you intend to marry him?"

"Not if I can help it."

Mary's grip on Caroline's hand tightened. "Maybe we should try to escape! I don't mean to sound cruel, but surely you realize that your brothers are probably dead! That's why Spotted

252

Horse won't tell you anything about them!"

"No!" Caroline cried desperately. "They aren't dead!"

"How can you be so sure?"

Caroline was silent for a moment, then in a tense voice, she said, "I feel deep down in my soul that they are alive! Call it intuition or whatever, but I know they aren't dead. Walter and Daniel are alive, and they need me! I've got to help them, I've just got to! No matter what!"

Mary didn't try to dissuade her, for she believed in premonitions. She had known instinctively that her sons were dead before anyone told her. She had felt their passing deep down in her soul, as Caroline was now feeling that her brothers were alive.

Mary had never told Caroline about the day her family was murdered. The tragedy still hurt too much to even think about, let alone to discuss. But, now, empathizing with Caroline, she gathered the courage to talk about that tragic day.

"My husband and I had a small homestead outside Albuquerque. My mother-in-law lived in town. She was ill, so I packed a bag and went to stay with her. I was gone two days when our home was attacked by a band of renegade Apaches. They wanted to steal our horses, and ransack our house. The Indians killed my husband and sons, stole what they wanted, then set fire to the house. The smoke was seen by our neighbors. By the time they got there, the house was smoldering ashes. They found my husband's body, and the bodies of my sons in the front yard."

Mary paused, and tenuously controlled her emotions. "My family was murdered at midday; at that same time, I was preparing my mother-in-law's lunch when suddenly, I had this strange foreboding. I knew that something terrible had happened to my husband and sons. Don't ask me how I knew, but I did! Later, when the men who found their bodies came to tell me what had happened, I knew what they were going to say before they even said it." All at once, crying, she covered her face with her hands, and sobbed, "My family was a part of me, and you can't lose a part of yourself without somehow knowing it!"

Caroline placed a consoling arm about her shoulders. She wished she could think of comforting words, but what could she say?

After a time, Mary's tears abated. Her eyes red with grief, she looked at Caroline, saying intensely, "Follow your instincts. If you feel that your brothers are alive, then believe in your intuition. And, Caroline, I'll help you in any way I can!"

She was deeply touched. "Thank you, Mary."

Although Caroline was indeed grateful, she nevertheless wanted Mary safely back in Dry Branch. She looked over at Spotted Horse, who was seated at the campfire, watching her closely. Could she possibly persuade him to set Mary free? El Zarango was only about an hour away. Would Spotted Horse agree to let her leave in the morning? If so, Caroline decided she would let Mary use her pinto, for she could always ride double with Leading Cloud, or even Spotted Horse.

Caroline made up her mind to talk to Spotted Horse. She would take a stand, and insist that he give Mary her freedom. He no longer needed a hostage, for they weren't being followed. She decided to confront him later, after everyone was asleep.

* * *

Ross and the others hadn't traveled very far from El Zarango when, Juan, riding in the lead, pulled up.

Ross, reining in, watched the huge Mexican carefully. He already knew what was going to happen, but he was prepared.

"Amigo," Juan said to Ross, smiling as he drew his pistol. "There is no reason for you and your cousin to go any farther. Hand over the money."

Ross calmly pitched him the small carpetbag.

Juan opened it quickly, looked inside, then bellowed, "It is empty!"

"Is it?" Ross said flippantly. "Well, what do you know about that."

"Where is the ten thousand dollars?" Juan demanded, pointing his pistol at Ross's chest.

"It's safely hidden. Sánchez will get his money when I get the woman."

Juan laughed, but his eyes were filled with wrath. "So you are not a fool, s?"

"Let's just say I'm not very trusting."

"You are sly, amigo. Maybe, though, you are not too smart. Sánchez does not like to be double crossed."

"Neither do I," Ross said, his tone deadly serious.

Juan was faced with a dilemma. Sánchez had told him to take the money, then send whoever delivered it back to Parker with the message that he'd be notified as to when and where he could pick up his daughter. But, obviously, Bennett had second guessed him. Juan didn't see where he had any choice but to take Ross and his cousin with him to Sánchez's hideout.

Alfredo blurted out Juan's very thoughts, which

255

irritated the huge Mexican, causing him to grumble, "Alfredo, if I want your advice, I will ask for it!"

Slipping his pistol back into its holster, Juan eyed Ross harshly. "Sánchez will be very disappointed, señor, when he learns you do not have the money."

Ross responded with an easy smile. "I'm sure he's been disappointed before."

Juan was through bantering. "If we ride through the night, we will reach Sánchez by tomorrow afternoon." He slapped the reins against his horse's neck, and took off at a fast gallop.

Alfredo and the other man followed close behind. Ross and Kirk, their horses trotting abreast, brought up the rear.

Leading Cloud, taking the first watch, was standing off in the distance. Mary and One-Who Laughs were asleep in their bedrolls, and Spotted Horse was sitting at the campfire. Caroline was also lying on her blanket, but she wasn't asleep. She had been waiting for a moment such as this one to talk to Spotted Horse. She got up and moved quietly to the fire.

"Spotted Horse," she began in the Apache tongue, "I must talk to you."

Standing, he said, "Come; we will take a walk."

They strolled away from the fire. The sky was cloudless, and the moon, encircled by a myriad of sparkling stars, cast a soft light down upon the quiet prairie.

Caroline, stopping, turned to Spotted Horse, and asked, "In the morning, will you please set Mary free? She can use my pinto to ride to El Zarango."

The warrior's eyes turned icy cold. "You worry

256

too much about the white woman. You no longer think or act like an Apache!"

"I never did," she argued. "Not really. My past was always haunting me, and I knew I didn't belong with the Apaches. When my memories finally returned, I could think of nothing but going home!"

"Your home is with me!" he said angrily.

"No!" she cried. "Spotted Horse, you can't make me love you!"

"We will see!" he replied. Moving with incredible speed, he reached out, grabbed her shoulders, and pulled her into his arms.

She fought against him, but her struggles were helpless against his superior strength.

"I have waited long enough to make you mine!" he said, his tone unyielding. "Tonight, you will become my woman!"

He forced her to the ground, and his body covered hers, trapping her beneath him. Spotted Horse was incensed with rage, as well as passion. He felt he could no longer hold back his passion. He had already waited for five long years, believing that, with time, White Raven would become an Apache in heart and spirit. Now, he was afraid the transformation would never take place. "White Raven," he threatened, "if you fight me, I will have to hurt you!"

Caroline refused to surrender, and trying to squirm free, she said furiously, "I'll never submit to you, Spotted Horse! Not now, not ever!"

Her rebellion fueled his anger, and with one hand he held her arms over her head. He was reaching down to rip at her clothes when, suddenly, Caroline screamed.

"White Raven!" he said raspingly, "you belong to

me! Screaming will not help you! Leading Cloud knows you are mine, and he will not interfere!"

She winced as though his words had hit her physically. Would Leading Cloud forsake her, and leave her at Spotted Horse's mercy? Did he feel that she was Spotted Horse's property to do with as he pleased? Fear renewed her will to fight, and she began to struggle wildly. Despite her efforts, however, the warrior's hold was too strong, and she couldn't free her arms.

Suddenly, Spotted Horse groaned wretchedly, which caused Caroline to cease fighting. He was now gazing down into her face, and his eyes were no longer angry, but filled with torment. "I cannot hurt you, White Raven. I love you too much. But I will not set you free. We belong together, and someday you will know this is true. You will then learn to love me." He truly believed it was so.

All at once, though, Leading Cloud's voice rang out unexpectedly, "Spotted Horse, let her go!"

He leapt to his feet, turned to Leading Cloud, and said furiously, "This does not concern you! Go away!"

Caroline rose quickly, but Spotted Horse clutched her arm, keeping her at his side.

One-Who-Laughs and Mary were standing behind Leading Cloud. The warrior was carrying his rifle, and aiming it at Spotted Horse, he ordered, "You will set White Raven and the white woman free." Leading Cloud's patience with Spotted Horse was over. He still loved his nephew, but he no longer respected him. A trace of tears misted the warrior's eyes, and his voice turned melancholy, "Spotted Horse, I am glad that my brother, your father, is not alive to see what you have become. You are no longer a proud warrior, or a man of his word. You lied to White Raven, and you tricked her." He spit, emphasizing his disgust. "I am ashamed to be kin to you."

One-Who-Laughs was infuriated. White Raven was an evil spirit, turning uncle against nephew! Deciding it was time to kill her, One-Who-Laughs lurched for Leading Cloud's rifle. She took him by surprise, and almost had the gun in her hands before he could pull it back.

"Give me the rifle!" she raged, fighting for the weapon. "I will kill White Raven! She is evil, and she must die!"

The woman was struggling so strongly that Leading Cloud was compelled to grip the gun with one hand so he could draw back an arm to shove her away.

Taking advantage of his one-handed grip, One-Who-Laughs made a final, desperate attempt to win control of the rifle. Frantic, she grabbed blindly for the gun, her finger hitting the hair-trigger, causing the Winchester to discharge.

The fired bullet whizzed through the air, and plunged into Spotted Horse's chest. The powerful blow knocked him off his feet; airborne, he fell to the ground with a solid thump.

As One-Who-Laughs screamed hysterically, Caroline knelt beside Spotted Horse. Leading Cloud, keeping his rifle with him, hurried over. He dropped to his knees, took one look at Spotted Horse's wound, and knew sadly that his nephew was dying.

Sitting, Caroline cradled Spotted Horse's head in her lap. Like Leading Cloud, she knew there was no hope.

Blood, pouring from Spotted Horse's chest, was

draining life from his body, and the icy fingers of death embraced him, causing his limbs to turn numb with cold.

"Spotted Horse," Caroline cried desperately. "What happened to my brothers? Please tell me! Please!"

He didn't answer; he was dead.

Leading Cloud touched her arm gently. "He is gone, White Raven."

Hard, racking sobs shook Caroline's shoulders. Now, she would never know what happened to her brothers!

She wept uncontrollably.

Ross and the others, traveling nearby, heard the rifle shot. Juan was content to ignore it, but the Bennetts insisted on investigating, for they knew that Caroline and her party could very well be in the vicinity. The Mexicans had no choice but to accompany them.

As they rode up to the empty campsite, Caroline's deep, heartbreaking sobs could easily be heard. Dismounting, the men hurried to the area where they found Caroline weeping over Spotted Horse's body.

Leading Cloud, hearing them, leapt to his feet. Juan and his friends had their pistols drawn, leaving Leading Cloud no option except to surrender his rifle. Walking over, he handed it to Kirk.

Ross moved slowly to Caroline, who was now staring at him incredulously. She was ghostly pale; Ross was the last person she had expected to see.

Ross, placing his hands on her shoulders, drew her gently to her feet. There was no jealousy in his heart, only pity. He knew he'd never forget the sound of her wretched sobs. Apparently, she had loved Spotted Horse very much.

"I'm sorry," he murmured.

She fell into his arms, for she needed him desperately. He drew her close, and his kindness renewed her tears. Between sobs, she told him what had happened. She didn't mention, however, that Spotted Horse had come close to forcing himself on her. After all, the warrior had had a change of heart, he hadn't hurt her; deep inside, Caroline had always known that Spotted Horse could never harm her.

Meanwhile, Kirk went to Mary, and asked, "Are you all right?"

She was overjoyed to see him, and almost threw herself in his arms; instead, she smiled warmly, and murmured, "Yes, I'm fine."

Juan, impatient with the delay, muttered gruffly to Ross, "Señor, we must be on our way." He turned his beady eyes to Leading Cloud, considered killing him, then decided not to bother. The Indian posed no threat.

One-Who-Laughs had made her way to Spotted Horse's body, and falling over him, she began to weep hysterically.

Leading Cloud went to her, grasped her shoulders, and drew her to her feet. Turning her so that he could see into her face, he shook her roughly. His harsh treatment quieted her.

"One-Who-Laughs," he said firmly, "you and your brother were very close. Did he tell you what happened to White Raven's brothers?"

Leading Cloud was speaking in Apache; Caroline, as well as Ross, understood his words.

When One-Who-Laughs refused to answer, Lead-

261

ing Cloud shook her again, harder this time. "Tell me! The spirits gave White Raven back her memories so she could find her brothers! You must not defy the spirits!"

One-Who-Laughs shuddered to think she might anger the gods, for when she entered the spirit world, they would certainly punish her.

She hung her head, and answered meekly, "Stalking Bear traded the boys for rifles."

Caroline asked anxiously, "Who did he trade them to?"

"Sánchez," she replied.

Ross's arms were still around Caroline. She moved out of his embrace, and asked, "Have you contacted Sánchez yet?"

"No. I'm on my way to see him now."

"Then I'm going with you."

"You'll do no such thing! It's too dangerous. I'll ask him about your brothers."

Juan intervened, "We will let the Indians go, but the women come with us." His gaze swept thoroughly over Caroline and Mary. They were too beautiful to set free. He was sure Sánchez would have the Bennetts killed, then Sánchez would no doubt take the golden-haired woman for himself. Juan intended to ask his boss if he could have the other one.

Ross was firmly against the women accompanying them. He was about to make that fact perfectly clear; but, Caroline, reading his intent, said strongly, "If you refuse to take me to Sánchez, then I'll find someone else who will!"

He knew Caroline meant what she said. He silently cursed her stubbornness. If only she wasn't such a hard-headed little vixen! Apparently, she was bent on talking to Sánchez. At least, if he was with her, he could take care of her.

"All right," he said quietly. "You can come with me, but I want you to promise me something."

"What's that?" she asked, regarding him cautiously.

"That you'll do as I tell you."

"I'll try," she replied. "But I'm not promising."

Juan, his patience gone, bellowed grumpily, "I have heard enough talk. Come; we must leave!"

Caroline went to Leading Cloud, and embraced him tightly. "Goodbye," she whispered. "Give my love to Basket Woman and Sweet Water."

"You will need another horse. Take Spotted Horse's." He looked at her sadly.

Caroline merely nodded, then followed the others back to the campsite. She was familiar with Apache custom, and she knew the ritual Leading Cloud would perform after they were gone.

Ross's thoughts were the same as Caroline's, for he was also well acquainted with Apache ritual. He had always found it odd that the Apaches, who were such a militant people, had such a horror of death. When a band member died, he was quickly buried, his dwelling and possessions burned. Then the mourners purged themselves in sagebrush smoke and moved away from the immediate area to escape harm from the ghost of the deceased. Leading Cloud would no doubt bury Spotted Horse, purge himself and One-Who-Laughs, then leave as expeditiously as possible.

Caroline gave her pinto to Mary, and took Spotted Horse's stallion for herself. The horse was spirited, but Caroline's scent was familiar, and it accepted her weight on its back. Although her control was not as firm as Spotted Horse's, the stallion nonetheless responded obediently.

Ross was riding at Caroline's side, and she asked him, "What do you suppose Sánchez did with my brothers?"

"He most likely sold them."

"Sold them?" she gasped.

"There are always childless couples hoping to adopt a son or a daughter, and your brothers were still very young. Especially, Daniel. I don't imagine it's that hard to find a couple who will buy a child."

"Then there's no telling where my brothers are."

She sounded terribly disheartened, and he said soothingly, "We'll find them, Caroline."

She prayed he was right.

Chapter Twenty

Sánchez's hideout was located in a box canyon surrounded by high bluffs. There was only one way in, a narrow path that ran over the cliffs and down into the valley. It would be impossible to enter or leave without being seen.

Sánchez and his Comancheros had used the hideaway for years, and its location was carefully guarded. Visitors, such as Ross and the others, were always blindfolded miles before reaching the canyon. Thus, the trip over the rocky bluffs was a little scary, for the bandanas over their eyes didn't keep them from knowing that they were climbing a steep terrain. The trail was so narrow that they had to travel in single file.

Caroline, blindfolded and riding the high-strung stallion, was more than scared — she was terrified. The precarious path, layered with small rocks and pebbles, caused her horse to lose its footing several times. The skittish horse was so nervous she could actually feel it trembling beneath her.

Ross was riding behind her, and his horse kept bumping into hers. The stallion, on the verge of panicking, would continuously stop, then prance in place. Ross, afraid for Caroline, called out, "Hold up!"

Juan, who was in front of Caroline, reined in, looked back at Ross, and asked, "What is wrong, se-ñor?"

Ross, impatient with his blindfold, was tempted to remove it. He controlled the urge, for he knew it was in his own best interest to wear it. The Comancheros' hideout was a carefully guarded secret, he doubted if anyone who saw his way in, would live to see his way out.

"I want Caroline to ride with me," Ross said to Juan. "Her horse is about to panic."

Juan saw no reason to refuse. Besides, the gringo was right, for he, too, had been wary of the skittish stallion. "All right, amigo," he said, dismounting. He went to Caroline, helped her down, then led her to Bennett. He lifted her into his strong arms, and placed her on the saddle in front of Ross. Then, taking the stallion's reins, he got back on his horse.

As they continued their gradual climb, Caroline snuggled closer to Ross. She was sitting side-saddle, and Ross's arms, encircling her, made her feel secure. Ross's Appaloosa, well-trained and sure-footed, made its way carefully.

Ross enjoyed having Caroline snuggled next to him, but he wished he could gaze into her beautiful gray eyes, and he silently cursed his blasted blindfold.

"Are you nervous?" Caroline suddenly asked.

"Nervous? About what?"

"About seeing Emily again."

"No, I'm not. But I do hope she's all right."

"So do I," she murmured sincerely.

They rode in silence for awhile, then Ross said considerately, "You're holding up very well. I admire you."

Giving in to her feelings, she replied pathetically, "I'm not holding up nearly as well as you think!"

"It takes time to get over losing someone you love," he told her, referring to Spotted Horse.

Thinking he was speaking of her brothers, she said firmly, "I certainly don't intend to give up. I'll find Walter and Daniel if it kills me!"

"I wasn't talking about your brothers. I meant it'll take time for you to get over losing Spotted Horse."

"Why do you say that?" she questioned, confused.

"You were in love with him, weren't you?"

"No, of course not."

"Then why were you crying so hard over his body?"

"I was crying because he died without telling me what happened to Walter and Daniel."

Ross smiled, and he felt as though a heavy burden had been lifted from his heart. "If you weren't in love with Spotted Horse, then why did you break him out of jail?"

"He said he'd tell me about my brothers. But he tricked me."

Ross cradled her gently against his chest. "You poor darling," he murmured with deep feeling.

Caroline, reveling in Ross's closeness, placed her head on his shoulder. She was content to leave it there. The blackness behind her blindfold made it seem as though she and Ross were the only two people in the world.

Their course suddenly took a drastic change, and instead of climbing, they began a steep descent. Going down was much faster than going up, and they were soon off the mountain and onto flat land.

Juan ordered everyone to pull up, then he told Al-

267

fredo and the other man to remove their visitors' blindfolds.

They did so at once. Caroline blinked against the bright sunlight, and it took a moment for her eyes to focus. She looked about with amazement. She had expected the Comancheros' hideout to consist of campfires and tents. She was shocked to find dozens of adobe huts, several with children playing in front of them. Corrals, filled with horses, were spaced sporadically. Chickens, geese, and even a few turkeys had free run, and in the distance, a large herd of cattle grazed contentedly. Gardens, overflowing with vegetables, were plentiful. Caroline, turned her eyes to the waterfall cascading down the far cliff, and understood why the area was so fertile.

A large, two-story home stood back from the settlement. Made of white adobe, it had a red tile roof, and an intricately carved veranda. Located close to the house were two filled corrals, a bunkhouse, and several small out-buildings.

Caroline, her gaze sweeping impressively over the valley, said with awe, "I wonder how many people even know this place exists."

Juan, hearing her, said, "You will not find this valley on any maps, señorita. But the Apaches, they know about it, for they were the ones who found it. A hundred years ago, they called this place their home. But, for some reason which no one knows, the shamans suddenly decided it was taboo. They said that it is haunted by evil spirits. The Apaches will not come within miles of this place. They now call it the Valley of Ghosts." He laughed somewhat uneasily. "When the wind is blowing, especially at night, it does sound as though the ghosts are wailing." He shrugged tersely. "But, of course, it is only the wind sweeping down into the valley."

Caroline smiled. "You don't sound too certain. Are you sure you don't believe in ghosts?"

He laughed, but it wasn't a very hearty chuckle. "I respect the Apaches' beliefs, but if there are ghosts here, then they are friendly, for we have been here a long time."

Juan slapped the reins against his horse, and the others followed. He led them to the large adobe house. Caroline wasn't surprised, for she had already ascertained that the home belonged to Rolando Sánchez.

Their host stepped out onto the veranda to greet them. Caroline couldn't tell if Sánchez was surprised to see Ross, for his expression was inscrutable. She closely perused the famous outlaw. There was no denying that he was sensually handsome—his tall, lithe frame was perfectly proportioned, and his black hair and dark eyes were devilishly attractive. He smiled roguishly, revealing pearly white teeth.

"*Amigo!*" he said heartily to Ross. "I did not expect you." His eyes swept over the others. "Nor did I expect so many to come with you." He looked at Juan, and asked with a note of anger, "Why did you bring them here?"

"Señor Bennett, he has hidden the ransom money. His cousin was already with him, but the women, we found them later." He pointed at Caroline. "She insisted on coming with us. She says she must talk to you."

Sánchez remembered Caroline. "So, señorita, we meet again." He descended the porch steps, stepped to Ross's horse, and helped Caroline down. Desire lurked in his eyes. "Do you need to talk to me, señorita?"

269

"Yes, I do."

He suppressed his curiosity, and said, "Then, we will talk later. First, I must have a serious chat with Señor Ross."

Dismounting, Ross remarked calmly, "I don't think we have much to discuss. You give me the woman, and I'll give you the money."

Rolando fanned his hands in the air as though exasperated. "Ah, señor, you make it sound so simple. But you will soon see that it is not as simple as you think."

"Why is that?" Ross watched him carefully.

"There is a slight complication, but nothing we cannot work out. Come; we will go inside and have a drink." His invitation included Kirk and Mary.

Entering the house, Rolando called loudly, "Maria!"

A plump, middle-aged woman hurried in from the kitchen.

"Prepare four bedrooms for our guests," he told her.

As the woman left to carry out Sánchez's request, Ross said, "We weren't planning on staying, Rolando."

"But you must stay for at least one night," he argued, showing his visitors into the parlor. "It will soon be dark, and it is too late for us to settle anything."

Sánchez quickly poured brandy for the men, and glasses of sherry for the women.

Caroline sat on the sofa beside Ross. She looked about the room with interest. It was tastefully furnished, the decor exclusively Spanish.

A pair of matching high-backed chairs were placed close to the sofa, Mary and Kirk went to them, and sat down. Like Caroline, Mary was impressed with

Sánchez's home. She also noticed that it was very clean. The tables were polished to a glossy shine, and the hardwood floor was spotless. Sánchez's housekeeper apparently took great pride in her job.

Rolando served the drinks, eased into his favorite chair, and said to Ross, "I never imagined you would be the one to bring the ransom. But, then, I shouldn't be surprised. After all, you are a hired gun."

"I was," Ross admitted. "But I'm not doing this for the money. I happen to be personally acquainted with Emily."

"Sí, I know. She told me. Still, I didn't think her father would send you to get back his daughter."

"He thinks you and I are friends, and he hopes that will go in Emily's favor."

"Thinks we are friends?" he questioned with emphasis. "But we are not really friends, are we, señor?"

Ross didn't answer.

Rolando, smiling expansively, didn't press the issue. He returned to the matter at hand, "There was no reason for Señor Parker to be worried. I never intended to harm his daughter. I only want the ten thousand dollars."

"I'll take you to it tomorrow morning."

"And?" Sánchez coaxed. He knew there had to be more to it.

"My friends and Emily will leave with us."

"I see. Surely, you do not expect me to go with you alone."

"You can bring two men with you." Ross grinned disarmingly. "You can trust me, Rolando, and you can have the money. I only want the woman."

"Yes, but that is where we have a problem. I am not sure that the woman will cooperate."

"Why not?"

271

Rolando put down his drink, stood, and motioned for Ross to get up. "Emily is asleep in her room. I will take you to her." He glanced at Caroline, saying, "Señorita, you may come also if you wish."

She did indeed wish to accompany them. She was very curious about Emily, and was anxious to see the woman who had broken Ross's heart.

They climbed the stairway, and went down the hall to the second bedroom. The door was closed, and Rolando opened it quietly. The room wasn't very light, for the floor length drapes were drawn.

Sánchez, gesturing for Ross and Caroline to stay back, stepped softly to the bed, where Emily lay sleeping. She was lying on her stomach with a sheet drawn up to her shoulders. Carefully, Rolando sat on the edge of the mattress, reached out a hand, and caressed Emily's long curly tresses.

"Wake up, *querida,*" he murmured gently.

Her head, resting on the pillow, moved slightly. She moaned throatily, like a purring cat. "Rolando," she whispered, turning to lay on her side. She held out her arms to him, and beckoned sweetly, "Kiss me, my darling."

Leaning over, he met his lips to hers. She laced her hands about his neck, and responded fervently.

Caroline turned her eyes away from the lovers to look at Ross. She wished she knew what he was thinking, but his expression was unreadable.

Rolando, releasing Emily gently, said with an amused smile, "There is someone here to see you." He was enjoying himself. Although Rolando loved women, he had little respect for them. To him, they were simply objects of pleasure.

Sánchez moved to stand beside the bed, giving Emily a clear view of Ross and Caroline.

Emily, staring shockingly at Ross, turned deathly white. Her mouth agape, her eyes wide with surprise, she sat up with a start. The sudden movement caused the sheet to slip, and her bare breasts were revealed. Quickly, she drew the cover up to her shoulders. "Ross," she gasped, "what are you doing here?" Her gaze suddenly went to Caroline, and she asked irritably, "Who are you? And what are you doing in my room?"

"They are both in your bedroom at my invitation," Rolando told her. "Your papa sent the ransom with Señor Bennett." Sánchez chuckled as though unconcerned. "But, Bennett, he has hidden the money." He turned back to Ross, grinned, and said, "This, *amigo,* is the complication I mentioned. It seems the señorita does not want to return to her father. She wants to stay here with me."

"If she wants to stay, that's fine. But you don't get the ten thousand dollars."

"Rolando," Emily said quickly. "Let me talk to Ross alone."

Sánchez had no objections. Besides, it would give him a chance to spend time with Caroline. He went to her, took her arm, and said, "Come with me, señorita."

Caroline was reluctant to leave, but there was no reason for her to stay. Her eyes flitted back and forth from Emily to Ross. The pair were staring at each other; Ross's eyes were slightly turned to anger, and Emily's blue eyes were flaming with defiance.

Rolando, aware of the tension, chuckled softly, then whispered in Caroline's ear, "Let us go before the fireworks start." With a firm grip on her arm, he led her from the room, closing the door behind them.

The fire went out of Emily's eyes. She preferred to

avoid an altercation. Besides, she was sure she could wrap Ross around her little finger. She screwed her pretty face into an attractive pout, and said sullenly, "Ross, you have no right to keep Papa's money. You must give it to me."

"I don't intend to keep it, but I'm not giving it to you."

"Why not?" she asked, still pouting like a spoiled child. "You know why. Parker sent that money to buy your freedom. Well, apparently, you aren't a prisoner."

"But that's not so!" she argued. "I was indeed kidnapped!"

Ross raised his eyebrows a trifle. He was obviously skeptical.

She patted the mattress, summoned a dazzling smile, and murmured, "Sit beside me, Ross." When he didn't move, she said daringly, "Are you afraid to be close to me? Don't you trust yourself?"

"It's you I don't trust," he replied. Nevertheless, he accepted her challenge, went to the bed, and sat on the edge. He couldn't help but admire her sensuous beauty. Her long, curly hair was temptingly silky, and her delicate features were perfectly carved. He had never made love to Emily, but they had shared many passionate embraces, and he was familiar with the exquisite curves of her body.

"Ross," she began curiously, "that woman who was here, who is she?"

"Her name's Caroline Hanley."

"And what is she to you?"

"Does it matter?"

She sounded a little peeved. "Honestly, Ross, you've always had an exasperating habit of answering a question with a question! You

274

shouldn't do that, you know!"

"Emily, let's understand each other. Are you going to tell me about the kidnapping, or not?"

"Yes, of course I am." She slipped her hand into his, as though she needed comfort. "Papa and I had a terrible argument. I left the house, went to the stables, and saddled my horse. I thought a brisk ride might make me feel better. But because I was overwrought, I wasn't thinking prudently, and I wandered too far from the ranch. Suddenly, I found myself surrounded by Rolando and five of his men. One of these men, he's called Pedro, used to work for Papa. He recognized me and told Rolando how wealthy Papa is. That's when Rolando decided to kidnap me. He forced me to write a ransom note, took me into Mexico, then blindfolded me, and brought me here."

"When did you two become lovers?"

She eyed him coquettishly. "Are you jealous, Ross?"

"Just answer my question."

"We became lovers after he brought me to his home. I couldn't help myself. After all, Rolando is very handsome and charming."

"I don't understand why you want to stay with him. I thought money meant more to you than love."

She smiled brightly. "With Rolando I can have both! Soon now, Rolando will be rich. The Revolutionists have contacted him, and they will pay him handsomely to help them overrun Diáz. Afterwards, Rolando plans to build a huge hacienda, and become even wealthier."

"Are you planning to share his wealth as his mistress or his wife?"

She looked offended. "As his wife, of course!"

Ross laughed aloud.

"How dare you make fun of me!" she snapped, fuming.

"Emily, you're a fool if you think Rolando will marry you."

"We'll see about that!" she said sharply. "You're just jealous because I didn't marry you!"

Standing, Ross smiled down at her; his eyes, however, were devoid of humor. "You might as well plan to leave with me in the morning. Given a choice, Rolando will choose the ten thousand dollars over you."

As he started for the door, she threw a pillow at his back. Her aim was terrible, and she missed him completely. Bending down, and picking it up, Ross tossed it onto the bed. He left the room, and headed toward the stairway. He wondered why he had ever thought himself in love with a spoiled brat like Emily!

Rolando escorted Caroline onto the veranda to a wrought iron bench. Sitting beside her, he reached into his pocket, and brought out a cheroot. "Do you mind if I smoke?" he asked.

She had no objections.

He studied her speculatively. "You are jealous, *si?*"

"What do you mean?"

"Emily told me that she and Ross used to be engaged. Do not worry, little one, you'll not lose Ross to Emily. He is no fool. Why would he want Emily when he can have you?"

"What makes you think I'm Ross's for the taking?"

"It is in your eyes every time you look at him. Which puzzles me a bit. I thought you were Spotted Horse's woman."

She appeared confused.

"That night when you came upon my camp, you

told me you were supposed to marry Spotted Horse. Remember?"

"Yes, I remember. But I only told you that because I believed it would keep you from harming me."

Sánchez chuckled good-humoredly. "I would never harm you. But I would like to make love to you."

She stiffened noticeably.

"Do not be afraid, señorita. There is no man I respect more than Señor Bennett. I would never try to steal his woman."

"You must like him very much."

"Almost as much as I fear him."

"Why do you fear Ross?"

"Maybe fear is not a good word. Let's just say that I would not want to find myself facing his gun. But enough talk about Ross. Why did you want to see me?"

"Five years ago, Spotted Horse's friend, Stalking Bear, brought you two boys. Their names are Walter and Daniel. At the time, they were five and two years old. Stalking Bear traded them to you for rifles. Do you remember the transaction?"

"*Si,* I do."

Hope filled her heart. "What happened to them?"

"Why do you want to know?"

"They are my brothers!" she cried. As quickly as possible, she told Sánchez about the day she and her family were attacked by Spotted Horse and his warriors. He asked several questions, and she answered them. Eventually, everything was explained.

Rolando, thinking back, was silent for a long moment. "Sí, now I remember what happened to both of them. I sold the youngest boy to Fernando Mendoza."

"Mendoza!" she interrupted, astonished.

"Do you know him?"

277

"I met him once. At the hotel in El Zarango." She inhaled deeply. "He had his son with him! My God, was that Daniel?"

"Sí, it must have been. The only son he has is the one he bought from me. Mendoza and his wife cannot have children. He wanted a son so badly that he was willing to buy one. Mendoza and I do not like each other, and it galled him to do business with me. But a son meant more to him than his pride."

Caroline thought about the child Mendoza called his son. Recalling the boy vividly, she could once again see him hiding behind his mother's skirts. He had smiled at her, and she had returned his bashful smile. Suddenly, tears flooded her eyes. Dear God, she had actually seen Daniel!

She was so choked up that she could barely speak. "Where is Walter?"

"He is with Roberto."

"Who is Roberto?"

"He owns the restaurant in El Zarango. He bought the boy to work for him. He calls him Carlos."

An anguished groan sounded deep in her throat.

"You have also seen Carlos, *sí?*"

"Yes!" she cried. "God help me, why didn't I recognize him?"

"Five years is a long time in a child's life. A boy at five does not always look the same at ten." He placed his hand on hers to offer comfort.

She threw his hand aside, bounded to her feet, and said angrily, "Don't touch me! You're a vile, contemptible monster! How dare you sell children as though they were cattle!"

"You forget, señorita, that I am an outlaw." His smile was devil-may-care. Standing, he stepped to the door, opened it, and waved Caroline inside. "I will

278

have Maria show you and the other lady to your rooms. I am sure you would both enjoy a rest and a bath."

Caroline stared at him with wonder. Rolando Sánchez was indeed an enigma. She had never met anyone like him. She hoped she never would again.

She brushed past him, and went into the house.

Chapter Twenty-one

Sánchez's housekeeper provided Caroline with a bath, and brought her a change of clothes. She explained that Sánchez kept women's attire in his home, for he was always prepared for a lady's unexpected visit. Caroline accepted the housekeeper's explanation without comment, but she suspected that Rolando was a womanizer, and that the wardrobe was purchased for the use of his lovers, including Emily Parker. But she was glad for the change of clothes, for her riding attire was coated with trail dust.

Maria left to assist Mary, but she told Caroline that she'd return later, gather up her dirty clothes, wash them, and hang them by the kitchen stove to dry.

Alone, Caroline looked closely about the bedroom. It was sparsely furnished, but comfortable. Like the rest of the house, it was immaculately clean. She went to the dresser, where a brush and comb rested on a mirrored tray. She sat down, and picking up the brush, began to run it briskly through her long golden tresses. She did so absent-mindedly, for her thoughts were elsewhere.

She could hardly believe that she had actually seen

Walter and Daniel! She was very sorry that she had not recogized them. But, then, five years is a long time, and at that age children change rapidly. She supposed she shouldn't be too hard on herself.

She wanted to go after her brothers without delay. Would Ross agree, or would he insist that first they deliver Emily to her father? But, then, Emily might refuse to leave Sánchez. If she did, Caroline knew Ross wouldn't hand over the ransom, he'd take it back to Parker. Would Sánchez try to take the money by force? She supposed it was possible. A worried frown creased her brow. Everything was so uncertain. Ross's life, as well as Kirk's, could very well be in jeopardy. The Bennetts weren't the kind to back down, they would stand their ground. But would they be so reckless as to defy Sánchez and his Comancheros? She hoped not! Parker's ten thousand dollars wasn't worth their lives!

Caroline's thoughts drifted back to Emily. She was absolutely beautiful! No wonder Ross had fallen in love with her. How did he feel about her now? Had it hurt him to see her in Rolando's arms? If so, she hadn't been able to tell by looking at him, for his expression had revealed nothing. Exasperated, Caroline sighed heavily. Her grandfather would say that Ross had a poker-face, and he would be right. Ross's thoughts were always his own!

She put down the brush, stood up, and looked at herself in the mirror. Maria had brought her a blouse and a skirt that closely resembled the ones Ross had purchased for her in El Zarango. The ruffled blouse, designed to be worn off the shoulders, was snowy white with dainty red roses, and the long, swirling skirt was bright red. Maria had also brought her a pair of black velvet slippers that fit perfectly. A scarlet ribbon came with the outfit, and Caroline used it

281

to hold her heavy tresses back from her face. Remaining in front of the mirror, she gave her reflection a final appraisal. Red was most assuredly her best color, for it brought out the blush of her cheek and contrasted stunningly with her deep gray eyes. The Mexican-styled clothes enhanced her slender frame, and softly hugged her delicate curves. Her flowing hair, falling to her waist in silky waves, provided a sensuous picture, but as Caroline left to go to Mary's room, her appearance wasn't on her mind, for she had never thought of herself as especially beautiful.

After Mary had bathed and dressed they went downstairs, where they found the men sitting in the parlor. Caroline and Mary, dressed similarly, were incredibly alluring. The gentlemen got quickly to their feet, their gazes traveling admirably over the women.

Sánchez poured glasses of sherry, and more brandy for himself, Ross, and Kirk. The group had finished their drinks before Emily finally made her entrance. Her dress, though simply made, was exquisite. Pale blue, it had a buttoned-up bodice and a lace-trimmed collar. Emily had left the top three buttons undone, revealing the soft hollow of her throat. Her silky tresses, pulled back from her face with a pair of matching combs, cascaded past her shoulders in an abundance of curls. She was sensually evocative, yet, at the same time, innocent-looking.

Caroline, wondering if Ross was enthralled with Emily's appearance, cast him a sidelong glance. Sure enough he was staring openly at her. Apparently, he was finding his former fiancée very attractive indeed!

Ross turned to Caroline and was a little surprised to see that she was watching him. She quickly looked away. In his opinion, Caroline was much prettier than Emily. He supposed a casual observer would find the women equally beautiful, but Caroline, unlike Emily, had a shining beauty that came from within. As far as Ross was concerned, Emily Parker couldn't hold a candle to Caroline Hanley.

Sánchez, with Emily at his side, led the way into the dining room. Despite the diners' doubts and apprehensions, the talk around the table remained trivial. No one wanted to discuss what was really the issue.

Following the meal, they returned to the parlor for coffee and brandy. Kirk, longing to talk alone with Mary, took this opportunity to ask her to step outside with him for a breath of fresh air.

She accepted readily, for she found the house confining. Kirk, taking her arm, escorted her through the foyer and onto the veranda, where they sat on the wrought-iron bench. A constant breeze made it a pleasant evening to sit outdoors.

Kirk gave Mary a surreptitious gaze. He thought her extremely lovely. He knew she wasn't beautiful in the same exotic way as Caroline and Emily, but Mary could hold her own with any woman, even those much younger than herself. Her auburn hair, freshly washed and worn naturally, radiantly framed her face. He liked the dusting of freckles on her cheeks. He found them not only attractive, but also flattering. Her body was slim and graceful, but quite voluptuous. Kirk couldn't recall ever desiring a woman as much as he desired Mary. He longed to possess her completely. He wanted her heart, body, and her love. The difference in their ages didn't bother him, though he knew that it bothered Mary a great deal. Kirk believed when two people cared for each other, love was the only important factor. But how could he convince Mary of this?

Mary looked at Kirk, and smiled warmly, for she

liked him very much. She supposed if she were younger, and if her heart wasn't so bruised, she would fall madly in love with him. Why not? He was not only handsome, but had a winning personality. He was also the kind of man a woman could depend on. Her smile suddenly widened, and a bright twinkle came to her green eyes.

"What are you thinking about?" Kirk asked.

"I was remembering that night when I first met you. I didn't like you. I thought you were very brusque and discourteous."

"And now?"

She laughed lightly. "Well, let's just say I was very wrong about you."

Encouraged, Kirk subtly placed his arm on the back of the bench, then let it slip down to Mary's shoulders. She stiffened immediately.

"Why do you keep fighting it?" Kirk asked impatiently.

"Fighting what?"

"This attraction between us."

"Kirk, I thought I made my feelings perfectly clear on that subject. I'm not only too old for you but . . . but . . ."

"Go on," he persisted.

She drew a deep breath, then continued, "It's not just the seven years between us, it's much more than that. Kirk, I loved my husband and sons with all my heart. When they died, a lot of me died with them. Oh, how can I make you understand? Don't you see? I have nothing to offer a man. I'm . . . I'm dead inside. You deserve a woman who is young and vivacious."

Kirk got to his feet, looked down at her, and said, "Mary Murphy, you're a coward. You're just spouting excuses because you're afraid of me."

She rose stiffly. "I beg your pardon! How dare you say such a thing! Why, that's preposterous!"

"Is it?" he challenged, a brow raised questioningly. Moving quickly, he brought her into his arms, bent his head, and kissed her with a punishing sweetness.

She didn't want to respond, but she had no defense against Kirk, and she found herself returning his ardor. She shifted closer to him, and surrendered to the pleasure his kiss was evoking.

Kirk released her gently. "Dead inside?" he questioned. "I hardly think so. Nothing died with your husband and sons, you're still very much alive. If I were an older man, you might give me a chance. But you're afraid of me, aren't you? You're scared that someday I'll leave you for a younger woman. Why don't you admit it to me, as well as to yourself?"

His words hit a sensitive chord, one that Mary wasn't ready to deal with.

Kirk took her arm, and led her to the door. "Think about what I said. And while you're thinking about it, think about this." With no warning, he once again drew her close and kissed her. It was a wild, hungry caress, and it left Mary trembling but longing for more.

He opened the door abruptly, ushered her inside, and back to the parlor. She went to the sofa, and sat beside Caroline. Her heart was pounding.

A short time later, Caroline, tired, decided to go to bed. She had hoped that Ross would ask her to take a walk so they could be alone, but, giving up, she excused herself and left the room. Mary, followed suit and trailed close behind. Emily had already retired.

"Another brandy?" Sánchez asked, his eyes flitting from Ross to Kirk.

They both declined.

Rolando eased back in his chair, stretched out his long legs, and regarded Ross unflinchingly. "I admire you, *amigo*. You are very cool. One would think that you have the upper hand. But what is to prevent me from forcing you to tell me where the money is hidden?"

"I suppose you could find a way to force it out of me, but you won't."

"Why not?" he asked. The faint beginning of a smile was on his lips.

"Emily doesn't mean that much to you."

His smile broke into a good-natured chuckle. "You are right, *amigo*."

"She thinks you're going to marry her, you know."

Ross's words brought a hearty laugh. "Marry her? She is a beautiful woman, and very passionate. But any man who marries her is a fool. She will make him miserable, for she will never be satisfied with what he can give her. She will always want more. You are very lucky, *amigo,* that you did not marry her."

Ross didn't argue, for he agreed wholeheartedly.

"You are even luckier, *amigo,* to have found a woman like Caroline."

Again, Ross agreed, but he didn't say anything. He wasn't about to discuss his personal life with Rolando. "I'd like to leave early in the morning," he said. "I want to get this matter with Emily settled as soon as possible."

"I have no objections, *amigo*."

Ross stood. "Then I'll turn in for the night. I'll see you in the morning." He looked at Kirk. "Are you coming?"

Suppressing a yawn, he answered, "I'm right behind you. I'm so tired, I'll probably fall asleep before my head hits the pillow."

The Bennetts were climbing the stairs when Juan and Alfredo came into the house. The two Comancheros waited until the men were upstairs before heading to the parlor.

"Patrón," Juan said to Rolando, "after we kill the Bennetts, can I have the red-haired woman?"

"There will be no killings. If you want a woman, there are several *putas* in El Zarango."

Juan was surprised. "You mean, you are going to let the Bennetts live?"

"Why not? They are no threat to us. In the morning, Ross will take us to the money. We will make the exchange, they will go their way, and we will come back here." Standing, Rolando said firmly, "That is the deal I made with Señor Bennett, and I see no reason to go back on my word." Leaving the room, he said over his shoulder, "Go to the bunkhouse and get some sleep. We will leave early in the morning."

Sánchez moved down the hall to his study. Going inside, he was surprised to find Emily waiting.

"I figured you'd come here before retiring," she said.

"What do you want?"

"What do you think I want? Are you going to send me back to my father?"

"Yes, I am."

She was furious. "You contemptible devil! You never intended to marry me, did you?"

"I don't recall ever mentioning marriage."

"No, but you led me to believe it would happen."

"It was all in your mind, señorita."

Her rage exploded, and she drew back a hand to slap him, but he caught her arm in midair, twisted it behind her back, and held her body flush to his.

"Let me go!" she fumed.

"You were a fool to turn down a man like

Ross. You should have married him."

"And live the rest of my life in poverty!"

Rolando turned her loose. "Poverty? Ross is not poor. He has made much money selling his gun. He plans to build a ranch. Someday he will be very prosperous. He will be as rich as your father, perhaps more so."

Emily was dumbfounded. "Ross has money? Why didn't he tell me?"

"Maybe he wanted to surprise you on your wedding night." Amused, Rolando smiled. "I know what you are thinking, señorita. But you can forget it. Ross is now in love with Caroline Hanley."

She lifted her chin smugly. "She's obviously his second choice. If I wanted Ross back, I could have him with a snap of my fingers." With that, she moved swiftly to the door.

"Emily," Rolando called.

She stopped, and turned back to look at him.

"Tonight will be our last night together. Later, I will come to your room."

"Oh?" she questioned. "What makes you think I won't lock my door?"

"Lock it if you want, beautiful one. But a locked door will not keep me out."

"I hate you, Rolando Sánchez!" she lashed out, hands on hips. "Stay away from me!"

She stormed out of the room, hurried up the stairs, and moved quickly down the hall, but when she came to Ross's room, she hesitated. She placed a hand on the doorknob. Should she go inside? She was certain Ross would be pleased to see her. Confident, she opened the door a crack, and peeked inside. The room was empty. Where was he? Was he with Caroline?

She closed the door softly, and went to her own

chambers. She considered locking the door, then changed her mind. After all, Sánchez was a superb lover, so why not enjoy him one last time?

Losing, Rolando was a big disappointment, but one that Emily knew she could deal with. It wasn't as though she were head over heels in love with him.

She sat in a rocking chair that was placed close to the window. She rocked back and forth, and the motion was soothing. Her thoughts turned to her father. He would undoubtedly send her to St. Louis to live with her aunt and uncle. She had met them twice, and didn't like them. Certainly, she had no desire to live with them. They were such devout Baptists that all they lived for was the Church. It wouldn't be any fun staying with people like that.

Her musings drifted to Ross. Except for Rolando, he was the only man she had ever really wanted. She would have married him if she had known that he had money. Wealth meant everything to Emily, and she'd not marry a man who couldn't provide for her in the style to which she was accustomed.

A look of determination crossed her face. She'd take Ross away from Caroline Hanley! Although Caroline was very pretty, she didn't consider her much competition. She was sure Ross had merely turned to Caroline on the rebound, and that he was still desperately in love with her.

Earlier, Ross had been in his room, but he had soon left, for he knew his mind was too troubled for sleep. He had decided to go outside and have a smoke.

Now, finishing his cheroot, he went back into the house. He hurried upstairs, and down the hall. His steps halted in front of Caroline's room. He wanted to be with her, but by now she was probably sound asleep. He dropped his gaze to the thin crack beneath the door, and seeing a stream of light, he hoped she was still awake. If she were asleep, she would certainly have extinguished the lamp.

He knocked on her door. "Caroline?"

She was in bed, but despite her fatigue, thoughts of her brothers and Ross had her wide awake. "Come in," she called.

He came in quietly, closed the door, then decided to lock it. The lamp, its wick burning low, cast shadows across the room. Ross moved slowly to the bed, drew up a small chair, sat down, and said, "We need to talk."

Caroline was surprised, but delighted. Ross didn't seem to be in a hurry to begin a conversation, and she looked curiously into his brown eyes. She was thrilled to see desire smoldering in their dark depths, and she became suddenly very physically aware of his nearness. She shivered imperceptibly.

Meanwhile, Ross was trying to keep his passion under control, but the need to make love to her was overpowering, for she was temptingly provocative. The covers, drawn up past her breasts, left her soft shoulders bared. Underneath, he was sure she was beautifully nude. Taking her hand, he turned it over, and placed a light kiss on her palm.

The touch of his lips sent her heart pounding, and her voice quaked ever so slightly as she whispered, "Ross, I need you."

In one swift move, he was on the bed beside her, his mouth claiming hers feverishly. His questing tongue set fire to Caroline's passion, and tremors of ecstasy coursed through her. Her arms encircled him tightly, and she held him as close as possible.

"Caroline," he murmured raspingly, "you're so

beautiful, so desirable. God, I want to make love to you!"

"Yes, Ross!" she cried. She craved him with every fiber of her being.

He kissed her endearingly, then, rising, he began to disrobe. Caroline watched his every move. He was so handsome, this man she loved with all her heart. Admiration shone in her gray eyes as she perused him boldly. He unbuckled his gun belt, and placed it on the bedside table. Then with impatience, he quickly removed his boots, shoved them to the side, and took off his shirt. She sighed at the sight of his smooth bronzed chest, the broad muscles as hard as rock. He shed the rest of his clothes, then stood before her completely nude. Caroline's gaze traveled hungrily over his tall, lithe, and tightly muscled frame. For a moment, her eyes rested on his erect manhood, and glorying in the pleasure it would soon bring her, she held out her arms to him.

Ross flung the covers aside, and as he had suspected, she was naked. He went into her arms, and kissed her with passion. Slowly he took his lips from hers, then raising up to lean on one elbow, he allowed his gaze to roam over every inch of her. He thought her lovely beyond compare. Her breasts, though not large, were full and well-rounded. She had a tiny waist, curvaceous hips, and perfectly-shaped legs. Leaning over, he very lightly kissed the golden-colored triangle between her thighs, then moving his mouth upwards, he suckled her breasts, his tongue circling the taut nipples.

Caroline moaned with unspeakable pleasure, and placing her hand to the nape of Ross's neck, she pressed him ever closer.

Her response was encouraging, and Ross thoroughly relished her lovely breasts before moving his mouth up to hers, kissing her with sweet, loving torment.

Engulfed in total rapture, they intimately explored each other's body, their skimming hands, warm lips, and flickering tongues driving one another gloriously wild.

Ross, his erection throbbing for release, moved over Caroline; she slid her long legs about his waist, and waited breathlessly for his exciting entry.

He plunged into her deeply, and his inserted manhood caused wondrous chills to prickle her flesh. Trembling with desire, she thrust her hips upward, wanting him as far inside her as possible.

"Caroline," Ross whispered. "I love you."

"My darling," she cried. "I love you, too!"

The pair, now wrapped securely in the warm bunting of their love, surrendered blissfully to their passion, and happily abandoned themselves to love's rapturous joy.

Later, as Caroline and Ross lay snuggled close, he said, "You know, I came in here to talk to you. Although I wanted this to happen, I didn't plan on it."

She smiled pertly. "Well, I'm certainly glad that it did happen. But, you're right, we should talk."

"Let me explain my plan, then if you don't agree, we'll discuss changing it. Rolando told me where your brothers are—after I give him the ransom, I'll send Emily back to Dry Branch with Kirk and Mary. You and I will go to El Zarango and get Walter. From there, we'll travel to Mendoza's hacienda."

"Your plan sounds fine to me."

"Caroline," Ross began hesitantly, "persuading Mendoza to give us Daniel won't be easy. In fact, it might be impossible."

"But Daniel isn't his to keep!" she remarked.

"That doesn't matter. Honey, we're in a foreign country, and Mendoza is a powerful man here. We can't just go to his home, take Daniel, and leave."

"Then what can we do?"

"I don't know, sweetheart."

"Daniel is my baby brother, and I won't give him up! I won't!"

Ross knew she meant it.

Chapter Twenty-two

Ross and the others had again been blindfolded, then guided over the mountain from the hidden valley, and forced to ride several miles before their blindfolds were finally removed. The sun was setting, and, Sánchez, growing impatient, asked Ross, "Where is the money, *amigo?*"

Ross, riding at his side, answered, "It's only a few miles from here, but we'll have to get it in the morning. It's buried, and I don't think I can find the spot at night."

"It will soon be dark. Where do you want to make camp?"

"There's a good place up ahead, we'll stop there."

Sánchez agreed.

Ross glanced over his shoulder to check on Caroline. She and Mary were riding directly behind him. Emily was next in line, followed by Kirk. Juan and Alfredo were bringing up the rear.

Catching Ross's glance, Caroline smiled at him. He winked, returned her smile, then looked straight ahead. His gaze, plus his wink, made her feel warm and tingly inside. She was so much in love that her face was actually glowing.

Mary, seeing this, said gaily, "Caroline, it's so

294

obvious that you're in love. I think I envy you."

Caroline and Ross had discussed Kirk and Mary, and they both suspected that Kirk was hopelessly in love. Caroline was certain that Mary was uneasy because of the difference in their ages.

"Young love is so romantic," Mary said dreamily, remembering her youth.

"Mary," Caroline began, "one doesn't have to be young to be in love."

Mary was instantly on her guard. "What do you mean by that? Has Kirk been talking to you?"

"I didn't mean anything in particular. And, no, Kirk hasn't said anything to me. Why do you ask?"

"Well, he has this foolish notion that he and I should become romantically involved."

"Why is it foolish?"

"I'll be forty years old next week. Kirk is only thirty-three."

"So?"

"You don't understand, do you?" she said impatiently. "I'm too old for him. Furthermore, he's never been married. I was not only a wife, but I was also a mother."

"You shouldn't worry about the difference in your ages. Kirk's seven years younger, true, but he's a grown man. And you're wrong to consider yourself too experienced for him."

She sighed heavily. "Caroline, you're only eighteen years old. What could you possibly know about it?"

She believed she knew enough, but she didn't say anything. She felt a little sorry for Kirk. Mary's mind was obviously set, and it wasn't going to be easy for him to change it.

Meanwhile, Emily, riding behind Mary and Caroline, wondered what they were talking about. She tried to overhear their words, but they were speaking too softly. They were probably discussing Ross. Emily smiled cunningly. Well, if they were, then Caroline was wasting her time! Ross would never marry her! Emily was quite confident that he was still in love with her. In her opinion, his love was obvious — hadn't he rushed to her rescue? He had to know the danger involved, yet, he had risked his life to save her from the Comancheros. She thought about the way he was now treating her. His behavior was cold, true, but understandable. After all, learning that she was Sánchez's lover had shocked him. A worried frown wrinkled her brow. Undoubtedly, it had also lowered Ross's opinion of her. She considered the problem, then dismissed it with a shrug of her shoulders. She'd get Ross back, regardless.

Kirk, riding behind Emily, was also deep in thought. He was remembering the way Mary had responded to his kisses. He was somewhat aggravated with her, and his patience was wearing thin. It was apparent that she desired him; still, she was determined not to become involved. He was beginning to wonder if he should give up, go to Arizona, and build his ranch. He had better things to do with his time than fight a losing battle!

Shortly thereafter, they set up camp. As Emily sat off by herself, Caroline and Mary prepared supper, which consisted of bacon, beans, biscuits, and coffee.

Following the meal, the travelers sat about the campfire. Sánchez waited until he had finished his second cup of coffee before suggesting that they post guards through the night. Ross agreed, and he offered to take the first watch.

As everyone spread out their bedrolls, Ross took his rifle and walked into the distance. He found a good spot beneath a cottonwood, sat down, and placed his

Winchester at his side. It was a beautiful desert night, for the sky was etched with thousands of twinkling stars, and a full moon was shining brilliantly against the dark heavens. A coyote's faraway howl, sounding forlorn, was soon answered by its mate. The pair began to wail in unison, and their canine music carried for miles. After a time, their howling ceased, and except for the occasional movement of a nocturnal creature, silence was prevalent.

Ross suddenly detected footsteps, and he placed a cautious hand on his rifle, though he wasn't alarmed. He was sure it was someone from camp. He listened closely, the steps were light. He smiled, it was probably Caroline.

"Ross?" a voice called.

His smile faded instantly. Getting to his feet, he said, "I'm over here, Emily."

She emerged from the dark shadows, and into the moonlight. She moved gracefully, yet there was a stalking intent in her walk. Ross braced himself for a confrontation. He wasn't sure what she wanted, but he knew he wasn't going to like it.

Emily summoned a radiant smile. "Ross, do you mind if I talk to you for a few minutes?"

"What about?" He sounded curt.

She wasn't discouraged. She stood close to him, gazed up sweetly into his eyes, and murmured, "You hate me, don't you, Ross?"

"I don't hate you, Emily."

"Of course, you do. And I don't blame you. I treated you abhorrently. But, Ross, I'm not the same girl who broke your heart. I'm much wiser now, and I'm no longer under my father's rule. I now have the courage to stand up to him." She brought tears to her eyes. "I was such a fool to let him influence me! Ross, I truly loved you! I never really stopped loving you!"

Ross raised a brow, and his expression was clearly skeptical.

"I know what you're thinking," she said quickly. "But it's true, I do love you!"

"What about Rolando?"

"I never loved him, not really! I was just infatuated with him. After all, he is quite charming."

"Yes, and he very charmingly cast you out of his life, didn't he?"

She pouted attractively. "Ross, don't be mean. Besides, now that I've had time to think about it, I realize that I never really wanted to marry Rolando. Underneath it all, I was merely rebelling against my father."

Ross grinned humorously. "That's quite a story, especially since it only took you one day to come up with it."

"Ross, please don't make fun of me." She flashed her most alluring smile.

"Emily, if you're here to get back into my good graces, then you're wasting your time. It's over between us. I'm in love with Caroline, and I plan to ask her to marry me."

She wasn't surprised, for she knew she would have to persuade him to forget Caroline and to come back to her. She moved subtly closer until her body was almost touching his. "Ross," she said sensually, "I think you are still in love with me."

"You're wrong," he answered calmly.

"Then prove it."

He looked at her inquisitively. "How can I prove it?"

"Kiss me, then tell me you no longer love me."

"Emily, what kind of game are you playing?"

"It's no game. I just don't think you can kiss me, then let me go."

"Then you thought wrong."

"Prove it," she dared him, smiling inwardly and feel-

298

ing victorious. Once he kissed her, he would certainly be hers for the taking! She had charmed him once, she would do so again!

Ross was hesitant. He wasn't afraid of falling back in love with her, he simply preferred not to kiss her, or any woman, except Caroline.

She egged him on. "Well, Ross? Do you have the nerve to take me in your arms and kiss me? Are you afraid?"

"Fear has nothing to do with it. I just don't want to kiss you."

"Yes, you are afraid," she argued. "You're afraid of reviving old feelings. You still want me, why don't you admit it?"

Ross, perturbed, said testily, "Damn it, Emily! If I kiss you, then tell you that I don't give a damn about you, will you believe me?"

"Yes, of course I will."

"In that case . . ." Roughly, for his patience was gone, he reached out and jerked her into his arms. He bent his head, and pressed his lips to hers. She quickly slid her hands about his neck, then thrusting her thighs against his, she attempted to turn their kiss into one of passion.

A few minutes after Emily had left the campsite, Caroline, wanting to be alone with Ross, crawled out of her bedroll. She moved quietly away from the fire, and headed in the direction Ross had taken. She stepped softly through the darkness, and was about to call out to Ross when, suddenly, she found him. Her heart pounded, and she felt a sickening sensation in the pit of her stomach. Ross wasn't alone, Emily was with him! She looked on with disbelief as Ross brought Emily roughly into his arms and kissed her.

Caroline had seen enough. She whirled about, and headed back toward camp. At first, she was filled with a heavy, sodden dullness, and her emotions were strangely numb. Returning to her bedroll, she lay down feebly, completely wrecked. The heaviness in her chest felt like a millstone, threatening to drag her down into a bottomless pit of depression. But Caroline's innate spirit fought back furiously. She'd not give in to despair! Ross wasn't worth it! If he wanted Emily, then he could damn well have her! The miserable, low-down, lying scoundrel!

Only seconds after Caroline had whirled away, Ross forcefully broken his embrace with Emily. Holding her at arms' length, he gazed down into her eyes, and said evenly, "Emily, I don't love you, in fact, I don't even like you. Now, go back to camp, and, hereafter, stay the hell away from me."

She wasn't about to give up — not yet. "Ross, you enjoyed kissing me, didn't you?"

"No, I didn't," he replied truthfully. His patience gone, he continued harshly, "Damn it, Emily! Can't you get it through your thick skull that I'm in love with Caroline?"

She looked hurt. "You don't have to yell at me, and you don't have to be so mean."

"I'm sorry," he murmured. "Go back to camp. Please."

"All right," she answered. "But, Ross, it isn't over between us, not by a long shot." With that, she twirled gracefully about and started back to camp.

Caroline, lying on her blanket, saw Emily return. The woman's bedroll was placed on the other side of the fire, and as she lay down, she happened to glance across the flames, and their eyes met. Caroline's gaze was filled with rage.

Emily wondered if Caroline knew where she had been. Had she seen her and Ross together? Had she caught them kissing? Emily was delighted. Of course she had! Otherwise, she wouldn't be staring at her so furiously. Emily cast Caroline a catty smile, then drawing up her top blanket, she rolled to her side, and turned her back to the fire.

Caroline was fuming, and it took a lot of effort for her to control her temper. Emily's spiteful smile had been like a slap in the face. Her rage was simmering. Damn Ross for falling prey to Emily! Couldn't he see the selfish, inconsiderate, and spoiled woman that lay behind the pretty face? Was his love that blind? Apparently, it was indeed!

She drew a protective cloak over her heart. Well, he'd not hurt her again! She'd not let him get that close!

Two hours later, Ross returned to camp, went to Kirk and awakened him, for he was taking the second watch. Ross had stashed his rolled up blankets beside the fire, he picked them up, looked about, and was tempted to make his bed close to Caroline. Her back was facing him, and he wondered if she was asleep. He decided to spread his blankets next to Kirk's, for if he got too close to Caroline he'd want to sleep with her snuggled in his arms — and this wasn't the place for such intimacy.

He made his bed, lay down, and folding his arms beneath his head, gazed up at the myriad of twinkling stars. He thought about Caroline's brothers. He wasn't too worried about reclaiming Walter. If Roberto tried to cause any trouble, he'd be taking on more than he could handle. The man was obviously a bully, and Ross was itching for a fight. It'd give him great satisfaction to plow his fist into Roberto's ugly face!

Reclaiming Daniel, however, was a different story.

301

Mendoza was an aristocrat — a personal friend of President Díaz's. It would be impossible to get Daniel back through threats. Ross was deeply worried. Mendoza thought of Daniel as his son, and Ross couldn't imagine Mendoza giving him up — regardless of the circumstances.

Fernando Mendoza stood at the hotel window, looking down at the rowdy street scene below. The expression in his eyes was hard, and his prominent patrician nose was wrinkled, the nostrils flaring, as though he smelled an offensive odor though there was nothing in the air — he was merely finding El Zarango distasteful. He loathed the lawless town, and, as always, he could hardly wait to leave. He remembered his last visit to El Zarango. He had come here searching for Alfredo, the man who had killed his sister. Once again, Alfredo was his reason for being here. The man had been seen in town, but, like the other time, he had disappeared. Mendoza was hoping he would return.

Turning away from the window, Mendoza's gaze fell across his son, who had chosen to sit in a hard-backed chair that occupied a corner of the room. A deep frown crossed Mendoza's face. Sometimes, Ricardo reminded him of a skittish mouse trying to hide in nooks and crannies.

The youngster, feeling his father's gaze, met the man's eyes for only a moment. He looked away, and stared down at his hands, which were folded in his lap. He seemed to shrivel beneath his father's scrutiny.

Mendoza was tempted to lash out at his son and tell him to sit up like a man! The boy was intolerable! From the first day he had brought the youngster to his hacienda, he had been a mother's boy. At the time, Mendoza hadn't been overly concerned, for he was sure the child would outgrow his dependency on his mother. On numerous occasions he had tried to become the most influential person in his son's life. His attempts had failed. The boy obviously feared him, and was only happy when he was with his mother.

Mendoza's frown deepened. His wife had died three weeks ago, and now that the boy had lost his mother, he was even more withdrawn.

The door to the adjoining room opened, and Mendoza watched as Ricardo's nurse, Belita, joined them. The woman was young and very beautiful. She had been the boy's nurse now for over a year. Belita came from a good family who had fallen on hard times. The woman was educated, polished, and aristocratic. Mendoza had desired her from the first moment he set eyes on her. However, he had never tried to make love to her, for she was a lady. Now that he was a widower, he hoped to court her, but he wasn't sure if she would accept him as a suitor. Belita had never done or said anything to make him think she shared his feelings.

Belita, moving elegantly across the room, was very aware of Fernando's admiring gaze. Although she had liked Mrs. Mendoza, she wasn't grieved over the woman's death. Fernando was now free, and she had every intention of becoming the next Mrs. Mendoza. She knew, though, that to win Fernando's love and respect, she must behave demurely. He would not marry her if he believed she was fast, which she wasn't. Belita was a virgin, and she intended to remain one until her wedding night.

She went to a chair and sat down. She was well-poised—her feet together, her back ramrod straight. Inwardly, she was confident. She wasn't blind, and she knew that Fernando was attracted to her. She was certain that, following a respectful period of mourning, he would ask her to be his wife.

She cast Fernando's son a furtive glance. She wasn't surprised to find the boy sitting in a corner. When he was in his father's powerful presence, he always tried to be inconspicuous. A small scowl creased her brow. She thought the child insufferable! She knew he was adopted. He wasn't really Fernando's son, so it was no mystery why the boy wasn't anything like Mendoza.

A cold determination filled her heart. When she married Fernando, their son would be his heir, not this adopted waif!

The group was going to dinner, and Mendoza escorted Belita and his son from the room, through the lobby, and down the street to *Roberto's Restaurante*.

The proprietor, impressed to have such aristocratic patrons, personally showed them to his best table, and took their order.

"Ricardo," Fernando said harshly, "sit up straight!" The boy was slumped in his chair, his small shoulders curved.

Obeying his father, he sat with good posture. Tears smarted his eyes, but he forcefully held them back. He shuddered to think what his father would do if he caught him crying in public. Ricardo was deeply depressed; he had loved his mother dearly, and now she was gone. He felt abandoned, lost, and completely alone.

A movement caught Ricardo's eye, and he watched as a boy not much older than himself approached their table. He was carrying a tray laden with a bottle of Roberto's best wine, and two long-stemmed glasses.

Carlos, feeling Ricardo's eyes on him, glanced curiously into the boy's face; but, as he did, he tripped over a loose plank in the floor, causing him to stumble forward. He lost his balance, and the tray tipped, sending the open bottle of wine, along with the glasses, tumbling into Mendoza's lap.

304

Fernando, bellowing angrily, bounded to his feet. Grabbing a napkin from the table, he wiped his wet trousers vigorously, but to no avail. The wine had soaked completely through.

Hurrying over, and apologizing profusely, Roberto assured Mendoza that he'd bring him another bottle of wine, and that the wine and dinner were free of charge. Considering what happened, it was the least he could do.

Mendoza's temper cooled, and returning to his chair, he calmly accepted the proprietor's apology.

Roberto then turned to Carlos. The boy was so scared that he was trembling. The man pressed his lips together, and his broad features twisted into a maddening leer. He was furious! Mumbling under his breath, he told Carlos, "Go to the woodshed and wait for me!"

The lad whirled about weakly, and moved away on wobbly legs. He knew Roberto would beat him for being so clumsy. The man had lashed his buttocks before, and he knew what to expect. Roberto would get his shaving strop, make him lower his pants, then he would lash him until he bled. It would take days for the lacerations to heal.

The woodshed was located behind the restaurant, and Carlos went into the kitchen, for he intended to go out the back door.

The cook, standing at the stove, had heard the commotion in the dining room. "What happened?" she asked Carlos.

He quickly told her.

She came close to weeping, for she knew Roberto would discipline the lad severely.

"You were wrong when you said God would save me!" Carlos yelled to the cook. "God is not going to save me! He does not care if I live or die! No one cares!" With tears gushing, he rushed outside and went to the woodshed to await his punishment.

Mendoza, having little appetite, merely picked at his food, but he drank quite a few glasses of wine. By the time they left the restaurant, he was noticeably tipsy.

Returning to the hotel, Belita took Ricardo to the room she shared with him, and got him ready for bed. Their quarters were next to Mendoza's, and she knocked lightly on the adjoining door, opened it a crack, and asked, "Patrón, may I talk to you for a moment?"

"Yes, of course," he said. He was at the dresser, pouring himself a glass of tequila.

"Señor," she began, "I don't mean to be forward, but at dinner, you seemed very preoccupied. Are you all right?"

He smiled warmly. "Yes, Belita, I am fine. Maybe, though, I am a little lonely."

Meanwhile, Ricardo had left his bed to listen at the closed door. He felt somewhat guilty, for he knew it was wrong to eavesdrop, but, despite his tender age, he was suspicious of Belita's motives. He had a feeling that she was planning to become his stepmother. He didn't like her, and he hoped his father wouldn't marry her. Pressing his ear against the door, he listened closely.

"Belita," Fernando was saying, "I am a very lonely man. I have been this way for a long time. Although I loved my wife, she was sickly for years and . . . and . . ."

A blush colored Belita's cheeks. "I understand, Patrón."

The liquor loosened his tongue. "Belita, I find you very beautiful and very desirable. I have wanted you for a long time. I know you are a lady, and I respect you

306

very much."

She knew what he was leading up to, but she wasn't about to succumb. She wanted to be his wife, not his mistress!

"I am also very unhappy. My son is a very big disappointment. He is nothing like me."

"But, Patrón, that is because he isn't really yours. You bought him from the Comancheros."

Ricardo, still listening, could hardly believe his ears. Mendoza wasn't his father? He had bought him from the Comancheros? It made no sense to him.

"There is no telling who his real parents are," Belita proceeded. "He does not have the Mendoza blood or bearing, and he will always be a disappointment to you. But do not be depressed, Patrón. You can marry again and have children of your own. You were married before this time, were you not? Your first wife gave you a son, yes?"

He nodded. "He was stillborn. A few hours later, my wife died. Then, as you know, my second wife was barren."

"You are still a vigorous man, and you can have many sons. You must marry a young, healthy woman who can bear these sons for you."

"A woman like you?" he asked.

She raised her chin proudly. "Yes, a woman like me."

He hurried to her side, and drew her into his arms. "Belita," he said huskily. "I will marry you, but we must wait until my period of mourning has passed."

"I know, Patrón."

"Call me Fernando."

He kissed her then, passionately and eagerly. "Belita," he whispered, "I am so starved for love. Please let me make love to you. Please!"

"I cannot," she said. "It would be wrong. We must wait until we are married."

Mendoza felt as though he couldn't wait. "Then to hell with tradition!" he said suddenly. "Come; we will go to the little village called Zaragosa. It is only five miles from here, but it has a church, and a priest. I will marry you tonight."

Belita, proud of herself, smiled complacently. "Very well, Fernando. What about Ricardo? Should I awaken him?"

"No, let him sleep. In the morning, we will tell him that he has a new mother."

Chapter Twenty-three

Ricardo was in bed pretending to be asleep when Belita came in to get her shawl. She was anxious to marry Fernando, and she didn't dally, but quickly grabbed her wrap and returned to the other room. Ricardo, listening closely, heard Belita and his father leave.

He remained in bed a long time, forcefully fighting back tears. Fernando had told him many times that it wasn't manly to cry. He had instilled the belief in the child so strongly that Ricardo hadn't even cried when his mother died, but had kept his tears bottled up inside.

Ricardo tried to fall asleep, but he was too troubled. He didn't want Belita to be his stepmother. He wasn't sure why he disliked her; she had never been cruel to him. But there was an aura of coldness about the woman that was chilling to a seven-year-old child.

Following an hour of tossing and turning, Ricardo flung the covers aside and got out of bed. He knew he wasn't supposed to leave his room, and he rarely disobeyed his father, but he wanted to go outside. The boy at the restaurant had been on his mind, and he hoped that he might find him. Ricardo had seen the fury in the proprietor's eyes, and he was certain that the boy had been harshly punished. He felt sorry for him; but his feelings went farther than that — for some reason, which he couldn't possibly understand, there seemed to be a some kind of bond between himself and the boy.

Ricardo dressed and left his room. He didn't question this strange link between himself and Carlos, for he was too young to be consciously aware of it. He was simply reacting spontaneously; at the moment, finding Carlos seemed like a good idea. He was lonely, and wanted to talk to someone close to his own age.

He made his way down the wooden sidewalk. It was crowded with townspeople, rovers, and drunks. Music, laughter, and loud voices were coming from the packed saloons, and the main thoroughfare was filled with horsemen, most of them shouting vociferously, some shooting their pistols into the air.

Ricardo, reaching the restaurant, was surprised to find that it was closed. It must be later than he thought. Disappointed, he turned and started back to the hotel. A narrow alley ran beside the restaurant, it led to Roberto's woodshed and his dilapidated barn. A lantern was lit inside the barn, and someone was moving about. Hoping it was Carlos, Ricardo headed down the alley. He approached the barn quietly, went to the open door, and looked inside.

Carlos was there, packing provisions on a burro. Catching a movement, he whirled about warily, for he was certain he was about to come face to face with Roberto. He was indeed relieved to see it was only a youngster.

"I didn't mean to scare you," Ricardo said, for he had seen Carlos's fear.

"Who are you, and what are you doing here?" Carlos asked. "I remember you! You were in the restaurant with your rich papa and mama." Carlos's expression turned a little bitter, for he couldn't help but envy the boy—he had everything Carlos wished he had.

Tentatively, Ricardo moved farther into the barn. "Your papa was very angry when you spilled the tray. Did he punish you?"

"He isn't my papa, he is my uncle. Yes, he punished me. He whipped me with his razor strop." He regarded his young companion uncertainly. "Why do you ask? What is it to you?"

Ricardo shrugged.

Suddenly, Carlos laughed. "You are a strange one. You better go back to your papa and mama before they come looking for you."

"She is not my mama, she is my nurse. But she and Papa are getting married." He paused, looked down at his feet, then raising his gaze back to Carlos's, he murmured desolately, "He is not really my papa."

"How do you know?"

"Belita, my nurse, she said that Papa bought me from the Comancheros." He looked confused. "I'm not sure I understand what that means."

"You are foolish to worry about it. Your papa loves you, and he takes good care of you. You know, it is strange, but my uncle bought me from the Comancheros, too."

Ricardo was astounded. "Really?"

"Yes, really! My mother married a gringo, and they had a home across the border. They were attacked by the Apaches, who took me and sold me to the Comancheros. My uncle found me, and bought me back."

"Do you remember being captured by the Apaches?" Ricardo asked, enthralled.

"No, but I think I remember being with the Comancheros." A thatch of dark hair was falling across his brow, he brushed it back distractedly. "I only know what Uncle Roberto has told me."

Noticing the packed burro, Ricardo asked, "Are you

311

going somewhere?"

"Yes, I am running away."

"But why?" he asked, surprised.

"My uncle is meaner than the devil, and I hate him! If my mother married a gringo, then maybe I have kin across the border. I plan to look for them."

Ricardo was impressed, for he thought the older boy was very courageous. He wished he had the nerve to strike out on his own. Why not? he suddenly thought. He was unhappy with his life, and with Belita as his new mother, he knew he would be even unhappier. Besides, he told himself, Fernando wasn't really his father—although he still wasn't sure exactly what that implied. But if he was sold by the Comancheros, then maybe he also had kin across the border.

"I want to run away with you!" he remarked, the decision making his heart beat rapidly.

Carlos was shocked. "Are you crazy? Your father will come looking for you."

Ricardo wasn't so sure. "He doesn't like me. And now that he has Belita, he will probably be glad that I am gone."

"No, you cannot come with me. You are too young. By morning, you will be crying for your papa!"

"Never!" Ricardo exclaimed. "I would never cry for him! I hope I never see him again!" He raised his chin proudly. "I am not a cry-baby! It is unmanly to cry! I did not even cry when my mother died, and I loved her very much."

"All right," Carlos gave in. "You can come with me, but if you change your mind, you will have to come back by yourself."

Ricardo held out his hand. "It is a deal."

Smiling, Carlos shook the boy's hand. He wasn't sure why, but he liked the youngster. "Come; we must leave quickly. I want to be miles away before my uncle

312

misses me."

Ricardo's face brightened. "I will not be missed for hours, for Papa and Belita have gone to Zaragosa."

"You will have to wear what you have on. We can't take time to go back to the hotel."

"That's all right. I don't mind." Ricardo was determined not to be a problem.

Carlos extinguished the lantern, took the reins to the burro, and with Ricardo following, they left the barn. Keeping to the back alleys, they made their way out of town.

Carlos wasn't sure which direction would take him to the border, nor did he know how far away it was. However, he wasn't about to tell this to Ricardo, for he knew the boy was depending on him.

The full moon kept the night from being quite so dark and threatening. Nonetheless, both boys found their shadowy surroundings a little frightening; but they didn't dare admit such weakness to each other.

Despite their fear, they trudged onward, slowly putting more and more distance between themselves and El Zarango.

The sun had barely crested the horizon when Caroline awoke with a start. She had been dreaming about her brothers. Now, awake, she tried to remember exactly what she had dreamt, but she couldn't recall a thing. Still, she was troubled, for she knew that the dream hadn't been pleasant. Again, she sensed that her brothers needed her.

She sat up, and looked about the campsite. The others were still in their bedrolls. The fire was only embers, she went over and added more branches, then prepared a pot of coffee. She tried not to think about Ross and Emily, but she might as well have willed herself not to breathe. How could she help but not think about them? Ross had been her future, her reason for living, and, now, it was all over. She couldn't recall ever being more disillusioned.

All at once, sensing a presence behind her, she glanced over her shoulder. It was Ross. He had gotten up so quietly that she hadn't heard him.

"Good morning," he said, smiling.

She was tempted to slap that smile off his face. Anger simmered within her like a living thing. "There's nothing good about this morning!" she spat.

Ross was bewildered. "Caroline, honey, what's wrong?"

"Don't call me 'honey'!" she said sharply, bounding to her feet. She preferred to confront him at eye level.

"Do you mind telling me what the hell's wrong with you?" His own temper was surfacing.

"As if you didn't know!"

"If I knew I wouldn't ask."

Suddenly, Sánchez came into view. He had taken the last watch, and was returning to camp. Smiling at Ross and Caroline, he called cheerfully, *"Buenos dias."*

"Haven't you heard?" Ross asked with an irritated note. "There's nothing good about the morning."

"You are wrong, *amigo*. It is a fine morning, for I will soon be ten thousand dollars richer."

The others began to awaken and leave their bedrolls. Ross leaned closer to Caroline, and said in a quiet, firm tone, "Later, you can tell me what's bothering you."

"With pleasure!" she lashed out.

"I hate to sound impatient," Rolando butted in, speaking to Ross, "but when do I get the money?"

"After breakfast," he replied tersely.

Sánchez didn't argue — he could wait a little longer.

Mary helped Caroline prepare the morning meal. Emily, who considered such work beneath her, sat be-

314

side Ross and flirted with him.

Emily's actions grated on Caroline's nerves. The woman was impossible! But, apparently, Ross didn't think so! Why couldn't he see that she was a phony? Evidently all he could see was a beautiful woman who had him totally bewitched. Caroline's opinion of Ross dropped immensely. Furthermore, she felt that she no longer respected him. She hoped, with time, she could stop loving him!

Following breakfast, Ross went to the pack mule, got a shovel, and motioned for Sánchez to join him. Together, they walked off into the distance.

"The money must be buried close by," Mary said to Caroline. She gathered up the dishes to wash them. A pot of hot water was simmering on the fire.

"Don't wash those dishes," Caroline told her. "It's about time Emily did something. Last night, we cooked supper and cleaned up, and this morning we cooked breakfast. Now it's her turn." She looked at Emily, who was sitting at the fire doing nothing.

"Miss Parker," she called, a cold smile on her face.

"Yes?" Emily responded.

"It's your turn to do the dishes."

Their gazes locked heatedly. "As far as I'm concerned, you can throw the dishes away."

"That wouldn't be very smart. You and the others will need these dishes for the remainder of your journey. Unless you intend to eat off the ground."

"The remainder of 'our' journey?" Emily questioned. "Aren't you coming with us to Dry Branch?"

"No, I plan to go to El Zarango."

"With Ross?" She smiled cattily, as though she knew for a fact that he wasn't going.

"I plan to go alone." Actually, Caroline's thoughts hadn't gotten that far. But it didn't matter, after what happened last night, she wanted to get away from Ross.

315

She'd get her brothers back without his help.

Speaking to Mary, Emily asked sweetly, "You don't mind washing the dishes, do you?"

"Yes, I do mind. I agree with Caroline. You should start doing your fair share."

"Very well," Emily conceded, "I'll wash the dishes." She looked back at Caroline, saying, "I suppose I might as well get used to it. I'm sure it'll be awhile before Ross can afford to hire servants." She suddenly put her hand over her mouth, giving the impression that the statement had accidentally slipped out. "My goodness!" she gasped, feigning embarrassment. "I must learn to think before I say things."

Caroline felt that she had won the battle, but had lost the war. In her own spiteful way, Emily had been victorious. She moved to her pallet, knelt, and began rolling the blankets.

Kirk, joining her, kneeled at her side, and said softly, "Caroline, I don't know what's going on between you and Emily, but Ross isn't planning on marrying her."

"Oh?" she questioned. "How do you know? Have you asked him?"

"No," he replied.

"Then how can you be so sure?"

"I know Ross."

"Well, maybe you don't know him as well as you think you do."

Kirk didn't pressure her. He left to tend to the horses, and shortly thereafter, Ross and Sánchez returned. Rolando was smiling, for he was carrying the bag containing ten thousand dollars.

Working quickly, everyone packed their gear, the fire was smothered, and the horses were saddled.

Sánchez said his goodbyes, and was mounting his horse to leave when he was suddenly stopped by the sounds of approaching riders. He stepped away from his horse and watched as the group drew closer. He considered grabbing his rifle, but prudently changed his mind, for he and the others were greatly outnumbered. He estimated at least twenty men arriving. Recognizing the man riding in the lead, caused anxiety to writhe in his stomach. He had confronted the man on more than one occasion, but he had always had his Comancheros to back him up. Now, with only two of his men to stand behind him, he hoped the man wasn't here to cause trouble.

Ross and Caroline also recognized the man leading his vaqueros. Caroline, however, could hardly believe her eyes. Now, she didn't need to go to Fernando Mendoza, he was coming to her!

Meanwhile, Alfredo, already mounted, sent his horse into a sudden run. He, too, had recognized Mendoza, and he knew the man would kill him for murdering his sister. He hadn't gotten very far before a bullet from Mendoza's rifle slammed into his shoulder, throwing him to the ground.

Two men rode out to get Alfredo, and the rest pulled up their horses. Mendoza dismounted, stepped to Belita's horse, and helped her down. He kept an arm about her waist.

Fernando's gaze, sweeping over Ross and the others, rested briefly on Sánchez. But at the moment, the outlaw's presence didn't interest him. He turned his gaze back to Ross. "Señor Bennett, it is a pleasure to see you. May I introduce my wife? This is Belita. We were married last night."

"Married!" Ross gasped.

"*Sí*, but then you don't know, do you? My wife, Leonora, died a few weeks ago."

Ross didn't say anything about the man's brief mourning, for he didn't consider it his business.

Mendoza continued, "We are looking for my son,

Ricardo. He ran away last night."

"Ran away!" Caroline cried, evidently alarmed.

"Sí, señorita." He regarded Caroline curiously, for he couldn't imagine why she seemed so upset.

The two men, one of them Roberto, returned with Alfredo. Caroline was astonished to see the restaurant's proprietor. Why was he riding with Mendoza?

"Why did you shoot Alfredo?" Sánchez asked Fernando.

"I have been looking for him for a long time. He killed my sister. Now, I will kill him. If you try to intervene, señor, I will be forced to kill you as well." His tone left no doubt.

Sánchez wasn't about to interfere. As far as he was concerned, Alfredo was on his own. "Señor Mendoza, if it is all right with you, I would like to leave." He pointed at Juan. "He will leave with me."

Fernando had no objections. "Go; I do not care. But, Sánchez, I will give you some advice I hope you will heed. Do not become involved with the Revolutionists. Díaz will not be overthrown. If you get involved, you will die."

Rolando smiled easily. "I will remember what you said, señor." He went to his horse, mounted, and with Juan at his side, they galloped away from the area.

Fernando said to Ross, "Señor, if you should come across Ricardo and another boy, I will pay you handsomely to deliver them to me."

"Another boy?" Caroline asked, cutting in. "Did Ricardo run away with Carlos?" She wondered if that was why Roberto was here.

"What do you know about Carlos?" Mendoza questioned. He was somewhat perturbed, for he thought the señorita was too forward.

"I know Carlos works for Roberto," Caroline replied.

318

"When I was looking about town for Ricardo," Mendoza explained, "I found Roberto searching for Carlos. It would seem that the boys ran away together."

Caroline, her eyes fighting mad, said strongly, "Well, if I find the boys, I'm not bringing them back to you, or to Roberto!"

Mendoza was taken aback. "Señorita, who do you think you are to make such threats?"

"I'll tell you who I am! I'm their sister! Carlos and Ricardo are my brothers! The Apaches kidnapped them five years ago, then traded them to the Comancheros for rifles. You and Roberto bought them as though they were cattle! Well, they don't belong to either one of you! I'm taking them home to their grandfather! Now, if you want to threaten me like you threatened Sánchez, then go right ahead! But the only way you're going to stop me from claiming my brothers is to kill me!"

"Kill you? That can be arranged, señorita." Mendoza's expression was deadly serious.

Chapter Twenty-four

Ross clutched Caroline's arm, and drew her close. "Control that damn temper of yours," he whispered angrily. "Haven't you ever heard of diplomacy?"

"Diplomacy?" she spat, wresting free. "What would a two-timing snake like you know about diplomacy?"

She was pushing Ross too far, and his patience was wearing thin. He couldn't imagine what was bothering her, but he was determined to find out. However, this wasn't the time. "Try to be quiet," he said softly to Caroline. "And let me handle this."

She responded with a defiant glare.

Ross turned to Mendoza. "Fernando, we apparently have a lot to discuss, but first I think we should concentrate on finding the boys."

He agreed. "*Sí,* señor. We will ride together. But before we leave, I have some business to take care of with Alfredo."

Ross knew what Mendoza had in mind, and he didn't want the women to witness the execution. "Why don't I ride ahead with the ladies?"

"There's no reason, señor. This will not take long." He moved to Alfredo, who was being held forcefully by two vaqueros. "You are lucky that I am in a hurry,"

Mendoza said to his prisoner. "Otherwise, you would die slowly at the end of a rope."

Alfredo was shaking. "Please, Señor Mendoza, don't kill me! Your sister's death was an accident! I didn't mean to hurt her!"

"You liar!" Fernando raged, drawing back an arm and slapping the man across the face. He took his pistol from its holster, aimed it at Alfredo's head, and pulled the trigger. The man was dead before his body hit the ground.

"Leave him for the buzzards!" Mendoza ordered.

Ross urged Caroline to her horse. She moved stiffly, for she was somewhat in shock. Everything had happened so quickly. Within a matter of seconds, a man's life was over!

"Caroline," Ross said, keeping his voice low, "Mendoza might be an aristocrat, but he can kill without blinking an eye. Remember that, and tread cautiously."

"He wouldn't kill a woman, would he?"

"Yes, if he considered her a serious threat."

A shiver ran through her. "He's worse than Sánchez."

"But Sánchez is considered a renegade, Mendoza is a wealthy landowner, and a personal friend of Díaz's. He has the law on his side."

Caroline sighed miserably. "He'll never agree to give me Daniel!"

"I don't think it's hopeless."

"Why do you say that?"

"I happened to be looking at Belita when you told Mendoza who you are. I could be mistaken, but I think she was happy to learn that Daniel's your brother."

"Why would that make her happy?"

"Fernando's wife, Leonora, couldn't have children, but Belita's a different story. I'm sure she hopes to give Mendoza several children, especially sons."

Caroline understood. Her eyes shining, she said excitedly, "She doesn't want her sons to share Mendoza's wealth with Daniel!"

"Exactly. And more importantly, Daniel's the oldest, which means, he'll be Mendoza's first heir."

"I'll try to find an opportunity to talk alone with Belita and feel her out."

The others were mounted and ready to leave. Ross quickly helped Caroline onto her horse, then hurrying to his appaloosa, he swung into the saddle.

The riders pulled out, leaving Alfredo's body where it had fallen. A flock of buzzards had already congregated, and they hovered overhead, their wings flapping noisily. The carrion-eating birds sent a repulsive shudder through Caroline, and her stomach churned uneasily.

Mendoza told his vaqueros to spread out and search in different directions, while he stayed with Ross and the others. Kirk, leading the way, looked for signs of the boys' passing.

They stopped at noon to rest their horses. Caroline was growing extremely concerned. She tried not to think of the dangers that could befall Walter and Daniel in this vast desert terrain.

Noticing that Mendoza was occupied talking to Ross and Kirk, Caroline decided to talk alone with Belita. The young woman was sitting beneath a tall mesquite, and Caroline went over and joined her.

"May I speak to you as one woman to another?" Caroline asked.

Belita eyed her a little suspiciously. "What about?"

"My brother."

"I think you should discuss Ricardo with my husband."

322

"Please, Belita, I need your help!"

"I do not see how I can help you."

"If you feel the way I think you do, then you can help me a great deal."

Belita looked at her questioningly.

"Don't you want your firstborn son to be Fernando's heir? You can be honest with me, Belita. It's only natural that you should feel that way."

"*Sí*, I do," she admitted.

"Then you should let Fernando know how you feel. Maybe he feels the same way."

Belita wasn't so sure.

"Are Ricardo and Fernando close?"

She shook her head. "No, not at all. Ricardo was very close to his mother. I do not think the boy even likes his father."

"Why not?"

"They are too different. Ricardo is a very quiet and studious child."

"Just like Papa!" Caroline remarked. "As a boy, my father was like that. He became a minister."

"Then Ricardo must take after his real papa, *sí*?"

"So it would seem. Tell me, Belita, do you think Fernando loves Ricardo?"

She shrugged. "I am not sure. I was Ricardo's nurse for over a year. During that time, I never saw them embrace like father and son. Ricardo avoids his father whenever possible."

Caroline stood up quickly. "Thank you, Belita. You have been very helpful." She headed toward Mendoza, and there was a purposeful intent in her walk. He was still conversing with Ross and Kirk, his back was facing Caroline.

"Mr. Mendoza, I must talk to you," she said firmly.

He turned with a quick snap of his shoulders. "What do you want, señorita?" he asked, his tone testy.

323

Her eyes, fearless, stared into his. "I want you to give back my brother. You don't love him, and he doesn't love you. There's no reason for you to keep him. Furthermore, you just married a young woman who can give you sons of your own. You don't need Daniel, and when you have children of your own, you won't even want him. He's nothing like you, so you'll never understand him. As he grows older, you two will grow even farther apart."

"Señorita," he cut in brusquely, "have you been talking to Belita?"

"What if I have?" Her eyes were defiant.

If Mendoza was upset, she couldn't tell, for his expression was inscrutable. "You have made your point, señorita. I will think over what you said."

Caroline decided not to pressure him. Besides, she was sure that, for now, he had no more to say. Taking Ross's earlier advice, she diplomatically thanked him, then walked away.

She went over to Mary, who was drinking out of a canteen. She handed it to Caroline, who took a couple of deep swallows. She handed the canteen back to Mary, and said, "I'm awfully worried about Walter and Daniel. I can hardly bear to think of them out there somewhere all alone!"

Mary managed an encouraging smile. "We'll find them, and I'm sure they'll be all right."

Caroline, responding, smiled a little shakily. "Mary, you're a wonderful friend. Considering all the trouble I've caused you, I wouldn't blame you if you refused to talk to me."

"Trouble? Whatever do you mean?"

"Thanks to me, you were taken hostage by Apaches, then you were blindfolded and taken to Sánchez's hideout, and now you're caught up in all of this."

"Caroline, please don't worry about it. I'm holding

up just fine. And I don't blame you for anything that has happened."

"Well, I do!" Emily said, appearing suddenly. She had walked up to the women so quietly that they hadn't heard her.

"I really don't care what you think!" Caroline retorted.

Emily wasn't dissuaded, she was determined to speak her mind. "Thanks to you, we're wasting time searching for two runaway boys. Did it ever occur to you that some of us might not like it?"

"Some of us?" Caroline questioned. "Are you referring to yourself and Ross?"

"Well, I am anxious to get this journey over with, and I'm sure Ross feels the same way."

"Then I suggest you take your complaint to him."

"Oh, I will. You can count on it." Her smug expression had an air of victory about it.

"We're pulling out!" Ross called, getting their attention.

Emily moved away, and walked to her horse. Ross was standing close by. "Ross," she said, smiling sweetly, "will you give me a hand?"

Obliging, he assisted her onto her horse.

Watching, Caroline seethed inwardly. Since Mendoza's arrival, she had been so involved with finding her brothers that she hadn't really thought about Emily and Ross. But, now, their clandestine kiss flashed painfully across her mind. It brought tears to her eyes, but she willfully controlled them. She would never let them see her cry! Never!

She went to her own horse, and Ross hurried over to help her mount. Turning on him with sudden fury, she said harshly, "I can manage by myself, thank you!"

Ross, fed up, said angrily, "Fine!" He wheeled about abruptly.

Their curt exchange didn't escape Emily's watchful eyes, and she smiled complacently. She was confident that Ross would soon be hers!

Carlos sat under a cottonwood, watching Ricardo sleep. The boys had stopped to rest, and Ricardo had fallen asleep almost immediately. Carlos was also fatigued, but troubled thoughts were keeping him awake. He was lost, completely. He had no idea of their location, or in which direction lay the Rio Grande. He knew in order to cross the border, he had to find the river. He supposed it would be somewhere to the north, and he thought they had been traveling in that direction. But he couldn't be sure if their course had veered. He had packed enough food for three or four days, but that had been with only himself in mind, and now, he was sharing his rations with Ricardo. He wasn't sure how long their water would last, but it was already getting low.

He leaned back against the tree's trunk, and looked vacantly about the area. Clouds of yellow dust, stirred by a gentle breeze, were the only movement across the cactus-dotted land. Clumps of sun-dried grass, intermingled with prickly sagebrush, added a dreary aspect. The surrounding tableau was stark and dismal.

Carlos sighed wearily, his spirits drooping. Reluctantly, he admitted to himself that running away had been a mistake. He and Ricardo would probably wander aimlessly for days until, finally, they died from lack of water. The prospect was frightening, and Carlos shivered in spite of the heat. Suddenly, he thought of something even worse than dying of thirst. What if they were captured by Apaches? The mere chance caused his heart to beat rapidly. Why hadn't he considered all this before running away? He grew angry with

326

himself, for he had acted very foolishly. But at the time, all he could think of was getting away from Roberto.

He shifted uncomfortably, for sitting was uncomfortable. Roberto had lashed his buttocks severely, and the lacerations were painful. He knew it would be days before they healed.

Suddenly, the sound of galloping horses sent Carlos leaping to his feet. A hard fist of fear grew in his stomach, and his whole body tightened. He watched wide-eyed as a group of riders came into view. They had obviously spotted him, for they were charging in his direction. He started to awaken Ricardo, who was still sound asleep, but his mouth was so dry from fright that he couldn't speak. He prayed that Roberto wasn't among these riders who were quickly advancing. However, he had no more uttered the prayer than he recognized Roberto's white stallion. Carlos's heart sank, and he knees weakened, causing him to sway precariously.

He leaned against the tree, for he was so scared that he needed support to stay on his feet. He knew Roberto would punish him viciously for running away.

The group arrived, and Carlos's fear was momentarily supplanted with curiosity as he recognized the señorita called "Caroline." He couldn't imagine why she was here. His puzzled gaze swept quickly over the others. The vaqueros were searching a different area, and Mendoza drew his pistol, sending three shots into the air — a signal that the boys had been found.

The shots brought Ricardo awake with a start, and he sat up rigidly. His gaze met Fernando's, and he winced as though he had been physically struck. His heart thumped against his rib cage, and he tried to stand up, but his legs felt like jelly.

Caroline dismounted quickly. The obvious fear in

the boys' eyes tore painfully into her heart. Her instincts had been right—her brothers did need her!

She didn't know which boy to embrace first, but Daniel was closer, so she went to him. Kneeling, she drew him into her arms, hugging him tightly.

The child was understandably confused. He had no idea why this lady was holding him, but he didn't resist, for her arms were comforting.

Taking Daniel's hand, Caroline moved to Carlos. She ached to embrace him also, but in an effort to avoid her, he took a step backward.

"Try to remember me," she told him.

"I remember you, señorita. One day, you came to the restaurant."

"My name is Caroline. Does that name mean anything to you?"

"I think maybe I have heard it before."

"What about the name Walter?"

He shrugged. He wished he knew why she was asking these strange questions.

"Your name is Walter," she said. "You and Ricardo are my brothers." She looked at Ricardo. "Do you speak English?" Caroline's English had improved tremendously.

He nodded. "Sí, señorita. I speak a little."

"Five years ago," she told both boys, "our family was attacked by Apaches. Our parents were killed, I was abducted, and you two were traded to the Comancheros for rifles." She spoke directly to Carlos. "You were sold to Roberto." She then spoke to Ricardo. "You were sold to Mr. Mendoza."

Ricardo was able to follow what she said, and her words didn't come as a complete shock to him or Carlos, for they already knew part of it. They were, however, shocked to learn that this lady was their sister, and that they were brothers.

328

For a long moment, a tense silence hung in the air. It was finally broken by Carlos, who dared to ask, "Señorita, will you take me home with you?" Bravely, he cast Roberto an oblique glance. The man was glaring at him.

"Of course I'm taking you home." She turned to Mendoza, who was still on his horse. "I hope to take you both home."

He dismounted slowly, moved closer to Caroline, and said, "I am sorry to disappoint you, señorita, but Ricardo is mine. I intend to keep him."

"No!" Ricardo yelled. It was spontaneous, and he was instantly sorry, for he feared his father would punish him for being impertinent.

Mendoza eyed the boy sternly. "You will do as I say! You are my son."

"He isn't your son!" Belita suddenly exclaimed. Getting down from her horse, she hurried to Fernando. "He is not your son by blood, nor is he your son in his heart. He does not love you, Fernando! Let him go! I will give you sons who will love you, and who will be worthy of you! Please do not force our sons to share your name and your estate with Ricardo! Don't you see? Ricardo is not worthy of your love—he does not even want it! He would rather leave with his sister!"

Ross, dismounting, said to Mendoza, "Your wife is right. Everything considered, it would be better if you let the boy go."

Fernando turned to Ricardo. "Is that what you want? Do not be afraid to tell the truth."

Ricardo swallowed heavily, drew upon all his courage, and answered softly, *"Sí,* it is what I want."

Mendoza, his voice touched with sadness, said to no one in particular, "I am not a man without feelings. In my own way, I love Ricardo. But I am reasonable, and I know he and I can never truly be as father and son.

Adopting him was a mistake. He could never be a Mendoza. He belongs with his own family." He looked at Caroline, and said without a trace of anger, "Take your brother. He is yours."

Belita touched her husband's arm, saying kindly, "You will not be sorry, Fernando. You have made the right decision."

"Sí, I know. As soon as my vaqueros get here, we will leave."

"In that case," Ross remarked, "we'll be leaving too. We still have a long way to go."

"Wait a minute, señor!" Roberto said, swinging down from his horse. "What about Carlos? He belongs to me! If the señorita wants him back, she will have to pay me!"

"Roberto," Ross began, his tone threatening. "If you value your face, you'll keep your mouth shut."

The man, familiar with Bennett's reputation, backed off. He had hoped the señorita would offer him some money, but he wasn't about to insist on it.

"Caroline," Ross said, "Daniel can ride with you, and I'll take Walter."

She agreed, and taking Daniel by the hand, she led him to her horse. As they walked past Fernando, he almost reached out to embrace Ricardo, but he couldn't quite go through with it.

Ross motioned to Carlos, and he hurried over. "Señor," he began, obviously hesitant, "can my burro come too? His name is Pecos, and he is like a pet."

Ross chuckled. "He's more than welcome." He lifted Carlos, but as he placed him on the horse, the boy winced painfully. "What's wrong?" Ross asked.

"Nothing, señor," he answered, unable to meet Ross's eyes. He didn't want anyone to know that he was too sore to ride horseback, for he was afraid they would leave him behind.

But Ricardo blurted out the truth, "His bottom hurts, and he cannot ride."

Gently, Ross lifted him down, then taking his arm, he led him to the other side of his horse, where the others couldn't see. He drew down the boy's trousers, and the sight of the child's deeply cut buttocks enraged him. Somehow, he managed to keep a hold on his temper long enough to ask Kirk to cut branches from the cottonwood to make a travois.

Then, going to Roberto, and moving with the quickness of a striking snake, he struck him across the jaw. As the man's head snapped back, Ross smashed a fist into his opponent's stomach.

Roberto stumbled forward, and Ross finished him off with a vicious uppercut that broke the man's nose. He fell limply to the ground, his face covered with spewing blood.

"Get up, you son of a bitch, and I'll kill you!" Ross said, his tone deadly serious.

The man wasn't about to move.

Ross went to Caroline, who was sitting on her horse with Daniel. "That ugly bastard beat Walter unmercifully." His voice took on a note of wonder, "Caroline, you always knew your brothers needed you and I'll be damned if you weren't right!"

She smiled beautifully. "Yes, and thank God, I found them!

Chapter Twenty-five

Alex went quickly to Bryan's office. He was enthused, and could hardly wait to tell his brother about the man he had just met. Bryan was sitting at his desk when Alex barged inside. "Jake Mackenna's in the saloon! Him and I just got through talkin'!"

"Mackenna?" Bryan questioned, failing to place the name.

"Yeah! It was him and his brother who got into a shootout with the Bennetts in El Zarango."

"Yes, now I remember."

"Well, he's lookin' for Ross. He intends to kill 'im. I told 'im not to be too eager, 'cause we might be able to use 'im."

Bryan was upset. "Damn it, Alex! When are you going to learn to keep your big mouth shut?"

"What are you so mad about?"

"We don't know this Mackenna. He's probably a damned blackmailer. Exactly what did you tell him?"

"I didn't tell 'im nothin'."

"I find that hard to believe. You must have told him something."

Alex's enthusiasm was faltering. "I just told 'im not to do anything rash 'cause we might need his services. I didn't say anything specific. Hell, Bryan, I ain't stupid!"

"That's highly questionable!" Bryan remarked.

"Well, what do you want me to do? You want me to tell 'im that we ain't gonna need 'im?"

"No. I'm sure that Jake Mackenna is dangerous, and you have no doubt raised his curiosity. He probably sees a chance to make himself a great deal of money. He's not going to simply go away. Also, we might need his services, although I don't foresee it. You better tell him to lay low and that we'll keep in touch with him."

"But where can he stay?"

Bryan thought for a moment, then decided, "I have a vacant room upstairs. He can stay there."

"But what if we don't need 'im?"

"Then we'll pay him for his time."

"That's kinda wastin' money, ain't it?"

"Yes, thanks to you! From now on, keep your damned mouth shut!" A firm knock sounded on the door. "Who's there?" Bryan called out.

"Bill," came the reply.

Bryan told Alex to take Mackenna upstairs, then he invited Bill inside.

Alex mumbled a quick hello to his stepfather before dashing out of the office.

"Bryan," Bill began, "have you seen Rebecca?"

"Not today," he replied.

"That's strange. She's supposed to have dinner with you."

An uneasy pang settled in Bryan's stomach. Damn it! Alex's incompetence was hard enough to deal with, and now Rebecca was obviously up to something!

"She told me you two had a dinner date," Bill explained. "After she left the Bar-H, I started thinking

333

about how I've been neglecting her lately, so I decided to come to town and join you for dinner."

Bryan ran a hand nervously through his hair. "I completely forgot I was supposed to have dinner with Mother!" he lied, pretending embarrassment. He glanced at his watch, and acting as though he were relieved, he said, "But it's still early. I'm not late. Mother probably got a room at the hotel. Why don't you stay here and have a drink, and I'll go get her?"

"No, that's all right," Bill replied. "If she's rented a room, then I can wash up before dinner." He moved to the door, opened it, and said over his shoulder, "I'll see you later."

Bryan's uneasiness intensified. Why had his mother lied about a dinner engagement? What the hell was she up to?

Disgusted, he slammed his fist against the desk top. He had a feeling that Alex and Rebecca were going to ruin everything!

Rebecca, lying naked in Parker's arms, stretched with sexual contentment. Henry was such a superb lover! Their encounters always left her wonderfully fulfilled, yet anxiously awaiting the next time.

Henry leaned up on an elbow, looked down at her, and admired her bared beauty. Although he cared nothing about her emotionally, he was drawn to her physically, for she was a very provocative woman. Also, she was a ravenous lover who knew how to please her partner. Yes, Henry was well-satisfied with Rebecca, however, he wasn't pursuing a long term involvement. She was just a passing fancy. Furthermore, he didn't see how any man could take her for a very long period of time. She was too passionately wild—he had several scratches on his back to prove it. Even if she were free, he wouldn't want her for a mistress, for she was too demanding and uncontrolled.

"Why don't you go to your room, get cleaned up, and I'll take you to dinner?" Henry suggested.

"Do you think we should be seen together?"

"I'm sure no one will think anything of it. When you go home just be sure and mention it to your husband. That way, if he hears about us having dinner, he won't think we were trying to hide anything."

"But he thinks I'm having dinner with Bryan."

"Tell him Bryan couldn't make it."

Agreeing, she got out of bed and hastily put on her clothes, which were strewn here and there. Earlier, she had been eager to remove them, and hadn't cared where the garments had fallen.

Henry slipped on a robe, took Rebecca's arm, and escorted her to the door. Her appearance was unkempt, for she hadn't bothered to completely button her dress, and her hair was falling about her shoulders in disarray.

Rebecca's room was directly across from Henry's. He opened his door, peeked down the hall, and finding it empty, turned to tell her it was safe to leave. Rebecca, taking him by surprise, impulsively threw herself into his arms and kissed him fervently.

It was at this moment that Bill entered the hallway. The desk clerk had given him Rebecca's room number, and he was on his way to see her. The sight of his wife in Parker's arms brought his steps to a sudden halt. Shocked, he looked on as Rebecca kissed Parker passionately while moving a hand down under his robe to fondle him intimately.

Hanley, his anger now raging, went to the lovers; his hand descended heavily on Rebecca's shoulder, jerking her out of Parker's arms.

"Bill!" she cried, her face paling.

Henry, his body rigid, cold perspiration suddenly layering his brow, uttered with uncanny calm, "Mr. Hanley, I don't know what to say."

"If you want to stay alive, you won't say anything!" Bill said fiercely. He turned his fury on Rebecca. "I told you after your last lover that if you ever cheated again, I would divorce you! I meant what I said, Rebecca! I want you to go to the ranch, pack your clothes, and leave my home for good!" He wheeled about abruptly and moved quickly down the hall.

Rebecca brushed past Henry, and went back into his room. He followed her inside, closing the door.

"I'm glad he found us," she remarked strongly. "Once I'm free, we can get married."

"Married!" Parker exclaimed.

"Yes! Isn't that what you want?"

He guffawed. "You can't be serious! Marry you?"

"Why not?" she asked, her voice almost a screech.

"I don't marry whores."

"How dare you! I'm not a whore!"

"Aren't you?" he taunted. "I know all about you, Rebecca. Remember the lover you had in Albuquerque? He happens to be a close friend of mine. He liked talking about you, and he told me your whole sordid past. I know that you were a prostitute working in New Orleans when you met the father of your sons. He lived with you, but he never married you. He was a riverboat gambler, and one night he was killed in a card game. You put your sons in a boarding school and returned to prostitution. Eventually, you had a falling out with the Madam, and she threw you back on the streets. That's when you decided to move to Dry Branch and live with your

336

brother. You took your sons out of school, came here, and pretended to be a widow. Then, when you met Hanley, you set out to marry him for his money."

"My past shouldn't be a factor between us. You desire me madly, and you can't get enough of me! If you don't want to get married, we can remain lovers." She was confident that, in time, she could persuade him to marry her.

"I don't want you as a lover any more than I want you as a wife. Our relationship is a passing fling. Besides, there's a woman back in Albuquerque who I am seriously considering marrying. She's a true lady, Rebecca—in every sense of the word."

"You don't love her!" she spat, unable to admit that she hadn't totally bewitched him herself.

"In my own way, I love her very much," he replied. He sounded like he meant it.

With terrible suddenness, Rebecca was struck with the truth of the situation. She had no control over Henry, and he couldn't care less about her. She was consumed by fury, and she lashed out viciously, "You heartless cad! Don't you realize what you have done? Thanks to you, Bill plans to divorce me! I'll be lucky if he agrees to give me a pittance of support! My God, I wasted years of my life on that man! And what do I get for my effort? Nothing! And it's all your fault!" Enraged, she drew back her arm and slapped him soundly across the cheek.

The sharp smack reddened his face, and put fire in his eyes. He was furious, causing the veins in his forehead to stand out and his features to twist into a malicious sneer. He controlled the urge to slap her back, for he had never hit a woman. He prided himself on being a gentleman, but he knew his restraint was tenuous. Afraid he would indeed strike her if she

337

remained, he grabbed her arm, and forced her to the door. Opening it, he ordered gruffly, "Get out of here before I forget you're a woman and knock the hell out of you!" That she actually had the gall to slap him was infuriating. The cheap little floozy! Who did she think she was?

When she didn't leave of her own accord, he shoved her into the hall. She lost her footing, and fell heavily to the floor.

"I'm warning you, Rebecca! Stay away! I'm through with you!" He slammed the door closed with a solid bang that echoed through the corridor.

Crying, Rebecca got awkwardly to her feet, and stumbled to her own room. She washed up, combed her hair, and still sobbing, she left to visit Bryan. She dreaded telling him what had taken place, but she knew he would find out sooner or later, so she might as well confront him now.

Bryan was standing at the bar with Alex when Rebecca walked into the saloon. Bryan knew at once that something was wrong, for his mother's face was haggard. With Alex tagging along, they went to his office, where Rebecca recounted everything that had happened.

Bryan was furious, and he shouted angrily, "Damn you, Mother! You've ruined my whole future! For years, I've stayed in this rat hole of a town waiting for the Bar-H! Now, thanks to you, it was all for nothing!"

"Don't you think I feel the same way?" she rejoined, her own anger raging. "My God, I've wasted the best years of my life waiting for Bill to die! But thanks to you and Alex, he's still alive! Neither of you did anything to get rid of him!"

"We had to wait for the right time!" Bryan retorted sharply.

"Maybe this is the right time," Alex intruded.

"Stay out of this!" his brother snapped. He turned back to Rebecca, and said irritably, "Couldn't you have been more discreet? I can't believe you were actually stupid enough to get caught!"

"Don't you dare talk to me like that!"

"I'll talk to you any way I damned please!"

"Stop it!" Alex butted in strongly. "Fussin' back and forth ain't gonna settle nothin'. Don't you see? We gotta get rid of Bill, and we gotta do it now!"

Bryan eyed him impatiently. "And just how do you suggest we do that?"

"We don't do it. We hire Mackenna to do it for us. Hell, he's a killer, ain't he?"

Bryan was impressed. "Alex, sometimes you amaze me. Of course, you're right. We'll hire Mackenna."

"Who's Mackenna?" Rebecca asked.

Bryan quickly told her who the man was and that he was staying in a room upstairs.

"I'll go get 'im," Alex offered. He went to the door, but as he opened it, he came face to face with Hanley.

Barging inside, Bill said to Rebecca, "I thought I'd find you here. Come on; I'll take you to the ranch, then in the morning I want you to pack your things and leave."

Bryan, putting an arm about Rebecca's shoulders, asked Hanley, "May I have a moment alone with my mother?"

Bill moved to the door. "Of course. I'll wait outside for her."

The moment he was gone, Bryan said enthusiastically, "Hanley just played right into our hands."

Rebecca looked questioningly at her son.

"I'll have Mackenna ambush Hanley on the trip back to the Bar-H. But, Mother, you must give Mackenna time to get ahead of you, which means you'll have to find a reason to stop somewhere."

"Stop somewhere? However am I supposed to manage that?"

"I don't know!" he replied testily. "My God, do I have to think of everything?"

"Hell, Ma, you're a woman, ain't you?" Alex asked slyly. "You can get Hanley to stop. When was the last time you loved up to 'im, huh?" He chuckled heartily. "If you're real sweet and passionate to Hanley, we might not have to kill 'im. After you get through givin' it to him real good, the old man will probably keel over from a heart attack."

Rebecca went to Alex and slapped him across the face. "How dare you be so disrespectful!"

Rubbing his stinging cheek, Alex mumbled sullenly, "You didn't have to do that. I didn't mean it like it sounded."

"What did I ever do to deserve a son like you!" she moaned miserably.

Alex didn't say anything, he merely crawled back into his inner shell, which was the only armor he had against Rebecca and Bryan. All his life, he had been forced to hide within himself. The pair always treated him as though he were an imbecile. Well, one day he just might get enough of their criticism—and, then, by God, he'd get even!

Assuring Bryan that she'd detain Bill, Rebecca left the office and went outside. Her husband was standing beside the buggy, and he gave her a hand up. Joining her, he took the reins, turned the conveyance around, and headed out of town. The horse he had ridden into town was tied to the back of the carriage.

Bill and Rebecca didn't see the man standing at the upstairs window watching them. Actually, he had given Hanley only a passing glance; it was Rebecca's beauty that had held his undivided interest. He tried to imagine the woman naked and beneath him. The picture was so sexually arousing that he felt his manhood stiffening in his trousers. He grew uncomfortable, and was turning away from the window when a knock sounded on his door.

Answering it, he found Alex standing in the hall, shifting nervously from one foot to the other.

"Mr. Mackenna," he said, "my brother wants to see you. He has some work for you."

He raised a bushy eyebrow, his expression curious. Jake Mackenna wasn't handsome, not by any stretch of the imagination. His brawny build was verging on obesity, and his face was covered with a scraggly black beard. His eyes were too small for his broad face, and his nose, which had been broken more than once, was grotesquely crooked.

"Your brother wants to hire my services, huh?" he said gruffly. "Well, I don't come cheap."

Jake Mackenna reminded Alex of a wild grizzly, and he knew he was just as dangerous. "He intends to pay you a fair price."

Mackenna walked into the hall, slamming the door closed behind him. "Let's go talk to this brother of yours. I could use some money."

Rebecca was tense and uneasy. How in the world was she to delay their journey home? She completely disregarded Alex's advice—Bill was in no mood to be seduced. The sun, dipping into the west, was also a problem. Jake Mackenna would need daylight to shoot accurately. Suddenly, she was overcome with

341

apprehension. What if the man missed and hit her instead? It was a terrifying possibility. It sent her heart racing, and her stomach churning.

Nausea struck quickly, and putting a hand over her mouth, she groaned wretchedly, "Bill, stop the carriage. I'm going to be sick!"

He pulled up, and she immediately jumped to the ground, leaned over and gagged violently. Her stomach finally settled, but the spell left her feeling weak.

"Bill," she began pleadingly. "May we please rest for a little while? If I get back into that buggy now the motion will make me ill again." It was true, she did believe she'd get sick, but her malady most assuredly fit into her plans. Now, she didn't have to conjure up a reason to hold up their trip.

A small cluster of trees stood in the distance. "We'll stop ever there," Bill said, pointing toward them. "That way, you can rest in the shade."

She climbed back into the carriage, and Bill guided the horses to the shaded area. Unfolding a blanket from the buggy, he spread it beneath a tree, and Rebecca went to it and laid down.

Hanley sat beside her and leaned back against the tree's trunk. He didn't say anything, but remained buried in thought. He felt humiliated, and he also felt like a fool. He was determined, though, to end his marriage. It had been a mistake from the beginning, and he saw no reason to try and keep it together. Furthermore, he no longer loved Rebecca— he hadn't really loved her for a long time.

Rebecca was also lost in thought. She still feared that Mackenna might shoot her by mistake. When she and Bill continued their journey, she must not sit too close to him.

The silence between the two hung on for several

minutes before Bill finally asked, "Do you feel well enough to leave?"

She needed to play for more time. "I still feel terribly nauseous. May we please stay a little longer?"

Bill considerately obliged, and he patiently waited nearly thirty minutes before insisting that they had to leave because it was getting late. He wanted to be home before dark.

Rebecca was certain sufficient time had passed, and she folded the blanket, then followed Bill to the buggy. He helped her up onto the seat, joined her, and started for the Bar-H.

As they approached a area well surrounded by boulders and undergrowth, Rebecca scooted subtly to the far side of the seat. She had a feeling this was the spot where the ambush would take place.

Rebecca's feeling was right, and a loud shot suddenly rang out, sending a thunderous bang rumbling across the countryside. Bill's body snapped back in the seat, then like a child's rag doll, he fell forward limply.

The shot startled the horses, causing them to take off with a bolt. Somehow, Rebecca found the strength to push Bill's limp body aside, grab the reins, and bring the skittish horses to a stop.

Realizing how easily she could have been injured or killed in the runaway buggy was making her heart pound rapidly; and, once again, she was feeling sick to her stomach. She breathed in deeply, the spell passed, and her heart began to slow back down to normal. She looked cautiously at Bill. He had fallen sideways on the seat, and his head and shoulders were lodged behind her. She moved so that she could see him better. The front of his shirt was covered with blood, and the sickening sight sent a repulsive shudder through her. Grimacing, for she preferred not to touch him, she lifted his wrist and felt for a pulse. She couldn't find one, and she quickly dropped his hand. Thank goodness, he was dead!

Hearing a rider approaching, she got out of the buggy and watched as the man drew closer. She was certain that it was Jake Mackenna. He dismounted slowly, his beady eyes raking over Rebecca lasciviously.

She found the man forbidding, and a cold chill ran up her spine. "Are you Mr. Mackenna?" she asked, her voice quavering slightly.

"In the flesh," he replied, a cruel smile on his lips. He gestured toward Hanley. "Is he dead?"

"Yes, he is," she answered. She tried to appear composed. "Your job is complete, Mr. Mackenna. You may leave now. I'll untie my husband's horse, ride back to town, and inform the sheriff that we were ambushed. Naturally, I'll tell him that I didn't see who shot my husband."

"I ain't done with my job just yet," he said, ogling her with his deep-set eyes.

She flinched as though his gaze was physically touching her. "What do you want, Mr. Mackenna?"

"I want a little of you," he uttered, coming closer.

"Stay away from me!" she ordered desperately. "If you lay a hand on me, my sons will kill you!"

He laughed outrageously. "Neither of those milksops you call sons are man enough to kill me. Why, if they cross me, I'll snap their scrawny necks in two."

She turned about to flee, but moving speedily for a man his size, Jake grabbed her about the waist. Lifting her off the ground, he carried her to a patch of grass, and threw her down roughly.

The hard impact knocked the breath out of her, and for a moment she came close to passing out.

344

Kneeling beside her, Jake doubled his huge hand into a fist, waved it in front of her face, and threatened, "If you fight me, bitch, I'll turn that pretty face of yours into bloody meat. You understand me, gal?"

"Yes," she whispered frightfully. Valuing her beauty above all else, she wasn't about to put up a struggle. She would submissively let him have his way with her. After all, it would soon be over, and a long, hot bath would cleanse her again.

Jake's rough hands lifted her skirt, and drew down her undergarment. He pitched it to the side, then spreading her legs, he moved in between them, undid his trousers, and entered her with a brutal fury.

His entry was painful, and she cried out sharply.

"Shut up, you bitch!" he growled. He pounded into her aggressively, his hips pumping madly. Despite his ugliness and brutality, she found herself responding to his large erection, which was amazing in size. Aware of her response, he laughed under his breath, draped her legs over his shoulders, and sent his huge member plunging even deeper.

Later, his manhood spent, he stood, and buttoning his trousers, he said with contempt, "You enjoyed it, didn't you, bitch?"

Sitting up, she reached for her undergarment. "of course not!" she spat out with no real conviction.

He smiled largely. "You lyin' little tramp."

She stood up shakily. "If you ever try anything like this again, I'll find a way to have you killed! That's a promise, Mr. Mackenna!" Now, totally appalled that she had actually responded to such a vicious and unattractive man, she felt as though she would indeed carry out her threat.

Jake merely laughed at her, went to his horse, mounted, and rode quickly away.

Rebecca, her emotions a wreck, hurried to Bill's horse, and was untying it when two of the Bar-H wranglers rode into view.

Pulling up, they rushed to Rebecca. "What happened?" the one named Carl asked. The other man went to check on Hanley.

"We were ambushed," she replied. "I was just on my way to town for the sheriff."

"How's Mr. Hanley?" Carl asked.

"He's dead," she cried, forcing tears to her eyes.

"No, he ain't," the other wrangler called out. "He's still alive."

"Get in the buggy, Mrs. Hanley," Carl said, taking her arm and urging her to do so. "We gotta get Mr. Hanley to the doctor."

Numbly, she got up onto the seat, and allowed Carl to place her husband's head on her lap. Bill was alive? But she hadn't felt a pulse! She inwardly cursed herself for being so incompetent! Why hadn't she been more thorough? If she had known that Bill wasn't dead, Mackenna could have finished him off!

Carl jumped up on the other side of the seat, took the reins and sent the team into a fast gallop.

Rebecca sighed miserably. How was she to face Bryan and explain this travesty to him? He would be furious! She glanced down at her husband, and his grave condition gave her hope. He might not be dead now, but his survival was highly unlikely! He probably wouldn't live to reach town.

Chapter Twenty-six

Caroline sat between her brothers, both ensconced in their bedrolls, sound asleep. She had talked with them for a long time before their fatigue took its toll. She thought about returning to the campfire and having a cup of coffee, but there was such tranquility here with her brothers that she didn't want to leave; not even to move only a few feet away. At last, the three of them were together! What a glorious miracle! A lovely, radiant smile crossed her face as she tried to imagine her grandfather's happiness. She knew he seriously doubted that the boys were still alive, which would make their return all the more amazing.

"You look as though you're thinking about something very pleasant," Ross suddenly said, walking up to her quietly.

"I am," she replied. "I'm thinking about my grandfather, and how happy he'll be to see Walter and Daniel."

Ross sat beside her. "You and your brothers had quite a long conversation. Were you three getting to know each other?"

"Yes, we were. Ross, both of them have been so unhappy, especially Walter. Roberto told him that his father was white, but that his mother was a Mexican.

347

That's why he was running away—he hoped to find his father's kin across the border." Her eyes turned angry. "Roberto beat Walter often. He was a tyrant!"

"That's putting it mildly."

"These past five years were easier for Daniel. Leonora was a good mother, and she loved Daniel very much. Fernando tried to mold Daniel into a small replica of himself, but Daniel's too much like Papa to be another Fernando."

Ross reached over and held her hand. "Well, it's all over now. The boys will soon be home with you and Bill, where they belong."

She tensed, and drew her hand away.

"What's wrong?" Ross asked impatiently. "Why have you suddenly turned on me?"

A spark of anger flickered in her eyes. "I'm not a fool, Ross Bennett, and I wish you'd stop treating me like one!"

Ross stood, bent over, grabbed Caroline's arm, and drew her to her feet. "You're coming with me!" he said sternly.

She tried to pull away, but his grip was too firm. "I'm not going anywhere with you!"

"The hell you aren't!" he retorted, forcing her to walk beside him.

"Where are you taking me?" she asked angrily.

"Where we can be alone. You're going to tell me what's got you all riled."

Caroline, deciding it was best to get her feelings in the open, didn't argue. The full moon made it easy for them to see their way, and Ross took her quite a distance from camp before stopping.

He folded his arms across his chest, eyed her severely, and said, "Now, tell me what's wrong."

Caroline wished the moon wasn't so bright, for it

348

would be easier for her to control her emotions if she couldn't see him so clearly. His countenance, though stern, was nonetheless strikingly handsome. He was hatless, and a thatch of dark hair fell sensually across his brow. His dark eyes, their depths the color of ebony, were mirror brilliant. She looked into his finely-sculpted face. His pronounced cheekbones, which attested to his Apache heritage, added to his good looks. Yet, there was something about his features that was durably boyish, and totally irresistible.

Caroline's scrutiny continued, and her gaze raked over his tall, lithe frame. His buckskin shirt and trousers fit perfectly, the pliant leather emphasizing his broad shoulders, narrow waist, and long, muscular legs. Her eyes rested on the gun strapped to his hip, worn low in the typical gunslinger's tradition. It lent a dangerous air about him that threatened men, but excited women.

Impatient with her silence, Ross mumbled testily, "Well? Are you going to tell me what's bothering you?"

She met his eyes, managed to keep a flimsy control on her emotions, and answered evenly, "I know what's going on between you and Emily. If you insist on making a fool of yourself, then go right ahead. But you're not going to do it at my expense. I'll not play second-fiddle to your former fiancée."

Ross was befuddled. "What the hell are you talking about?"

Caroline's anger came alive. "Don't you play innocent with me, you two-timing rake! I saw you kiss Emily!"

Amusement suddenly lurked in his eyes. "Is that what's got you all steamed up?"

His flippant attitude was infuriating. "How dare

you act as though it's all right for you to kiss another woman! How would you feel if you saw me kissing another man?" Her anger escalating, she continued, "That was a foolish comparison, wasn't it? You wouldn't even care if I kissed someone else!"

"I would care very much," he replied. "Caroline, I can explain why I kissed Emily, and I assure you it didn't mean a thing to me."

"Stop treating me as though I'm a complete fool! I saw the way you swept her into your arms and kissed her!"

"What else did you see?"

"Wasn't that enough?"

"Did you hear any of our conversation before or after the kiss?"

"No! I'm not an eavesdropper! I came upon you two quite by accident. I didn't stay—I left as quickly as possible!"

"If you hadn't left, you'd have heard me tell her that she doesn't mean anything to me, and that I'm in love with you."

She eyed him skeptically. "Then why did you kiss her?"

"She kept egging me on. She didn't believe I could kiss her, and not fall back in love with her. Finally, I agreed just to get rid of her; permanently, I hope."

"Surely, you don't expect me to believe something so outlandish?"

Ross was becoming impatient. "Caroline, I'm telling you the truth!" A note of pleading entered his voice, "Don't you know me at all? Do you really think I'm capable of that kind of deceit? Without faith, how do you expect our love to survive?"

His reasoning made headway, and Caroline pushed her jealousy aside to think logically. She began to feel ashamed of herself for jumping to conclusions. She did know Ross Bennett, and he was right, he wasn't capable of such deceit. If he loved another woman, he would tell her face to face. He wouldn't sneak around behind her back.

"Ross," she said softly, "I guess I did misconstrue what I saw. But the kiss you shared with Emily was so romantic—so intense! What was I supposed to think?"

"Apparently, you thought the worst, which I suppose is understandable. But, Caroline, we have to learn to trust each other. And if we have any doubts or insecurities, we should bring them out in the open and candidly discuss them. Otherwise, they will only fester and grow." He placed his hands on her shoulders, gazed tenderly into her eyes, and said with intense feeling, "I love you, Caroline Hanley. You mean everything to me. I've never felt so much love for anyone." He kissed her lips softly, then asked, "Will you marry me?"

Caroline's happiness was ecstatic, and flinging herself into his arms, she answered, "Yes, I'll marry you! Oh Ross, I love you so much!"

When he bent his head to seal their engagement with a kiss, she met his lips halfway. As her body moved against his in a suggestive caress, he drew her even closer, pressing her hips flush to his. His mouth, moving hers in a sensuous exploration, sent her senses fluttering.

Ross had to struggle against the need to take her completely, and he released her with a tearing reluctance.

Caroline's passion was so aroused that she was actually trembling. "Oh Ross!" she moaned, her torment raging. "I want you so badly!"

He smiled hesitantly. "I know, sweetheart. I feel the same way."

Suddenly, she blushed profusely. "My goodness, I'm very wanton, aren't I?"

"I wouldn't have you any other way," he replied, taking her back into his arms. He kissed her again, passionately and intensely. Then, with his lips hovering above hers, he whispered thickly, "If we stay here another moment, I won't be able to control myself."

"Then let's stay," she taunted saucily.

Ross, worried that they might be discovered, scanned their surroundings for seclusion. Spotting the ideal place, he lifted her into his arms, and carried her to an area bordered densely by overgrown shrubbery. Placing her on her feet, he quickly shed his shirt and spread it on the ground. Next, he removed his holster, then very gently he eased Caroline down onto the shirt.

He longed to strip away all her clothes and feast his eyes upon her lovely body, but he feared possible discovery, and knew they might have to dress quickly. Lying beside her, he took her into his arms, and kissed her demandingly.

She responded with a fervor that equaled his, and their heated kiss sent fire through every fiber of her being.

When his hand reached for the band of her riding skirt, she helped him unbutton it and slip the garment past her hips. He placed the article aside, then he deliberately removed her underwear slowly, inch by inch, so he could thoroughly relish the sight of her. The golden moon, shining luminously, clearly revealed her creamy thighs, and the delectable mound between them. He kissed her there, softly but completely.

His intimacy was wonderfully ecstatic, and she surrendered totally to his rapturous, exciting possession of her.

Soon Ross's need to consummate their union became overpowering, and moving over her, he undid his trousers. She arched her hips, and he penetrated deeply, and she accepted his full length with wondrous abandon.

At first, his thrusts were slow and measured, and their bodies blended together in love's erotic rhythm. Steadily, their fiery passion burned gloriously higher until, uncontrollably, a firebolt of ecstasy rocked their senses with utter fulfillment.

Afterwards, the lovers remained entwined in each other's arms, basking in the wonder of their union, and savoring its sweetness.

Reluctantly, however, they came back to reality, drew apart, and prepared to return to camp. Ross slipped an arm about her waist, and as they moved away from the secluded area, Ross's thoughts went to Hanley, prompting him to say cheerfully, "I was just thinking about your grandfather. I can't wait to see the look on his face when he sees Walter and Daniel."

Caroline laughed merrily. "Neither can I! Oh Ross, he's going to be so happy!"

"He'll no doubt be the second happiest man in the world."

"Second?" she questioned pertly.

"Yes, second to me."

"Are you truly happy, Ross?" Her eyes watched him expectantly.

"I've never been happier. I'm going to marry the woman I love, and I feel like shouting with joy."

"I know what you mean," she replied, smiling delightedly. "I think Grandpa will be pleased to learn we're getting married. He likes you very much."

"The feeling's mutual."

"I've missed him terribly, and I can't wait to see him!" Caroline's heart was overflowing with joy, and she was indeed anxious to see her grandfather reunited with his grandsons!

Rebecca, along with Bryan and Alex, sat in the doctor's parlor, awaiting the prognosis for Hanley. Earlier, the wranglers had carried their boss to Doctor Gordon's spare bedroom, then Rebecca had sent them to the saloon to tell Bryan and Alex that she wanted them with her. The physician had now been in the room with his patient for over an hour, and the waiting was fraying Rebecca's nerves. She and her sons had the parlor to themselves, for the doctor's wife was assisting him. Sheriff Taylor had already arrived, asked several questions, and left.

Bryan, his nerves as shattered as his mother's, helped himself to a glass of brandy, swigging half of it in one swallow. Moving to the sofa to sit beside Rebecca, he said with quiet rage, "I can't believe you didn't make sure Bill was dead before Mackenna left!"

Rebecca scowled furiously. "I already told you that I thought he was dead! I couldn't feel a pulse." She sighed heavily. "I guess it was too weak."

"Apparently!" Bryan seethed.

"Let's not give up," she said hopefully. "He might still die. After all, his wound was horrid!" A repugnant shudder coursed through her. "And he lost a terrible amount of blood! The sight was ghastly. Just thinking about it makes me ill!"

"Ma's right!" Alex put in. "He ain't gonna live. A man his age can't lose a lot of blood without dyin'."

354

Bryan cast his brother a disgusted look, but he didn't say anything, for he didn't think Alex's statement warranted an answer. In his opinion, it was too stupid!

Hearing the bedroom door open, Rebecca said quickly, "Don't say anything, the doctor's coming."

As the physician entered the parlor, the threesome got hastily to their feet. The man's somber expression gave them reason to hope.

"How is he?" Bryan asked at once.

"Not good, I'm sorry to say. I was able to remove the bullet, and, thank God, it didn't puncture any vital organs. However, it's going to be touch and go for the next few days. I wish I could be more encouraging, but, in all honesty, his chances are very slim."

Concealing her delight, Rebecca moaned sadly, "Oh no!"

"I'm sorry, Mrs. Hanley," the doctor said sympathetically. He spoke to Bryan. "Why don't you take your mother to the hotel? She needs a good night's rest."

"But I can't leave Bill!" she cried, as though she sincerely meant it.

"There's nothing you can do for him, Mrs. Hanley. My wife and I will sit with him tonight, then in the morning, you can relieve us."

"Well . . . if you think that's best," she replied.

Assuring her his advice was best, he showed his visitors to the door. Deciding to have a small glass of brandy before returning to his patient, he went to his liquor cabinet. He poured the drink, and had it almost finished when a visitor's knock sent him back to the front door. He was somewhat surprised to find Henry Parker. Inviting him in, he asked, "Is anything wrong, Mr. Parker?"

"I'm not sure," he replied.

Gordon looked at him curiously.

"I heard that Bill Hanley was ambushed. How is he?"

"He's barely alive."

"Doctor Gordon, I need to talk to you confidentially."

"Of course," he said, ushering him into the parlor. "Would you care for a brandy?"

"No, thank you," he declined. Henry was nervous, and he distractedly kept rubbing his hands together as though they were cold, and he was trying to warm them. "Doctor Gordon, I think Mrs. Hanley tried to murder her husband."

"What!" the doctor exclaimed. "Why, that's preposterous!"

"Please, hear me out. It's not as preposterous as you might think." As quickly as possible, Henry told Gordon about Rebecca's past, her reason for marrying Hanley, and that she had once had an affair with his friend in Albuquerque. He then confessed his own infidelity with Rebecca, explained that Hanley had caught them, and that he had threatened to divorce Rebecca.

The doctor listened closely to his story, and when he finished, he said calmly, "You haven't said anything to make me believe that Mrs. Hanley had anything to do with her husband being shot."

"She has the motive—she wants his money. And she's cold-hearted enough to kill for it."

"Tell me, Mr. Parker, why are you so concerned about Bill? You certainly weren't thinking in his best interest when you seduced his wife."

"Conscience, I suppose. I feel guilty about what I did. Mr. Hanley's a nice person, and I acted like a real

356

heel. But Rebecca's a very provocative and persuasive woman, and I didn't have the will power to turn away."

"If Mrs. Hanley did hire someone to shoot Bill, what do you expect me to do about it? Why come to me instead of the sheriff?"

"I intend to talk to the sheriff, but I came to you first because I don't think you should leave Bill alone with Rebecca. Or with her sons, for that matter. A pillow over Bill's face will finish what she and her sons already started."

Gordon was astounded. "Mr. Parker, you're full of accusations, aren't you? Not only do you accuse Mrs. Hanley, but her sons as well."

"For Bill Hanley's sake, I hope you take my accusations seriously."

"I believe people are innocent until proven guilty, Mr. Parker. However, I don't think your suspicions are totally unfounded. I'll send to the Bar-H for Inés. Instead of Rebecca, she can help my wife and me tend to Bill."

"Inés?" Parker queried. "Isn't she Hanley's housekeeper?"

"Yes, and she's a very proficient nurse."

"Thank you for your time, Doctor Gordon. Now, if you'll excuse me, I intend to take my suspicions to the sheriff."

The doctor showed his guest out. He wondered if Parker's accusations were true. He had never really liked Rebecca—there was a coldness about her that warded off any attempts he and his wife had made toward friendship. Also, he knew for a fact that she hadn't made Bill happy, and he always suspected that she had married him for his money. But murder? Was she capable of that? More astounding, were her sons

357

also involved? Gordon, a man dedicated to saving lives, found it hard to accept something so gruesome. A mother and her sons plotting murder? The thought alone sent a cold chill through him. The more he pondered the matter, however, the more he realized that Parker might be right.

With grim determination, he decided to stick by his promise to Parker—his patient would not be left alone with Rebecca or her sons!

The next morning, Bryan went to the hotel, and took his mother to the dining room for breakfast. They gave their order to the waiter, then over coffee, Bryan said eagerly, "I have it all planned out!"

Rebecca raised a brow questioningly. "You have what planned out, Bryan?"

"There's no reason for us to wait around for Bill to die. You'll be sitting with him this morning. All you have to do is smother him with a pillow. Doctor Gordon won't even be suspicious. He'll think he simply died. After all, he doesn't expect him to live."

"I don't think I can do that!" Rebecca said, finding the idea distasteful. "The mere thought makes me ill."

"Damn it, Mother! Everything makes you ill!"

"I don't like violence."

"You mean you don't like to be the perpetrator! You want someone else to do the actual killing!"

"I can't help it if I'm squeamish."

"No wonder Alex can never do anything right! He takes after you!"

"That's enough! How dare you!"

Bryan's face contorted into a sinister, maddening leer. "I'm warning you, Mother, either you smother that son of a bitch, or I'm going to leave this town,

358

and you'll never see or hear from me again!"

"You can't do that! If you leave, I'll be all alone!"

He chuckled coldly. "You'll have Alex!"

"God forbid!"

"Then you'll do what I want?"

"Yes, I'll do it," she gave in. The thought of being without Bryan was more frightening than smothering her husband.

Bryan escorted his mother to Doctor Gordon's house. He planned to go in with her to see Bill, then he'd leave to go back to the saloon. He was certain that the doctor and his wife would leave Rebecca alone to watch over her husband.

They were shocked to find Inés sitting with Bill. Rebecca ordered her to return to the Bar-H, but the woman flatly refused. Doctor Gordon had taken her into his confidence, and she wasn't about to leave Bill's side. Furthermore, her suspicions were as strong as Henry Parker's.

Rebecca was about to fire Inés for her insolence when Doctor Gordon, accompanied by Sheriff Taylor, entered the room.

"Is something wrong?" the doctor asked Rebecca.

"Yes! I'd like to be alone with my husband, but Inés refuses to leave!"

"Bill's condition is so grave that I've decided either myself or Inés must be close by at all times. As you know, Mrs. Hanley, Inés is experienced in caring for the ill."

Rebecca gave Bryan a look of defeat. There was nothing she could do.

Seething inwardly, Bryan cursed their rotten luck.

"Bryan," Sheriff Taylor spoke up, "I understand

that Jake Mackenna was in your saloon yesterday. He was seen by someone who recognized him."

Bryan shrugged. "I wouldn't know. I've never seen Mackenna, and I wouldn't know him if I met him on the street. Why do you ask?"

"He's wanted for murder in several towns across the west."

"Then why are you standing here? Why aren't you out looking for him?"

"He'll probably show his face again," the sheriff answered. "I'll be watchin' for him."

Bryan, his nerves strained, walked stiffly out of the room. He had an uneasy feeling that the sheriff was suspicious of him. Well, let him be suspicious, he thought. He couldn't prove anything. And, as for Mackenna, the man had apparently left town, for he hadn't seen him since he paid him to shoot Hanley. Bryan hoped he'd stay gone—permanently!

Meanwhile, Rebecca, knowing she must play the role of the concerned wife, drew up a chair and placed it close to Bill's bed. She sighed wearily, for she knew it was going to be a long day. She certainly didn't relish sitting in this room for hours. If only Bill would hurry up and die!

Chapter Twenty-seven

Caroline and the others arrived in Dry Branch at midday. First, they stopped at the sheriff's house to drop off Mary, then they planned to take Emily to her father before riding to the Bar-H.

Sheriff Taylor had gone home for lunch, and was walking out the door when the travelers arrived. Happy to see his niece, his face broke into a large smile. Mary, dismounting, rushed to embrace him, and sweeping her into his big arms, he hugged her warmly.

The others remained mounted, and as the sheriff released Mary, his gaze went over the group.

Ross, indicating Emily, said, "This is Parker's daughter." Then grinning expansively, he gestured toward the boys, and continued, "These are Caroline's brothers, Walter and Daniel."

Walter, who no longer needed a travois, was riding double with Kirk, and Daniel was with Caroline.

Sheriff Taylor seldom expressed his emotions openly, but the sight of the boys brought tears to his eyes. Bill Hanley had waited so long for this day! His condition was still grave, and so far, he hadn't regained consciousness. Doctor Gordon feared that he might slip into a coma and never awaken; that is, not in this world. Dear God, the sheriff lamented, was Bill destined to die before seeing his grandsons? Would he never learn that they were still alive, and evidently in good health? He prayed fate wouldn't be that cruel.

Taylor looked at Caroline, and said gently, "I have some bad news for you, dear. Your grandfather was shot a couple of days ago. His condition is very serious. He's at Doctor Gordon's house."

Sudden fear coursed through her. "Grandpa's been shot?" she uttered, her voice weak from shock.

"Who shot him?" Ross asked.

Taylor shrugged. "I'm not sure. He and Rebecca were on their way to the ranch when he was shot by a sniper. Rebecca claims she didn't see who did it."

"Claims?" Ross questioned, picking up on the implication.

"We'll talk about it later. You need to take Caroline to see her grandfather. Why don't you leave Walter and Daniel here?"

Ross agreed, and as Mary showed the boys into the house, he asked Kirk to take Emily to her father.

Caroline, her feelings numb, kept her horse abreast of Ross's as they rode the short distance down the street to Doctor Gordon's home.

Ross dismounted and went to Caroline and helped her down. With an arm wrapped securely about her waist, he led her to the front door and knocked firmly.

Doctor Gordon wasn't in. They were admitted by his wife, who took them to Hanley's room. Inés, in attendance, was sitting beside Bill's bed.

Caroline crossed the room on legs that felt too

362

weak to support her. She paused at the bed, and as she looked down at her grandfather, tears welled from her eyes. He appeared gravely ill—his complexion pale, his cheeks sunken, and his breathing dangerously shallow.

Inés, bounding from her chair, took Caroline into her arms, holding her tightly.

"Oh Inés!" Caroline sobbed. "We're going to lose him, aren't we?" On the brink of hysteria, she continued wretchedly, "It isn't fair! It just isn't fair! I brought Walter and Daniel home, and now he won't even see them! Oh God, why . . . why?"

"Sh . . . sh . . ." Inés murmured soothingly. "We will not lose him. Bill, he is a strong man, and he is a fighter. He will pull through this. Now, wipe away those tears, señorita."

Caroline was calmed by her words. She pushed gently out of Inés's arms, gazed deeply into the woman's eyes, and was suddenly aware that Inés was in love with Bill Hanley. The truth was written clearly on Inés's face. Caroline was saddened. If only her grandfather had fallen in love with Inés instead of Rebecca, his life would have been so much happier!

Ross moved to Caroline, touched her hand, and said, "I need to talk to the sheriff. I'll be back shortly."

She nodded. "All right."

He leaned over and kissed her cheek. "I love you," he whispered.

Inés, watching, heard Ross's whispered endearment. The moment he walked out of the room, she turned to Caroline, and said with a heartwarming smile, "He is a good man, señorita. I am happy that you found someone like him. Your grandpapa, he will be happy too."

She watched the woman speculatively. "Inés, why haven't you ever married?"

She returned to the chair, dropped her gaze to her lap, and murmured, "I never met the right man."

"You mean the right man married someone else, don't you?"

She lifted her gaze back to Caroline's. "You know what is in my heart, sí?"

Placing a consoling hand on Inés's shoulder, Caroline answered tenderly, "Yes, I know."

Sheriff Taylor told Ross about Parker's suspicions, and he also warned him that Jake Mackenna had been seen at the saloon. Knowing that Mackenna had a vendetta against Ross, he advised him to be cautious.

Ross hoped the ugly bastard showed his face, for he was anxious to tangle with him. They had a score to settle, and until they did, he knew Mackenna wouldn't stop stalking him. Ross was uneasy, though, for Jake was the kind to shoot a man in the back. He had every intention of heeding Taylor's advice — he would stay alert.

Leaving the sheriff's office, Ross headed straight to the hotel. He had some questions of his own to ask Parker. He hadn't been surprised to learn about Parker's and Rebecca's affair, for he had always sensed that Rebecca was a woman on the make. As for Parker, making love to another man's wife lowered his opinion of him even more. But their illicit union wasn't any of his business, and he wasn't planning to confront Parker on that point. He intended to question him about his suspicions of attempted murder. That he did consider his business!

The desk clerk gave Ross Parker's room number. He hastened upstairs, went to the door, and knocked rapidly.

It was answered by Emily.

"Where's your father?" he asked, entering.

She closed the door. "He isn't here, but he'll be back soon. He's at the mercantile buying me some more clothes. All I have with me is the riding attire that I'm wearing."

"When does Parker plan to leave?"

"I'm not sure. He said he wants to stay and see if Mr. Hanley pulls through. I can't understand why he's so concerned about the man."

Ross knew why—guilt!

Emily gestured toward her father's liquor supply. "Would you care for a drink, Ross?"

He said that he would, and she moved to pour him a glass of brandy. Her thoughts were churning turbulently. Since that night she had taunted Ross into kissing her, his manner toward her had turned cold, brusque, and, in her opinion, inexcusably discourteous. She supposed she should accept defeat, and chalk up Ross as unattainable; however, she wasn't quite ready to give up. Surely, there was some way she could win him back! After all, he had once loved her so desperately!

Taking Ross his drink, she walked toward him lithely, like a cat stalking its prey. The expression in her eyes was starkly licentious, and she actually licked her lips as though she were about to devour him. She paused before him, her body mere inches from his. She handed him the glass, dropped her voice to a husky octave, and said, "You know, Ross, you and I have never made love."

"So?" he asked, arching a brow.

"So, aren't you the least bit curious? Don't you want to know what it would be like?"

"I hate to disillusion you, Emily, but I'm not in the least curious."

She smiled confidently. "I don't believe you."

"Then that's too bad." He finished his brandy in two large swigs, gave her the glass, and said abruptly, "I'll come back later when your father is here." He went straight for the door.

She laughed tauntingly. "You're a coward, Ross Bennett! You're afraid to be alone with me, aren't you? That's because you still want me!"

He opened the door, turned back, and said calmly, "I'm not leaving because I'm afraid. I just can't stand being in the same room with you. Now that we have that understood, will you do me a favor, and stop trying to seduce me? You're making a complete fool of yourself."

Emily, her temper aroused, drew back her arm to throw the glass at him. Reacting quickly, Ross slammed the door just as the glass hit. He heard it shatter into pieces.

Bryan, pacing his office, was seething inwardly. It was beginning to look as though he would never own the Bar-H. Ross, damn him, had returned with Caroline and the boys! To make matters worse, Mackenna had shown up! Bryan, believing he had seen the last of Mackenna, was indeed shocked when, earlier, the man had barged into his office, asking for a place to stay. He was angry about his arrival, but he kept his wrath concealed, for he was afraid of Mackenna, who at this moment was

366

watching his every move. Sitting at his desk, and feigning composure, he said, "Mr. Mackenna, I can't hide you indefinitely; however, you are more than welcome to spend the night upstairs." Nervous, he folded his hands together, they were clammy.

A smile that closely resembled a sneer, crossed Jake's homely face. "I'll stay here as long as I need to," he mumbled. "Bennett's back in town, and I got a score to settle with 'im. After I take care of that, I'll be on my way."

Alex was also in the room. He was standing at the window, but, now, turning away, he looked at Mackenna, and said, "If you want to get even with Ross Bennett, I can tell you how to do it."

"I ain't plannin' on gettin' even, I plan on killin' im."

"But wouldn't you like to see 'im really suffer 'fore you kill 'im?"

Jake, as well as Bryan, stared curiously at Alex. Knowing his idea was a good one, Alex continued eagerly, "Ross is in love with Caroline Hanley. All you gotta do is kidnap her, wait for Ross to come save her, then you can kill Caroline in front of 'im. After that, you can finish off Bennett."

Bryan, pleased with Alex's plan, said with enthusiasm, "My brother's right! If you want to get Ross where it really hurts, kill the woman he loves." Still, he couldn't help but feel a pang of disappointment—he had always hoped for an opportunity to enjoy Caroline's lovely body, but now . . . ? Well, at this point, he told himself, her death was more important!

"Just how am I supposed to kidnap this woman?" Mackenna was finding the scheme to his liking.

It was Bryan who answered. "Wait until late to-night, go to the Bar-H, grab her, and leave Ross a note, telling him where he can find her."

"It might not be that easy to break into her house."

Smiling, Bryan opened his desk drawer, brought out a key, and handed it to Jake. "Here; all you have to do is unlock the door, and walk in. Caroline's room is upstairs, second door on the left."

He took the key, put it in his pocket, and said, "I'll think it over." Standing, he crossed the room, went to the door, and mumbled over his shoulder, "For now, I'm gonna get some shut-eye. I'll talk to you about this later."

The moment he was gone, Bryan turned to Alex, smiled pleasantly, and said, "I have to give you credit, Alex. Your idea is good, damned good! Mackenna gets rid of Caroline, then all we have to do is find a way to eliminate Walter and Daniel."

"You reckon all these killings might arouse too much suspicion?"

"No, because we can wait awhile before killing the boys. They're still too young to take possession of the Bar-H. With Caroline dead, Mother will be in charge of Hanley's estate until they come of age. So we have plenty of time to get rid of them."

"But what if Hanley doesn't die?"

Bryan frowned testily. "That old man's going to die—one way or another!"

Caroline sent Inés to the sheriff's home to get Walter and Daniel. She was hoping, praying, that somehow the three of them could get through to Bill's unconscious state. If he could somehow know that she and his grandsons were at his bedside, it might be the miracle he needed to pull him through.

Inés returned promptly with the boys; Mary, worried about Hanley, accompanied them. As they were entering the house, Ross arrived. He and Inés took Walter and Daniel to see their grandfather. Mary remained in the parlor, not wanting to intrude.

Caroline gathered her brothers close, one on each side. Keeping an arm about them, she said softly, "This is your grandfather. He loves you both very much. Talk to him, maybe he'll hear you."

Walter, studying Hanley, tried very hard to remember him. The first five years of his life still eluded him. He couldn't recall anything, nor could he recognize this man who was fighting for his life.

Daniel shifted closer to Caroline, placed his head on her shoulder, and peeked cautiously at his grandfather. In the eyes of a seven-year-old child, he looked terribly old and withered.

Caroline, sensing her brothers' feelings, told them gently, "Your grandfather is very robust and hearty. I know he doesn't look that way now, but you must realize that he's very ill." Tears filled her eyes, and she cried heartbrokenly, "He loves us so very, very much! We must try to save his life! He needs us! Please, please talk to him!"

Walter touched her arm consolingly. "I will talk to him."

She smiled through her tears.

Leaning over the bed, Walter placed his hand on Hanley's. *"Abuelo,"* he began, using the Mexican word for grandfather.

"Call him grandpa," Caroline interjected. "He'll find it familiar."

"Grandpa," he began again. "It is me, your grandson, Walter. Please do not die!"

Caroline encouraged Daniel to move closer to the bed. He was a little hesitant, but he loved his sister very much, and didn't want to disappoint her. If speaking to this old man would make her happy, then he would comply. "Do not die, Grandpa," he murmured. "We want you to live." He quickly moved back to Caroline, and snuggled against her.

Caroline fully understood the boys' feelings. She hadn't expected them to love their grandfather on sight, especially under these grave conditions. But she knew if Hanley survived, it wouldn't take him long to win their affections.

She took Bill's limp hand into hers, leaned over him, and said clearly, "Grandpa, I found Walter and Daniel. They're here with me. Didn't you hear them talking to you? Grandpa, please hear us! Please!"

His hand, resting in hers, moved feebly. Caroline was ecstatic. "You understand!" she cried happily. "Grandpa, you can hear me!"

His eyelids fluttering, he whispered almost inaudibly, "Caroline . . . Caroline . . . I hear you."

"Thank God!" she praised.

"I will get the doctor!" Inés exclaimed, leaving quickly. She headed for the kitchen where she knew he was having coffee.

Bill's eyes opened, and staring lucidly into Caroline's face, he murmured hoarsely, "Walter and Daniel . . . are they here? . . . did I only dream I heard them?"

"They're here," she told him at once. "Oh Grandpa, they're both fine!"

Doctor Gordon, followed by Ines, came into the

room. Caroline and the boys moved away from the bed, giving him ample room to examine his patient.

Ross was standing at the door, Caroline went to him, and flung herself into his arms. He held her as close as possible.

Following a short examination, Doctor Gordon was glad to report, "His pulse is much stronger, and his breathing isn't quite so labored." He looked at Inés. "Get him a small bowl of broth, he needs nourishment."

The physician moved to Ross and Caroline, and said too quietly for his patient to hear, "He isn't out of danger, but his chances are greatly improved." He smiled largely. "Bill's got a lot of grit, and he just might pull through."

"He's going to make it!" Caroline said, refusing to think otherwise. "He'll live, I just know it!"

Mary was still in the doctor's parlor when Kirk knocked at the door. She let him in and they sat on the sofa, both anxiously awaiting news of Hanley's condition.

Kirk liked Bill Hanley a lot, and although he was sincerely concerned about him, he nonetheless was acutely aware of Mary's closeness. He longed to draw her into his arms, but certain of rejection, he suppressed the urge. Kirk wasn't one to give up easily, neither was he one to fight a losing battle. He had fallen deeply in love with Mary, but he reluctantly admitted to himself that it was a lost cause. She considered the seven years between them insurmountable, and no argument on his behalf was going to change her mind. Kirk, deciding to bow out gracefully, told her evenly, "Mary, I have land in Arizona, and I'm anxious to build a ranch and settle down. I've sowed my wild oats, and I've drifted long enough. I plan to leave in the morning, so I guess this is goodbye."

"I wish you all the luck in the world, Kirk." Her calm voice totally belied the sudden tension she felt. Kirk was leaving? She knew she would miss him unbearably. But her feelings toward marrying him were still adamant. He deserved a young woman who was full of freshness and vitality.

"I wish you would marry me, and come with me," Kirk said softly. "But I know you're firmly against being my wife, and I'm not going to pressure you. I also know all the reasons why you won't marry me. If I could add seven years to my age, I would."

She smiled wistfully. "Kirk, I think that's the sweetest thing anybody has ever said to me."

"Is that right?' he remarked, anger in his voice. "Well, I never wanted you to think of me as sweet, I wanted you to desire me like a woman passionately in love."

"Kirk, I didn't mean to upset you."

He rose from the sofa, looked down at her, and said gruffly, "I'm thirty-three years old, damn it! What I feel for you isn't a school boy crush!"

"I don't think it is," she replied.

"The hell you don't!" he grumbled. He headed for the door. "Tell Ross I'll be at the saloon."

"Kirk, why are you leaving? Is it something I said?"

"It's not only what you say, but the way you act! If you ever get up the courage to face your feelings honestly, let me know! I'll be in Arizona!"

With that, he left, closing the door soundly behind him.

Alex, moving stealthily, stored two cans of kerosene behind the saloon. Standing, he looked at the fuel as though it were some kind of great discovery. And, in a way, it was, for Alex was uncovering a new image of himself. He had been the one to plot Hanley's ambush, and, now, finding a way to kill Caroline had also been his idea. For the first time in his life, Bryan was listening to him, and taking his advice! Yes, Alex was very proud of himself. Now, his newest plan, in his opinion, was the best.

Bending over, he ran his fingers across the cans of kerosene as though he were actually caressing them, but suddenly he was struck with a touch of insecurity. Maybe he should include Bryan and Rebecca in his latest scheme. He thought about it for a moment, then dismissed it. No, he would do it on his own, then accept their praises, which he was sure would be forthcoming.

Mackenna had returned to Bryan's office, and had told him that he would abduct Caroline. Bryan had been so pleased that he had actually patted Alex on the back for coming up with the idea. The compliment had thrilled Alex, and it had also built up his confidence. However, he didn't agree with Bryan about waiting to kill Walter and Daniel. He thought they should die now. Getting rid of the boys was his newest plan. He knew it would be easy—a piece of cake! Tonight, he would pour kerosene over the house, then set fire to it! He didn't think Bryan would be upset about losing the house, for he'd have plenty of money to build another one.

He supposed he could also get rid of Caroline in the fire, but he thought Mackenna kidnapping her was better. The man would no doubt force himself on her before killing her, and Alex found the brutal act justifiable. In his estimation, Caroline was a haughty bitch who deserved such a vicious fate. He wished he could watch it happen!

Rebecca, he knew, was planning to spend the night in town, so tonight was the ideal time to burn down the house, along with its occupants. Later, he'd go to the ranch, hide in the woodshed with the kerosene, then after Mackenna grabbed Caroline, he'd start the fire.

He laughed gleefully. By this time tomorrow, Caroline and her brothers would be dead! And, if Hanley was still alive, he'd find a way to get rid of him too!

He moved away with a proud swagger. After tonight, Rebecca and Bryan would never again treat him like an imbecile!

Chapter Twenty-eight

Caroline was sitting at Hanley's bedside when Rebecca came in. There was no one else there, for the boys and Inés were having dinner in the kitchen with Doctor Gordon and his wife; Caroline had eaten earlier.

Inés had talked frankly with Caroline, and she knew about Rebecca's affair with Parker. She also knew that Bill had threatened divorce, which led Parker to suspect that Rebecca was involved in her husband's attempted murder. Although Inés was ready to find Rebecca guilty, Caroline was more lenient. She didn't believe in passing judgment hastily; she was, however, firmly against leaving Bill alone with Rebecca or her sons. Like Doctor Gordon, she didn't think Parker's suspicions were totally unfounded.

"Hello, Caroline," Rebecca said. "I just came from the kitchen. Walter and Daniel seem to be in fine health. Your grandfather will be so pleased." She forced a smile. "Doctor Gordon said that Bill regained consciousness this afternoon. That's wonderful! Is he awake now?"

"No, he's sleeping." Although Caroline was tempted to interrogate Rebecca, she didn't say anything. She knew the woman wasn't aware of Parker's accusations, or that he had voiced them aloud.

"If Bill's asleep, then I won't disturb him," Rebecca said. "Caroline, I was planning to spend the night in town, but I've changed my mind. If you're going to the ranch, may I ride with you?"

"Ross is at the saloon, but he'll be here shortly to take us to the Bar-H. We'll be leaving within the hour. Can you be ready by then?"

"Yes. It'll only take me a moment to pack, then I'll go to the livery and get the buggy. I'll be back as soon as possible."

She left the house quickly. She didn't relish riding to the ranch with Caroline and the others, but traveling alone was out of the question, for it would soon be dark. As she hastened toward the hotel, she considered stopping at the Watering Hole and letting Bryan and Alex know that she was going home. Pressed for time, however, she decided not to bother.

Rebecca had found staying at the hotel unbearable. Henry Parker's proximity was agonizing; she still wanted him desperately. She had hoped to weave him back into her web, but his daughter's return had thwarted any such plan, for Emily now monopolized his time. Thus, Rebecca had decided she might as well go home.

Ross, enjoying the cool night, stood on the front veranda of the Bar-H. He was smoking a cheroot and thinking about the ranch he planned to build for himself and Caroline. His land, which was ideal for grazing, stretched for several miles. A log cabin now stood in the area where he intended to build his future home. Ross was anxious to set his plans in motion, and as soon as Hanley was out of danger, he planned to leave. First, he would buy his cattle, then after the house was finished, he would return, marry Caroline, and take her to their new home.

The front door opened, and Caroline stepped outside.

"Are the boys asleep?" Ross asked, pitching his smoked cheroot over the porch railing.

"Yes. They were so tired they fell asleep almost instantly."

Ross slipped an arm about her waist, drawing her close to his side. "I was just thinking about our future."

She smiled brightly. "I can hardly wait to become Mrs. Ross Bennett. Caroline Bennett — sounds wonderful, doesn't it?"

"Sounds perfect," he said, kissing her tenderly. He embraced her tightly, whispering, "I'm going to miss you."

"Miss me?" she questioned, pushing out of his arms. "Whatever are you talking about?"

"As soon as we know Bill's out of danger, I plan to leave for Tucson. I have a ranch to build, remember? At present, there's nothing there but empty land and a log cabin."

"Ross Bennett!" she fussed, placing her hands on her hips. "If you think for one moment that you're leaving me behind, then you're out of your mind!"

"But, honey, I can't ask you to live in a cabin. I want to give you a home as grand as this one."

"And no doubt you someday will! But, in the meantime, our home will be a log cabin. My goodness, Ross! For five years I lived in a wickiup! Don't start treating me as though I've been pampered all my life." She went back into his arms, and holding him close, she said merrily, "Besides, living in a cabin and helping you build our future sounds very adventurous and romantic. I wouldn't miss it for the world."

"Are you sure you don't mind roughing it?"

"I've never been more sure of anything."

He bent his head, and his lips brushed against hers. It was a tantalizing invitation for more, and taking the initiative, Caroline turned their kiss into one of passion.

Releasing her, and holding her at arms' length, he studied her thoughtfully. He found her more beautiful than words could describe, and perusing her leisurely, he looked deeply into her gray eyes, which were veiled by thick, graceful lashes. He reached out and twirled a golden silky curl about his finger. He loved the color of her hair, so rich and vibrant.

Stepping back so he could see her better, his admiring gaze meandered over her trim, softly curvaceous frame. She was still wearing her riding attire, and the outfit, spotted with trail dust, reminded him that it had been a long day for Caroline. Knowing that she must be very fatigued, he kissed her lips softly, then said, "You need a good night's sleep, so I'll be on my way. I'll come back in the morning."

"Ross, you can spend the night here."

A worried frown knitted his brow. "I think I'd better get back to town. When I left, Kirk was at the saloon drinking pretty heavily. I'm a little concerned about him."

"What do you suppose is bothering him?"

"I'm not sure, but I think he's given up on Mary."

Caroline sighed impatiently. "Mary's such a fool! I can't believe she's going to lose a good man like Kirk simply because he's younger than she is."

"Maybe she doesn't love him."

"No, I'm sure she does." Hopeful, Caroline suddenly smiled. "Surely, she'll come to her senses."

Caroline took a long, relaxing bath and was slipping into her robe when she heard a knock at the front door. Wondering who could be calling at this late hour, she hurried downstairs.

Opening the door, she was surprised to see a young Mexican woman. The visitor was obviously apprehensive, for she kept shifting her weight nervously from one foot to the other.

"Señorita Hanley?" she asked.

"Yes. What can I do for you?"

"I was told that I might find work here. I am all alone, señorita. My parents, they were killed by the soldiers, and I have no kin to take me in. I am a good worker, and you do not have to pay me much money."

"How old are you?"

"I am sixteen."

Caroline looked about, expecting to find a buggy, a horse, or even a donkey, but none were in sight. "How did you get here?"

"I walked. I was able to hitch a ride to Dry Branch, then I got directions here, and I have been walking all day."

Caroline wondered why she hadn't come across her on her way home. "I came from town myself a few hours ago. I'm surprised I didn't see you on the road."

"I stopped to rest, and I fell asleep. Maybe that is why you did not see me."

Caroline told the vagrant girl to come inside. A small, badly worn carpetbag was at her feet, she picked it up and stepped into the house.

The girl's eyes widened with amazement. "Señorita, your home, it is very beautiful!"

"What is your name?"

"Lucía," she answered.

Caroline felt sorry for the girl, and smiling gently, she told her, "Lucía, we have a housekeeper, but she's getting on in years, and could probably use some help. I'll give you a job on a trial basis and if it works out, you'll have a permanent position. Do you understand?"

Her dark eyes shone radiantly. "Sí, señorita! I understand!"

"Come with me," Caroline said, taking her arm. "We'll go to my room, and you can tell me more about yourself."

They started up the stairs, but Caroline suddenly hurried back down, saying, "I forgot to lock the door. I'm not expecting trouble, but as my grandfather always says—it never hurts to take precautions."

A few minutes later, Mackenna, using Bryan's house key, unlocked the door, opened it furtively, and came inside. Stepping lightly for a man his size, he crept soundlessly up the stairs, and moved quietly down the hall. Bryan had said Caroline's room was the second on the left, but as he passed the first one, he heard someone moving about. He stopped, squatted, and peeked through the keyhole. He immediately recognized Rebecca, who was pacing back and forth. He seriously debated barging inside and taking her forcefully. He laughed to himself—it wouldn't take much force! The woman was as hot as a bitch dog in heat! He continued to watch as Rebecca went to her bed, slipped off her robe, and lay down. Reaching over, she extinguished the lamp, and the room became pitch dark.

Jake pushed aside temptation. This was no time to think about sexual thrills—his vendetta against Bennett was too pressing. He moved quietly to Caroline's room, pressed his ear against the closed door, and listened closely. The sounds of two voices made him frown with misgivings. Damn it, he had thought Caroline would be alone! He wasn't too upset, for she was evidently talking to another woman, and he didn't really consider the second person a threat. Handling two women should be easy.

He drew his pistol, placed the other hand on the doorknob, then stormed inside. Caroline was sitting on the edge of the bed, and, Lucía, occupying a chair, were speaking when they were interrupted by Jake's sudden intrusion.

Holding his gun on them, he threatened, "Scream, and I'll kill ya!"

Caroline, her heart pounding, got shakily to her feet. She had seen Mackenna at the restaurant in El Zarango, and she remembered him. She knew he was a cold-blooded killer, and she was very frightened.

Jake's gaze swept over Caroline's sleeping attire—she couldn't ride dressed like that! "Put on some clothes!" he told her gruffly. "And make it fast!"

She grabbed her riding garments, for they were within easy reach. Earlier, when she had undressed for her bath, she had discarded them, letting the articles fall beside the tub, which was still in her room. She knew asking for privacy would be a waste of breath, so she turned her back to Jake, and tried to dress while showing as little flesh as possible.

"What do you want with me?" she dared to ask.

"Never mind! Just hurry up, and keep your damned mouth shut!"

Meanwhile, Lucía, who had bounded from her chair, was terrified. Did this man plan to kill her, then kidnap the señorita? "Please, señor!" she begged, tears flowing. "Do not kill me!"

Jake wasn't sure what he intended to do with her. He hadn't planned on her being with Caroline. The moment he left with his captive, she would no doubt alert the whole household, plus every wrangler on the Bar-H. He considered killing her, then decided to hell with it. He'd simply knock her out. The blow itself might kill her, but if it didn't, she'd remain unconscious for a long time.

Caroline finished dressing, slipped on her boots, then turned back to Jake. She caught a glimpse of Lucía, though, and the girl's obvious fright touched Caroline deeply. "Mr. Mackenna," she said, her tone pleading, "I'll do anything you say. But please don't harm Lucía. She hasn't done anything to you."

Jake raised a bushy eyebrow. "So you know who I am, huh?"

"Yes, I do."

"Well, let me give you some advice, gal! I'd just as soon kill ya as look at ya! You give me any trouble, and I'll break your pretty little neck. You do as I say, and we'll get along just fine. You ain't nothin' to me but bait, but if I have to, I can catch Bennett without bait. You understand what I'm a-sayin'?"

"I understand perfectly. Now, about Lucía — with your permission, I'll tie and gag her." Caroline's voice was a lot steadier than her nerves.

"I got a better idea," Jake said, grinning cruelly. He stepped quickly to Lucía, and before the young woman had time to react, his pistol crashed against her forehead. The vicious blow sent her dropping face down onto the floor.

"My God!" Caroline cried. "You've killed her!"

Jake shrugged. "Maybe not—after all, these Mexicans got thick skulls."

Caroline rushed to Lucía, knelt beside her, and gently turned her over. She gasped deeply. Lucía's eyes, though open, were sightless. It was obvious that she was dead. "You monster!" Caroline raved, staring at Jake with rage.

"Shut the hell up!" he ordered, his beady eyes filled with cruelty. Taking a piece of paper from his shirt pocket, he moved over and propped it on the dresser.

"What's that?" Caroline asked.

"It's a note to Bennett, tellin' 'im where he can find you." He clutched Caroline's arm, and drew her away from Lucía. "Come on, gal! We're leavin'!"

He opened the door carefully, and finding the hallway empty, he forced Caroline to walk at his side. "Don't make any noises," he whispered gruffly. "If anyone shows his face, I'll blow it off!"

Caroline prayed that neither Walter nor Daniel would leave their rooms.

Keeping a firm grip on her arm, Jake led her outside, where two horses were saddled. He helped her mount, then taking her reins, he swung up onto the other horse.

As they galloped away from the house, Caroline fought back a wave of grayness that was trying to wash over her. She had never fainted in her life, but she knew she was very close to doing so. But, then, she had never been so frightened—dear God, she was at the mercy of Jake Mackenna!

She managed to take control of herself; she'd not faint! Quite the contrary, she would stay alert, and hope for a chance to escape!

Alex, hidden in the woodshed, waited until Jake and Caroline had ridden out of sight before venturing into the open. Carrying the cans of kerosene, he sneaked to the front of the house. Jake had left the door unlocked, but it didn't matter, for Alex had a key.

Going to the parlor, he opened one of the cans, and splashed the fuel haphazardly over the furniture, letting some of it spill onto the rug. Then, hurrying, he emptied the other can in the entryway, struck a match, and pitched it to the floor. The flames, catching immediately, swept across the foyer and into the parlor.

Alex ran from the house to his horse, mounted, and rode away at a fast speed. He would have enjoyed watching the house burn, but he couldn't chance being seen.

Meanwhile, Carl, who was asleep inside the bunkhouse, woke up with a start. Sitting up, he wondered what had awakened him. Had he heard a noise? He listened acutely, he could hear nothing except a few snores here and there from his bunkmates. He lay down, and was on the verge of falling back asleep when, suddenly, he became aware of a crackling sound. He sat up with a bolt, got out of bed, slipped on his trousers, and darted outside.

By now, the front of the house was a burning inferno. Carl froze for an instant; then, reacting, he rushed back into the bunkhouse. His urgent yells quickly brought everyone awake. As the wranglers, tried to clear their sleep-laced thoughts and stumbled out of their beds, Carl hastened back outside.

He headed toward the house, running at full speed. As he drew closer, heat from the raging fire hit him full force. He kept on going, lifting an arm over his face, for the fire was so intense that it singed his eyebrows. Knowing he couldn't enter through the front, he hurried around to the back.

The first two wranglers to arrive spotted Carl and followed him. The rear of the house wasn't in flames, and the men threw their bodies against the door, breaking it off its hinges. Barging inside, they were confronted with smoke swirling thickly through the kitchen. Going to the back stairs, they made their way to the second floor. The smoke was less dense here, and as the other two wranglers hurried inside Walter's and Daniel's bedrooms, Carl made his way farther down the corridor. He was almost to Caroline's room when, suddenly, a gust of flames flew up the stairway, and like a fiery red ball, rolled rapidly down the hall.

Turning away from the oncoming blaze, Carl had no choice but to retreat. His friends had found Walter and Daniel, and with the boys held tightly in their arms, they carried them down the rear stairs. As Carl followed, he felt physically ill. God, if only he could have gotten to Caroline's and Mrs. Hanley's rooms, but it had been impossible! The fire had so quickly consumed that part of the corridor!

They hastily made their way through the smoke-filled kitchen and outside into the night air. Carl thought he heard a woman's agonizing scream—he shuddered visibly—it sounded like Mrs. Hanley!

The rest of the wranglers were congregated in the front yard, and as Carl and the others came around

385

the side of the house, they asked if they should go inside.

"No!" Carl told them, coughing to clear his congested lungs. "The fire's out of control!"

The two wranglers put the boys on the ground, but Walter made a beeline for the house. Catching him, Carl forcefully drew him back.

"Let me go!" he shouted frantically. "My sister is in there!"

"I know," Carl groaned. "But I couldn't get to her!"

Walter struggled wildly. "I can get to her! Turn me loose!"

At that moment, the house, now totally engulfed in flames, began to cave in. The top floor gave way, and breaking up like so many jigsaw pieces, it tumbled downward.

Walter, crying uncontrollably, looked away from the conflagration. Cautiously, Carl turned him loose. He hurried to his brother and took him into his arms.

Daniel held on tightly but his eyes were dry. It was unmanly to shed tears—Fernando had implanted the belief in the boy so deeply that he had simply forgotten how to cry! Inside, though, his heart was breaking, and the pain was excruciating.

Chapter Twenty-nine

Sheriff Taylor had been on the brink of sleep when he thought he heard a noise in the parlor. Not wanting to disturb his wife, he got up carefully and slipped a robe over his nightshirt. His gun belt was hanging on the back of a chair, he unholstered his pistol, opened the bedroom door, and moved cautiously down the hall.

The moonlight shining through the parlor window revealed Mary instead of a burglar. Smiling, the sheriff entered the room, saying, "Honey, I thought you were an intruder." He lit a lamp, placed his gun on a table, and turned to look at his niece. She was sitting on the sofa, a robe over her nightgown.

"I'm sorry I woke you," she murmured.

"That's all right. I wasn't asleep. Why are you sitting in the dark?" His eyes studied her with care.

"I was just thinking," she replied.

Taylor sat beside her. "What's troubling you, Mary?"

She wondered if she should tell him what was on her mind. Deciding it might help to talk about it, she said softly, "Kirk Bennett wants me to marry him."

Taylor smiled pleasantly. "Honey, I think that's wonderful. Kirk's a good man."

"Yes, I know, but . . ."

"Go on," he encouraged.

She sighed heavily. "I think he's too young for me."

"Too young?" he questioned. "That's poppycock!"

She couldn't help but smile. "But it's true, Uncle Jim! Furthermore, he's a bachelor. Why would he want to marry a widow, a woman who has had two children?"

"I think he wants to marry you because he loves you."

"But will he love me ten years from now when I'm fifty, and he's only forty-three? A man in his forties can be very attractive, but when a woman reaches her fifties, she . . . she . . ." Mary's voice dropped to a whisper. "At fifty, she's old."

Jim guffawed. "Don't let my wife hear you say that!"

Mary blushed. "I'm sorry. But Aunt Lisa is different."

"Why do you say that?"

"Well, she's still so vivacious and good looking."

"That's because she's in love."

Mary regarded him dubiously.

"Lisa and I might not be all that young, but we can still love with a passion." Taylor's eyes twinkled. "We've been married for forty years, have three children, and seven grandchildren; yet Lisa's an exciting woman." He reached over, took her hand, squeezed it gently, and said, "And Lisa's four years older than I am."

"What?" Mary exclaimed. "I never knew that!"

"Well, its true. And Lisa's no longer in her

388

fifties, she's well into her sixties."

"She certainly doesn't look her age."

"And neither do you, but that's not the issue here. If Kirk really loves you, none of that matters."

"If I could only be sure that he does."

"I've had a few long talks with Kirk, and he's a man who knows his mind. He grew up at a young age, you know. He was only eighteen when he worked as a deputy. At the same time, he took care of Ross, who was only thirteen. He sent 'im to school, and made a home for 'im. Kirk's been around, Mary, and he's seen and done a lot in his thirty-odd years. I'm sure he's had chances to marry women a heck of a lot younger than you are, but you gotta realize that he didn't marry any of 'em. He was waiting for the right woman. Apparently, you're the one."

"But why me?" she pleaded. "Why not one of those younger women?"

" 'Cause when you love someone, age hasn't got anything to do with it. Mary Murphy, you're a very attractive woman, and you've got compassion, honesty, and integrity. Why wouldn't Kirk love you?"

She considered his words carefully. "Kirk's leaving in the morning," she said so quietly that Jim barely heard her.

"Don't let him go. Men like Kirk Bennett are few and far between."

She didn't say anything.

"Do you love him?"

"Yes, I do." She looked worried.

"Why are you troubled? You should be overjoyed."

"If I could only be sure!"

"Sure of what? That you'll always be happy? There are no guarantees, Mary. You should know that as well as anybody."

He was about to say more, but was interrupted by a sudden knocking at the door. "Who could that be at this hour?" Jim grumbled, getting up.

He was surprised to find that it was one of Hanley's wranglers. "Come in, Carl," he said. The man's face was haggard, and Jim knew at once that something was wrong.

"Sheriff," Carl began, "I got some real bad news."

"What is it?"

Mary hurried over and stood beside her uncle. She prayed nothing had happened to Caroline or the boys.

"There was a fire at the Bar-H," Carl said, his tone rasping. "The house burned to the ground."

"Was anyone hurt?" Mary cried.

"We got the boys out, but Mrs. Hanley and Miss Caroline . . ." Carl's voice broke. It was a moment before he could continue. "I swear to God that I tried to get to Mrs. Hanley and Miss Caroline, but the fire was out of control!"

"Dear God!" Mary exclaimed, horrified. "Are you saying that Caroline is dead?"

"Yes, ma'am. Her and Mrs. Hanley."

Shocked, Mary's knees gave way, and as she swayed precariously, Jim caught her in his arms. He helped her to the sofa.

Deep, heartbreaking sobs tore from her throat. The sheriff's wife, awakened by the commotion, hastened into the parlor. Jim told her what had happened, and as she tried to comfort Mary, he drew Carl aside.

"Go to the saloon and tell Bryan what has happened, then meet me at my office. I'll ride back to the Bar-H with you."

Taylor was halfway to his bedroom before Ross entered his thoughts. That Ross was in love Caroline was evident, for Jim could see it in his eyes every time he looked at her.

As he slipped on his clothes, Jim's heart was heavy indeed, for he knew he must tell Ross about Caroline before going to the Bar-H.

Ross went to his room at the hotel, lit the bedside lamp, and sank into a chair near the window. Although he was tired, he knew he had to wind down before sleeping. He had spent hours at the Watering Hole with Kirk. He had never seen his cousin so depressed, nor had he ever known him to drink so much. He felt sorry for Kirk, and wished he could help him, but there was nothing he could do. Kirk was suffering a broken heart that only time could heal.

Following hours of drinking, Ross had finally convinced him to leave the saloon. Kirk's steps had been unsteady, and Ross had helped him across the street and to the hotel. He unlocked Kirk's door and guided him to the bed where Kirk had promptly fallen into a whiskey-laced sleep.

Now, as Ross tried to relax, he steered his thoughts away from Kirk. He wanted to think about something pleasant, so he daydreamed about the ranch he and Caroline planned to build.

He was deeply submerged in his reverie when the sheriff rapped at his door.

"Who's there?" Ross called out.

"Sheriff Taylor."

Ross went to the door quickly. A visit from the

sheriff this time of night could mean only one thing—trouble!

Jim entered the room hesitantly. He dreaded what lay ahead.

"Is something wrong, Sheriff?" Ross asked at once.

Taylor drew a deep breath, then explained as gently as possible, "Bill's wrangler, Carl, just came to the house. There was a fire at the Bar-H. The house is completely destroyed. He said . . ."

"Caroline and the boys?" Ross cut it anxiously.

"Walter and Daniel are fine, the wranglers were able to get to them."

An icy snake of fear coiled in Ross's stomach. "Caroline?" he asked, his voice a rasping whisper.

"I'm sorry, Ross, but she's dead. The wranglers couldn't get to her or to Mrs. Hanley."

Ross felt as though he were encountering a nightmare beyond his imagination. Caroline dead? It was more than his mind could accept. "No!" he moaned. "I don't believe you!"

"It's true, Ross. God, I'm sorry!" Jim's grief was sincere. "I'm so damned sorry!"

Ross's body tensed, his feelings grew numb, and his heart went into shock. Caroline's death was beyond his comprehension. He headed for the door.

"Where are you going?" Jim called.

"To the Bar-H! Caroline's there, and she's alive!"

Jim stepped to him, and placed a hand on his shoulder. "Ross, don't do this to yourself."

He flung off the man's hand. "I tell you, she's alive! Damn you, don't you tell me otherwise!"

Jim followed Ross into the hallway. He knew Bennett was in shock. In his occupation, he had dealt often with death, and had witnessed this kind of shock before. It was nature's way of making such a loss bearable until the heart and mind were strong enough to accept it.

Bryan paced his office restlessly. His body was tense, and his nerves were on edge. He wondered how much time had passed since Alex had delivered his shocking news. Two, three hours perhaps, but to Bryan's troubled mind, it seemed much longer. He was sure any minute now, the sheriff or one of Hanley's wranglers would show up to tell him about the fire.

So far, Bryan had refrained from stating an opinion. He knew Alex expected him to be pleased, and if everything worked out to his advantage, he would be gratified. Losing the house didn't bother him, for he would build another one on an even grander scale. However, Bryan was upset with Alex for setting the fire without first talking it over with him. He would never have given his permission; arson was too risky. Furthermore, the boys probably escaped, and Alex's plan more than likely resulted in nothing more than a heap of ashes.

Bryan's thoughts went to Caroline, and her abduction appeased his nerves somewhat. He knew for a fact that she was eliminated, for Alex had seen Mackenna whisk her away.

He stopped his pacing, and wondered if he should go to the hotel and let his mother know what Alex had done. He considered it for a moment, then decided against it. If the sheriff were to find Rebecca awake at this hour of the night, it would certainly arouse his suspicions. Uneasiness, mingled with a touch of irritation, sent him back to pacing.

Alex wished his brother would sit down. Bryan's

393

pacing was getting on his nerves. He couldn't understand why he was so upset — everything would be all right. Walter and Daniel were dead, and soon Caroline would join them. After years of waiting and plotting, the Bar-H would undoubtedly be theirs! Why wasn't Bryan celebrating instead of acting like a man about to face the gallows?

A knock suddenly sounded at the door. Although they had been expecting it, they nonetheless jumped as though they had been shot. Bryan sat at his desk, composed himself, then told Alex to answer the door.

The brothers weren't at all surprised to see Carl. Alex waved him inside, and the man came into the office with halting steps. He hated being the bearer of such ill tidings.

"What can I do for you, Carl?" Bryan asked calmly.

"I got some bad news for you and Alex," he murmured.

"Oh?" Bryan questioned, his expression showing concern. "What is it?"

"There was a fire at the Bar-H. The house was completely destroyed. We were able to save the boys, but Miss Caroline and Mrs. Hanley . . ." Carl's face was anguished. "I'm sorry, but your mother and Miss Caroline died in the fire."

Bryan leapt to his feet. "You must be mistaken! Mother's at the hotel. She's spending the night in town." He was so distraught that Caroline's reported death failed to sink in.

"She came home," Carl explained. "I saw her arrive with Miss Caroline and the others."

"Are you absolutely sure?" Bryan demanded, his eyes bulging.

"Yes, sir, I'm sure." Carl, not wanting to intrude

on the brothers' grief, mumbled his condolences and left.

The instant the door closed, Bryan came at Alex like a madman. Grabbing him by the shirt collar, he jerked him forward. His face livid, Bryan uttered in a rasping, blood-chilling whisper, "You idiot! Do you realize what you have done? You killed our mother?"

Alex, trying to wrest free, moaned piteously, "I didn't know she was home! God, Bryan, how the hell was I supposed to know?"

Releasing him abruptly, Bryan struck him with the flat of his hand. The blow was short but vicious, sending Alex's head snapping backwards.

"Damn you, Bryan!" Alex raved, murder in his eyes. "You ever hit me again, and I'll kill you! So help me God!"

Alex's threat didn't scare him. "You stupid, blundering moron! The boys are alive, but Mother's dead!" Suddenly, Bryan blinked in utter astonishment. "Didn't Carl say that Caroline died in the fire, too?"

"Yeah, he sure did," Alex replied, remembering. "But I don't understand! I tell you, I saw Jake take her away!"

"Come on; we're riding out to the ranch. If the sheriff's there, you keep your goddamned mouth shut! You hear me?"

Alex merely nodded. Now that he had made a mess of everything, he decided it was best to be compliant.

The brothers, heading out of town, met up with Sheriff Taylor, Ross, and Carl. The group rode to the Bar-H together. They made the journey speedily, and without much conversation. Ross, still in shock, said nothing at all.

The house, now a pile of smoking rubble, was a heart-rending sight to Ross. Dear God, had Caroline died in this mass of destruction? The question tore into him without mercy. Two bodies, covered with sheets, were placed in the front yard.

The riders reined in. Ross dismounted and started toward the covered bodies when, suddenly the sheriff caught up to him, grabbed his arm, and deterred him.

"Let me go!" Ross shouted. He tried to fling off the man's grip, but it was too firm.

"Don't do this to yourself, Ross! It won't change anything! Besides, Caroline wouldn't want you to see her like that! My God, man, remember her as she was, not like she is now!"

Hanley's wrangler, Joe, who had placed the sheets over the corpses, said gently to Ross, "They were burned beyond recognition, Mr. Bennett. It ain't gonna do you any good to look at 'em."

"Then how do we know for sure that one of them is Caroline?" Ross asked desperately.

The wrangler replied, "We found one body in the bedroom that's Mrs. Hanley's, and the other one in Miss Caroline's room. The top floor caved in, but we recognized the bedrooms by the furniture that wasn't completely burned."

Ross still couldn't accept it. "How would you know whose bedroom is whose?"

"I do a lot of carpentering for Mr. Hanley, and I've worked in every room in the house." He placed a sympathetic hand on Ross's shoulder. "Besides, only Mrs. Hanley, Miss Caroline, and the boys were home tonight. There was nobody else here."

Ross turned toward the bodies, looked at them

for a moment, then whirled around. Taylor was right, Caroline wouldn't want him to see her this way! His steps sluggish, Ross moved toward the bunkhouse where Walter and Daniel were sitting on the porch steps. He sat between them, and Walter, bursting into tears, went into Ross's arms.

Never in his life had Ross been forced to face such a tragedy. He wasn't sure if he was strong enough to deal with it. Caroline had been his life, his heart, and his very reason for living! How was he to go on without her? Furthermore, he wasn't sure if he even wanted to go on!

His pain was agony, and it cut torturously into his heart. He groaned aloud, a wretched, pathetic sound.

Daniel, sharing Ross's pain, touched his arm gently. "Why did God let this happen?"

"I don't know," Ross murmured. He looked closely at Daniel, and noticing that the child's eyes were dry, he said, "You're holding up very well."

"Fernando says it is unmanly to cry." The boy was obviously fighting tears.

"Fernando's wrong. Sometimes, crying makes you more of a man. There's nothing unmanly about showing your feelings, whether it's through laughter or tears. Don't keep your grief bottled up inside, son. Let it out!"

Wrapping his arms about Ross's neck, Daniel set his emotions free, and hard, racking sobs shook his small body. Ross, drawing both boys close, took his own advice, and surrendering to his sorrow, he grieved along with Walter and Daniel.

The sheriff, standing at a distance, watched as Ross and the boys drew comfort from each other. His own eyes were misty, and wiping at the wetness, he moved toward the rubble that had once been a beautiful home. Carefully, he made his way through the ruins, his boots protecting his feet from the hot debris.

Spotting what appeared to be a gallon can, the sheriff studied it closely. It was black and charred, but identifiable—it was a can of kerosene. He searched a little farther, and came up with another one. Evidently, the fire had been started intentionally! Taylor was at a complete loss. Who would do such a thing? And why?

For a moment, he suspected Bryan and Alex, but quickly dismissed the notion. They would benefit from Caroline's and her brothers' deaths, true, but he didn't believe they would kill their mother. He didn't care much for the Rawlins—in his opinion, they weren't very likeable—but he was certain that they had loved their mother. The threesome had always seemed very close. Ruling them out as suspects, he tried to think of someone else who might have set the fire. He concentrated deeply, but could think of no one.

He reached down to pick up one of the cans, it was still hot. He quickly untied his neckerchief, wrapped it about his hand, and lifted the evidence. Getting the other can, he carried them to the woodshed, and placed them out of sight. Until he had time to investigate, he preferred that no one know about the kerosene.

Meanwhile, Alex and Bryan, having no inkling that the sheriff had found incriminating evidence, were standing close to the covered bodies.

The brothers were alone, for the wranglers had walked away. "You reckon we oughta take a look and see if it's really Caroline?" Alex asked.

"You heard what Joe said—the bodies are burned beyond recognition. Apparently, Caroline got away from Mackenna, and came back to the house. She probably rushed inside to try and save her brothers."

Alex smiled inwardly. "A lot of good it did her."

Bryan frowned irritably. At the moment, he hated his brother. His stupidity had taken Rebecca's life, and Bryan knew he would never forgive him. Afraid he might lose his temper, he said gruffly, "Alex, get the hell away from me before I knock you to the ground!"

"What's wrong with you? What did I say to get you all riled?"

"You're an idiot, Alex! Go back to town and wait for me in my office."

Alex left to do as he was told, but he was raging inside. He was sick and tired of Bryan treating him like dirt! As he headed away from the ranch, his mother's death barely fazed him. Years of jealousy had hardened his heart toward Rebecca—Bryan had always been her favorite—and he had resented her for that.

Chapter Thirty

The sheriff returned home at mid-morning. He had Walter and Daniel with him. The boys were exhausted, and Mrs. Taylor considerately took them to the guest bedroom.

Mary followed her uncle into the kitchen, where she poured him some coffee. "Where's Ross?" she asked, placing his cup on the table.

"I don't know," he replied wearily. "When we were loading the bodies into a buckboard to bring them to town, Ross suddenly mounted his horse and took off." He rubbed a hand over his brow. "I've never seen a man more tormented. He must've loved Caroline an awful lot."

"He did," Mary murmured. "Does Kirk know what has happened?"

"I don't think so."

"Someone should tell him. I'm sure Ross needs his support. He and Kirk are very close." She started out of the kitchen, saying over her shoulder, "I'll go to the hotel and tell him about the fire." She was still in her robe, and hurrying to her room, she dressed quickly.

The town was bustling with its usual morning activities as Mary hastened to the hotel. She went to the desk clerk and asked him for Kirk's room number. She was surprised when he told her that Kirk had checked out an hour ago.

She hurried to the livery, where she hoped to catch Kirk before he left town, but she was too late. The sheriff owned four horses, and he kept them stabled at the livery. She wasn't dressed for riding, but knowing she didn't have time to go home and change, she ordered one of the horses saddled. She swung up onto the roan gelding, her full skirt flaring.

She kept the horse at a steady walk, but the moment she was out of town, she kneed it into a fast gallop. The liveryman had said that Kirk left about thirty minutes ago. She should be able to catch him.

Kirk, riding at a leisurely pace, heard a rider advancing from the rear. He turned his horse about, and pulled up. His hand went cautiously to his holstered pistol, but as Mary drew closer, he recognized her. He spurred his horse forward and met her halfway.

Dismounting, he went to her side and helped her down. Her face was flushed, and she was trembling. He had a sinking feeling that something was terribly wrong.

"Oh Kirk!" she cried, and taking him unawares, she flung herself into his arms. He held her tightly, and she clung to his strength. She started crying; she couldn't help it.

"Mary, what's wrong?" he asked, his tone gentle despite his anxiety. Had something happened to Ross?

"Kirk, why were you leaving without saying goodbye? What about Ross? Didn't you want to see him before you left?"

"I told Ross last night that I was leaving this morning." He held her at arms' length. "Why did you come after me?"

"There was a fire at the Bar-H. Caroline and Mrs. Hanley are dead. They died in the blaze! The wranglers were able to save Walter and Daniel, but they couldn't get to Caroline and Mrs. Hanley!"

"My God!" Kirk groaned. "Does Ross know?"

"Yes! Uncle Jim said he's taking it very hard!"

Kirk was silent for a moment, then he exclaimed in a ravaged tone, "Caroline was still so young, and she had so much to live for! Aw God! Why, Caroline?"

They went into each other's arms, both drawing comfort from the other. It was a long time before Kirk finally released her. "Where can I find Ross?" he asked softly.

"We don't know where he is. He was at the ranch, but Uncle Jim said he left without telling anyone where he was going."

"He probably needs time alone." Taking her arm, he led her to her horse and helped her mount. "I'll ride back to town with you. Ross will show up sooner or later, and when he does . . ." A shiver ran through Kirk. "Ross and I have seen each other through a lot of hard times, but this time . . . ? It's not gonna be easy to help him through it. He loved Caroline as much as it's possible for a man to love a woman."

Mary and Kirk stopped at the sheriff's house, but Ross wasn't there. Neither was the sheriff, for he was at Doctor Gordon's home. They went there also, and were admitted by Inés, whose eyes were red and swollen. Mary held the woman gently as, together, they wept for Caroline.

Doctor Gordon gathered his guests in the parlor, a solemn silence hovered over the group. Mrs. Gordon served coffee, then she left to sit with Hanley.

Clearing his throat, Doctor Gordon said, "Bill isn't strong enough to be told. The shock would kill him. We'll have to wait until he's stronger."

"But he'll wonder why Caroline and Rebecca don't come to see him," Taylor replied.

"We'll tell him that Caroline has a bad cold, and I forbade her to see him. In Bill's condition, if he were to catch a cold, it would probably turn into pneumonia. As for Rebecca, the day he was shot he told her he wanted a divorce. He won't even care that she doesn't come to see him. I doubt if he'll even ask." He turned to Mary. "You'll have to talk to Walter and Daniel, and explain how vital it is that they don't tell their grandfather about Caroline."

"I will," she answered.

Kirk spoke to the sheriff. "Do you have any idea where Ross is?"

"No, I don't."

Kirk sighed heavily. "I'm gettin' awfully worried about him."

The sheriff left his chair, crossed the room, and said, "I have some business to take care of. I'll see you all later."

He went outside, mounted his horse, and headed toward the general store. Recently someone had purchased two cans of kerosene — he intended to find out who it was!

Mackenna had taken Caroline to an abandoned cabin. There was no furniture, and she was forced to sit on the floor, her hands tied behind her. She was uncomfortable—the floor was hard, and her hands were bound so tightly that the rope was cutting off her circulation.

Mackenna, holding a bottle of whiskey, was seated beneath a window, the pane was cracked in several places. Periodically, he would pour some whiskey into a tin cup and drink it slowly. So far, he had been a man of little words, and Caroline's attempts to talk to him had failed. She was hopeful, however, that eventually the whiskey would loosen his tongue. She wanted to find a way to convince him to untie her—escape was impossible with her hands bound.

She decided to make another attempt to draw him into a conversation. "Exactly what did you say in the note to Ross?"

"I told 'im he had until sunset to come and get you. I also told 'im if he didn't come alone, you'd be dead."

"What makes you so sure that Ross will come for me?"

Jake grinned slyly. "I know you're Bennett's woman. The Rawlins boys told me all about you."

"You mean, Bryan and Alex?"

"Yep, I sure do."

Caroline was astounded. "But why would they do something like that?"

"You see, we kinda made a deal. They gave me the bait I needed to trap Bennett, and, in return, I get rid of you for them. They're a-itchin' to own the Bar-H."

"I suppose they hired you to shoot my grandfather."

404

Jake merely laughed.

Caroline's thoughts raced—there must be something she could say or do to escape! She came up with a plan, but she knew it would take time. First, she must plant a seed of doubt in Mackenna's mind.

She spoke calmly, "Mr. Mackenna, Bryan and Alex have used you. Ross Bennett and I are not lovers. In fact, he left last night for Tucson. They simply tricked you into getting rid of me without having to pay you."

"You don't fool me, little gal. You're just tryin' to get me to set you free 'fore Bennett gets here. You know I'm goin' to kill 'im."

Caroline decided not to say anymore. She had planted the seed, and she hoped it would take root. She prayed that Ross wouldn't show up before sunset. With time, she just might be able to escape. She lowered her gaze to her lap. The pouch of sleeping powder was still in the pocket of her riding skirt. The garment had been cleaned at Sánchez's house, but the next morning, Caroline had slipped the pouch back into the pocket. There, it had remained. Last night, when she had undressed for her bath, she hadn't thought to remove the powder.

She hoped to find a way to convince Mackenna to untie her so she could slip the powder into his cup. Her nerves tightened, and her heart began to pound. She was afraid that Ross would come after her without delay. If he showed up before she had a chance to use the powder, she was sure Mackenna would kill him!

Alex was in the saloon at a corner table with Bryan when his friend, Nick, came through the bat-

405

wing doors. Seeing the brothers, he hurried over, pulled up a chair, and sat down.

Bryan glowered at the young man. In his opinion, Nick was as worthless as Alex. A deep frown knitted his brow as he remembered the way Alex, Nick, and Alfredo had blundered ambushing Caroline and the Bennetts. They claimed the sun had blinded them! What idiots!

"Alex," Nick began, sounding anxious. "I was just at the general store, and the sheriff was there askin' if anyone had bought two cans of kerosene. I heard the owner say you had bought some yesterday. The sheriff seemed real interested. I don't know if this means trouble or not, but I thought I oughta let you know."

"Goddamn it!" Bryan hissed, jumping to his feet. "Alex, let's go to my office!" He whirled about stiffly, motioning for his brother to follow.

"Did I say somethin' I shouldn't have?" Nick asked, having no idea why Bryan was upset.

Alex didn't answer, he simply moved away. Replying was impossible—fear had his throat so dry that he couldn't talk.

The moment they entered the office, Bryan slammed the door shut, then turned on Alex with a maddening fury, "You stupid ass! Didn't you get rid of those kerosene cans?"

"I figured they'd burn up in the fire." His voice not only squeaked, but wavered as though he were gurgling his words.

"Do you realize what you have done? You've ruined everything! Taylor will be here any minute to arrest you, and knowing you, you'll spill your guts! He'll get everything out of you, and then he'll be arresting me!"

"Well, if I have to go to prison, I ain't gonna go

alone! You're right! I'll tell 'im everything! I'll tell 'im how you hired Nick and Alfredo to kill Caroline and the Bennetts, and I'll also tell 'im that you hired Mackenna to shoot Hanley! Goddamn it, I ain't in this alone, and I ain't gonna take the full rap!"

Enraged, Bryan pulled back his arm, and slapped Alex across the face. The sharp whack resounded throughout the room.

Alex's anger erupted, and drawing his pistol, he said with murderous intent, "You hit me for the last time!" Fiery hate burned in his eyes. "You'll never again treat me like dirt!"

Bryan was scared. "Now, Alex, don't do anything foolish! Put away the gun, and we'll talk everything over. Don't worry, you won't go to prison. I'll hire you a good lawyer. I promise."

Alex's mentality didn't disappoint Bryan. "You reckon a good lawyer can get me off?"

"Of course," Bryan lied.

"You serious?"

"I'm very serious." Bryan held out his hand. "Give me the gun, Alex. We're brothers, and we stick together." He forced a smile. "Through thick and thin."

Convinced, he foolishly handed over the pistol. Taking it, Bryan pointed it at Alex, and within the blink of an eye, he fired the gun, sending a bullet straight into his brother's heart.

He rushed to the door, opened it, and yelled to his bartender, "Don't be alarmed! Alex was fooling with his gun, and it accidentally fired. There's a hole in the floor, but no one's hurt."

Moving quickly, Bryan went to his wall safe, removed the painting covering it, and took out all his money. He knew he had only one option—he had to leave town at once. If he traveled fast and hard, he might cross the border into Mexico before the sheriff caught up to him.

He went to his brother's body, stood over it, and looked down at it with disgust. Damn Alex for ruining everything! There wasn't a lawyer on the face of the earth who could have saved him! Bryan knew Alex would have gone to prison or to the gallows, and he also knew that his brother would have implicated him. His own arrest would have been as certain as Alex's.

He stepped over his brother's body, put his money in a briefcase, and left by the back door. He felt no remorse. Quite the contrary, he was glad to be rid of Alex once and for all!

From Caroline's position, she could see the window at Mackenna's back, and she watched as the sun dipped farther and farther into the west. It would soon be dark! She had thought Ross would be here before now. At first, she had hoped that he wouldn't show up before she could escape, but all attempts she had made to get Mackenna to untie her had failed. Finally, she had given up, praying that Ross would somehow save her without losing his own life.

Where was he? Why hadn't he come to her rescue? The note had certainly been found, for Mackenna had left it on her dresser. He had even propped it up in clear sight.

No, she was sure Ross had received the note. So why hadn't he come for her? She didn't want to lose faith in him, but as the sun crept farther down the horizon, she began to doubt Ross's love. She didn't want to feel this way, but she couldn't help it.

"It don't look like Bennett's comin'," Jake grumbled. "I guess he don't figure you're worth it, huh?'

Despite her turmoil, Caroline took advantage of Ross's absence. "Mr. Mackenna, I already told you that Ross and I aren't involved. Maybe now you'll believe me. Bryan and Alex lied to you. They merely used you to get rid of me. They tricked you, and you fell for it."

Jake scowled harshly. "Nobody uses me and gets by with it!"

"Apparently, Bryan and Alex did just that. But, Mr. Mackenna, if you set me free, then their trickery will have been for nothing."

He seemed to mull it over, and Caroline was hopeful. Suddenly, though, a lewd expression fell over his face, causing Caroline to grow apprehensive.

"You know, you sure are a pretty little gal. And I just might let you go, but not until you and me have some fun. You know what I mean?"

She understood exactly, and the thought alone sent a revolting shudder through her.

"I'll give Bennett another hour, but if he don't show up, then you and me are gonna get to know each other real good. If you're real sweet and cooperative, afterwards, I just might let you go."

Revulsion, mixed with fear, stirred within her. She felt as though she'd rather face death than have Mackenna touch her in such a way.

The next hour was an agonizing one for Caroline. She was torn between despair and dread. She couldn't understand why Ross hadn't come to save her. She felt betrayed, and as the minutes ticked by, she became more and more despondent. Through it all, Mackenna's lecherous intentions loomed ominously.

As the gray shadows of dusk faded into night, Caroline gave up on Ross. She knew she had to save herself—her only resources were wit, instinct, and the hidden pouch in her pocket.

Jake had been sitting beneath the window, he got up, turned to Caroline, and said, "He ain't comin'."

"I knew he wouldn't," Caroline replied, trying not to sound as disillusioned as she felt. "Mr. Mackenna, will you please untie me? Before we get to know each other better, I'd like to have a couple drinks of whiskey."

He moved toward her. "A little gal like you shouldn't drink hard liquor, it might make you sick." He laughed menacingly.

"It won't make me sick," she replied. Then, with a suggestive smile, added, "But it might make me more cooperative. You know, relax me a bit?"

A lustful grin curled his lips. "Yeah, I know what you mean. And if you want a couple of drinks, then you can have 'em. Ole Jake here, he knows how to treat a woman."

"I just bet you do," she murmured, still smiling. Inside, her stomach was turning. She didn't need whiskey to make her sick, Jake's nearness alone was enough to bring on a bout of nausea. She swallowed heavily, conquered the need to gag, and turned so that Jake could untie her hands.

He removed the ropes quickly, and Caroline rubbed her wrists in an effort to get her blood circulating freely. Her hands were numb, but feeling soon returned. Jake had the whiskey bottle, but had left the tin cup behind.

Caroline stood up swiftly, and before he could stop her, she moved away, saying, "You forgot the cup."

He watched her closely as she went to it, stooped

over, and picked it up. "If you're thinkin' 'bout dashin' for the door, you'll never make it."

"I'm not planning to make a run for it," she replied. She moved back to him, gestured toward the floor, and said, "Shall we sit down?"

They were about to do so when, all at once, Caroline acted as though something had caught her attention. She stood rigid, her ear cocked toward the door.

Jake was immediately on guard. "Did you hear somethin'?" he asked gruffly.

"No, I . . . I . . . didn't . . . hear . . . a thing," she answered, her hesitancy obvious.

Naturally, he didn't believe her. "Stay here!" he grumbled.

The moment he walked away to check the window, then the door, his back turned, Caroline slipped the small pouch from her pocket, and sprinkled its contents into the cup. There wasn't much left, but mixed with the whiskey he had consumed, the combination should put him out for hours. She certainly hoped so!

Deciding no one was lurking about, Jake returned. Caroline sat down, and he joined her. She poured a good amount of whiskey into the cup, and handed it to him.

She smiled, and the moonlight that was now shining through the window illuminated her face. "I prefer to drink straight from the bottle," she said, tilting it to her mouth and taking a large swig. The liquor burned her throat, but through sheer will power, she managed not to choke.

Jake was staring at her dubiously, and she daringly took another big drink. The second swallow seemed to burn less.

"You're a gal who likes her spirits, ain't ya?"

"Yes, and I also like a man who can drink right along with me. So, are you going to just hold that cup, or are you going to join me?"

"Bottoms up, little gal," he said, touching his cup to her bottle.

Caroline dreaded taking another drink, but she had no choice. She quaffed down the third gulp. Meantime, Jake tipped the cup to his lips and drained it. He belched, thrust the cup toward her, and said, "Fill it up, baby doll. We'll have another drink, then we'll get down to some serious lovin'. What do you say, huh?"

"Sounds good to me," she replied, praying the powder would soon take effect. She filled his cup.

Caroline's fourth swallow of whiskey went down easy, and settled warmly in her stomach. She was beginning to feel a little light-headed. She certainly didn't want to get drunk, for she needed full control of her faculties. But if Mackenna didn't soon fall asleep, she feared she'd be inebriated.

The sleeping powder hit Jake all at once. The cup was halfway to his mouth when it tilted forward, then slipped out of his hand, falling onto his lap. He leaned back against the wall, his head bowed, causing his long, ragged beard to rest on his chest. A low moan sounded deep in his throat, then, following a moment of silence, he began to snore loudly.

Caroline leapt to her feet. She fled outside and swung up onto her horse. She didn't want Jake to follow, so she reached over and took the reins to his mount. Leading the horse behind her, she rode away swiftly.

As she steadily covered the miles to town, Ross occupied most of her thoughts. Why hadn't he come for her? Was he sick? Had he been injured?

Or did he not love her enough to risk his life? The last question tore through her heart, and brought tears to her eyes. She had believed that Ross's love was as strong as her own! Could she have been wrong? It was a heart-rending possibility, and she wanted to dismiss it. But how could she? The note had given Ross plenty of time to get to the cabin, but he hadn't come! Why? God, if she only knew why!

Chapter Thirty-one

Mackenna awoke slowly. The effects of the drug and alcohol muddled his thoughts, and as he got awkwardly to his feet, his head was spinning. Woozy, he almost collapsed, but somehow managed to keep his balance. He stumbled to the door, swung it open, and stepped outside. The night air refreshed him, and his thoughts began to clear. Caroline Hanley! Damn it, he had let her slip away! Having no idea that she had drugged him, Jake couldn't understand why he had passed out. He blamed it on the whiskey, although he hadn't drunk all that much.

He was still on the porch, recovering, when a lone rider approached. He moved a hand toward his holstered pistol, but stopped at the unmistakable click of a rifle being cocked.

"Don't move!" the rider called out, coming closer, his Winchester aimed and ready to fire.

The man rode into the moonlight, and Jake recognized him; at the same time, the rider recognized Mackenna.

"What are you doing here?" Bryan asked, coming upon Jake quite by accident. He pulled up and dismounted.

"I brought that Hanley bitch here," Jake grumbled.

"Here?" Bryan questioned. "But that's impossible! There was a fire at the Bar-H last night, and she died in the blaze."

"I don't know nothin' 'bout no fire. But I had her here with me for hours, but Bennett never came." Jake was fuming, but he didn't show it. He believed that Rawlins had double-crossed him. He had known all along that Bennett wouldn't try to save Caroline Hanley! He and his brother had simply used him to get rid of her. Well, she was still alive, and it served them right!

"Did you set Caroline free?" Bryan was indeed confused. If Caroline was alive, then whose body had been mistaken for hers?

"Nope, I didn't set her free. She slipped away while I was dozin'," Jake explained. "I reckon I drank too much whiskey."

"It doesn't matter," Bryan replied heavily. "I've given up on the Bar-H, and I really don't care if Caroline's alive or not. In fact, I'm on my way to Mexico."

"Runnin' from the law?" Jake asked, grinning.

Bryan didn't answer, but looking about, asked, "Where's your horse?"

"That bitch took it."

"That's too bad. If you had a mount, I'd invite you to ride with me, but I'm in a hurry and riding double would slow me down."

"I understand," Jake replied, smiling calmly.

Bryan moved carefully to his horse, his rifle aimed at Mackenna. He found it clumsy, however, to mount and hold Jake at gunpoint. He made a fatal mistake when he let down his guard to swing into the saddle.

Moving with lightning speed, Mackenna drew his pistol, aimed, and fired. The bullet hit its target, and Bryan was struck in the chest. He dropped to the ground with a solid thud.

Jake hurried over, grabbed the rifle, and leered down at the man he had shot.

Bryan, still alive, was writhing in pain.

"Nobody double-crosses me and gets by with it!" Jake uttered gruffly. "You knew all along that Bennett wouldn't show!"

"That's . . . not . . . true," Bryan groaned weakly.

Jake shrugged. "It don't really matter. I'd have killed you anyway, 'cause I need your horse."

"Please," Bryan pleaded piteously. "Get me to a doctor. Don't let me die! Oh God! Jake! I'm in terrible pain! Help me! Please!" He was petrified by fear. He didn't want to die!

"I'll help you, Mr. Rawlins," Jake said, a cruel grin curling his lips. "I won't let you suffer no more." He chuckled heartily. "I'm what you call a humani . . . hu-man-i-tar-i-an. Yeah, that's the word." He was proud of himself for coming up with it. "I'll get you out of your pain, Mr. Rawlins. Yes, siree!" He pointed his pistol at Bryan's head.

"No!" Bryan cried feebly. "No! Don't do it! I beg you!" Tears filled his eyes, and spilled down his cheeks.

"Farewell, Mr. Rawlins. I'll see you in hell!" Jake pulled the trigger. He didn't miss, and Bryan died instantly.

Laughing, for he enjoyed killing, Jake holstered his pistol and went to Bryan's horse. He had seen the briefcase, and was curious about its contents. Finding it filled with money was a pleasant surprise indeed. There was enough to tide him over for a quite a spell, especially in Mexico where things were a lot cheaper. First, however, he still had a score to settle with Bennett. Caroline had said that Bennett left for Tucson but he wasn't sure if he believed her. He had a feeling that Ross was still somewhere around Dry Branch. If he didn't find him there, then he'd head for Tucson.

Slipping the rifle into its sheath, Jake mounted the horse, turned it about, and rode away.

Kirk had rented a room at the hotel directly across from Ross's. He sat on the edge of the bed, his door open so he'd see his cousin should he return. Kirk was gravely worried about Ross, no one had seen him since he mysteriously rode away from the Bar-H. Kirk supposed Ross needed time alone, but, damn it, he had been missing for over twelve hours! He was growing more concerned by the minute.

Kirk frowned uncertainly. Maybe he should have joined the posse who were chasing after Bryan Rawlins. At least he would be doing something besides just sitting and worrying. He had stayed behind, though, because he wanted to be here when Ross came back.

Restless, Kirk went to the window and stared blankly outside. He thought about Bryan and Alex. The sheriff had concluded that Alex didn't know his mother was in the house. After all, when the brothers had learned of their mother's death, Bryan had exclaimed to Carl that Rebecca was at the hotel. Apparently, she had decided to return to the Bar-H without telling her sons.

Kirk wondered why Bryan had shot Alex. Was it out of hate because he had killed their mother, or did he simply want to get rid of him?

Suddenly, the sound of footsteps sent Kirk whirling about. He was pleased to find Mary coming into his room.

"Did Ross show up?" she asked.

"No, not yet," Kirk replied. He pulled up a chair for her, then sat on the edge of the bed. "Has the posse come back?"

417

She shook her head.

Kirk sighed deeply.

Watching him, Mary held back an impulse to take him into her arms. He looked so tired, and so worried! She knew Ross's absence was very upsetting. "Kirk, try not to worry. I'm sure Ross is all right."

"Yeah, I know," he murmured. "I just hate this damned waiting!" Nervous, he got up and began to pace.

Mary went to him, and placed a hand on his arm. "Kirk, why don't you try to sleep? I'll watch for Ross."

"Sleep!" he grumbled. "That's not what I need!"

"Then what do you need?"

His strong hands suddenly gripped her shoulders. "I need you! I need your love! I need to feel your body next to mine! I want us to make love now before something happens to rip us apart! Life's too damned uncertain to gamble with happiness! I love you, Mary Murphy, and God knows I don't want to lose you! How can you throw our love away when Ross's and Caroline's has been taken away so cruelly? Don't you realize that we've got to hold onto each other, and be thankful for every moment of happiness that comes our way? No man will ever love you as much as I do, but because of seven lousy years, you're going to reject my love as though it were nothing!"

"Oh Kirk, that's not true! Your love means everything to me! I'm just so afraid!"

"Of what?"

"That I'll grow old before you, and that you'll regret you married me! Someday, you'll long for a younger woman, one who can give you children!"

"To start with, what makes you so sure that we won't have children? Why are you so sure it would matter to me whether we do or not? This country's full of orphans we can always adopt. Hell, if you want, we can adopt an even dozen! We both have a lot of love to give, why not give it to kids who really need it."

"Why not?" she responded, smiling brightly.

Kirk was taken aback. "Mary, are you . . . are you saying . . . ?"

"Yes!" she cried, flinging herself into his arms. "I'm saying that I love you, and I want to be your wife with all my heart and soul!"

He held her tightly. "Mary, I love you! Please don't worry that I'll leave you for a younger woman. You're all I want, and I'll want you until the day I die!"

"I believe you," she whispered truthfully, casting her doubts aside.

He kissed her then, passionately and from the bottom of his heart.

"Kirk," she murmured in a trembling voice. "You were right when you said we need to make love now before anything can rip us apart. We'll never need each other more than we do right this minute. For a little while, let's leave reality behind, and lose ourselves in each other's arms. I want to escape, don't you? This day has been too unbearable!"

"Sweetheart," he whispered, holding her close. "I feel the same way. I've never needed love as much as I do right now." He kissed her softly, then going to the door, closed and locked it.

He went to the lamp, turned the wick down to a romantic glow, returned to Mary, and kissed her again.

Leaving the real world behind, she was conscious only of his nearness, and the touch of his lips, which sent pleasure pulsing through every nerve in her body.

Now, with passion controlling their every move, they anxiously helped each other undress, both marveling at the perfection they found in each other.

Mary's eyes roamed boldly over Kirk, and she thought him admirably handsome. His tall, muscular physique was ideally proportioned, and she could hardly wait to touch, kiss, and thoroughly enjoy such male perfection.

Kirk was equally impressed, for Mary's slim and voluptuous frame was beautiful beyond compare, and he intended to relish every inch of her desirable flesh.

He swept her into his arms, carried her to the bed, and laid her down with care. Taking his place beside her, he drew her close, pressing his lips ardently to hers. She surrendered totally to the strength, feel, and scent of him, and wrapping her arms about his neck, she molded her body to his.

Wonderfully engulfed in ecstasy, they expressed their love through touching, kissing, and arousing gestures that set fire to their already heated passion.

Kirk, his desire raging, spread her legs, moved over her, and claimed her completely. His possession was rapturously exciting, and Mary's hips lifted in sensuous submission. As his hardness delved ever deeper, her passion was aroused to its fullest.

They gladly gave themselves up to the incredible power of their love, and leaving the real world behind, they soared happily into their own utopian paradise.

Ross's steps were quiet as he walked down the corridor. He stopped at his room and unlocked the door. He paid no attention to the room across from his, for he didn't know that Kirk had rented it. As far as Ross knew, Kirk had left this morning for Tucson.

Ross had taken one step inside when, down the hall, a door suddenly opened. He turned to look, and seeing that it was Emily, he turned away and went into his room.

Before he could close the door, however, she was there. "Ross," she said, sweeping past him and barging

nside. "I heard what happened to Caroline. I wanted
o tell you how sorry I am."

He left the door open, and stepped to the dresser,
where a full bottle of whiskey rested. He uncorked it,
put it to his lips, and took a big swig.

"Go away, Emily," he muttered, his tone strangely
hollow. But, then, Ross wasn't capable of feeling anything — his heart, thoughts, and emotions were numb.

Emily wasn't about to go away. Now, with Caroline
dead, there was no reason why she couldn't get Ross
back. She knew it wouldn't happen overnight — first
he'd have to get over losing Caroline. But she intended
o help him recover.

"Ross, where have you been? Kirk's been looking for
ou."

"Kirk?" he questioned, taking another swig of whiskey. "I thought he left town."

"No, he's here at the hotel. I saw him earlier. I also
saw you ride up. I was standing at the window. I really
don't want to intrude on your grief, but I did so want
o give you my condolences."

"Emily, just go away, will you?"

She watched as he gulped down more whiskey.
"Ross, how much have you had to drink tonight?"

"Not enough," he said flatly.

"Well, liquor is exactly what you need." She hoped
he'd get drunk, maybe then she could compromise
him. "If you drink enough, you'll be able to forget
Caroline — at least for a little while."

A sudden, fiery rage burned in his eyes. "There's not
enough liquor on the face of this earth to make me forget Caroline! Not even for a moment!"

"I'm sorry, Ross. I didn't mean to upset you. I was
just trying to be helpful."

He wasn't listening. He didn't give a damn what she
had to say. He felt he didn't give a damn about any-

thing or anybody! He swigged down more whiskey, wishing he could drink himself into oblivion!

Ross had spent the day by himself. After leaving the Bar-H, he had ridden to the old homestead that had been Hanley's original home. The clapboard house was in need of repair, but for the most part, the structure was still sound. It was unfurnished, and Ross had sat on the floor, where he had grieved in solitude. The quiet, grief-filled hours had failed to ease his pain.

Now, with Caroline's memory still torturing him mercilessly, he continued to drink. Forgetting that Emily was even in the room, he lumbered to the bed, sat down, and tilting the bottle to his mouth, he quaffed a huge amount. God, he wanted to die!

A low, mournful moan sounded deep in his throat.

Emily went to him, and placed an arm about his shoulders. She drew him close, and, Ross, completely unmindful to who was holding him, leaned against her.

"I love you, Ross," she whispered.

His mind was so crazed with grief and whiskey that, for an instant, he thought he was with Caroline. "I love you, sweetheart. I'll never lose you again. Never!"

Caroline was riding down the main street on her way to the sheriff's office when she saw Ross's horse tied in front of the hotel. She dismounted, flung the horse's reins over the hitching rail, and went inside. At the moment, no one was at the front desk, so she went up the stairs to the second floor. If need be, she'd knock on every door until she found Ross's room. He had a lot of explaining to do! Why had he left her at Mackenna's mercy?

Down the hall a door had been left ajar, and she decided to investigate. Moving quietly, she went to the

pen threshold, and the sight before her eyes hit her
ith terrible force. She looked on with horror as Emily
ut an arm about Ross's shoulders, drawing him close.

"I love you, Ross," she heard Emily whisper.

"Sweetheart, I love you. I'll never lose you again.
Never!"

Caroline, her heart breaking, wheeled about and
ashed down the hallway. She descended the stairs
uickly, darted through the lobby, and ran outside.

She didn't go to the sheriff's office, but rode speed-
y out of town. She headed toward the Bar-H. She
idn't want to see anybody. Not now! She needed time
o get her feelings under control!

Pain, mixed with anger, swirled through her turbu-
ently. Damn Ross! He was a two-timing, unfeeling
wine! Apparently, he didn't even care that Jake had
bducted her. He only cared about his darling Emily!
he was so enraged she felt as though she could send a
ullet into his stone-cold heart!

Caroline had barely dashed down the hallway when
Ross had come to his senses. Realizing he was with
Emily and not Caroline, he pushed her away and got to
is feet. His grief had him so confused that he was hal-
ucinating!

Ross and Emily didn't hear the door across the way
open, nor did they see Mary and Kirk step into the
all. Glad to see Ross, the pair started to rush into his
oom, but Emily's presence was a deterrent.

"Ross," Emily was saying, patting the mattress.
Come back, darling. Let me help you forget. You
vant my arms about you." She smiled sweetly. "You
now you do."

"The only reason I let you hold me is because I
hought you were Caroline. I'm so damned mixed up

that I don't know reality from a dream!"

"You told me you loved me."

Ross, his emotions crumbling, yelled, "I was saying it to Caroline! God, help me! I can't stand it! I'm losing my mind! Aw, God! Caroline!"

Mary barged into the room, and with tears flowing, she coaxed Ross into her arms. He held onto her as though if he let go he would sink to the floor.

Kirk told Emily to leave, and his tone brooked no argument. She cast him a petulant glare, then left in a huff.

Ross remained in Mary's comforting embrace for a long moment before moving away. He welcomed her sympathy, but it did little to ease his tortured heart.

"Ross, are you all right?" Kirk asked gently.

He nodded, mumbling, "Yeah, I'm okay." He rubbed a hand over his perspiring brow. He was suddenly feeling very warm, and the small room seemed to be closing in on him. These claustrophobic feelings sent him escaping to the door.

"Where are you going?" Kirk asked anxiously.

"I gotta get out of here! I need air—I need breathing space!" Before Mary or Kirk could stop him, he was moving quickly down the corridor.

"Oh Kirk!" Mary moaned. "I feel so sorry for him! He's in such horrible pain!"

"I don't think he should be alone. I'm gonna follow him."

"I want to go with you."

A faint smile touched his lips, and kissing her tenderly, he said, "We'll go together."

She hugged him tightly. "From this day forward, my darling, we'll always be together."

Carl was about to walk inside the bunkhouse when

Caroline rode into sight. At first, he couldn't believe his eyes, and he rubbed them as though he needed to clear his vision. Then, realizing there was nothing wrong with his eyesight, he ran forward to greet her.

Caroline, staring at the burned rubble that had once been a home, dismounted in a daze. She reached out, grabbed Carl's arm, and asked with fear in her heart, "Walter and Daniel—are they all right?"

"They're fine, Miss Caroline."

She didn't notice that Carl's face was as white as a ghost.

"Where are they?"

"They're staying with the sheriff and his wife."

"Do you know what caused the fire?"

He didn't answer, he merely stared at her, his mouth agape.

Impatient, Caroline asked, "Carl, why are you looking at me so strangely? Did you think Mackenna had killed me?"

"Mackenna?" he questioned. "We all thought you died in the fire."

"Died in the fire?" she repeated. "But, of course! The note burned up!"

"What note?"

Following more questions, answers, and explanations, all the pieces fell neatly into place. Although Caroline had never liked Rebecca, she was sorry that she had she had died in such a horrible way. That Alex had set the house ablaze certainly didn't surprise her. Thank God, Carl and the others had saved Walter and Daniel!

Caroline, her emotions jumbled, told Carl that she wished to be alone for a spell. She walked slowly toward the burnt ruins. The night sky was cloudless, and the moon's golden rays shone down upon the destruction. She felt sick inside. Her grandfather's home had

425

been so elegant, and filled with such fine furnishings. Now, everything was destroyed. She thought about her grandmother's portrait that had hung in the den. Gone—forever!

The veranda was still intact. She climbed the steps, and stood and with tears in her eyes, continuing to take in the heart-wrenching view. Everyone had believed Lucía's body was hers. It was certainly a logical mistake. She must leave soon, ride to town, and let everyone know that she was alive, especially Walter and Daniel! Her thoughts suddenly shifted to Ross, and her anger toward him intensified. The heartless devil didn't even grieve over her death, but had hurried straight into Emily Parker's arms! She hated him! She hated him with a fury! When she saw him again, she would . . . she would . . . ! She was so angry she didn't know what she would do—except slap him as hard as she could!

Chapter Thirty-two

Ross approached the Bar-H slowly. He wasn't sure why he wanted to return—perhaps at the ranch he somehow felt closer to Caroline. Laden with grief, Ross sat slumped in the saddle, shoulders drooped, his head bowed. The appaloosa, as though it were in tune with its master's mood, moved lethargically.

Ross rode past the bunkhouse. The windows were open and he could hear voices inside. Not bothering to lift his gaze, he kept his horse on a steady course which would take him to Hanley's destroyed home.

As he neared the burned ruins, he happened to glance up. He saw a woman standing on the veranda. The sight of her caused his body to stiffen, and his heart to pound erratically. *Caroline!* his thoughts cried. But it couldn't be! It couldn't! My God, was he hallucinating again? Had losing Caroline driven him totally mad?

He brought his horse to a stop. Gradually, as though she were moving in slow motion, the woman turned about and looked at Ross.

It took a moment for Ross's shocked mind to grasp what his eyes beheld. He sat rigid, not even his chest moved, for he was holding his breath. Then, suddenly, a wondrous exultation filled his whole being, and leaping from his horse, he ran to the woman he loved.

He swept her into his arms. Overcome with joy, he swung her about, exclaiming, "It *is* you! Thank God, it's you! You aren't dead! God, what a miracle!" He brought her back into his arms, holding her so tightly that she could barely breathe. "Caroline," he whispered, his voice quivering, "I love you! Oh honey, I thought I had lost you! God, I almost went crazy without you!"

She pushed out of his embrace, drew back an arm, and slapped his face soundly. "You liar!" she spat out. "Crazy? Yes, you went crazy all right! Crazy over Emily Parker!"

Ross's mind, still in shock, couldn't cope. Her vicious slap, and her scornful words failed to get through to him. He simply wasn't capable of thinking rationally.

"Caroline," he began excitedly, "where have you been? Why weren't you home last night? Whose body was mistaken for yours?"

"I've been with Jake Mackenna. He kidnapped me last night, and left a note to you in my room telling you where you could find us. But before I was abducted, I gave a job to a homeless Mexican girl. Jake killed her, and her body was mistaken for mine."

"You were with Mackenna?" Ross questioned. "Caroline, honey, I didn't know! The note was destroyed in the fire!"

"Yes, I already figured that out."

"How did you get away from Mackenna?"

"I laced his whiskey with sleeping powder."

Quickly, before she could stop him, he drew her back into his arms. "Caroline! Caroline, I can hardly believe you've come back to me!"

Putting her hands against his chest, she shoved him

428

aside. "I haven't come back to you, you two-timing, low-down snake!"

Ross was at a complete loss. "Caroline, what's wrong?"

"Don't play innocent with me!"

He gripped her arms, holding her firm. "Tell me what's wrong!"

"I saw you with Emily!"

"Emily?"

"Yes, in your hotel room!" She made a futile effort to wrest free. "Ross, please let me go. You're hurting me." He turned her loose, and taking a step backwards, she said calmly, "I'm through competing with Emily. You two can have each other with my blessing."

"Caroline, you have it all wrong. I don't want Emily."

She raised an eyebrow skeptically. "I heard you tell her that you love her."

"But I was saying it to you."

She frowned peevishly. "Ross, please! Surely, you don't expect me to believe something that outrageous." She turned about brusquely, and going down the veranda steps, she said decisively, "Ross Bennett, stay away from me. I don't want to ever see you again!"

Stunned, Ross stood motionless, and watched as Caroline walked away.

Jake had decided to avoid Dry Branch, and check out the Bar-H. He wasn't too hopeful that he'd find Ross there, but he thought he might as well give it a try. Approaching the ranch cautiously, he was indeed pleased to find Bennett. Obscured by the dark shadows of night, he looked on as Caroline and Ross carried on a conversation . . .

Jake slipped Bryan's Winchester from its scabbard and dismounted quickly. Moving stealthily, he crept closer. Ross and Caroline, totally involved in their discussion, were not aware of his stalking presence. Taking full advantage of their preoccupation, Jake, remained in the shadows and hefted the rifle to his shoulder. The Winchester had an extra rear sight for greater accuracy, and Mackenna used it to zero in on Bennett. He was about to pull the trigger when, suddenly, Caroline stepped in front of Ross, blocking Jake's view. Cursing softly, Mackenna watched as Caroline said a few more words before walking away. He grinned—Ross was again in the open. Carefully, he took aim.

Kirk and Mary had gone to the livery and rented a buggy, which placed them a distance behind Ross. Although Kirk had no way of knowing where his cousin might have gone, he decided to try the Bar-H.

As Kirk turned the buggy onto the lane that led to the Bar-H, an inexplicable chill prickled the back of his neck. He pulled up, and listened closely. He didn't know what he expected to hear, for there was no explanation for the way he felt. But he inherently knew something was wrong. Handing the reins to Mary, he said softly, "Stay here."

"Kirk, what is it?" she asked.

Getting down from the buggy, he replied, "I'm not sure. Maybe nothing's wrong, but I've got this feeling . . ." He drew his pistol. "Just stay here, please."

He moved away quietly. Keeping to the shadows and out of the moonlight, Kirk hurried down the lane. Kirk was an experienced stalker, and although he moved very swiftly, his footsteps were soundless. He hadn't gotten very far when he saw a man up ahead. The darkness of night didn't prevent Kirk from seeing that the man had a rifle.

Ross was stunned by Caroline's behavior, but not for long. She had taken only a few steps when he moved to go after her. At that same moment, a gun shot rang out. Speedily, Ross drew his pistol, lurched for Caroline, grabbed her arm, and pulled her behind him. Now, with his body shielding Caroline's, Ross took time to scan their surroundings. He saw a body sprawled close by, and Kirk was running toward it. He left Caroline behind and hurried over.

Carl and the other wranglers rushed out of the bunkhouse. They reached Kirk and Mackenna at the same time as Ross.

"Mackenna was goin' to shoot you," Kirk told Ross, holstering his pistol. He was a little shaky. Mackenna had been about to pull the trigger on Ross when Kirk shot him. Another second, and Ross would have been dead!

"You saved my life," Ross said. "Thanks."

Kirk was about to make light of the incident when he suddenly caught a glimpse of Caroline approaching. Shocked, he was struck speechless.

Ross grinned expansively. "I didn't lose her, Kirk! She wasn't in the fire!"

Kirk went to Caroline, took her into his arms, and hugged her tightly. "Thank God, you're alive!"

At that moment, Mary arrived, and seeing Caroline, she jumped to the ground, hurried to her, and embraced her enthusiastically.

After asking several questions, and receiving answers, Mary and Kirk had a clearer understanding of what had happened.

Carl and two wranglers took away Mackenna's

body, while the others returned to the bunkhouse.

Kirk, still flabbergasted, said heartily, "Caroline, I didn't think that cousin of mine was going to survive losing you. He really had me worried."

Kirk was puzzled to see Caroline frown testily. "Survive, you say? If you ask me, he was enjoying himself!"

"Caroline!" Mary exclaimed. "That's not true!"

"Oh, isn't it?" she said, an eyebrow raised sharply. "Apparently, you and Kirk don't know Ross very well!"

Ross spoke up, "She saw Emily and me together in my room." His patience was wearing thin. He looked at Caroline although he was still speaking to Mary and Kirk, "Naturally, I told her the truth, but she won't believe me!"

"Caroline," Mary began, "Emily doesn't mean anything to Ross. Kirk and I saw them together too. You must have left just as we came out of Kirk's room." She quickly repeated everything Ross had said to Emily.

Silence prevailed as Caroline thought over Mary's words. She suddenly felt terribly ashamed. Twice now, she had found Ross guilty when he was innocent! Tears came to her eyes, and turning to him, she murmured, "Ross, can you ever forgive me?"

"Sweetheart, there's nothing to forgive," he replied, bringing her swiftly into his arms.

Kirk and Mary moved away discreetly, wanting to give them time alone.

Caroline, with tears flowing, clung to Ross. Almost incoherently, she cried, "Oh Ross, I'm so sorry! . . . You thought I was dead! . . . Then I treated you so hatefully! . . . I even struck you! . . . I'm sorry! . . . I'm so sorry!"

"Caroline, when I thought I had lost you, I wanted

to die too! I think in a way, I did die! I felt so empty inside!"

She controlled her tears, and murmured soothingly, "It's all over now, darling. We're together, for now and always."

"Yes, for always," he whispered thickly. He kissed her with great tenderness.

The sheriff was in town when Carl and the wranglers brought in Jake's body, and a short time later, Ross and the others arrived. Carl had told Taylor that Caroline was alive, so seeing her again didn't shock him, but it made him very happy indeed.

The sheriff let them know that he and the posse had found Bryan's body in front of an abandoned cabin. Caroline had already ascertained that Jake had killed Bryan, for he had been riding Bryan's horse. She had also recognized Bryan's briefcase, which was filled with money. She handed the money over to the sheriff, telling him to use it for a charitable cause.

Caroline, anxious to see her brothers, didn't dally at the sheriff's office. Walter and Daniel believed she was dead, and she wanted to take away their grief without further delay.

Caroline and the others went to the sheriff's house, and after his wife recovered from seeing Caroline, she invited them in. She was ecstatic, and hugged Caroline repeatedly.

When the woman finally calmed down, Caroline asked about her brothers.

"They're in bed," she replied. "By now, they should be sound asleep."

"It doesn't matter," Ross said. "Caroline's return is too wonderful to wait for morning. I think we should tell them now."

Caroline was hesitant. "Ross, maybe you should go to them and let them know that I'm alive. Seeing me all at once would be such a tremendous shock."

Ross agreed, and as he went to the boys, the sheriff's wife showed everyone into the parlor, then left to prepare coffee.

Kirk and Mary sat on the sofa, but Caroline was too tense to sit down. She anxiously paced back and forth.

Only a few minutes had passed when the sound of footsteps hurrying down the hall carried into the parlor. Caroline, knowing it was her brothers, fled to meet them halfway.

They met in the foyer. Caroline knelt and drew both boys into her arms. Tears of happiness filled her eyes, rolled down her cheeks, and mingled with those of her brothers. It was indeed a joyous occasion!

Caroline, sharing Mary's room, spent the remainder of the night at Sheriff Taylor's. Ross and Kirk went to their rooms at the hotel.

The cousins returned early the next morning, and following breakfast, Ross, Caroline, and her brothers visited Doctor Gordon's home. The doctor and his wife were delighted to see that Caroline was still alive, and Inées actually wept with joy. They were all thankful that Bill Hanley hadn't been told that his granddaughter had died. The shock might very well have killed him.

The doctor had decided though that someone should tell Bill about the fire and Rebecca's death. The sad task fell to Caroline and Ross.

They went to Bill's room, where they found him awake and sitting up in bed.

"Caroline," he said, smiling. "Is your cold better?"

"Cold?" she questioned, confused.

"Yes. Doctor Gordon said you couldn't come see me because you had a bad cold."

Ross and Caroline exchanged knowing glances.

"I'm fine, Grandpa," she assured him, pulling up a chair. She placed it beside the bed. Ross stood behind her, his hands resting gently on her shoulders.

"Where are my grandsons?" Bill asked. "I'd sure like to see them."

"They'll be in shortly. But first, I have something to tell you."

He regarded her closely. "Honey, you seem troubled. Is everything all right?"

As kindly as possible, Caroline told her grandfather about the fire and Rebecca's death. She also gave him a full account of Bryan's and Alex's crimes, and the way in which they had died. In addition, she described her abduction and escape.

Hanley listened to her story with few interruptions. Rebecca's death saddened him, but he had stopped loving her, and his grief wasn't one of a bereaved husband. Bryan's and Alex's greed and cold-hearted ways didn't surprise him all that much—he had never really like either one of them. He was unhappy about losing his home, but Bill knew material things could be replaced. He was just thankful that Caroline and the boys hadn't died in the fire. That Rebecca had met with such a terrible fate was tragic.

Bill didn't say anything for a long time, and Caroline become worried. She asked, "Grandpa, are you all right?"

He smiled ruefully. "Yes, dear, I'm fine. I'm just a little sad. I wish things could have been different. Rebecca and her sons—their greed destroyed them. Such a shame! Such a tragic shame!"

Caroline slipped her hand in his, and squeezed gently.

435

His thoughts remained on his wife and stepsons. "They tried to kill me, as well as my grandchildren. Dear God!"

"Grandpa, please try not to think about it. It's all over now."

"Yes, of course. You're right." He smiled bravely, and changed the subject. "Well, I guess we'll be living in the old homestead until I can have a new house built. You don't mind, do you?"

Caroline's eyes brightened. "You'll have to make do with Inés and your grandsons. I'm going to Tucson! Ross and I are getting married!"

"Well, I can't say I'm surprised. I always figured you two were in love." He looked at Ross. "You make sure she visits me often, you hear? Tucson's not that far away."

"I hope you'll come to see us too," Ross replied.

"I will, you can count on it." He held out his arms. "Come here, Caroline, and give your old grandpa a big hug."

She did so at once, and holding her tightly, Bill whispered in her ear, "If you two are just half as happy as your grandmother and I were, you'll have it all."

"We'll be happy, Grandpa. We love each other so much."

Bill offered Ross his hand, "Congratulations, son." Ross quickly accepted his handshake.

Hanley, his eyes twinkling, said cheerfully, "I can't wait to see my first great-grandchild."

Grinning, Ross replied, "On that point, sir, I'll sure try to accommodate you." He winked at Caroline.

She blushed, but her smile told Ross that she could hardly wait.

Ross and Caroline decided to ride out to the old

436

homestead and start cleaning it up. On their way out of town, they rode past the hotel. Henry and Emily Parker looked on as their luggage was stored in a buckboard. They were just about to leave.

Parker flagged them down, and they reined in.

Speaking to Caroline, he said, "I understand that your grandfather is out of danger."

"Yes, he is."

"I'm glad to hear that." By now, Caroline's return was the talk of the town, and Parker, as well as Emily, had heard the news. "Miss Hanley," Henry continued, "your return was quite a shock, to say the least. May I say that I'm glad you're all right?"

Caroline didn't harbor ill feelings toward Parker. His affair with Rebecca was in the past, and she saw no reason to be bitter. "Thank you, Mr. Parker," she replied politely. She turned her attention to Emily. The young woman wouldn't meet her eyes. "Goodbye, Miss Parker," she said clearly.

Emily, her expression sullen, barely glanced at Caroline. "Goodbye," she mumbled. She ignored Ross.

Parker slapped the reins against the team, and with his two wranglers following, they started out of town.

Smiling pertly, Caroline remarked to Ross, "Emily didn't look happy at all, did she?"

"I guess she's a poor loser."

"And I'm the happy winner!" she declared.

Chapter Thirty-three

It was a beautiful sunny morning, and Bill awoke feeling great and raring to go. Caroline was getting married today, and Doctor Gordon had given Bill permission to get up, dress, and attend the wedding. He had been convalescing now for three weeks, and he was not only anxious to see his granddaughter married, but was also impatient to get on with his life. After all, he had a ranch to run, a new house to build, and two grandsons to raise. Having so much to do made him feel younger and more vigorous.

All the same, he got out of bed gingerly, for he knew his full strength hadn't returned. Gordon had said that he must take it easy for at least another month. Bill had every intention of following the doctor's orders, for he didn't want to suffer a relapse; he had too much to live for! Running his ranch, building a new home, and taking care of his grandsons were indeed reasons to want to live, but there was more — he had fallen in love with Inés.

He wasn't sure when he had stopped thinking of her as just a friend, but now she was the woman he wanted to marry. For the past three weeks, Inés had practically been his constant companion, and somewhere during that time, he had fallen in love. He couldn't help but wonder if he had always been in love with her, but had been too blind to see into his own heart. He didn't know, but he did know that life was too short to spend it regretting the past. He still had a present and a future, and he hoped to share it with Inés. But he wanted her as a wife, not a housekeeper!

Carefully, for his legs were a little wobbly, Bill slipped his robe on over his nightshirt. He washed his face, combed his hair, then sat on the edge of the bed. It was time for Inés to bring his breakfast.

Keeping to her schedule, Inés arrived promptly. She was pleased to find Bill looking so well. Placing his tray on the bedside table, she said cheerfully, *"Patrón,* you are feeling much better, si?"

"I feel as fit as a fiddle," he replied heartily.

"That is good, for today is a very special day. Doctor Gordon said you can walk Caroline down the aisle."

"Well, I was going to, whether he said I could or not."

Inés smiled warmly. "Doctor Gordon knew that is what you would say. That is why he is letting you do it. He knew he could not stop you." She gestured toward the food. "You must eat your breakfast before it gets cold."

He didn't move. He merely stared at her with an expression she couldn't understand.

"Patrón, is something wrong?"

"Inés, do you remember that night when you told me I should imagine my life without you? You said I should think about it when I'm lying alone in my bed."

She blushed. "I should not have said that. Please, señor, let us forget it."

He reached out a hand. "Come here, Inés, and sit beside me."

439

She did so hesitantly.

"I have tried to picture my life without you, and I know if I were to lose you, I would lose not only my best friend, but also the woman I want to marry."

Inés was shocked. "You want to marry me, señor? But why?"

"Because I've fallen in love with you. You love me, too, don't you?"

Her happiness overflowed. "Oh *sí,* señor! I have loved you for many years!"

"I never knew," he replied. "But that night when you finally spoke up to me, I began to think. When I was gravely ill, you barely left my side. That was when I knew for sure that you loved me."

Gently, he drew her into his arms. "As soon as I'm completely well, we'll be married." A worried frown knitted his brow. "I hope you won't mind being a grandmother to Walter and Daniel. The boys are still very young, and it's going to be up to us to raise them."

Inés smiled happily. "I do not mind, *Patrón.* I already love the boys as though they were my own."

"I wish you'd start calling me Bill. After all, I am your fiancé."

"Sí, I will call you Bill." Blushing somewhat, she continued, "But I have always dreamed of calling you 'darling.' Just once, I would like to say it."

Grinning, Bill replied, "You can say it as often as you wish."

She hugged him tightly, exclaiming, "I love you, darling!"

They had barely sealed their commitment with a kiss when, all at once, Walter and Daniel barged into the room. Guests at the doctor's house, they had spent a great deal of time with their grandfather—both boys had learned to love him dearly. Inés, as well as Bill, overlooked their intrusion, and cheerfully welcomed them.

Caroline was rooming at Sheriff Taylor's house—he had plenty of space, for Mary was no longer living there. She and Kirk had now been married for almost three weeks. They were staying at the hotel, but the day after tomorrow, they planned to leave for Tucson with Ross and Caroline. Kirk didn't have a log cabin on his land, but there was a boarding house in town where he and Mary could stay until their house was built.

Caroline had taken a bath in her bedroom, and was toweling herself dry when Mary knocked on her door, asking to come in.

Caroline slipped on her dressing gown, opened the door, and drew Mary inside. Her face glowing, she exclaimed, "Oh Mary, I'm so excited! I wonder if all brides are as anxious as I am!"

Her friend laughed lightly. "You're supposed to be anxious. This will be one of the happiest days of your life!"

"What time is it?" Caroline asked.

"Almost time for you to get married. I'm here to help you get dressed."

Caroline fled to the wardrobe, removed her bridal gown, and placed it carefully on the bed. It was a beautiful dress. Last week, she and Ross had gone to Albuquerque so she could find a wedding gown. She had insisted on shopping by herself, for she didn't want Ross to see the dress before they were married. The gown had been expensive, but her grandfather had given her plenty of money to spend.

Caroline put on the new crinolines she had bought in Albuquerque, then with Mary's help, she slipped into her white satin wedding dress. A pair of dainty white, slippers complimented the gown. Caroline sat at the vanity, and Mary arranged her long hair into a lovely, upswept style. The veil was still in its box. Mary took it out and placed it atop Caroline's golden curls.

Standing, Caroline gazed into the mirror, giving her reflection a thoughtful appraisal.

"You're absolutely beautiful!" Mary exclaimed.

Caroline was indeed a stunning bride. Her bridal gown was adorned with intricately woven seed pearls, and the flowing skirt was cut into scallops along the front, where again the tiny pearls were repeated. Her veil, made of fine silk, was the crowning touch.

Suddenly a knock sounded at the door, followed by Bill's voice, "Caroline, honey, it's time to leave for the church."

She let him in, and as his gaze fell across his granddaughter, sentimental tears came to his eyes. "Caroline," he praised, "you're a beautiful bride!" Hugging her close, he whispered, "You look so much like your grandmother. She, too, was a beautiful bride."

"Yes, and I'm certain you were a very handsome groom."

"Talking about grooms," he said, taking her arm, and ushering her toward the door. "The last I heard, your groom was already at the church. I get the feeling he's kinda eager to get married."

Caroline laughed gaily. "So am I!"

Following the wedding, the Taylors gave a reception at their home. There was plenty of food and lots of dancing, and everyone had a wonderful time. Ross was a graceful partner, and Caroline loved waltzing in his arms.

Although the bride and groom were indeed enjoying themselves, they nonetheless longed to be alone. Finding the Taylors, they thanked them for the reception, then very discreetly slipped away.

Ross lifted her into the buggy, sat beside her, and slapped the reins against the team. Caroline thought they would spend the night at the hotel, but Ross passed it by.

"Where are we going?" Caroline asked.

"You'll see," he said, smiling secretively.

"Well, I'm glad my bag's in the buggy," she replied. "It has a change of clothes, and also what I plan to wear to bed."

"Oh yeah?" he said, arching a brow. "Is it something revealing?"

"Yes, I think you'll find it very revealing," she replied saucily. "I bought it Albuquerque just for our wedding night."

"I can hardly wait to see it on you."

"Ross, please tell me where we're going. I can't stand the suspense!"

"I want us to be alone, really alone. The hotel's too full of people."

"But you still haven't told me where we're going."

"Be patient, Mrs. Bennett. You'll find out when we get there."

"Mrs. Bennett," she said dreamily. "Doesn't that sound heavenly?"

Holding the reins in one hand, he slipped an arm about her shoulders. "You're heavenly."

"Flattery will get you everywhere with me."

"Promise?"

"Cross my heart."

"I'm going to hold you to that," he said, a twinkle in his eye.

Caroline snuggled close, and time passed quickly as

she enjoyed being with her husband. When Ross turned the buggy toward Hanley's old homestead, she sat straight up in the seat.

"Is this where we're going?"

"I came here earlier today, and got everything ready."

He brought the team to a stop, jumped down, then lifted Caroline from the buggy. He carried her to the door, and over the threshold.

"Stay here," he said, putting her down. He moved away. The house was dark and she could barely see him. He struck a match, then lit a candle.

Caroline looked about the room with amazement. The house was still unfurnished, but Ross had made a big pallet and padded it with several blankets. A bottle of champagne rested in an ice bucket, and two long-stemmed glasses were beside the bed. There was also a packed picnic basket, which he told her held their breakfast.

Caroline didn't say anything, and Ross began to have second thoughts. Maybe she would rather have gone to the hotel.

"We don't have to stay here," he told her. "I guess my idea was a lousy one."

"No!" she exclaimed. "I think it's a wonderful idea! Here, we really are alone! And it's so peaceful and quiet — in town it's always so noisy. "

Ross was relieved. "For a moment there, I thought I'd made a big blunder." He hurried outside, got Caroline's bag, and brought it to her.

Taking it and a candle, she went to another room, where she quickly took off her formal attire, and got ready for bed.

Ross, stripped down to his trousers, was sitting on the pallet when she returned. Caroline's presence sent him leaping to his feet. She was standing before him totally unclothed, wearing only one red garter. The lone candle cast a luminous glow over her silky flesh, and her husband's gaze traveled hungrily over her full breasts, tiny waist, and shapely thighs. He dropped his gaze to the red garter—it was indeed a sexy touch. His passion was raging.

She pointed at the garter. "This is what I bought for our wedding night. As you know, darling, I prefer to sleep in the nude."

Ross grinned from ear to ear. "Come here, you little vixen." His dark eyes were glazed with desire as his wife very gracefully crossed the floor and came to his side. Sweeping her into his arms, he kissed her passionately.

"Caroline," he whispered. "Did I ever tell you that you're a very provocative young lady?"

"I don't think so," she replied, pressing her body seductively against his. "Did I ever tell you that you are a very sensual man?"

"I don't remember," he said softly, holding her so close that they seemed inseparable. "I love you very much, Mrs. Bennett."

"And I love you, Mr. Bennett." Twirling away, she went to the pallet, and lay down. "This provocative wife needs her sensual husband."

Ross, his grin askew, replied, "Whatever you say, darling."

Within the blink of an eye, he was on the pallet with Caroline in his arms. His lips sought hers in a long, love-filled exchange that left them breathless, but hungry for more.

Ross quickly stripped away the remainder of his clothes, then holding Caroline's body tightly to his, he kissed her again. Expressing their love with whispered endearments, fiery kisses, and tender fondling, they brought each other to the peak of their passion.

Ross moved over, brought her thighs flush to his, and possessed her fully. His hips moved rapidly, and with each deep thrust, she trembled with ecstasy. Wondrously, he took her with him to a rapturous, heart-stopping climax which left them gloriously fulfilled.

He kissed her softly, then moved to lie beside her. She cuddled against him.

"Caroline," he whispered. "I love you with all my heart."

"I know you do, darling. Believe me, I feel the same way."

He raised up, and with a big smile, asked, "Honey, will you do me a favor?"

"Yes, of course."

"Will you wear that red garter for me on every one of our anniversaries?"

"Even after we've been married fifty years?"

"Yes, even then."

She laughed merrily. "I have a feeling the romance will never go out of our marriage."

He reached down and snapped her garter. "Not as long as you wear that!"

Laughing, they went into each other's arms.

THE LIVES AND LOVES OF THE WEALTHY
AND BEAUTIFUL

DESIGNING WOMAN   (337, $4.50)
by Allison Moser

She was an ugly duckling orphan from a dusty little town, where the kids at school laughed at her homemade dresses and whispered lies about her fortune-telling grandmother. Calico Gordon swore she would escape her lackluster life and make a name for herself.

Years later she was the celebrated darling of the fashion world, the most dazzling star the industry had seen in years. Her clothes hung in the closets of the beautiful and wealthy women in the world. She had reached the pinnacle — and now had to prevent her past from destroying her dreams. She had to risk it all — fortune, fame, friendship and love — to keep memories of her long-forgotten life from shattering the image she had created.

INTERLUDES   (339, $4.95)
by L. Levine

From Monte Carlo to New York, from L.A. to Cannes, Jane Perry searches for a lost love — and discovers a seductive paradise of pleasure and satisfaction, an erotic and exotic world that is hers for the taking.

It's a sensuous, privileged world, where nights — and days — are filled with a thousand pleasures, where intrigue and romance blend with dangerous desires, where reality is *better* than fantasy. . . .

FOR WOMEN ONLY   (346, $4.50)
by Trevor Meldal-Johnsen

Sean is an actor, down on his luck. Ted is the black sheep of a wealthy Boston family, looking for an easy way out. Dany is a street-smart kid determined to make it any way he can.

The one thing they all have in common is that they know how to please a woman. And that's all they need to be employed by Debonaire, Beverly Hills' most exclusive escort service — for women only. In the erotic realm of pleasure and passion, the women will pay any price for a thrill. Nothing is forbidden — except to fall in love.

Available wherever paperbacks are sold, or order direct from the Publisher. Send cover price plus 50¢ per copy for mailing and handling to Pinnacle Books, Dept. 17-546, 475 Park Avenue South, New York, N.Y. 10016. Residents of New York, New Jersey and Pennsylvania must include sales tax. DO NOT SEND CASH.

HISTORICAL ROMANCE FROM PINNACLE BOOKS

LOVE'S RAGING TIDE   (381, $4.50)
by Patricia Matthews

Melissa stood on the veranda and looked over the sweeping acres of Great Oaks that had been her family's home for two generations, and her eyes burned with anger and humiliation. Today her home would go beneath the auctioneer's hammer and be lost to her forever. Two men eagerly awaited the auction: Simon Crouse and Luke Devereaux. Both would try to have her, but they would have to contend with the anger and pride of girl turned woman . . .

CASTLE OF DREAMS   (334, $4.50)
by Flora M. Speer

Meredith would never forget the moment she first saw the baron of Afoncaer, with his armor glistening and blue eyes shining honest and true. Though she knew she should hate this Norman intruder, she could only admire the lean strength of his body, the golden hue of his face. And the innocent Welsh maiden realized that she had lost her heart to one she could only call enemy.

LOVE'S DARING DREAM   (372, $4.50)
by Patricia Matthews

Maggie's escape from the poverty of her family's bleak existence gives fire to her dream of happiness in the arms of a true, loving man. But the men she encounters on her tempestuous journey are men of wealth, greed, and lust. To survive in their world she must control her newly awakened desires, as her beautiful body threatens to betray her at every turn.

Available wherever paperbacks are sold, or order direct from the Publisher. Send cover price plus 50¢ per copy for mailing and handling to Pinnacle Books, Dept. 17- 546, 475 Park Avenue South, New York, N.Y. 10016. Residents of New York, New Jersey and Pennsylvania must include sales tax. DO NOT SEND CASH.